ᴛʜᴇ EMPRESS GAME
CLOAK OF WAR

Also available from Rhonda Mason and Titan Books

THE EMPRESS GAME

EXILE'S THRONE
(August 2017)

THE EMPRESS GAME
CLOAK OF WAR

RHONDA MASON

TITAN BOOKS

The Empress Game: Cloak of War
Print edition ISBN: 9781783299430
E-book ISBN: 9781783299447

Published by Titan Books
A division of Titan Publishing Group Ltd
144 Southwark Street, London SE1 0UP

First edition: October 2016
10 9 8 7 6 5 4 3 2 1

A CIP catalogue record for this title is available from the British Library.

Printed in the USA.

What did you think of this book? We love to hear from our readers. Please email us at: readerfeedback@titanemail.com, or write to us at the above address.

To receive advance information, news, competitions, and exclusive offers online, please sign up for the Titan newsletter on our website: www.titanbooks.com

This book is dedicated to my amazing husband, James Douglass. Not only is he my biggest supporter and best friend, but he also gave me the greatest gift a writer could ask for: Time.

Dear James, I hope you hear all of the unspoken words in my heart when I say, "I love you."

THE EMPRESS GAME

CLOAK OF WAR

1

Kayla Reinumon lay wide awake in the darkness of a bedroom, on a bed too comfortable to be her own. A high window gave a glimpse of the city skyline of Falanar at this late night hour. Things looked muted, quiet.

And foreign. Nothing like her homeworld of Ordoch in Wyrd Space. Or the slum side of Altair Tri, where she'd been exiled for the last five years. It was somewhere in between, a place as alien to her as she was to it.

A place she found herself stranded in.

As it often did, the night's quiet weighed on her, like a g-force on her chest, breaking loose questions she couldn't answer, doubts she ignored during the flurry of her waking hours.

"Who am I?" she whispered to the dark.

She'd always known, since the moment of birth, who she was. She was a Wyrd, member of an advanced race of psionics. More importantly, she was a *ro'haar*. She was one half of a bonded pair, trained in martial arts to protect her *il'haar*—her twin, Vayne—as he protected her with his superior psionic gifts.

Kayla Reinumon, *ro'haar*.

A title that meant everything. An empty title now. A title that mocked her.

Vayne was long gone. He and their younger brother Corinth had blasted off from Falanar two weeks ago, headed for sanctuary.

What was a *ro'haar* without her *il'haar*?

Just a Wyrd.

Wyrds had psi powers, though, and she had lost hers. What was a Wyrd without her powers?

Just a person. Nothing more.

So, who was she supposed to be now?

The comm in the room buzzed with an incoming transmission. "Princess Isonde? Are you awake?"

Princess Isonde, Kayla's assumed identity, while the real princess died slowly in a coma. Was that the only identity Kayla had left?

Kayla rolled out of bed and absently retrieved her kris from beneath her pillow. Its mate sat atop the shelving unit near the door. She gave the dagger a pat before thumbing the comm's switch.

"What is it, Orna? I'm sleeping."

No, she wasn't, and hadn't since her brothers had fled Falanar and left her in the wake of their hyperstream. She strapped one kris to her bare thigh.

"Ambassador Bredard of Geth needs to speak with you; he says it's quite urgent." Her junior aide sounded harried. "The word 'emergency' was mentioned more than once."

Kayla blinked dry eyes at the chronometer. "At three in the morning?" He wouldn't be the first person to come seeking an audience with her in the dead of night—not even the dozenth. Oh-three-hundred on Falanar was another planet's mid-day commodities market crash, or a dinnertime peace accord crisis.

Isonde, she was learning, lived an exhausting life.

Kayla couldn't decide if she wanted to be left alone with her demons, or saved from them by hours of mind-numbing political wrangling.

"Ambassador who?" The name wasn't familiar at all. The province of Geth she remembered—a contentious nation on a

Sovereign Planet, pushing for dominance and threatening military force. Isonde's home nation had cut diplomatic ties with them.

"Bredard." The aide was very clear on the name, and none too pleased, by the sound of it.

Kayla looked back at the bed—Isonde's bed, her own private battleground—even as her mind spun on the name. "Can he be put off?" She hated going in blind. Playing the part of Isonde took more than a convincing hologram and an air of authority. It took research and study to be up to date on the latest political situations, to gain at least a basic understanding of the players involved.

"I don't think he's leaving, Princess. I could barely contain him in the front lounge. A few more minutes and he'll make a run for your room."

If Orna couldn't put him off, it couldn't be done. The girl was a master at screening the various political entities clamoring for Isonde's time and only allowing the most important through.

That settled it. Kayla wasn't here on Falanar just to make appearances as the triumphant princess, fresh from her victory in the Empress Game. She was here to act as Isonde while the princess was still in her coma, until Malkor—*her* Malkor, Senior Agent Malkor Rua of the IDC—could find someone better suited for the job.

And Isonde, Kayla knew, would be knowledgeable of the importance of such a visit from this Ambassador Bredard of Geth. She wouldn't hesitate to take the meeting.

"Tell him I'll be down shortly." The sleeping tunic and robe she'd been wearing would be the most comfortable, but Isonde never arrived anywhere looking less than micro-precise in her attire. Kayla sighed and headed to the dressing room.

Fifteen minutes later she arrived at the lounge, looking elegant, if austere. Her sole consideration for comfort had been swapping out a long skirt for leggings so that she could strap a kris to each thigh.

Rawn, her favorite of Isonde's guards, stood sentry outside the front lounge.

"How did you pull the midnight shift?" she asked him with a smile.

"Ethan had a rough afternoon with the new baby, so I sent him home to get some extra sleep. I was due to start in a few hours anyway."

"You're a big softie, Rawn, you know that?" Not to mention big in general, with a physique that would have frightened her a month ago if she hadn't gotten used to dealing with the larger males.

He returned her smile. "Just don't tell anyone."

Kayla straightened her shoulders and gave him the nod to open the doors.

Bredard waited in the shadows near the bank of windows, silhouetted against the sleeping city. Lights dotted the night behind him like a swath of electronic stars across the backdrop of towering buildings, with the exception of a dark blot mid-center. A power outage uptown? A single lamp illuminated the room, its weak light spinning out a web of intimacy—or secrecy.

Imperials did love their games.

After a day like hers had been she was too weary for such affectations. The lounge doors slid shut behind her and she tapped the base of a second lamp, bringing up enough light to make her squint for a moment. His gaze fell immediately to the kris and she pretended not to notice.

"Princess Isonde." Bredard gave the traditional Piran greeting, touching right fingertips to right shoulder, then lowering his arm, palm up. "Thank you for agreeing to meet with me."

If the Gethans had a traditional greeting she certainly didn't know it. "Good evening, Ambassador. Unusual circumstances."

His gaze drifted again to her kris. "I apologize for the lateness of the hour. I fear this is known as the only way to have a moment of your time without scheduling weeks in advance."

Lovely. She'd have to tell Orna to be stricter or they'd be deluged with visitors.

She gestured toward chairs arranged opposite each other

across a low table—it was what Isonde would do. Left to her own instincts, Kayla would prefer to stand, one hand resting on a kris's handle, her back to the door she knew Rawn guarded from the other side. The tenor of the room, Bredard's posed stance near the dark embrasure of the windows, set her slightly on edge. What sort of meeting did he intend?

He took a winding course to the chairs, tapping the base of the first lamp as he went, powering it down, and sat facing the windows. She took the seat opposite, annoyed to find herself looking into the only lit lamp in the room directly behind him.

She stared him down. *Let him start the conversation.* That would work much better than her demanding, "Well, what do you want?" in a perfectly Kayla tone. He was well-dressed and handsome, she supposed, in the blunt-featured, craggy way of some imperials. He seemed to have more in common with Trinan and Vid, IDC agents from Malkor's octet, than he did with most diplomats.

A minute ticked by. Two. She resisted the urge to sigh with impatience—barely. What sort of quasi-cloak-and-dagger nonsense had he roused her from bed for? Hopefully he would be quick. She had more not-sleeping to do. She could be lying awake, worrying over the whereabouts of her brothers, the war crime charges levied against her people, and best of all, the fractured state of her relationship with Malkor.

On second thought, maybe Bredard could drag this out all night.

The silence stretched to uncomfortable levels and she cracked first. "You have my full attention, Ambassador."

"The full attention of Princess Isonde?"

His reply put her on guard. She nodded once. "Of course."

"That's odd, because the Princess Isonde I know wouldn't come to a meeting armed with daggers."

"The Isonde you knew hadn't survived a terrorist attack and a brush with death at her own attempted wedding, either." Radical elements from within the empire had tried to infect the planetary rulers of the galaxy with the incurable Tetratock

Nanovirus after the Empress Game. Kayla had thwarted the attack and avoided infection by the slimmest margin.

"The Isonde I know," he said, "wouldn't come to a midnight meeting with a Gethan—period."

Stars burn it! What else didn't she know about Piran's involvement with Geth? She should have put him off until the morning and spent the night researching. Damn Orna for being intimidated into summoning her.

"Things have changed," Kayla said. "I am no longer simply one of Piran's representatives on the Sovereign Council, I have wider concerns." At least, Isonde would, if she ever woke from her coma, married Prince Ardin and took her place on the elite Council of Seven at his side. Bredard didn't need to know those concerns stretched beyond the empire, to the fate of Kayla's homeworld in Wyrd Space.

"Things have indeed changed," Bredard said, "and not for the better, I fear." His gaze switched to the windows behind her for a moment and an uneasy feeling prickled across her skin, the sensation of being watched from the shadows. She casually lowered one hand from the chair's armrest to sit atop a kris.

"I wouldn't be here like this if they hadn't," he said. "Things were rolling along smoothly. The results were... promising. However, your recent activities have forced my hand."

He'd have to be more specific than that.

In the last few months Kayla had impersonated one of the most influential women in the empire, perpetrated that fraud throughout the entire Empress Game, won the rank of Empress-Apparent and a seat on the Council of Seven, helped uncover a clandestine division working within the Imperial Diplomatic Corps, freed prisoners of war that had been experimented on for five years, and killed the empire's Grand Advisor of Science and Technology.

To name a few of her activities.

He couldn't know about any of those, though. She and Malkor's octet had kept all of the details tightly contained, so he must mean one of the more mundane aspects of her charade as Isonde. Which, though? Which of her recent political maneuvers would affect Geth?

And why couldn't he have scheduled this meeting with her in advance so she could have prepared?

With no notion of how else to go on, she went for the most controversial of her decisions in the past week.

"Piran stands behind its decision to boycott Timpania's sale of gallenium ore until they improve conditions in the refineries." Anything that impacted the empire's supply of the precious fuel resource would have everyone riled. "If you came to change my mind about it, I'm sorry to say my father and I are quite in accord on this." Star travel depended on gallenium ore. As the largest supplier, Timpania had the rest of the empire in an economic stranglehold over it.

"If I cared about gallenium I would have arranged a meeting with Isonde's father to discuss it."

The bastard knew about the identity switch—why else would he refer to her in the third person—but how?

Bredard lifted one finger from where it had lain on the armrest. "I've come about something more personal."

Suddenly the air felt close, thick—too shallow for two people. His attention shifted past her again in a way it shouldn't have if they were alone. As she drew breath to question him, a hand clamped over her mouth from behind with the force of a vacuum seal. Bredard sat at ease as an arm encircled her throat, locking her against the chair and holding her prisoner.

Her kris were already in her hands by the time the arm secured its grip. She slashed one wavy blade across the hand at her mouth, catching her cheek with the tip and spilling a warm rivulet of fluid down her chin in the process. The hand held firm. She swung her other arm overhead backward, hoping to sink her blade in the flesh of her attacker's shoulder, if she wasn't lucky enough to hit his jugular. Instead her blade shanked off something harder than it, tearing a line through flesh as the blade slid aside.

The arm about her throat tightened, constricting blood flow

to her brain as the hand bruised her lips against her teeth. She tried to twist and drop beneath her attacker's arm but it held like a garrote and about as tightly. A scent like... *lubricant?* hit her right before Bredard drew a pistol from his pocket.

"Enough."

She desperately sucked air in through her nostrils, breathing what little she could get down her trachea, and raised her hands, kris away from her body. Even with the pistol trained on her, it was hard not to kick her feet out and keep struggling with the arm strangling her closer to darkness each passing second. The lubricant smell was everywhere and a clear fluid glistened on one of her hands in the weak light.

She tried to still her rampaging heart and focus.

Where had the second man come from? She flashed through her memory since arriving—the black spot of the city's landscape, as seen from the windows. Not a power outage, a cloaking device of some sort, used to hide another person's presence. A cloak that couldn't flawlessly render the complicated scene behind it, presenting the outline of buildings without the shifting lights.

A rushing sounded in her ears. In a second she was going to have to choose between getting shot for making a move or being passively strangled to unconsciousness.

"If you promise not to make a sound, I'll have Siño release you."

Blinking was all she could manage. Luckily, he took it in the affirmative. Siño released his grasp and she sucked in air, filling her burning lungs even as she studied Bredard's weapon.

The design of the pistol was unfamiliar to her—how in the void had he gotten it past her security filters? For that matter, how had Siño gotten past? And who the frutt did they think they were, assaulting her in her home?

"Knives, if you please." Pistol still trained on her, Bredard gestured and Siño came around from behind her chair. Blood rimmed the gash she'd opened on the back of his hand. More disturbing, though, was the clear fluid oozing out of it. The wound on his shoulder showed an equally small amount of blood, with a larger stain forming on his shirt.

"I find biocybes are a bit more effective in a fight than your average person," Bredard said. "Considering your current predicament, I'm guessing you agree."

If Siño had military biocybernetic enhancements, which she suspected he did, that was some *seriously* high-level tech for an "ambassador."

Siño reached out his injured hand for her weapons, and through the cut she caught sight of a series of flesh-colored tubes, some severed, running beneath his skin. Her stomach gave a sick roll as she imagined biocybernetics threaded through her own body.

She had the urge to stab her kris through his outstretched hand. She'd been taken by surprise like a novice, brought down by an imperial and his mechanical monkey in less than three minutes. Her chest burned with wounded pride. It didn't matter that Wyrd training couldn't save her from a pistol blast at close range; she should never have been caught in this position in the first place.

Life on Falanar was making her soft.

She handed over her kris with the feeling of being declawed, and turned her attention back to Bredard. His satisfied expression begged for her fist.

"That's better. Here's the way of it: we're going to have a little chat. You alert the guard outside to our presence, I'll shoot you." He said it so matter-of-factly that she didn't doubt him. "Siño—the door."

Siño must have brought a pack of gear, hidden by the cloaking device, because he disappeared from view before returning with what looked like a mini towel rack. He affixed it to the door, one square mount on each side of the door's center seam, a ten centimeter bar connecting them. Depending on the sealant, the lock bar could hold against a powered jack.

Finished, Siño positioned himself beside her chair.

"I've come with a message for you, *Princess Isonde*."

"Ever heard of a comm device?"

He quirked his lips, then nodded to the biocybe.

Even prepared for it, the backhand snapped her head to the side. It opened the cut on her cheek she'd given herself earlier.

"I find comms lack the appropriate tone."

She tried to loosen her muscles and roll with the motion, but the second backhand still felt like a brick to the face. She forearm-blocked the third and Bredard raised the pistol a little.

"Come now, take it like a man. Or should I say, like a *ro'haar*.

"Oh yes. I know who you are, despite who you pretend to be—Isonde, Evelyn, Shadow Panthe—guises that hide the truth of your heritage." He lowered the pistol to rest on his knee, now that he had her undivided attention. This was about more than imperial power and politics, more than councils and empresses. It went deeper, into much more dangerous territory.

"What I do with that knowledge," he said, "I'll leave you to fear, especially if I don't get what I want."

She wasn't merely the woman impersonating Princess Isonde, the soon-to-be Empress-Apparent to the throne of the Sakien Empire. Kayla was one of the few surviving members of the royal family of the Wyrd World Ordoch. She was a sworn enemy of the empire, a fugitive in their lands, hiding in plain sight. If taken prisoner, she could be their greatest piece of leverage in the empire's struggle to dominate her homeworld.

Worse, if she were killed, she would never see her two *il'haars*, the brothers she'd been born to protect, again.

"What do you want?" Her face throbbed from Siño's blows, one side of her mouth already swelling, and the words came out stiffly.

"What I *want* is you and your twin, Vayne, in the same room, access to certain laboratory equipment which you destroyed, and the genius of the smartest man—Wyrd—I've ever known."

He could only mean one person, the exiled Wyrd and neurobiological engineer Dolan. She smiled with the half of her mouth she could still move. "Whom I killed."

"Precisely. What I'll settle for is the data from Dolan's complinks that you and your pet octet stole from me, data from five years of experiments that could change the nature of our brains."

Those experiments had been carried out on members of her family, including her beloved twin, for five years. Most of her family had not survived.

"I don't have access to it." And if she did, she'd destroy it before handing it over to anyone else.

"Not at the moment, no. Senior Agent Rua does, however, and I believe the two of you have something of an understanding."

She and Malkor had something of a sexual relationship, to be precise. Or they had, before everything went sideways.

"I would have taken it from him directly, but unlike you, the IDC pays more attention to the security of their buildings' exteriors, including the windows."

That at least explained how Siño had gotten in.

She gave him the only answer he'd ever get from her. "Frutt you."

He laughed, a soft chuckle, and stopped Siño with a gesture when the biocybe would have struck her again. "It's amusing to me that you think you have a choice." He rose. "You have one week."

The pistol lost its aim on her as he straightened his clothes, and she itched to attack. *Spring from the chair, one foot on the table, launch at him—*

"Oh," he said, the word freezing her in place, "if revealing your identity and cheating at the Empress Game isn't enough of a threat, know this: I have something you want."

She wanted three things from life right now: to be with Malkor, which Bredard couldn't affect, to free her homeworld from imperial occupation, which was beyond his means, and to be reunited with her brothers and remaining family. That last...

"I see you understand. I have the one thing you do not:

knowledge of your *il'haars*' location."

"My family escaped to Wyrd Space." Escaped, and left her behind.

Bredard arched a brow. "*Did* they?"

She stiffened as he approached. He forced the muzzle against her temple while Siño pulled something from a pocket.

"I'd sit still for this part, if I were you."

Electricity crackled in the air one second before pain shot through her from neck to brain to toes, and then she fell into darkness.

Senior Agent Malkor Rua of the Imperial Diplomatic Corps perched on the edge of a chair in Kayla's bedroom and studied her reflection in the mirror. He so seldom saw *her*, hidden as she always was behind the Isonde hologram, and it was a welcome sight.

Or would be, if she didn't have a split lip, a swollen, just-now-bruising jaw, and a slashed cheek. The biocybe hadn't been gentle. A frutting biocybe—how had Bredard found one of those rarities?

Kayla could take the beating, he knew, and even now she treated it like it was nothing while she began healing the damage with a medstick.

Neither of them mentioned the real threat screaming through the room—their cover was blown. Bredard, and who knew how many others, knew who Kayla was, knew that Malkor and Isonde had worked with her to fix the Empress Game.

That knowledge was a death sentence if it got out. Not to mention the end of years of planning Malkor, Ardin and Isonde had done. It was something they'd all known could happen when they began this, but now the danger was very, very real.

Kayla's fingers were sure and strong as she applied the medstick to the bruising, something she'd probably done thousands of times in her history as a *ro'haar*.

"Let me do that," he said. He had to do something. Fix something. Smash something. Anything to get away from this feeling of lack of control.

Kayla's gaze met his in the mirror, seeming to really see him for the first time. She held him suspended as he waited for her to relent. Supreme self-sufficiency had been her credo for the last five years and even now, despite the bond they shared, it took an effort for her to lean on him.

She nodded.

He hadn't come near her when he arrived twenty minutes ago to get her account of what happened with Bredard and Siño. Unlike most people who had been assaulted in the night, in the one place they should have been the safest, it wasn't her instinct to rush into a strong pair of arms for comfort. It wasn't her instinct to rush to anyone. He'd known from the set of her shoulders when he entered that what she needed was space and the chance to remind herself that she was strong.

"Sit."

She chose a stiff-backed chair beside the table that held the medical case with its assortment of medsticks. Her face looked worse up close, but its puffiness didn't soften the determined set of her features. She hadn't called him here in the dead of night to be a concerned lover, or even a friend. She'd summoned him as an IDC agent and a co-conspirator whose clandestine activities had been discovered.

Frutt. They were really into it now. How had Bredard found out? Had someone betrayed them?

And what of the evidence? The hologram biostrip that Rigger had designed, with Corinth and Kayla's help, was so advanced that no one would believe its possibilities if they didn't see it firsthand. Was it time to destroy the thing and all of Rigger's schematics? Without the hologram itself as evidence, maybe they could argue that such a switch during the Empress Game would have been impossible, given the empire's low-level tech.

He took the medstick from Kayla and focused its beam on

her jaw, working first on the hematoma. This, at least, was a problem he could fix.

"Hekkar's looking into it," he said. "I think you're right about the biocybe entering through the window." Hekkar Tial, his second in command, was studying the lounge where the attack had taken place. Rigger, his octet's tech specialist, was investigating how they had circumvented the outside security systems.

"Rawn found hydrofluoric gel around the edge of the pane," she said, "which explains how they got it loose without smashing it—they dissolved a thin line of the glass where it met the casing. Something tacky had held it in place by the corners once the biocybe entered, and I hadn't noticed in the dim light." He could almost hear the thought: *I should have.* "I bet it's also how they got the weapon in. They left the same way."

She stiffened when he touched her chin to tilt her head to get a better angle on her swollen mouth. He ignored the reaction, just like he'd ignored the stiffness between them since she had decided to leave him behind on Falanar. The broken state of their relationship would have to wait for a day when they weren't being blackmailed with their lives in the balance.

She waited for him to finish the first round of healing on her mouth before speaking. "I've never seen a pistol like it before."

"I think we both know where he would have gotten tech for a new weapon design."

The *kin'shaa*, Dolan. The most sophisticated neurobiological engineer ever born in the Wyrd Worlds. He'd gone too far in his experiments, warping the minds and destroying the free will of innocent people, and had been stripped of the psionic powers inherent to all Wyrds as a punishment. He'd been banished from Wyrd Space and defected to the Sakien Empire, bringing with him a level of technology the imperials wouldn't have reached in a generation. He'd been doling out that technology to clandestine groups in the IDC and the government and continuing his research with their support.

At least he had been, until a few weeks ago when Kayla had

staked him through the throat and Vayne pulverized his body.

She batted Malkor's hand away so she could talk. "Bredard said, 'Did they?' when I told him my family had escaped to Wyrd Space. '*Did they*.'" For the first time since Malkor had arrived, something akin to fear showed in her gaze. "What did he mean?"

"He was bullshitting you." Only, Malkor wasn't sure. Couldn't be sure. And that uncertainty would never be enough for Kayla.

"I can't ignore it."

He could see she couldn't stop thinking about it. Her finger tapped a staccato rhythm against one of the kris strapped to her thigh. Thankfully Bredard had left those behind.

"There's nothing we can do about it tonight," he said.

"There's nothing we can do about it at all. Damnit." She pressed her lips together in frustration and the split he hadn't finished healing yet dribbled blood. "It's only been two weeks," she said. "They haven't reached the edge of Imperial Space yet; they could be anywhere. They would have had to drop out of their hyperstream periodically—anything could have happened."

"Or nothing could have happened." But Imperial Space was a treacherous place.

"Then why haven't we heard from them?"

It's true; he'd expected to have heard from her two brothers at least, even if the other rescued members of her family or the Ilmenans hadn't thought to assure her of their progress. They might have at least sent her a final farewell.

"I'm sure we will."

Her fingers tapped faster. "That assurance is useless to me."

He set down the medstick with a snap. "We have more immediate concerns right now." He had entirely too many concerns at the moment.

She frowned fiercely at him but didn't argue.

"I know you're worried about your brothers. I'm worried too. Their lives aren't the ones in immediate danger, though."

"Bredard wouldn't have killed me, not while he thinks he can get Dolan's research data from me."

"And when he realizes he can't?"

"We'll have to think of something before then."

"Bah." He reached for the medstick again and directed it to her lip. They sat in silence while he worked, she not looking at him, he trying not to stare at her. This was at most the third time they'd been in the same room in the last few weeks, and then only because she'd been attacked. They were both too busy to steal quiet moments together, and in truth, the awkwardness between them was more than he wanted to deal with right now.

She loved him, as much as he loved her. Apparently that hadn't been enough to keep her here. Kayla had chosen to leave him behind with no more than a word about it on her way to the spacedocks. She'd chosen life with her brothers over a life with him. If the Wyrds hadn't been forced into an emergency departure she'd be with them now.

How did he reconcile his feelings for her with knowing he'd always be a distant second choice to her brothers, so far behind that she hadn't even consulted him before making the decision to leave? Intellectually he understood her choice, if not her methods. None of that eased the rift between them.

He finished healing her mouth and returned the medstick to its case.

"I'm going to start skimming vessel logs for the last two weeks," she said, "see if I can find any mention of the Ilmenans' starship." The words came out fuzzy, the numbing effect of the medstick having reached her lips. She was already heading in the direction of the complink.

"Sleep's a better option right now, Kayla." Stars knew she had an impossibly full schedule tomorrow in her charade as Isonde.

"I slept already, remember?"

"Being stunned into unconsciousness for an hour before Rawn cut the lounge doors open and revived you doesn't count as sleeping."

She winked. *Winked*. After what happened... So Kayla.

He took a syringe from the medcase. "Sleep, or I'll sedate you myself."

Her eyes narrowed, judging his seriousness, so he waved the syringe around a little. He must have looked convincing because she grumbled and changed course for the bed.

She was asleep in less than five minutes.

2

Early next morning, Kayla and half a dozen politicians gathered in Archon Raorin's sumptuous office—one of hundreds of offices tucked into the wings of the Sovereign Council seat. While informal, the breakfast meeting was in some ways more important than the emergency session of council starting in an hour. Everyone seated in the padded hover chairs looked ill at ease, despite the micro-fine controls that adjusted every aspect of the chairs for maximum comfort.

Coffee was poured, fruit and pastries delicately selected, small talk made. Kayla tilted her seat upright so as not to get too comfortable. She'd gotten maybe three hours of sleep and fatigue ground her down, despite the high stakes of this morning's meeting. Also, her jaw ached. A medstick had healed the soft tissue damage but the joint remained stiff.

Those gathered spoke in low tones, a side conversation here or there, an air of expectant waiting hanging about the room. Archon Raorin's gaze flitted first to the door, then the chronometer embedded in the wall. He caught her watching him and gave her barely noticeable smile that she took as encouragement. Encouragement for Isonde. Kayla was back to wearing the hologram and playing her part as a member of the Sovereign Council representing the Sovereign Planet Piran, betrothed to Prince Ardin, and soon to take her seat on the exalted Council of Seven.

Isonde's seat. Isonde's soon-to-be husband.

Not if Malkor finds a replacement for me first.

He'd needed Kayla's elite training as a *ro'haar* in order to win the Empress Game. With that done, Kayla recommended a more politically savvy person be found to impersonate Isonde. That outcome seemed less and less likely as the days passed and he didn't mention any possible candidates.

Archon Raorin cleared his throat and the room fell to silence. He looked much as he always did in understated grey robes, with his long black hair knotted into an intricate braid: thoughtful, attractive and approachable. It was that combination, intelligence and charisma, that made him one of the most influential members of the Sovereign Council despite his home-moon's relatively small role on the imperial stage. "I was hoping for one more, but it appears he's changed his mind."

Raorin was a close confidant of Isonde's and Kayla had spoken with him several times in the last two weeks. Even after those talks, she was surprised by some of the people Raorin had called together this morning.

She had counted on seeing the scarred visage of General Yislan—a retired general and military hero from the imperial army—and the diminutive Sovereign Councilmember Siminia. They'd been vocal in their support of Raorin's proposal for imperial withdrawal from Ordoch. The attendance of elder stateswoman Councilor Gi, however, was unexpected. Her white braids twisted into ropes on either side of her head and her mahogany skin smelled of an antiseptic powder some people preferred to bathing. She hailed from the Sovereign Planet Wei-lu-Wei, known isolationists, their leaders only vaguely concerned with the goings-on beyond their planet. What help Gi might be was a mystery. She looked as formidable as her reputation implied, though, her strong features stamped with determination and her skin showing deep lines only years of frowning could cause.

She reminded Kayla of one of the separatist leaders from Ordoch's southeastern continent.

If Gi's presence was curious, the attendance of both the Low Divine of Falanar and Commander Parrel—a high-ranking officer in the IDC and Malkor's superior—was extraordinary. Parrel had frowned upon seeing Kayla when he entered, reminding her that while he respected and trusted Malkor, he was certainly no fan of hers. He looked stern and alert amidst the politicians and the Low Divine. His indigo IDC uniform was precise, every millimeter of jade piping along the seams aligned perfectly, the bars of his rank polished to a shine.

When the Low Divine had arrived, General Yislan had bowed low and risen to escort her to a chair as if the young woman couldn't cross the distance of ten meters on her own. The pale fifteen-year-old looked delicate in a gown of gold lamé. The cap sleeves, rounded neckline and belted waist suited her trim figure perfectly, while the skirt flowed to the floor and trailed behind her like a river. The image, no doubt calculated to the last detail, evoked ancient goddesses and reverence.

Very well done, Kayla admitted to herself.

How Raorin had persuaded the Low Divine to attend she couldn't imagine. Raorin was famous for his opposition to the prevailing religion among the Sovereign Planets. On Falanar, the Low Divine's religious authority was third only to the Mid and High Divines', and the girl made no secret of disliking Raorin. Maybe the sheer novelty of him requesting her presence had intrigued the Low Divine enough to attend.

"Thank you all for coming this morning," Raorin said. "I appreciate the chance to speak with you before the Sovereign and Protectorate Councils convene their emergency sessions today."

"Of course," Councilor Siminia said, "but perhaps you could make it brief? I have meetings with my staff to finish." Kayla liked Siminia. She was brisk, efficient and effective—much like Isonde was.

Is. Much like Isonde *is*. Isonde would get better—she had to.

Raorin inclined his head. "I'll come to the point then. The topic on all of our minds is the Tetratock Nanovirus; its spread and its possible eradication. Prince Trebulan's attempted release of the TNV at the Empress Game has finally, I'm convinced, made real the deadly nature of this threat to the Sovereign Council. We can't continue to pretend this plague is limited to the Protectorate Planets.

"Fear still rages on Falanar in the aftermath of the event. Those who were present took that fear home with them when they returned to their planets. I want to turn that fear into something positive: action. I want to use that frightened energy to drive our efforts to stop the TNV."

Siminia nodded in agreement. No one else spoke, letting him come to the point.

"Our best hope for a cure to the TNV still lies with the Wyrds and their advanced understanding of nanotechnology." Raorin shifted his gaze among those gathered, expressing his earnestness. "Now is the time to push the councils, to move for a full withdrawal from Ordoch. Only with the Wyrds' cooperation can we hope to end this plague. I gathered you here because I feel that a concerted effort on our parts can make this happen."

Kayla couldn't quite follow the intricacies behind Raorin's choice of "allies," not the way Isonde would have, but she approved of the plan.

General Yislan was the first to speak, as always. She couldn't fault his motives, driven as he was by a strong belief in the immorality of the empire's actions on Ordoch. Damn if he wasn't a pious, pompous hardliner, though. In Kayla's opinion, his value came from being one of the few members—or former members—of the imperial army willing to speak against the occupation of Ordoch.

"Whatever must be done to free the people of Ordoch," Yislan said, "we must do. The indignities they've suffered at our hands are too much to bear, and we have a moral obligation to see the occupation ended." He directed his words to Gi as if imparting a lecture.

Damn. Kayla could really use her psionic powers right now. She'd never regained them since the night of her family's death.

What had Raorin been thinking, bringing Gi into this? And what was Gi's reaction to Yislan's tone?

"Quite so," Raorin said. "There's more to it than that, though."

Yislan looked ready to object so Raorin continued without pause. "Siminia, I'm sure you can speak to the staggering amount of resources needed to maintain the occupation on Ordoch. Your planet has, since the beginning, been a major contributor of combat gear and defensive technologies for the army, among other things."

"That's true," Siminia said. "We're of course happy to do our duty to the empire, but we could use those resources at home. Especially if some of the Protectorate Planets are heading toward conflict, as they look to be."

Raorin switched his attention to Commander Parrel. "It's no secret that the IDC resented the Council of Seven's decision to end the diplomatic mission on Ordoch and initiate the coup. Since the takeover, the IDC's 'official stance' has been one of support for the occupation. You've never publicly agreed it was the right decision, interestingly."

"We want what's best for the empire." Parrel offered the well-worn line without inflection.

"Exactly," Raorin said. "And what's best for the empire is to withdraw from Ordoch. Councilor Siminia mentioned the growing hostilities between some of the Protectorate Planets. The IDC does what they can diplomatically to ease the situation, but sometimes it takes the presence of the imperial army to enforce the peace—an army which is spread too thinly among the planets, now that the bulk of our forces are needed to hold Ordoch.

"Add to that the panic from Trebulan's attempt. Suddenly everyone feels vulnerable to the TNV. Who knows what might happen in the face of such fear? Who knows who might take advantage of the lack of a military presence in the chaos? The IDC's mission of diplomacy would be much aided by the return of the bulk of the imperial army."

The Low Divine spoke, her childlike voice an odd counterpoint to the weighty issues being discussed. "I see no need for me to be here for such a meeting. I care not for politics; the Unity of our people is my only concern."

Now that was a barefaced lie. All three Divines schemed endlessly from the heights of their religious dominion. Isonde had repeatedly warned Kayla to be wary of them.

Raorin's smile was arch, as if he were aware of the games she played and more than willing to join in. "And that is why I asked you here today, Divine. Our people need guidance in the face of the TNV threat, lest their... Unity... be sundered by fear and distrust."

The Divine's lifted eyebrow said she heard his facetiousness.

"Their panic needs an outlet," Raorin continued, "needs to be shaped and shunted away from destructive paths. You could be the one to shape them, to lead them to greater Unity."

"I need not your counsel on how to best help my people."

"Of course not, I apologize. I only meant to suggest that our people might be best served if counseled to patience, toward a peaceful resolution with the Wyrds. Too often a threat to our person spurs an aggressive response. If, in their fear, the people clamor for stronger military measures to be taken on Ordoch, that could be disastrous for us all."

"The Divines take no stance on the matter of Ordoch," she said with hauteur.

"I ask only that you consider it. All of you." His gaze touched upon each person present. "You are the major voices in your spheres of influence. We could make a withdrawal from Ordoch a reality if we coordinated our efforts.

"Today's council sessions will be devoted to the TNV threat. Listen to the voices, the opinions. Ask yourself if anyone has a better solution. And then ask yourself which part you want to play in our impending struggle. Because rest assured, the TNV is coming for us. Isn't that right, Councilor Gi?"

Every head swiveled in Councilor Gi's direction. "You could not possibly know," she bit out.

"I doubt the secret will last out the day," Raorin countered. "They have a right to know."

It suddenly came together, what role an isolationist nation might play in Raorin's plan, what stake they might have.

"The presence of the TNV has been confirmed on Wei-lu-Wei," Raorin said. "The first Sovereign Planet has been infected with the plague."

Kayla gripped the bar with weak fingers, hanging on by sheer determination while sweat rolled down her temples. Beside her, Vid, one of Malkor's octet agents, seemed worse off than her, struggling to pull himself up.

"You can quit any time," she huffed out on a breath.

Vid's forearms flexed as he drew his chin to the bar. Again, damn him. "After you."

They were having something of a pull-up competition, which she'd foolishly agreed to in an effort to burn off her mental exhaustion from a long day at the Sovereign Council meeting. The haze hadn't dissipated after an hour-long workout, so here she was, dangling by hands that screamed to let go.

She hauled herself up for another count.

She'd come almost straight here to the workout space the octet favored when on Falanar, stopping at home only long enough to change and vent a string of curses Isonde would never have used at the intricacies of imperial politics. Life as a *ro'haar* with no expectation of ever ruling had not prepared her for this.

Kayla left Isonde's guards outside the workout space when she entered. Not surprisingly, she found Vid there doing his own workout, alone. He worked out more often than was good for him.

Vid had been severely injured a few weeks ago by Janeen, a traitor in their octet. Bad enough that he'd suffered; even worse for Kayla was the knowledge that he'd sustained the injuries fighting to save her brother from kidnap. She would forever owe him for that.

He was supposed to be resting.

He was supposed to be healing.

Instead he did another pull-up.

"Trinan's... gonna... kill you," she said, struggling to follow suit.

Her arms ached. The only reason she was still in the game at this point was because Vid's injuries weren't fully healed. She wouldn't have had a chance of keeping pace otherwise.

"Don't tell—"

"Vidious Con Vandaren!" Trinan's voice cracked across the room from the direction of the door.

"Thank the stars," she groaned, releasing the bar to land lightly on her feet.

Malkor entered the room behind Trinan. "Told you we'd find them here."

Vid had the grace to look sheepish, an odd expression on such a powerful person. Trinan's answering frown was only half for show. He really would be concerned.

"Wait a minute... Vidious? That's your name?"

"I *prefer* Vid, thank you very much."

Kayla grinned and reached for two towels with a rubbery arm. "I can see why." She wiped her face while tossing the other towel to Vid.

Malkor wandered toward them, studying Vid. "You're not overdoing it, are you?"

"No, boss." He stretched his shoulders, wincing a little. "Just getting a feel for my limits."

"With this one? She doesn't even have limits." Malkor turned to her. "You're a bad influence. We mere IDC agents can't match a *ro'haar*."

"Me? He started it." Well, maybe after a jibe or two from her. "I only went along to keep an eye on him." Okay, so it was a jibe or three.

"Riiiight. And you didn't trash talk at all, I'm sure."

"Would I do such a thing?"

He rolled his eyes. This was the Malkor she missed. The

comfortable, treat-her-as-one-of-the-guys, trade-insults-while-sparring Malkor. The Malkor she had almost left behind.

"How did the council session go?" he asked.

"It was…" Intense? Complex? Convoluted? Incendiary? Time-sensitive, scheming and a little overwhelming? "Eventful."

Malkor chuckled. "Don't worry, you'll get used to it."

"I hope not." She shot him a look. "You *are* searching for a replacement who understands this tangled maze you imperials call 'politics,' right?"

One thing had become abundantly clear to her in today's Sovereign Council session—the Sovereign Planets didn't give a damn about the Protectorate Planets. They saw them as founts of resources and that was about it.

"I'm looking," Malkor said noncommittally.

"Great." Just great.

Isonde had better revive damn soon.

"Come on," Malkor said to her. "We're late and you smell worse than Vid." They were meeting with Rigger about the data she'd collected from Dolan's machines—data Bredard wanted.

Last night's attack by Siño flashed into Kayla's mind. She felt the biocybe's arm locked around her throat, the hand suffocating her.

She took a deep breath to prove to herself that she could. Then another.

"Go on," she said, "I'll be there in twenty."

Kayla stood in the lobby of Rigger's condo tower, glaring at Rawn.

"Can't you stay here?" she asked, gesturing to the expansive space, which accommodated chairs, couches, vidscreens and even a bar staffed by a tender bot. She genuinely liked Isonde's favorite bodyguard, but damn! *She* was used to being the guard, not shadowed by someone else. And Rawn was there every time she turned around.

Rawn arched a brow and Kayla knew she'd erred. Isonde

would be used to being followed any time she left her house. Kayla pinched the bridge of her nose, feigning a headache. "Sorry, it was a long day at council and I was looking forward to relaxing with friends."

"You can relax perfectly well, Princess, while I stand outside your friend's door." He gave her the hint of a grin, and she had to like him. She would do the same in his place.

"Fine," she said. "I warn you, the walls are thin, and I want no mention of my hideous karaoke singing if the evening comes to that."

Rawn placed his hand over his heart. "I wouldn't breathe a word of it," he said, with mock seriousness.

She smiled, giving in, and took the maglift to Rigger's condo with Rawn at her side.

Malkor greeted her when she entered, and Rigger called a hello from the kitchen. Rigger's abode was a sleek space lodged somewhere in the middle of the condo tower. At least, it would have been sleek if the corners of the living area weren't crowded floor to ceiling with tech equipment. Not to mention the bedroom.

Rigger pushed an ancient-looking complink to one end of the table so the three of them could settle in the kitchen. At least Kayla thought it was supposed to be a complink. The side panel was open and electronic guts trickled out. It looked like a museum piece mid-dissection.

Rigger waved in its direction. "I'm addicted to hardware."

She synthed three plates of meat and veggies that tasted almost like the real thing. Kayla had lived off subpar calorie packs when she'd been hiding with Corinth on the slum side of Altair Tri. If she hadn't been spoiled rotten by eating real food everyday at Isonde's house for the last two weeks, she would have been in heaven with this meal.

"You splurge on high-end calorie packs?" Kayla asked, around another mouthful.

"Nah." Rigger patted her food synthesizer unit. "It's all about calibration."

"Why do you think I suggested meeting at Rigger's?" Malkor asked. "I'm here practically every other night."

"As is the rest of the octet," Rigger added. "Trinan and Vid alone double my calorie pack usage."

Not surprising. The two muscled agents were convinced food was a miracle remedy. Their love of food rubbed off on Corinth when they were watching over him.

As always, thoughts of her younger brother brought an ache to her throat. He'd been her only family for five years. She'd lived for him, sheltered him, and raised him the best she knew how. Now he was gone, on his way back to Wyrd Space with the Ilmenans and Vayne. It was all she'd wanted for five years, to get him home. It should have made her glad. Instead all she felt was lonely without him, and terrified to trust his welfare to anyone else.

"Kayla?"

Her name, so rarely used these days, caught her attention. "Sorry, what?" Apparently she'd left her fork hanging halfway to her mouth.

Malkor gave her an odd look. "Did Bredard say anything else last night, something you remembered afterward?"

"About the data we pulled from Dolan's system?" She shook her head. "Nothing, just that he wanted it, and he knew Dolan had been studying the transfer of psionic powers. Well, among many things, at least."

"I still haven't been able to unlock all of the data yet," Rigger said. "Our download was aborted midstream so some of the data is incomplete and some is trapped behind security protocols that can't ever be completed and rerouted. And the sophistication of the code he used…" Rigger half-shrugged. "I wish I still had Corinth's and Noar's help on this."

Noar was one of the Ilmenans who had come with Tia'tan to free Kayla's family from Dolan's captivity, and who now had charge of her brothers. He had better be keeping them safe, wherever they were.

"I did find the schematics for Dolan's mind-control

machine—which he'd apparently dubbed 'the Influencer,'" Rigger said. "Extracting the schematics and understanding them, however, are two different things."

Vayne had taken great pleasure in demolishing the original machine in Dolan's laboratory when they'd escaped.

"That's only one piece of what Bredard wants," Kayla said.

Malkor raised a brow. "What more would he need? With a machine that can control minds and access to the chambers of the Council of Seven, he could manipulate politics at the highest level. He would rule the empire, essentially."

Kayla finished the last bite of her food before replying. "The Influencer takes manual input on a basic level, and can control people superficially that way. Like, 'always wash your clothes on Tuesday,' 'never reply to the word hello,' that kind of stuff." She waved a hand in dismissal. "Parlor tricks. Practical usage requires a psionic." Kayla shuddered to think about the things Dolan had made Vayne do using that machine. And he'd only told her the barest of details. "Thoughts, emotions, morals… a thousand variables that can't be quantified well enough to be entered manually into the machine. You need to interface with it mentally to make the most of it, and it takes a Wyrd to do that."

Or, someone with the powers of a Wyrd.

Dolan had discovered how to rip the psionic powers from a Wyrd's mind and graft them onto someone else's brain. The only element missing had been permanence, and Dolan had meant to unlock that secret using her and Vayne.

"Dolan had been transferring psi powers to himself, a Wyrd to Wyrd translation. Could a Wyrd to imperial brain translation be successful?" Malkor asked.

"I have no idea," Kayla said. That level of science was way beyond her.

Malkor looked at his tech specialist. "Rigger?"

"I dunno, boss. I've found thousands of biomedical files and I've had limited time to go over them. Life as an IDC agent doesn't leave a lot of time for side projects."

Kayla frowned. It didn't leave a lot of time for anything else at all. Like relationships. Or finding someone to take over the role as Isonde so that Kayla could go after her brothers.

"Even if Dolan had discovered how," Malkor said, "there are no Wyrds left in the empire from which to harvest psionic powers."

Kayla gave him a mock-thoughtful look. "Bredard would need access to, say, a Wyrd planet that the empire controlled. Gee, where would they find that…"

"Point taken."

Rigger cleared away the dishes and passed out cups of rich qula-kava for dessert. They moved to the living room, each locked in their own thoughts for the moment. Kayla took a seat on the couch, the only two-seater in the room, and hoped Malkor would join her. Their relationship might be all kinds of frutted up, but if she could sit near him while planning together like they used to, she could pretend everything was all right.

Malkor chose the chair farthest from her. Rigger looked from Kayla to Malkor, then settled on the couch beside Kayla without comment.

Malkor was the first to break the silence. "Even without information on the Influencer, Dolan's files are priceless for the Wyrd-based tech schematics they contain. I've read through a few sections—it's clear he was feeding certain people weapon designs, spaceship modifications and a host of other advancements well beyond our current level of understanding. And what he'd released so far was only the tip of the iceberg."

"Who was he feeding them to, though?" Rigger asked. "Legitimate IDC channels? Corrupt elements within IDC? The imperial army?"

"At this point it's impossible to tell, and that isn't even our immediate concern," Malkor said.

Kayla had so many immediate concerns she couldn't keep track of them all.

Malkor's gaze switched to her. "We have to somehow keep Dolan's data from Bredard, while convincing him not to reveal Kayla's identity and the fact that we cheated to win the

Empress Game. If that gets out, our public execution will be the least of the damage."

"So let's talk plans," Kayla said. Her post-workout euphoria was fading, and seeing Malkor sitting across from her like a team member instead of a friend or lover depressed her. The urge to sink into the cushions of the couch was very tempting.

Sadly, her time was short. She was due for a late-night tea with Raorin to discuss the day's council session and plan their next move.

"Bredard is brother to the ruling warlord of Geth," Malkor said, "the third largest province on planet Sysar. Geth's military surpasses any other on Sysar, and they've been making aggressive moves to annex the neighboring province. None of which explains how he knows about Dolan's research or who he's working with."

Rigger nodded. "So he could conceivably be involved with anyone. It's going to take time to find a connection."

"Time we don't have," Kayla said. She finished her qula-kava and set the mug on the end table beside her. The knowledge that she was near-useless in this investigation galled her. Life as Isonde had her running around more hours of the day than she'd thought possible. Add to that her ignorance of the delicate interplay between imperial agencies and she was fully dependent on Malkor and the octet to find Bredard's weakness.

"Let's assume," she said, "that Bredard was working directly with Dolan, and is not a vulture intent on picking his technical corpse clean. It stands to reason that he would be connected to Dolan's other allies." And they all knew who she meant. Several people had been identified in Dolan's files, and each of them worked for the same agency.

"The IDC," Malkor said, his voice hard. She knew he still didn't want to believe that members from his own organization had sanctioned and supported the capture and years-long torture of the Ordochians.

Among other things.

The fact that a certain group of agents, commanders and

even chiefs had formed a clandestine alliance and used the IDC's power to forward their own ends was a secret to all but a handful.

"It's a place to start," she said, checking her chronometer and pushing herself to her feet. "I'll see if I can find out any more about him from the other councilors."

Malkor rose as well. "I've got mediation with Triumph and Victory in the morning." At Kayla's raised brow, he said, "They're from Altair Prime. Don't ask. After that I'll see if Commander Parrel has time to meet."

"I'm due at HQ all day for performance evals," Rigger said. "I'll see what I can wheedle from the data if I get a spare second."

They had all too few spare seconds these days.

Kayla climbed the stairs toward the second floor of Isonde's townhouse, more than ready for bed after her chat with Raorin. It was midnight and the last hour had resembled a military strategy session. So much to know and do and balance in imperial politics.

She reached the top step, hand already on her zipup to free her from her overtunic, when she caught the shift of shadow from the darkened end of the hallway. She instantly halted her movement and breath. Had Siño returned? Was the biocybe lying in wait?

One second later reality caught up with her paranoid brain: it was one of Prince Ardin's bodyguards, keeping watch outside of Isonde's sick room while Ardin was inside.

Relax, Kayla. Rawn doubled the security detail. No more biocybes. Problem was, she wouldn't recognize any of the new faces yet and Siño's arm was still strong about her throat. Damn this Isonde charade for disarming her of her kris.

She released the zipup's clasp and made her way down the hall. Prince Ardin, heir to the emperor, had arrived while she'd been meeting with Raorin. It wasn't like him to visit so late, or to stay so long. No doubt Isonde's staff already thought it odd that her fiancé came to visit "Lady Evelyn," who had supposedly been struck heavily with the Virian flu. Kayla tried to sit with him while he visited, to make it seem as if Ardin were keeping her company while she visited her unconscious "friend." It was too painful to stay for long, though. If Isonde's staff thought anything untoward was occurring, they were too loyal and too well-trained to remark on it.

Kayla nodded to the guard, relaxing when she realized it was the same guard who accompanied Ardin on most visits, not some stranger who could possibly be an agent from Bredard, bringing her another "message."

She entered the room and the doors slid shut behind her, locking her into the quiet, low-lit tomb. Isonde herself lay like a corpse in a medical pod in the center of the room, the blinking lights along its side the only indication that she still lived. The allergic reaction Isonde had suffered to Janeen's toxin still held her in its stony grip. Normally she wore Kayla's face, using Kayla's cover as Lady Evelyn of the Sovereign Planet Piran. Tonight Ardin had pulled the hologram biostrip off to see her true face, the face Kayla wore daily.

Ardin stood like a sentinel beside the pod, his back to the door, his jacket in hand as if he'd risen to go but couldn't make himself leave.

Who wasn't suffering through this masquerade they all perpetuated?

"Sometimes I think I hate you."

Ardin's words, so matter of fact, slapped her in the face. She couldn't move, couldn't even speak in response.

"She's dying, you know." His voice lacked any inflection, and barely carried to Kayla. "Toble told me tonight he doesn't think she'll last out the week."

Kayla had known it was bad, that the third of four possible antidotes hadn't worked like they'd hoped. Surely... surely the fourth would. Surely Isonde could hang on that long.

Surely she will free me.

"Toble wants to bring her to the institute," he continued in that flat voice, still not looking away from Isonde. "With the equipment there he thinks maybe, it's possible, he might be able to stabilize her for a little while longer." He choked out a grim laugh. "Stabilize her. Not heal her, not cure her, stabilize her. To leave her like this." He gestured with his free hand to encompass the woman Kayla had come to admire. A woman of drive and of ideals, who belonged to a future greater than the sum of Kayla's existence to date.

Kayla found her voice at last. "If he does that, everyone will know—"

He rounded on her then, his eyes as agitated in the dim light as his voice had been passionless. "Do you think I give one frutting damn, with Isonde dying?"

The words whipped her with their vehemence.

"It would mean our death," she whispered.

"I don't care!" His answering roar shook her. "I don't care," he said, more quietly this time. "She—" His voice broke. "She..."

Rage surged through Kayla. Rage and frustration and the sharp edge of doubt. "I never asked for this. For any of this. This was *your* plan."

He thrust his jacket down onto the chair he normally occupied, the fingers of his suddenly free hand flexing with strain. "This plan—it had seemed so possible when she was here. Now everything is frutted up."

Kayla took a step forward. "Then end it. Quit your moaning and end it. Save her, save the woman worth more than anything to you." It was almost a relief to say the words, to let someone take the awful decision of continuing the charade out of her hands. "Let Toble take her to the institute."

"I can't. Gods—" He balled a fist and for one second she thought he might try to strike her. Then his tension broke, his shoulders slumped, his fist lost its shape. "I can't."

How could the heir to the entire empire be so powerless?

He shook his head as if she didn't understand, as if she

could never understand. He turned back to gaze down at Isonde. "Isonde would forbid it, could she speak. Ruling by my side as my wife, on the Council of Seven, and the good we could do with that power means everything to her. More than you, more than me." He hung his head. "She would never, ever, forgive me for saving her if it meant the loss of all she'd worked for."

He fell silent.

Kayla, drained and aching, turned to go, catching his last words as the doors reopened:

"Sometimes I think I hate her."

3

At daybreak, Senior Commander Jersain Vega of the IDC sat at her desk in the home office of her townhouse in Falanar. Her official duties didn't start for hours. Naturally, she was already at work. Well, "at practice" would be more accurate.

She set her hover chair to stationary, placed both feet flat on the ground, rested her hands lightly on the chair's arms and sat comfortably, the chair supporting her back. She closed her eyes and focused on her breathing. A soft, cloying voice rose from memory—Dolan's voice, the voice of the Wyrd traitor who had served the empire. He exhorted her to breathe rhythmically and concentrate on her mantra.

I am in control.
I am in control.
I am in control.

The right state of mind, he always said, was essential for *beginners* learning to use psionic powers. Her lip curled at the memory of the condescending tone he used to emphasize "beginners." Smug bastard. He had certainly gotten what he deserved in the end.

A pity. Dolan was the best instructor on how to use psi powers—stolen psi powers—and she missed him for that alone.

At least she still had her thrall, Agira.

I am in control, she said again, and turned her mind inward.

She admired her mental shields for a moment. In her mind's eye they took the form of immense quadtanium walls, braced and gated and interwoven and locked a thousand times over. Dolan had laughed when he'd first probed them, testing her shield strength. The laughter hadn't lasted long when he found himself unable to break through. Of all their dealings together, that was perhaps her favorite moment.

"It would take an abnormally strong psionic to beat your shields," he finally admitted. "Unless you run into a Wyrd paragon, your secrets are yours to keep."

Imagine that. The leader of the subversive sect within the IDC, who had drawn in illicit elements from the imperial army and various politicians, being able to keep a secret.

Vega chuckled and slipped past her mental shields. She sank deeper and deeper, searching out the new source of power within. It appeared exactly as she remembered. The floor of her mind was the blue of an ocean abyss, and a fault ran through it, a giant crack glowing a fervent crimson that pulsed with violence. She sensed, rather than saw, the enormity of red-orange beneath that blue surface, a massive chamber of pure psionic energy ready to burst through the fault and incinerate her from the inside out.

A near invisible dome capped the fault off, kept it locked down. Vega took a steadying breath before reaching toward the shield dome. As she'd been taught, she punctured it, allowing a slim flow of power through.

The psi power hit her system like a drug, exhilarating, hypnotic, empowering. She widened the hole in the shield a fraction and opened herself for more. Her skin hummed with energy, the psi force tingling through her whole body, lighting her cells up.

A tremor went through her dome shield. She steadied it, applying another layer.

I am in control.

Time to practice.

She opened her eyes, took in the familiar setting of her

home office, the stylus and datapad in front of her on the desk. Slowly, carefully, with rigid restraint, Vega reached her mind out toward the stylus. The stylus rolled a centimeter when she brushed it with telekinetic force.

Gently, gently…

She wrapped a tendril of power around the stylus, shaking with the effort of translating the torrent of energy inside her to the merest thread of power outside. Her biggest challenge was controlling her strength, something few Wyrds struggled with because their powers grew steadily from birth, along with their ability to control them.

Not Vega's. She had stolen hers fully-formed.

She pushed all irrelevancies from her head and focused on the stylus.

Now to lift it. Gently, gently…

The stylus shot upward and bounced off the ceiling. It fell back to her desk with a clatter.

Damnit.

Not surprising, though. Most practice sessions began that way for her.

This time when she lifted the stylus she dialed back her power, though it tired her to do so, to hold so much inside and only let a little out. She was rewarded with a perfect ascent to eye level and only a slight wobble in its balance.

Getting better all the time.

Vega spent the next fifteen minutes spinning the stylus in various directions around various axes, before deciding to levitate the datapad simultaneously. Sweat dotted her brow. She let out a laugh of triumph when she had both the stylus and the datapad hovering at the same height and spinning in perfect synchrony.

Now for the real test.

Vega's shoulders trembled as she gripped the flow of power, painstakingly manipulating it to bring the point of the stylus to the surface of the datapad.

Gently, gently…

The point touched down. The stylus quivered slightly as Vega drew it across the screen, writing her name.

::Jersain? What are you doing awake?::

The mind voice ripped through her brain like a razorblade, shearing her tenuous hold on the telekinetic flow. The stylus punctured the datapad and flew through to the opposite wall, knifing into the organoplastic like a dart. The datapad crumpled in her grip. Without control of the force applied, Vega crushed the datapad.

"Frutt! Agira!" Vega flung the ruined datapad across the room to embed in the wall beside the stylus.

"Damnit." She ground her teeth and quickly repaired the translucent dome that shielded her from the strongest of her psi powers. With the flow contained, the reality of how drained she was hit her. She slumped back in her chair and muttered a weaker, "Damnit."

::Do you need me?:: Agira's mind voice was concerned.

Vega wrestled her anger back under control. Venting at the Ordochian thrall was like kicking a puppy—Agira couldn't help herself, not after all Dolan had done to her.

::I'm fine:: Vega told her. ::Go back to sleep, I'll be there in a minute.:: Vega sighed, letting out the last of her agitation. All in all, it had been a successful practice session, until that moment.

Her gaze fell on the stylus and mangled datapad lodged in the wall.

That was going to be a little tricky to explain to maintenance.

Morning found Malkor striding through the halls of IDC's headquarters, on his way to Commander Parrel's office. Parrel was his commanding officer. More than that, he was a respected, trusted mentor. A mentor Malkor had lied to on more than one occasion since his deception at the Empress Game. The knowledge that he hadn't lived up to his mentor's standards weighed heavily on his conscience as he commed the door.

"Enter," Parrel said, his habitual gruff tone coming through.

Malkor stood before his desk while Parrel finished reading something on a datapad. The strained silence intensified when Parrel set the datapad down and looked at him a moment without comment. Malkor felt every milligram of his disapproval in that gaze.

"Sir," Malkor finally said, nodding in deference to his rank.

Parrel motioned for him to sit. "Nice work this morning, Agent Rua, with Triumph and Victory. I read a summary of the transcript. No idea how you managed a full reconciliation between those two, but then, you always were my best."

Were. Past tense.

Now he was an IDC agent who had used the power of the organization for his own ends. He had betrayed his commander's trust and damaged the integrity of an organization they both proudly served. And worst of all, Parrel knew it. Knew it, and had yet to do anything about it.

"Thank you, sir." He settled stiffly into a chair.

"I'm glad you asked for a meeting—we need to talk about your new octet member."

"Excuse me?"

Parrel's neutral expression gave nothing away. "You're down a team member since Agent Nuagyn's betrayal." Janeen—Agent Nuagyn—was responsible for Isonde's current near-death state and the kidnapping of Kayla's youngest brother. To say she betrayed him was putting it mildly. "I'm putting together a list of candidates."

"I don't feel that we need another team member at this time." Malkor couldn't possibly risk the agents in his octet by bringing a stranger on board. They were all embroiled in the schemes over the Game, data lifted from Dolan's complink, Kayla's true identity… he couldn't trust anyone else. Not now that he knew Dolan had a network of corrupt IDC agents and officers running a shadow organization within the IDC.

It was hard enough trusting Parrel, who could still ruin him if he chose to.

Parrel arched a brow. "You don't feel that a seven-person octet needs an eighth? Is that because you want to continue running your octet as your own little autonomous band of agents?" Malkor winced inwardly as the words hit home. "A new agent, someone not on board with your plans, might throw a spanner in the drive, hmm?"

Precisely. How did one explain that without sounding like he'd gone rogue?

"With what we've learned about divisions within the IDC," Malkor said, "I don't rightly feel I could trust another agent at this time." As far as question-dodging went, it was at least truthful. "You had been compiling your own evidence on a secret cabal even before we secured Dolan's files linking his activity to several IDC agents and members of the imperial army. Who knows how deep the corruption runs?"

If Janeen, whom he'd trusted implicitly, could betray them, who else would?

"There are still agents and commanders I trust," Parrel said. Malkor shifted uncomfortably in his seat. Did he only imagine the rebuke in Parrel's tone? "Quit squirming, Rua, of course I mean you." Malkor would have felt better if he hadn't added, "To a point."

"Thank you, sir." It was probably more than he deserved. Suddenly the need to explain, to defend his actions, rose. "About the Game..." About the Game, what? *I'm sorry I did it?* Not likely. *I'd do it again tomorrow?* Probably. *It was the right thing to do?* How could he be sure, after all that had happened?

"Do you think I don't get it?" Parrel asked. "From day one I've known you'd make a great IDC agent. You had it in your eyes, that dedication, that driving need to do what was best not only for the empire itself, but its people. You have that look in your eyes still. I don't agree with your actions, but I can't disagree with your motives.

"You were not the only one—and certainly not the only IDC agent—trying to affect the outcome of the Game. You were only the best at it."

"Will you turn me in?" Malkor finally asked straight out. Tension over Malkor's choices had lurked between them these last few weeks, unaddressed.

Parrel snorted. "Don't be an idiot. More harm than good would come of revealing Isonde's treachery and the IDC's role in it at this point." He shook his head. "I hope she's as good as you think she is, because we're stuck with her."

Not exactly a ringing endorsement. And while the news gave Malkor some relief, he wondered if Parrel had other reasons for keeping the Empress Game deception a secret. He certainly had Malkor solidly in his pocket, now.

Stars. When had he become so distrustful?

"Time to make the most of this political situation you've gotten us into," Parrel said. "Do you have influence over her?"

Parrel knew Isonde was still paralyzed—he'd been instrumental in "coaxing" the formula for the possible cure out of Janeen—so he could only mean Kayla.

For a second Malkor couldn't answer. Did he have any influence over Kayla? Or was she one starship short of doing exactly what she wanted: leaving him and this whole mess behind to search for her brothers?

"She and I have similar goals," he finally said. No matter what else, they were united by their desire to free Ordoch from imperial occupation. That much he could count on.

Parrel snorted again. "What about Isonde? Once she recovers, can you influence her?"

No one influenced Isonde. You either agreed and rode her bow wake, or disagreed and got trapped in the undertow. "That's slightly less certain."

It was a surreal moment, discussing whether or not they could influence someone on the Council of Seven. Parrel would never have considered such an action previously. Then again, they'd never been in this situation before.

"Once she recovers," Malkor said. *When she recovers. She has to.* "You'll find Isonde's policies in line with our own interests. She'll be a strong ally in our fight to rid the IDC of corruption, and we couldn't ask for a better champion regarding the withdrawal of the imperial army from Wyrd Space."

Parrel raised a brow. "I never said that we should withdraw from Ordoch."

Malkor met his gaze steadily, on sure footing now. "No, sir, you never said it." He waited him out. It was another moment or two before Parrel nodded to concede the point.

"I've actually come about a more immediate matter," Malkor said.

"Something more immediate than the current TNV hysteria, the political reorganization brought on by the Game, and the Protectorate Planets taking advantage of both to start their own war?"

When put like that... "It's on something of a shorter timetable."

"Spit it out, Rua, I've got zero patience for mysteries." Parrel drummed his fingers on the desktop, rattling the pile of datapads waiting for his attention.

Malkor told him about Bredard, the blackmail and the one-week deadline—now short one day.

"Damnit, Rua! You're more trouble than three of Hanson's octets combined."

Which was generous, considering the bomb Malkor was about to drop on him. "He wants Dolan's data."

Parrel's frown conveyed his answer even before he spoke. "The personnel files Dolan had on the corrupt agents? He can't have it. That's internal IDC business." He wasn't likely to budge on that, either. Parrel loved the IDC and believed too strongly in the good the IDC could do to reveal the corruption within its ranks to the public. "He'd ruin us with it."

"Not to mention the councilors, imperial military personnel and aides that Dolan had under his thumb. Bredard could bring down a large section of the empire's elite with that data."

"Anything else you haven't told me? Did your octet gather any other data in the raid on Dolan's facility, something I need to worry about?"

"No sir," Malkor lied. Information on the mind-control experiments and the Influencer was too dangerous. Malkor couldn't trust the information to anyone else, not even Parrel.

His commander stared at him, a stare that had broken many an agent over the years. The waiting, the patience... Malkor kept his peace—barely.

Parrel finally pushed back from the desk, his chair groaning from the strain on its joints. "So let's talk plans."

They spent the next half hour debating how to gain leverage on Bredard. If he was in on Dolan's schemes, then he was high enough in the new power structure Dolan had been building to have some influence. Still low enough, however, to be sent like a thug to threaten Kayla for the information. The person pulling the strings wouldn't have gone themselves. That meant Bredard had a handler, someone in a greater position of power, someone with more to lose. Find a way to pressure that person and they'd bring Bredard to heel.

A lull hit. Their plans to stymie Bredard were getting nowhere. Parrel drew breath, then hesitated, debating something. Something big, if Malkor's stalwart commander wavered over sharing it.

Malkor wasn't sure he wanted to hear it.

"Senior Commander Jersain Vega is dirty," Parrel said. Regret flashed across his face. "That's who Agent Nuagyn compiled reports for."

Holy shit.

"You're certain?"

"Would I have said something, otherwise?"

What a disaster. Senior Commander Vega outranked Parrel, despite being younger. In the constellation of IDC power-players she ranked near the top, a few promotions short of leading the whole show. With the influence she already wielded...

"Shit."

"Exactly."

It had to hurt. Parrel had trained Vega when she became a commander. They'd worked side by side for years.

"Do you think Bredard's reporting directly to her?" Malkor asked.

"Not sure. That's where Dolan's blackmail personnel files come in."

"I haven't had more than a second to glance at those," Malkor said. He had too many other crises to deal with.

"Why don't you leave that to me? I have a trio of junior agents I've trained myself that I trust. They've been combing through the files and sending me briefs." Parrel flicked a finger in the direction of the stack of datapads.

Malkor arched a brow at the mention of junior agents. "Anyone I know?"

"Nah, fresh blood." He waved a hand, closing discussion on that topic.

If Parrel vouched for them, Malkor would trust them. "I'll go through what I have of Janeen's files, the ones she'd been preparing for Senior Commander Vega. If Bredard's handler is an IDC agent, Janeen might have something on them." Malkor stood to leave, feeling more in control of the situation than he had since Kayla had been attacked. "If it turns out we're looking for a councilor, I'll bring in, uh, 'Isonde's' help."

Parrel's gaze narrowed at the name. "Your involvement with her schemes had better be over now that she's won the Game, Rua. You're still an IDC senior agent—see that you remember that."

Across town, the hover car carrying Kayla to the Sovereign Council seat sank to the curb directly in front of the sprawling front steps of the building. A crowd awaited them, and she noticed with unease that the number of people waiting outside had multiplied since yesterday.

Media, fans, and politicos met her everywhere she went as Isonde. Isonde was powerful in her own right as the Princess of Piran and one of the councilors representing Piran on the Sovereign Council. Even more so now, as the soon-to-be

Empress-Apparent. It was also no surprise to have people gathered at the council seat during an emergency council session. Today's crowd had a mobbish feel to it, though, that put her on edge. There was a frantic energy, and for once she was thankful not to be the one on bodyguard duty.

Fear of the TNV was evident everywhere, as many in the crowd wore filtration masks and gloves of the tightest possible mesh weave and avoided contact with anyone else.

That won't save you.

The breathing filter and fine mesh might stop the TNV from penetrating at those two inlets, but unless you were covered head-to-toe in protective gear, the nanobots would find a way to burrow into the skin. Typical clothing fabric wasn't woven tightly enough to prevent TNV access to the skin, and in either case, the nanobots could cling to the surface of the protective gear and make their move once the gear was taken off.

Not to mention, with an actual outbreak confirmed on Wei-lu-Wei, any and all protective gear should be redirected there, not used to soothe fears on Falanar.

Rawn popped open his door and got out. He scanned the crowd, which was more or less contained beyond the double set of handrails leading up the steps, then gave it a second look before he let her exit the car. The questions hit her as soon as the sunlight did.

"How long have you know about the TNV infestation on Wei-lu-Wei?"

"Are they going to blockade the entire planet?"

"Is it true the Wyrds provided Prince Trebulan with the TNV in order to attack Falanar?"

"Do you think the Wyrds are responsible for the nanovirus on Wei-lu-Wei?"

The vid of yesterday's council session had been broadcast to the public once the session closed, as was imperial law. Raorin had been correct, news of the TNV plague on Wei-lu-Wei came out during the session, and the revelation had dominated the news vids ever since.

She ignored all the questions, including the ones on how long her wedding to Prince Ardin would be put off, and entered the council seat. Kayla hadn't played a large part in Ordoch's politics and the enormity of the entire imperial situation was daunting. Having people question her on imperial policy when she didn't know the right answers herself only worked to remind her of her inexperience.

I could really use your help right now, Isonde.

Or Malkor's. She could really go for having him at her side right now. His unwavering confidence always settled her, and his smile, the one that said, "You and me? No one stands a chance against us," would be perfect at this moment. She sighed on her way down the corridor. Why did things have to be so complicated between them?

She put that thought in a box and shoved it on a mental shelf beside concern for her brothers and the expectation of being revealed as a fraud at any moment. Worries for another time.

Rawn left her at the door to the council chambers and went to wait wherever it was bodyguards waited during session. Luckily, both council seats had been inspected and declared TNV-free, so none of the councilors had to worry about protective gear.

As Kayla entered at the back of the yawning chamber, the mantle of Isonde settled over her with eerie ease. She *was* the princess, and these councilors were her peers. The split-personality was becoming second nature to her in a way that would have been more disturbing if she didn't need Isonde's persona so much—Ordoch's freedom depended on it.

The square chamber was quadruple-story height and decorated in an antique imperial style that she admired for its artistry and gravitas. It made her feel small and transitory, a minor player in a rich history that had seen and would yet see orators of greater importance than her.

Deep, arched recesses running along the two side walls held many-paned windows that rose from the floor to third-story height. They were wider than the length of a hover car and light poured through them. The windows were topped with star-shaped cutouts filled with birefringence gel, through which the sunlight sparked rainbow fire. The arches themselves were each carved from a single piece of green stone, and worked over with a spiraling star motif.

A media gallery was embedded in the third story of the chamber's front wall, above and behind where the adjudicator sat. The huge stone archway that fronted the gallery had the same carved star pattern and rose gracefully toward the ceiling. The true masterpiece of the room, however, was the ceiling itself. Reliefs of the most notable moments from the founding of the empire, worked in the traditional indigo and jade palette of the empire, sprawled across the expanse. The Final Surrender of Wei-lu-Wei, the Signing of the Great Accord and the Launching of the *Intrepid* were all represented and intricately wrought in plaster sculptures. Gold and silver filigree ran through it all, adding opulence to an already astounding work of art. Chandeliers dripping plascrystals hung at regular intervals, lighting the curved rows of desks on the floor that held the councilors.

Archon Raorin lifted a hand in greeting from his place across the room, and she nodded in response as she took her seat among the councilors from Isonde's home planet, Piran.

From her hover chair in the Piranian section, Kayla faced the adjudicator's desk and the empty media gallery head-on. In the idealist opening days of the empire, media had been allowed to watch the proceedings of the Sovereign Council live. As things grew more strained with the addition of each Protectorate Planet, that access had been pulled, journalists replaced by the cams that recorded the session to be broadcast—and potentially edited—later.

Kayla made polite chit-chat with the Piranian councilor beside her. Raorin had warned Kayla that the councilor had known Isonde for years, and meeting him had been a worry for Kayla. Thankfully, Raorin was correct in his estimation that the councilor considered Isonde too young for the post, and Isonde considered him too conservative to be of any use to her, so they rarely spoke. Kayla made it a point to use him as a silent buffer between her and the other Piranian councilors, who would certainly know Isonde better.

Pockets of councilors around the room were debating or agreeing with each other when the adjudicator called the session to order. It took more than one electronic chime for everyone to finally settle into their seats. Tension thrummed through the room, and styluses scribbled furiously across the datapads embedded into the desktops as councilors continued their conversations silently.

The adjudicator consulted her list. "Councilor Araújo will speak first."

The lights from the chandeliers dimmed and a circular platform rose from the center of the room, the holotiles of its floor illuminated in a soft blue glow. Araújo activated his comm at his desk, and a three-dimensional hologram of him appeared above the platform. The hologram was pre-designed; every councilor had one programmed into the council's databank. Araújo's hologram wore the ceremonial garb of his prelateship—a profusion of gauzy citron fabric wrapped about his torso, over his shoulders, down his arms until it covered his hands, and around his legs in a tight skirt that would make walking challenging. He spoke from his desk and the hologram said the words, allowing every councilor to see and hear him clearly.

A silver dot blinked on her desktop. The message [not good] came across on her datapad, attached to Raorin's ID. Her instinctive response was a sarcastic, "Yeah, you think?" She refined her reply to fit Isonde's style with effort. She scribbled [perhaps he'll keep it short] with her stylus.

Not likely. Araújo was rabidly anti-Wyrd and could go on about their "evil" for days without stopping for breath. Thank the stars he was only allotted twenty minutes to discuss the policy proposal he'd filed yesterday before debate on the topic began.

Kayla called up the list of policy proposals on the table for the day. Since his was titled "Fair and Righteous Retaliatory Action for TNV Terrorist Attack on Falanar by the Wyrds from Ilmena," she had a good idea what to expect.

Fantastic. War-mongering. Just what they needed.

"It's clear that Prince Trebulan's TNV attack on the empire at the attempted wedding of our most honored Prince Ardin was masterminded by the Wyrds from Ilmena," Araújo's hologram began. "Even if you ignore the thorough findings of the military proving their guilt"—he flashed a look at Raorin, who had openly called the findings into question—"the fact remains that the Wyrds were the only ones with the technology to get the nanovirus past all of our scanning protocols and onto the planet's surface."

Which, in Araújo's defense, was a fair point. Trebulan, coming from a planet infected with the TNV and being somehow immune himself, certainly had access to the nanovirus. What he lacked was a way to get it onto Falanar, especially during the heightened security of the Empress Game.

"Though the attack was thwarted by our own Councilor Isonde, this terrorist action, this assault on the very heart of our empire, cannot go unanswered. The Wyrds showed their willingness to act without mercy, to kill innocents and civilians, and in a manner of unspeakable cruelty. We can do no less in defense of our great empire."

He went on to suggest that the military use Ordoch as a home base in Wyrd Space, a jumping-off point from which to attack Ilmena itself.

"We must bring the fight to these cowards, who would use our own people, our own disaster against us," he finished.

The number of councilors around the room who nodded in agreement with this idiocy gave her some alarm. That more than a handful even considered this proposal a viable option was beyond her.

Raorin's light blinked on her datapad: [well, that went worse than I'd hoped for]

Holographic Araújo winked out and the adjudicator opened

the floor to discussion. A hundred rebuttals came to Kayla's mind: How could anyone cognizant of the tenuous nature of the Ordochian occupation think the empire had anything like a "home base" there? Where would the extra troops come from? More importantly, how would that help stop the spread of the TNV in the empire? How would that help them find a cure? Rebuild the damaged planets? Keep the Protectorate Planets in line, who were themselves headed for a possible war?

Even if the Wyrds had planned Trebulan's attack—and she refused to think Tia'tan and Noar capable of that—how did the empire not see that they'd brought any such action on themselves by attacking Ordoch in the first place? The hypocritical self-righteousness of Araújo's speech stoked her ire.

Thankfully the majority of the councilors who joined the discussion shared many of her objections. The lack of resources to wage an intergalactic war on two fronts was mentioned, as well as the dearth of popular support for military actions in Wyrd Space at the moment. That could change in an instant, though, if the panic were great enough.

When Araújo's crony turned the tone of the debate into an "it's us or them!" dynamic, the adjudicator called the discussion closed and moved onto the next proposal.

There were a million and one policy proposals on the docket, only a handful of which were worth taking seriously. Many of the others would be tossed out by the adjudicator for their irrelevance. Councilors had used the emergency convocation of the council to put forth proposals for their own domestic issues, unrelated to the mandate of the emergency session, which was to decide on a plan of action for addressing the problem of the TNV.

Everyone had expected a proposal from Councilor Gi, or any of the councilors from Wei-lu-Wei, but despite news of their TNV outbreak becoming public, they remained silent. Hopefully Gi was thinking over Raorin's words from the meeting yesterday, considering that her planet's best hope was to throw their support in with Isonde and Raorin's plan.

Hopefully.

The day wound on with a long series of proposals that varied from blockading Wei-lu-Wei off entirely; cancelling all space travel to and from the planet; establishing aid stations on the as yet uninfected continents to house refugees; creating massive "firebreaks" around the infected areas—a method of containment that had only been mildly effective on other worlds; bombing the infected landmass to ash, and so on.

The number of proposals focused on finding an actual cure for the TNV was much lower. They were mainly focused on increased funding for the scientists currently trying to work on a cure—a cure they hadn't been able to find in a decade. One or two took the vein of attempting diplomatic negotiations with the Wyrds on Ordoch to see if they might now, after five years of occupation, be ready to help. Kayla made note of those councilors, as well as the councilors who seemed to respond favorably to the idea, with a mind to approach them later. If she had access to the imperial data stream, she'd download all the information she could find on them now. However, with the exception of the adjudicator, everyone was cut off from outside communication of any electronic sort while in chambers.

The proposals that worried her most were those put forth by councilors from Inja, the smallest of the Sovereign Planets, and from Hurruha's councilors, a planet that rivaled Piran for influence. They called for harsher military action on Ordoch, arguing that the empire hadn't applied enough pressure on the Wyrds there to force them to develop a cure. Those proposals were delivered well. The councilors laid out definitive plans of action and avoided over-emotionalizing the issue. People who didn't respond to the overt war-mongering from Araújo earlier seemed to at least be considering these proposals.

Kayla had been given the last speaking slot of the day, arguably the best position to be in. Councilors would end the session with her words ringing in their ears.

She activated her comm and Isonde's hologram sprang to life in the center of the room. Kayla had had a new hologram preprogrammed for this, her first council proposal since winning the Empress Game. In the image, her deep indigo gown sparkled, the sleek fabric shimmering from its high collar to its long skirt. Subtle jade accents flashed here and there, the message "I'm about to marry into the royal family" coming across clearly. Lastly she'd had Isonde's auburn hair braided and coiled about the top of her head like a coronet.

Discount the words of the Empress-Apparent at your peril.

She opened her notes on the proposal she and Ardin had crafted, and Raorin had refined. Everything was in readiness. Trebulan's attack and Wei-lu-Wei's TNV outbreak set the perfect stage from which to argue for a withdrawal from Ordoch. The immediate need for a cure would force the issue, and the inroads Isonde had been making into both councils for the last year would bear fruit.

Kayla stood, earning surprised glances from everyone. She was too full of passion on the topic to deliver her speech sitting down. This was for her people's freedom, perhaps their very lives. She could do this, she *would* sway these politicians.

She took a final calming breath. She was Kayla Reinumon, *ro'haar*, one of the last remaining heirs to the throne of Ordoch. She was Princess Isonde Veriley of Gangisha, Sovereign Planet Piran, soon to be Empress-Apparent.

"Esteemed councilors. Today—"

Her hologram winked out and her comm went dead as the chandeliers came back to full brightness.

The adjudicator's voice filled the chamber. "My apologies, Councilor Isonde, councilors. There has been an... incident." It sounded almost like a question, as if she wasn't sure what to call it. "The session is adjourned effective immediately, and you will be escorted directly outside upon exiting the chamber through the rear doors only. Security will see to your safety." With no more instruction than that the closing chime sounded and the adjudicator rose. She ignored questions from the councilors on all sides and ducked through the door at the front that led to her private rooms.

The skin prickled on the back of Kayla's neck when a message from the adjudicator flashed on her datapad: [Captain Arsenault, chief of security, is waiting to take you into custody. Present yourself to him immediately.]

4

[Captain Arsenault, chief of security, is waiting to take you into custody. Present yourself to him immediately.]

Kayla's skin flashed ice cold. Bredard. *That bastard!* He had said she had a week before he exposed her.

She could barely draw a breath, lungs locked tight at the shock of finally being discovered. What to do? For the second her mind answered only, "You're trapped! Trapped. Trapped..."

"Well, of all the preposterous—" the older councilor beside her grumbled. She blocked out the sound and searched the room's exits.

Isonde would accept her capture calmly. Isonde would rise gracefully from the hover chair, make her stately way out of the chambers and greet the soldiers waiting with a cool nod of her head, acting as though she'd done nothing wrong.

Isonde could kiss her ass.

Capture meant inquisition. Trial. Execution. Hers and Malkor's.

No frutting way.

Exit, she needed an exit.

All around her people rose from their seats, hundreds of obstacles that stood between her and a way out. They milled like leaves in an eddy, clumping here and there, more curious than concerned about the interruption. Very few actually headed for the doors at the rear. That gave her some time.

The side doors? There was a door set in a deep recess on either side of the room, both still closed. They were rarely used—would they still be guarded? Probably. If they knew who she really was and all she'd done so far, they wouldn't risk it.

The media gallery? Even if her hover chair could lift her three stories off the ground, there was no telling if the doors in the back of that balcony would be unlocked. Then she'd be trapped for sure.

Her gaze landed on the adjudicator's door. There had to be another entrance from there into the building proper. Would they think to guard that?

Didn't matter. The adjudicator's chambers were the best of her terrible options.

She cursed Isonde's prominent seat in the middle of the rows of desks. Councilors blocked the aisle to either side of her, and where she really needed to go was forward, across the rows to the front of the room. The main walkways of the chamber were clogged, all but impassable now.

Malkor's face flashed in her mind. No way to get a message to him. Damn the communications-blocking field of the council chamber!

She had to warn him. If she could reach him first, maybe they could run. Maybe one of them could escape at least. *It had better be him.* No way she'd let him be killed, not while there was any fight left in her.

And she had plenty of fight.

She toed off her dress heels and hit the altitude adjustment on her hover chair, shooting to the height of the desk. With a push off the shoulder of the councilor beside her she stepped onto her desk and immediately leapt to the desk one row ahead.

Thank goodness for embedded *ro'haar* training—she'd dressed in a loose, knee-length skirt with plenty of room for any necessary action. Her bare feet had perfect traction on the desk's aeroglass surface when she landed. A councilor from Trijika shrieked when Kayla stepped on her shoulder to launch herself forward to the next desk.

"What the void?" Councilors scrambled out of her way, some shouting, some pointing. She knocked the wig off of someone's head with her next jump and stumbled, nearly crashing into the back of the hover chair on the other side of that desk.

Two desks to go. Then a building full of security—and no doubt imperial military officers to blow through on her way out.

Malkor, you had better be ready to run when I get there.

She made the next desk easily and jumped for the last one without breaking her momentum. Thankfully no one knew enough to stop her. That and they were all too stunned to try.

At least she was ending her career as Isonde with style.

She hit the floor at a run and launched herself shoulder-first at the door to the adjudicator's suite. It burst open, sending her stumbling through an office and into private chambers beyond.

The adjudicator, deep in conversation with someone at a complink terminal, shot to her feet. "You shouldn't be here!" The face of a council security officer gaped at her from the screen.

A dry chuckle escaped Kayla before she could stop it. "No shit." There. Another room lay beyond this one, and through the passage she saw her way out.

"You should be with the guards! It's not safe."

"Lady, I haven't been safe in five years. This is just another day in my life." Kayla sprinted through the remaining room and opened the door to the corridor beyond.

Empty. For the moment. She grabbed her mobile comm from her belt as she took off down the hallway. The blackout field only covered the council chambers themselves. She punched in Malkor's code.

Please don't let me be too late.

"Kayla?"

"Thank the stars! Malkor, listen—you have to run, get out of there, wherever you are." She approached a T in the corridor at a full sprint. Left or right? *Damnit!* "They know about Isonde. They're after me."

She chose right, which turned out to be wrong as she slammed full-force into a security guard, sending them both sprawling to the floor and her comm spinning away.

"Princess Isonde!" The security guard got to his feet first, his face red as if with embarrassment. "I'm so sorry." He reached down to help her, babbling like a junior councilor in the presence of royalty. "I didn't think— The adjudicator said— I'm so glad you're safe." He seemed unaware that he still gripped her hand and that she gaped at him like an imbecile.

His words slowly penetrated the flight response fogging her brain. *Isonde?*

The young guard spoke into his comm. "I have Princess Isonde with me, sir; she's unharmed. Should I escort her to you?" He finally realized he still had her hand and dropped it, turning a darker shade of red.

"Yes, sir. Of course, sir." He gave her a smile that was half-comforting, half-star-struck.

The pounding need to flee thrummed through her, almost forcing her into motion. What was going on here? If this was an arrest, it was the worst arrest attempt in the galaxy. *And* he'd called her Isonde.

"What the void is going on?" she asked, balanced on the balls of her feet, ready for anything.

"I… I'm sorry, Princess. I thought you knew. They said you'd fled the council chamber so I assumed you'd received a threat on your life." When she remained mute, he continued. "Your bodyguard, he's been… well, he's been murdered. We suspect poison."

"Rawn?" The words tilted her sideways. It took a moment to reorient herself to the new landscape. She wasn't under arrest. No one was chasing down Malkor.

"My captain was waiting to take you into protective custody outside the chamber's rear entrance, since this was clearly an attack aimed at you. When you fled the chambers, we assumed you'd received a death threat and needed a quicker escape route."

She nodded like an automaton, her mind racing. "Yes. A

death threat. Exactly why I ran."

Her freedom, her life, weren't at risk. Malkor was safe.

Wait—Malkor. She dashed to where her comm lay and snatched it up. "I'm fine," she said, the words coming out on a rush of breath. "I'm fine. It's fine. We're…" She sighed, her heart finally beginning to slow. "We're okay."

Malkor's voice shouted at her from the other end. "What the frutt is going on? I thought you were at council? Where are you? Stay there. I'm coming right now. Where?" he demanded.

"Council," she said, "I'm safe." She was safe, but, Rawn? The full impact of the guard's words hit her. "I have to go." She cut the connection before he could object.

Rawn. Isonde's favorite bodyguard. *Her* favorite bodyguard. "He can't be dead."

The guard ducked his head. "I'm sorry, Princess. The medics have already seen him and pronounced the time."

"How is that possible?" Rawn had been in the council seat the whole time, hadn't he?

"We'll find out, trust me. For now, I have orders to take you to Captain Walsh. He'll keep you safe until—"

"No. Take me to Rawn."

"Pardon?"

"I've never been in this section of the seat, and I don't know where to find him." She'd never been in any other part of the council seat before, not that he knew that.

The young guard looked ill at ease. "That's not a good idea."

"If you won't take me, then point me in the right direction and I will go by myself." How could Rawn be dead? Who could even accomplish such a thing in the middle of all this security?

"Captain says I'm to keep you safe," the man tried.

As if he could do a better job than she could herself. Kayla picked a direction at random and started jogging. She had to see Rawn for herself.

"Princess! Wait!" He clearly didn't expect his shout to have an effect because he jogged after her right away, his boots loud against the floor compared to her barefoot tread. "It's this way."

They passed the rest of the way in silence and arrived at a cafeteria. People who could only be the other councilors' bodyguards were scattered throughout the room, talking in groups, being interviewed by council security.

Now that they were here, Kayla hesitated in the doorway. Dread crept up, curling around her legs, her stomach, freezing her chest. Silence fell, every eye turned to her as she struggled to move forward. It took all her willpower to put one foot in front of the other and approach the sheet-draped table near the windows.

She had to see. Had to *know*.

A guard moved as if to stop her. She halted him with a glance. This was her tragedy to own. Rawn was one of hers.

She stopped beside the table. The sheet outlined the shape of a man hunched over the tabletop, its pristine whiteness mocking the silhouette of death. She bunched a fistful of fabric in her hand and tore the sheet off.

Rawn lay collapsed across the table, his knees bent as if in the action of rising, his hands grasping the surface for support. He was turned toward her, his handsome face black as the vacuum of space, his blood-burst eyes popping out like two red giants.

She stared.

Stared and stared in the silence that no one dared break.

Every part of her wanted to deny it, to refuse to believe her eyes. If she denied it hard enough, could she change the truth? Because the truth was, the only reason to kill Rawn was to get at her.

Rawn had died because of her. She might as well have poisoned him herself.

A shrill squealing split the air, making her jump back. Around her people scrambled toward the door. Someone tried to pull her away but she shook them off.

The sound came from Rawn.

"It's a trap, Princess!"

Not likely, or it would have done its damage already. This was something else.

The squeal carried on and she finally located its source: Rawn's mobile comm. She gingerly pulled it off his belt and looked at the screen.

```
In case you hadn't
taken my threat seriously.
You have 5 days left.
```

Senior Commander Jersain Vega of the IDC stood with her back turned to the late afternoon sunlight streaming through the floor-to-ceiling windows, and considered slamming her skull into her desk. Repeatedly.

"Blinds. Full cover," she demanded, palms pressed to her temples. The glass instantly blackened, leaving her in the twilight of weak ambient office lighting. Even that she dimmed to almost nothing.

Damn these attacks.

The procedure had been months ago, she should have been over these spells by now.

The full couch in her office beckoned, promising the sweet relief of a few hours' unconsciousness. Vega refused to succumb. She was a senior commander of the most powerful organization in the empire, the youngest currently holding that post at fifty-three years old. She would *not* be brought low by a headache.

Spell. Headache. Paltry words to describe the pain of her brain going supernova. She wanted to crack her skull open, peel apart the edges and let the agony out.

Instead she sank into her desk chair, eyes slitted, palms pressing her temples, as if the vise-like pressure could counteract the torment.

Breathe, Vega. Breathe through it.

In. Out. Again. Palms pressing, pressing.

It'll fade. It always does.

How long would it last, though? If she were a praying

woman, now would have been the time. Her door chime sounded, blasting like a shot through her head. Rang again.

"Go away," she muttered. The person must have taken the hint. As she caught a deeper breath, hoping the worst was over, she made the mistake of looking at her complink. In the dark of the room, the power light blinking in the corner glowed like a sun, stabbing through her eye.

Ten steps to the bathroom…

She'd never make it.

Vega doubled over and vomited into her waste bin.

One hour, two pain injections and three rounds of dry-heaving later, the ache had subsided into something like the background roar of a waterfall. Constant, booming, but manageable.

"Frutt you, Dolan." Swearing at the dead man didn't give her any satisfaction. The Wyrd traitor had done his job, had transferred the psionic powers of his kind onto her brain somehow. She'd demanded the best. Vega *was* the best, she wouldn't settle for less, despite Dolan's warnings.

Her mistake hadn't been in trying to gain psi powers for herself, her mistake had been in choosing Vayne Reinumon— the strongest Wyrd in captivity by far—as her unwilling donor.

I'm the best, she reminded herself. *I can master this.*

All she needed was training. Practice.

Thank the void she still had Agira.

Vega remembered her conversation with Dolan, months ago:

"Even if you survive the transfer process," Dolan had said, in that oh-so-superior tone he favored, "I doubt you'll last a week with full-blown psi powers ripping through your mind. Psionic powers grow slowly in Wyrds from birth, bit by bit, layer by layer, giving us time to adjust, to learn step by step how to control them."

"You managed to handle a full transfer of psi powers," she'd pointed out.

His condescending smile deepened. "I have more training in controlling psi powers than you could achieve in several lifetimes."

Frutt, how she'd hated working with the smug bastard.

If he wasn't the only man standing between her and everything she'd wanted for a decade, she would have executed him like the traitor he was. Instead, the emperor housed him in high style, catered to his every whim, acceded to his every demand in exchange for Dolan's cooperation.

"I think I'll manage," she'd told Dolan. She'd been so certain.

Then again, overconfidence had always been her undoing.

"Vayne is too strong for you. As is Natali. I recommend we start with Effusa."

She would have been wise to heed Dolan's advice. Instead she'd said, "I want Vayne. Make it happen, or so help me, I'll turn you over to your own people."

And that had been that.

Now, since Dolan's death and the liberation of the Wyrd prisoners, she was left with the enthralled Agira and a psionic force that threatened to destroy her.

Enough bitching. The power wouldn't kill her today, and she had work to do, starting with a meeting with that lackey, Bredard.

Twenty minutes later she arrived at the massive grounds of the Basilica of the Dawn, the palace of the Low, Mid and High Divines. The extensive building and green space sprawled boldly in the heart of Falanar City's crown district. Here, the Low Divine—the darling of the masses—gathered the peoples of the empire to listen to the message of Unity, passed down from the High Divine himself.

How ironic. Meeting at the center of Unity while planning yet more schisms within the IDC and imperial army. Vega smiled as she entered the grassy park, the idea warming her and beating back the headache.

Her smile dimmed at the sight of Bredard, standing before

one of the dozens of metal sculptures on the grounds.

Frutting middle men.

High-level details held her interest. Politics. Conspiracies. Coups.

Petty blackmail? Better left to thugs.

Sadly, this blackmail scheme was too delicate to leave to anyone else. The fewer who knew she might gain Dolan's full cache of tech the better. Bredard was a necessary evil in the process, someone she could hang out to dry if plans backfired.

"Lovely, isn't it?" Bredard murmured when she reached his side. His gaze remained fixed on the twisted arc of metal in front of him. The sculpture's anodized niobium skin flashed a rainbow of colors in the late afternoon sun. Beautiful at another time—brutal to her headache right now.

She focused her attention on the bland stone base. "How go the negotiations?"

"Stalled. I've given them a little nudge, to get things moving."

"Did it work?"

"Eh." He shrugged his shoulders, less confident than she liked. "Give it time."

"We don't have 'time,'" she snapped. What good were her psi powers, all this pain, without Dolan's notes on the Influencer? "I want that data now."

Bredard looked her way for the first time. "Kayla Reinumon seemed pretty... secure in her position. How reliable is this blackmail you have on her, Agent Rua and Princess Isonde?"

"Top notch. We got it from Agent Nuagyn, the mole inside Agent Rua's octet." Janeen had provided extensive notes on Agent Rua's scheme to fix the Empress Game, though she didn't have the tech expertise to back it up. Once Vega knew where to look, however, her own forensic complink specialists could find the minute trail Rigger had left behind as she adjusted DNA, retinal and ID scans to switch with the activation of a biostrip hologram. Vega never would have found the evidence without Janeen's report. No one would.

Not to mention the hologram program itself—talk about

sophisticated. The Wyrds had to have helped Rigger with it because that hologram was advanced way beyond those currently available to the IDC, and the IDC had the very latest and greatest of everything.

Creating a fake image to cover a person, sure, they could do that. Making the image react to the clothing underneath, say if fabric got torn? Or respond to biologics, such as simulating blood on the hologram if the wearer started to bleed… no one Vega knew had access to that kind of complex tech.

"Maybe if we pressed them with the specifics of what we know," Bredard said, "how tightly we have them by the balls…"

"And give them time to find a counter to it? Not a chance." They would, too. Rua and the Wyrd princess would slip right through her trap.

Bredard shrugged again. "Then we're back to waiting."

Vega turned, giving him the full force of her gaze. "I don't do 'waiting.' I do results."

"Look. You like to bully people. I get it. How 'bout you stand down on the 'disappoint me at your peril' bullshit?" He gave her a cocky grin. "You need me, because you certainly won't get your own hands dirty."

She stared at him for a full minute in silence, watching his grin fade and the fidgets start. When she put a hand on his shoulder he flinched at the contact. "Bredard, I can have you killed before you reach the front gates." She didn't have to brag, it was a simple fact.

He swallowed tightly.

"Dolan's data files are worth more than your life. Keep that in mind during your 'negotiations,'" she said.

Vega left him staring after her, his face pale, as she exited the basilica's grounds.

5

Kayla, bracketed by two of Prince Ardin's royal guards, finally entered Isonde's townhouse three hours later. Other royal guards had already been dispatched to the house and had searched it top to bottom for any threats before Kayla had been allowed to return. More guards waited outside in the motorcade that had seen her safely from the council seat to the house.

She nodded wearily to one of Isonde's guards who stood at attention outside the front lounge. Where Rawn might have stood, on another day.

So many emotions assailed her that she couldn't even process them. Anger—overwhelming anger. Powerlessness. Exhaustion. Shock. And over it all, fear. A fear she hadn't felt since escaping the massacre on Ordoch.

The guard bowed to her. "Princess, Senior Agent Rua is waiting within, if you care to see him."

She wanted nothing more in that moment. She nodded at the guard to open the door. When her two new royal bodyguards made as if to precede her, she blocked them with a hand.

"Agent Rua is a trusted friend." Kayla summoned every ounce of Isonde's hauteur and tone of command. "I will see him alone."

"Princess—"

She cut the objection off with a raise of her brow. "You may wait here, or you may leave. Your choice." They silently stepped back.

She entered the room and hit the lock command on the door pad before turning to face him. Malkor stood in the room's center, arrested by her entrance. The furniture had been pushed askew as if he'd paced for hours and needed more room to go about the business. His indigo uniform jacket was thrown over the arm of a sofa and his hair was in disarray, his fingers no doubt having raked through it a hundred times. He looked tense and worried and ready to fight.

He looked beautiful.

"Malkor." Kayla peeled off the hologram biostrip and tossed it to the floor before rushing to him. He caught her in his arms, holding her as fiercely as she needed. She wrapped her arms around his waist, burying her face against his neck. He was her strength in that moment, his heartbeat was hers. She couldn't hold him tightly enough, couldn't convince herself that he was truly safe.

"I thought—" she started. She couldn't get out any more than that.

His arms tightened around her. "Me too."

It was a long time before she could loosen her hold enough to pull back and look at him. That face she loved, the eyes, so intense, shadowed by worry even though they were both safe—for the moment.

"He killed him, Malkor. Bredard killed Rawn." She rested her hands on his hips, needing the solid reassurance of him to face that fact. "And for what? To prove a point? Rawn wasn't even involved in this, he doesn't—didn't—even know what was going on." And such a horrible way to die. She might never get the image of his last agonized moment out of her head.

She took a deep breath, forced herself to put into words the fear that had haunted her since Rawn's poisoning. "It could be you next. And I— I can't—"

Malkor shook his head. "It won't be me. I have the data he wants, locked tight within IDC headquarters." He smoothed a hand over her hair. "He knows threatening you is a far more effective weapon than threatening me directly. You're his leverage, Kayla." He searched her face as if drinking in every detail, his eyes more worried than she'd ever seen them. "It's going to be you next."

"Let him try." She'd love a rematch.

"No." He gripped her by the shoulders and set her apart from him. "No," he said again, with quiet force. "Ardin and I are agreed, we're moving you into the royal palace tonight. Much higher security."

She couldn't argue with that. As Isonde, she was too important to risk. As a *ro'haar*, though, the idea of hiding behind royal walls galled her.

"What then, though?" she asked. "Who's next? The octet? What if he goes after Rigger, or Hekkar? Trinan and Vid?" Who else had to die to keep their charade secret?

"We'll be safe enough. We're not public figures, our itinerary isn't published like Isonde's is. And we spend a good deal of our day at IDC headquarters anyway. It's more secure than the palace." He gave her a little smile. "I'd move you there if I could, but I doubt we could survive the scandal."

That brought an answering smile to her lips. Oh, if only.

The fantasy of actually getting to spend any time with the man she loved dissolved as reality pressed in again. "We have to decide what we're going to do about the data."

"We're not doing anything with the data."

"Malkor. Five days left with no idea how to stop him."

He pushed a hand through his tousled hair. "I'm working on it." He didn't sound confident. "This morning Commander Parrel confirmed that Senior Commander Jersain Vega is corrupt."

At least Malkor was able to *do* something. All she could do was go on like nothing was wrong, make public appearances, all the while having a target on her back. "Is that significant?"

"Significant?" Malkor's tone implied the question was ludicrous. "She's one of the most powerful commanders in the IDC. Her influence, not to mention her available resources... it's much worse than *significant*."

"Hmm," she said, mulling that over. No doubt the commander

was untouchable. "What about Bredard, do we know where he is staying?" she asked. "Maybe if I could get to him—"

"You'll what, assassinate him?"

Was the idea as horrible as he made it sound? It would be retribution. It would keep Isonde in power, set the empire on a better path. Most importantly, it would keep Malkor safe.

She'd only killed a handful of people and each of them in the heat of battle for her life. Had Malkor, as part of his IDC duties, ever played the role of assassin?

Better to leave his past alone.

"If it comes to that."

"It won't," he said. She heard the hint of uncertainty he couldn't hide. "In the meantime, we need to get you to the palace."

Another wrinkle occurred to her. "What about Isonde?" The unconscious Isonde currently wore the hologram that made her look like Kayla in her role as Lady Evelyn, who had "caught the Virian flu." "We can't leave her here, unguarded, but if we bring her to the palace and it becomes clear how sick she is, they'll want to have doctors look at her." The biostrip would be discovered immediately, as would the true nature of her "illness."

A buzz from the door signaled someone overriding her lock code. She cursed and dove for her own biostrip where she'd left it on the floor. She had a microsecond to slap it on her throat before the doors opened to reveal Prince Ardin. He gave her an odd look where she knelt, hand still on her neck, before transferring his attention to Malkor. He spoke as soon as the doors hissed shut again.

"We can't move Isonde." His eyes were strangely bright, his body tense with suppressed energy. "Not yet."

Malkor frowned at his friend. "We were discussing—"

"You don't understand." Ardin verbally ran right over Malkor. "We have a plan." His voice almost shivered. "Toble and I. I've already contacted him, he's on his way here now."

"The attack—"

He waved Malkor's concern away. "My guards are here, it'll be fine. We'll tell them Isonde is too overwhelmed to move to the palace tonight." Ardin's lips twitched, the vaguest hint of a smile, as if he couldn't bear to let the expression cross his features but couldn't hold it in, either. "The fourth cure—we've augmented it. Well, Toble has." The smile broke free. "It could work. This could really work."

Could Toble really have created a cure this time? By the look of him, Ardin believed it, and that had her hoping, too. Could this save Isonde? Could this be the beginning of her freedom?

"Come on," Ardin said. "I told my guards to admit Toble when he arrives; we'll meet him in Isonde's room." Then he was back out the doors before she or Malkor could answer.

One of Isonde's guards still kept watch over the room she slept in. Maybe Ardin's guards had decided that "Lady Evelyn" wasn't in any real danger. Or maybe Isonde's guards knew more than they ever let on about the situation and refused to surrender the post. Kayla nodded at the familiar face and followed Ardin into the room.

Things looked as they always did: Isonde's medical pod quietly beeping away in the center of the room, the lights low, the window tinting turned almost opaque. The labored rasp of Isonde's breathing barely escaped the pod.

The tomb of Princess Isonde Veriley of Gangisha, Sovereign Planet Piran.

Ardin brought the lights to full, his energy breathing life into the room. He programmed the window tinting to transparent, letting in a view of stars and nighttime cityscape, breaking open Isonde's cocoon. He stood beside Isonde's pod and peeled off the biostrip that made her look like Kayla. For the first time in too long, hope lit his features as he brushed a hand across her forehead, and Kayla's heart clenched at the tender gesture.

Please let this last cure work.

Toble arrived almost immediately, bringing with him the same hopeful energy that fueled Ardin. He barely gave her and Malkor a hello before propping a silver case on the table beside the medcase he always kept here. He opened both and started setting out his instruments.

"Results on the last test were the same as the first ten," he said to Ardin. "One hundred percent disintegration." He grinned, the expression of a scientist with a breakthrough. "I think you've found the answer."

What had Ardin found?

"I wish we had more time to refine the serum," Toble continued. They all knew that was impossible. With Isonde's diaphragm solidifying, she could barely draw air into her lungs. Toble had already implanted a ventricular assist device into her heart to keep blood flowing. "There's no telling how long dissolution will take."

"This *will* work," Ardin said. He nodded at Toble, giving him permission to go ahead.

Malkor stepped forward, clearly about to interject. Kayla placed a hand on his arm. She gently pulled him back beside her and spoke low, for his ears alone. "Let Ardin make this decision. He loves Isonde more than anything; let him try this one last thing to save her."

Malkor frowned. "I don't even know what they—"

"It doesn't matter. It only matters that Ardin believes in it. It's right to place her final fate in the hands of the one who loves her best."

Malkor finally blew out a breath, shoulders relaxing, and she knew he understood. They went together to stand at the foot of Isonde's pod.

Toble punched codes into the console, no doubt setting parameters and serum distribution rates. That finished, he pulled a twenty-centimeter cube from his case. The liquid inside had a ruddy tinge, disconcerting when the previous three formulations of a possible cure had been clear. He plugged it into the specially designed receptacle, double-checked the fit, then started the process. The liquid was instantly sucked into the bowels of the medical pod, leaving an empty cube and four people holding their breath.

And holding it.

And holding.

When nothing on the pod's monitors changed even after a few minutes, Toble visibly relaxed. "No initial adverse reaction to the modified serum, that's good."

Ardin didn't take his eyes off of Isonde. "How long before we see a change?"

Toble flipped through a series of internal scans. "Full dissolution for each of the tests took some time, and that was only a small tissue sample. We could be in for a long wait."

"Good," Malkor said, "you'll have time to explain."

"This is Ardin's genius," Toble said.

"How does the crown prince of the empire acquire advanced medical knowledge?" Kayla asked, looking at Ardin. Not that she had any idea what his education was. He could be a genius for all she knew, born to be a scientist, trapped in the role of politician.

Ardin finally peeled his gaze away from Isonde, still holding her hand. "I don't, but I have a mind that can think and too many hours in a day since I can't rest knowing she's dying. You at least have things to do, meeting with the Sovereign Council. The Council of Seven is not convening until we have recommendations from the Sovereign and Protectorate Councils to work with. In between necessary public appearances I've been going over everything I can about the toxin."

Kayla had left that to Toble. Could she have been more help? "What did you find?"

"Well, Toble's analysis showed that Janeen's toxin combined the paralytic effect of dutrotase with the muscle stabilizer known as RDU-7. It should have produced a localized result. Instead, Isonde's extreme allergic reaction made it systemic. We've been assuming all along that the toxin contained a synthetic form of dutrotase. If that were the case, though, any of the other three cure formulations should have been able to break up the paralysis.

"I started examining Janeen's whole plan, starting with

where she might have gotten the toxin. I think she put the plan together after Malkor's decision not to let her act as Isonde's body-double for the Empress Game, the decision announced en route to Altair Tri. Once she'd seen Kayla fight, Janeen realized that disabling her was the only way to stop Kayla from winning the Game. It's likely she acquired the toxin on Altair Tri itself."

It would have been easy enough to do. The slum side of Altair Tri was a catch-all for human filth. All manner of illegal merchandise could be bought there on the cheap.

"I gained access to Tri's police records," Ardin said, "looking at criminal cases that involved poisoning and what substances were used. A few used a natural form of dutrotase refined from the leaves of the coinsis weed. Apparently it's an invasive species on the slum side." Ardin shrugged. "Why waste materials and credits synthesizing a pure form of the compound when you can basically get it for free?"

Toble joined in. "Assuming Janeen got a homemade batch on the slum side, it would contain impurities because a small percentage of plant cells would be mixed in with the dutrotase. Those cells are probably what triggered the allergic reaction."

"Whereas I," Kayla said, "have no allergy to that plant."

Toble nodded. "Exactly."

"That's all very interesting," Malkor said. "How does that help us?"

Toble gestured to Ardin. "The credit is all his, for tracking the information down."

"Being the crown prince does tend to get results when badgering scientists," Ardin said, with a half-smile. "I can't tell if I made new friends by pretending the empire was interested in obscure botany studies, or enemies by being an arrogant, insistent, curt bastard with them all." He shook his head. "Damn, scientists can go on and on about their research." He patted Isonde's hand, looking down at her with a mix of hope and love. "If this cure comes through, Father will find I've created a new position for a Royal Botanist of the Protectorate Planets. I'll name our first born after the woman."

Kayla barely refrained from saying, "Spit it out already."

"The coinsis weed is an invasive flora species taking a foothold in Altair Tri. It moves into an area, then overgrows and chokes out the natural flora that should grow there. One plant—the supposa flower—developed a defense mechanism against the encroachment. It sheds its petals regularly, which break down quickly, releasing an acidic compound into the soil. That compound denatures the proteins in the coinsis's cells, causing cell death." He looked to Toble to take over the explanation.

"Basically," Toble said, "we're using that acidic compound from the supposa flower to break down the coinsis cells in Isonde's body, because they seem to be the ones perpetuating the paralytic allergic reaction."

Kayla shook her head. "You lost me at invasive and I fell off the hover car at denature. You honestly think this will work?" It seemed... far-fetched. Plants fighting other plants with acid?

Ardin looked at Toble, and she felt Ardin's absolute need to believe. His hope radiated through the room. His eyes almost demanded that Toble proclaim this cure Isonde's savior.

"So far it's worked on small tissue samples," Toble said. "There's no reason to think it won't work on a larger scale."

Kayla kept her mouth shut. Ardin didn't need her skepticism, he needed her support. It would be what it would be, now that the compound was being fed into Isonde.

She touched him on the shoulder. "Isonde's lucky to have you fighting for her." Ardin smiled in return, and it might have been the friendliest moment ever between them. She moved away before he could remember she was a pit whore from Altair Tri and soon to be his wife if Isonde didn't recover.

Even with the serum pumping away, nothing happened. Despite Ardin's optimism, standing around Isonde's pod with the others made Kayla feel like a vulture waiting on a dying animal. Toble himself looked to be settling in for a long wait, so Kayla drifted over to a couch on the other side of the room, sank down tiredly and turned on the news vid feed.

After a few quiet words to Ardin, Malkor joined her on the couch. He sat closer than they had been in weeks, but not close enough to satisfy her chaotic emotions. She longed to be on his lap, his arms closing around her like a safety net as she waited on the cure that would decide her future.

Who would she be from this day forward—Isonde, or Kayla?

A picture of Isonde on the vidscreen caught her attention. Today's proceedings from both the Sovereign and Protectorate Councils had been released to the public, and the news feed was showing Kayla's mad dash from her desk in the council chamber to the adjudicator's room in a loop. Bare feet, skirts rucked up, lunging over councilors… Isonde might never live down the moment Kayla knocked Councilor Choo's wig off and sent it flying.

"You looked magnificent," Malkor said in a low voice, with warmth in his eyes. "Quick-witted, graceful, powerful." He studied her flight on the screen again. "Every centimeter the superb fighter you are."

Kayla smiled at his words. How many women would be flattered by the compliment, as she was? His octet thrived on efficiency and execution. To meet Malkor's high standards… she felt a touch of pride.

Well-deserved pride, of course.

The news feed showed the short interview she'd given after the attack, reinforcing her lie that the reason she'd run from the council chambers was because she'd received a death threat on her datapad at her desk and believed it was from someone inside the room. Combining that with Rawn's actual death made her mad dash legitimate.

The story flipped again, posting the news that both councils would be closed while security personnel in both seats were re-vetted. Apparently a single security guard from the Sovereign seat had been the instrument of Rawn's poisoning. The current empress—Ardin's mother—appeared on the screen, asserting to reporters that the empire would not be cowed by terrorism, and that the councils would reconvene as soon as the councilors' safety could be assured in both seats.

"I'm sorry for what happened to Rawn," Malkor said. "Bredard did us a favor in some ways, though."

The news feed showed her fleeing the council chambers again, with the caption "Princess Isonde flees attempt on her life" running along the top. She looked at Malkor. "How's that?"

"Your speech. The one you were poised to give at the closing of today's council session. Now people think your guard was assassinated and a threat made on your life to silence you. They're breathless to know what you plan to say that's so polarizing."

"It's nothing Isonde hasn't said before," she answered. "Withdraw from Wyrd Space because the tremendous resources going into the occupation are needed here."

"Now people will *really* listen. You have the attention of the entire empire."

She frowned. "No pressure." Her eyes drifted back to the medical pod. "If Isonde wakes, maybe she can—"

Malkor shook his head. "The councils will reconvene as soon as possible. Even if this cure works, Isonde won't be up and about by then, and certainly not ready to speak before the empire."

So even if this cure worked, Kayla would *still* be Isonde, at least for a little while.

Maybe the charade would never really end. Maybe her identity as Kayla would fade into nothingness beneath the needs of her people and the empire.

The thought was depressing, and with all the day had brought her, she suddenly felt exhausted. Across the room Toble rose to insert another cube of liquid into the medical pod, and Kayla relaxed back into the depths of the couch, settling in for a long, long wait.

* * *

She woke hours later, sometime around midnight, to find herself tucked against Malkor's side, his arms curled around her in sleep. Her instinct was to snuggle closer and drift back to unconsciousness, but voices caught her attention.

"Did you see that?" Ardin asked. "You saw it, right?"

"Let me run another scan," Toble said.

Had the cure worked? Kayla shook Malkor awake and dragged him over to Isonde's medical pod. Ardin's gaze was riveted on Isonde's hand as if it had performed a miracle.

Toble studied the readings from the scan, then let out a "ha!" He grinned, so ecstatically, that hope crystallized in Kayla.

"It's working?" she asked.

He nodded, eyes still on the pod's display. "The princess's heartbeat is stronger, and strengthening by the minute. Her oxygen saturation is increasing as well." He looked across the pod at Ardin. "I think we did it. I think we actually did it."

A sense of relief so great, a sense of thankfulness so large Kayla couldn't keep it inside, burst forth. She hugged Toble, then Ardin, then Malkor, then Toble again.

"There!" Ardin said, and this time Kayla saw it too: Isonde's index finger twitched. They had done it, they had saved Isonde.

Throughout the night and into the morning, Isonde made slow, steady progress. Kayla spent a few hours resting in her bed while Malkor slept on the couch, Toble dozed in a chair, and Ardin kept watch.

Kayla snuck back into the room with the sun's rise, needing to see for herself once again that the cure was actually taking effect. Ardin sat beside the pod, one hand holding Isonde's hand, while Malkor and Toble snored gently in the background. Ardin seemed weary beyond belief, but content, so content, just to sit beside her. There was a peace about him that she hadn't known he possessed.

"How's she doing?" Kayla whispered.

He smiled when she approached. "Better all the time. The

paralysis is easing." He shook his head the slightest bit. "I almost can't believe it."

"From what I've learned of her, Isonde is too stubborn to be defeated by anything," Kayla offered.

His smile turned rueful. "I don't think anything could stop her, once she's determined." His gaze traveled over Kayla's face, seeing the Isonde hologram she wore. "You're much like her, in some ways."

Perhaps she was. "Thank you."

"That's not always a compliment," he said. Quiet fell between them, not quite comfortably. He cleared his throat, looking away a moment, and Kayla thought that might be her cue to leave. Instead, his gaze returned to hers. "What I said, yesterday, about hating you… about—"

She waved her hand. "It has been a tough situation. On all of us."

"On you most of all," he said quietly. "You didn't deserve that. I had no right to vent my frustration and fear on you, not after all you've done for us."

They were the first words of gratitude she had ever received from him. His first recognition that she had suffered through this ordeal. Understanding passed between them, a moment acknowledging trials endured together.

A whispered word broke the silence.

"Ardin?" Isonde's voice was no more than a breath. Her eyelashes fluttered, her eyes struggling to open.

Ardin came to attention instantly. He leaned over Isonde, stroking her hair, touching her cheek. "I'm here, darling. I'm here."

Isonde's eyes peeled open slowly, as if with a great effort, and the breath caught in Kayla's throat. It was really happening. Isonde really was waking.

"Ardin," Isonde whispered again. Her gaze found him and the breath eased out of her like a sigh. "You're here." Her eyelids swept down as if she couldn't hold them up.

Somehow Isonde managed to open her eyes again. Her

throat moved as she swallowed. "You've been here all this time, with me." She swallowed again, the effort of talking clearly painful.

"Hush," Ardin murmured.

She looked into his eyes, seeming to gather her energy. "Thank you," she rasped, "for not giving up."

A profound sadness touched Ardin's face. Clearly, those were not the words of love he'd hoped to hear.

Kayla tiptoed out of the room. Isonde's wispy voice faded from her mind when the truth of the situation hit her. She leaned back against the doors, unable to hold all her weight. Her life shifted before her, everything suddenly new and open.

I'm free.

6

THE WYRD PLANET ORDOCH, WYRD SPACE

The shadows came and went, unpredictable. It was the silhouette of a body on the upper walk here, a momentary cloud over the sun there; each no more than a puddle. If Cinni knew the pattern she could skip like a stone across them all, finding a way in darkness to the street's other side.

Instead she hung back under the cover of the eastern flak tower, waiting like a starving child for a crust of bread that would never come. Her blaster's ion cell would decay before an easy path presented itself.

Atop the multi-story fortification the imperials had built around Ordoch's capital city, the indigo and jade pennants of the Sakien Empire undulated in the breeze, their fairly stable shadows offering her the best entry point. They'd betray her in a strong gust, but if the wind held steady she could make it halfway across the street without too many acrobatics.

She checked the charge on her transparency generator: still getting the orange "go" light. The mini-field was big enough to surround her and her alone, and while it offered decent cover in low-light areas and shadows, the cheap photon deflector couldn't successfully perpetuate an illusion in direct afternoon sunlight.

A glance up showed sentries pacing the tritinium decking

that lined the guard wall on this side of the street. Half of them faced outward, looking over the ruins of the city's suburbs. The others watched the storefronts, tripclubs and cyberbrothels inside the imperial compound with half-hearted attention. Cinni studied the movements of everything in the street, from the sanitation bot sucking scum from the sewers to the imperial soldiers strutting with full-on imperial arrogance.

She shrank back as the soldiers passed, resisting the urge to knife one in the jugular. A minute ticked by while she waited in shadow. Two. The stim she'd taken before heading out on this mission made patience—and even standing still—near impossible.

When the soldiers passed far enough ahead, she bolted into action. Her steps took her zigzagging to the middle of the street where she halted, waiting on a stab of sunlight that stole the next movement from her.

The pennant above swung back, giving her enough shadow to skip across. She tumbled on, halt-and-run-and-halt, trusting her transparency generator to hide her as she dashed from dark to darker to darkest, finally reaching the street's other side.

From there she sidled along the alleys, slipping through the shadows that adhered to the buildings' surfaces, making her way farther into the heart of the occupied city.

Hephesta would never expect her.

And that's exactly why Cinni, of all the Wyrd rebels on Ordoch, had been sent.

She ducked around the back of a VR lounge, one of dozens like it in the imperial compound. Five stories rose above it, apartments stacked atop each other. The building's sheer walls mocked her with organoplastic smoothness. Scale this? Only if the gecko pads she'd brought really had been overclocked to carry her full weight that long. She'd have to be quick about it. She pulled the pads from her pack and attached them to the toes of her boots, her knees, and lastly her hands. A running leap took her two steps up the wall and then she clamped on, holding herself with straining arms, starting her climb.

Cinni would never have chosen an infiltration like this in the daylight. The choice wasn't hers to make, however. Hephesta only slept during the height of day, always had. No one knew that better than Cinni.

The roof's stylish overhang shadowed this face of the building, allowing enough cover for Cinni to climb to the third story and enter through a hallway window. She landed lightly and stowed her gecko pads. Hopefully they had enough juice left for the climb down. Then again, if things didn't go as planned, she wouldn't need them again.

Straight ahead and around one right turn she found her destination: 338, Hephesta's new apartment. *Mishe, you better have gotten me the right door code.* She punched in the alphanumeric sequence she'd spent the morning memorizing, then breathed a sigh of thanks when the locks released and the door swung inward.

A jaded thanks, as Mishe had been forced to prostitute himself to an imperial officer for the chance to steal the information.

The imperial bastards would pay for that necessity. They would all pay—every last one of the frutters. Cinni wouldn't rest until Ordoch was free of the invaders, and if it took the death of every single imperial on the planet and in orbit, so be it.

She tiptoed into Hephesta's room, powering down the translucence generator along the way. The time for stealth was over. She found Hephesta asleep in her bed, tucked like an innocent child in need of comfort, a frown on her face even in sleep. It wasn't how Cinni remembered her. Once, Hephesta had had a ready laugh. Her smile had the power to charm anyone with its warmth, and she'd been carefree, almost to the point of irresponsibility.

Apparently turning traitor had taken its toll.

Cinni stood beside the bed. It seemed to her there should be some sort of last words. A farewell for the woman who had meant everything to her. Or maybe a reading of her crimes. Now that Cinni was here, the emotions she'd buried for so long rose with unbearable force. Betrayal burned so hot within that it choked her, brought the sting of would-be tears to her eyes.

Why! Why? How could you do this? Cinni resisted the urge to shake the older woman awake and demand answers. *We needed you,* she silently screamed. I *needed you.*

There could be no answer that excused a Wyrd for collaborating with the imperials.

Cinni wrestled with the hate and rage and pain and loss, her harsh breaths echoing in the quiet room with the effort. She could do this. She *needed* to do this.

She drew her ion pistol with a hand that trembled—whether from emotion or the stims, she refused to acknowledge it. She flicked the charge to life, calm returning with the hum of the weapon's ready power against her palm. She could do this.

Her aim was far from steady as she pointed the pistol at Hephesta's chest—not that it mattered at point-blank range. Cinni blinked away the last of the would-be tears.

In the second before she squeezed the trigger, Hephesta's eyes flashed open.

"Hello, Mother," Cinni said, and fired.

Blast.

7

THE *SICERRO*, HYPERSTREAM INSIDE IMPERIAL SPACE, PRECISE LOCATION UNKNOWN

Vayne Reinumon lay flat on the floor of his cabin aboard the Ilmenans' spaceship, *Sicerro*, his chest heaving, air sawing through his lungs. Sweat covered his bare back and shoulders and rolled past his temple as he rested. Had he done enough? His arms and abs and thighs and calves told him he had. But the carpet beneath his palms, the thin covering over the ship's decking, was identical in color to the carpet in one of Dolan's "playrooms," and remembrance drew him in. Forced him back into that room. Threatened to trap him there.

No.

Vayne pushed himself up violently, weight balanced on toes and palms, and began another set of push-ups.

One. Two. Three. Four.

The effort of it, the determination needed to push himself off the floor time and again, carried his mind away. There was only him, only his body, the smooth cycle of his motions, the rhythm of his exhalation.

Five. Six. More. Again. Again.

He lost count. There was nothing else. There was no one else. It was him and the strength of his body. Him and his fight.

Again. Again.

When one more push-up seemed like an agony his arms couldn't endure, he did three more, as his older sister Natali had taught him, then rolled onto his back. He stared at the low quadtanium ceiling of his cabin, heart slowing, each beat centering him in his body. The memories of his years with Dolan, too raw and gruesome to even acknowledge, were locked away again—for now.

He was himself, wholly himself. No one mind-controlled him anymore. He was free.

Then why doesn't it feel like it?

Suddenly the room was too small. Vayne ignored the question and fled.

First, a shower. Then, a meal. Hopefully he could accomplish both without running into anyone else at this hour of night. Or day. Or whatever time the ship kept while riding a hyperstream.

He grabbed a shower in one of the communal bathrooms without trouble. His luck ran out as he approached the lounge, sadly. Tia'tan, leader of the Ilmenans who had come to Falanar to rescue him and his family, headed for the same destination from the opposite direction. She caught sight of him before he could turn around, and he was forced to meet her at the door.

"Hi," she said, with a friendly smile. Or was it a calculating smile? A smile of calculated friendliness? His instincts for honest interaction were warped from his last five years as a mental experiment.

Friendly, he finally decided, and offered her a polite smile in return, even as he wished her to the void so he could eat in isolation.

"Haven't seen you in a bit," she said, sweeping the lavender bangs off her forehead with one hand and tucking them behind her ear.

What to say? Sorry, I avoid you because you treat me as an equal, as *human*, and after five years of degradation I don't know how to deal with it? Sorry, your gaze holds questions I never want to hear, let alone answer? Sorry, in another life I could see myself actually liking you and that scares the shit out of me?

"Sorry."

She shrugged. "We'll all get sick of one another on a ship this size soon enough. Lunch?" She stepped into the lounge and he followed. Too many heads turned in their direction as they entered. So much for avoiding people.

Joffar, the eldest Ilmenan of the four, stood near an expansive viewport, in conversation with Vayne's uncle, Ghirhad. They were of an age, and seemed to get along well enough. Corinth sat at a table with Noar. Guilt pricked Vayne at the sight. Noar had started training Corinth to control and expand his psionic skills, something Vayne should have been doing. Kayla had asked that of him. At the moment, though, Vayne couldn't handle his younger brother's silent resentment. Kayla had become Corinth's whole world, and Vayne had made the call to leave her behind, something Corinth hadn't forgiven him for.

Something he couldn't forgive himself for.

He nodded in greeting to them and followed Tia'tan to the bank of food and beverage synthesizers. He was conscious of Natali rising from her seat and pointedly not looking at him, just as he had avoided turning his gaze in her direction. She was out the door before he could enter a meal selection on the synthesizer.

Tia'tan glanced over at his plate as she queued for a drink. "That looks... appetizing."

The synthesizer delivered him a saucer full of what looked like egg patties and tentacles in a lukewarm brown gravy. "Still getting used to your codes." If the worst thing that happened to him in a day now was choking down sludge-covered tentacles, he'd eat it, like it, and be thankful. He did much better with the beverage and synthed a full-bodied ale that ought to at least wash down some of his dinner.

Plate and cup in hand, he hoped he could get away with that brief hello and run right back to his room, but Tia'tan grabbed a seat at an empty table and watched him, clearly inviting him to join her.

Damn.

He took the seat opposite her, facing the viewport. The soothing pink-green ribbons of the hyperstream washed by, carrying him away from his nightmares, from his captivity, from his past. *Faster*, he urged it. *Faster*. He couldn't sleep easy until they reached Wyrd Space, and even then it might take setting his feet down on Ilmena to truly feel free. Ordoch might have been his home once. Now, with the imperial occupation, he'd never go back. Not if it meant more strife and heartache. Ilmena, on the other hand, was untouched by the imperials. At peace. Safe.

"Any signs of pursuit?" he asked.

She nodded. "News of our supposed terrorist activity with the TNV travels a lot faster than our ship. When we dropped stream last night the imperial military stationed in this sector swooped in. Luliana barely skipped us out in time."

They'd been dogged since they left Falanar. Whoever had framed the Ilmenans for delivering the TNV to the imperial wedding must have been convincing. Dropping from the hyperstream to correct their course was a gamble every time.

"We could stay in the stream longer," he suggested, choking down a bit of tentacle-topped egg patty.

Tia'tan shook her head. "Hyperstreams meander too much in this region. Too long without course corrections and we could find ourselves in the heart of the empire, or worse. Don't worry, we'll keep ahead of the imperials."

They'd better. He hadn't left Kayla behind, at the mercy of those bastards, only to be captured and dragged back to a cell. Never again.

"How long until we reach Wyrd Space?"

Tia'tan glanced away. Doing the math on the distance? Fabricating an answer? Or maybe she found his stare too disturbing to maintain. Void if he knew.

"I'm uncertain about the particulars," she finally said. "Hopefully we won't be here much longer."

A *soon* would have satisfied him far greater. *Hopefully* didn't usually factor into space travel.

"Is there something—"

"I'll get you to Ilmena, Vayne. Trust me."

Ambiguity. It was in the way she said "trust me," like it was a request as much as an assertion that he could. The only person he trusted was his *ro'haar*, and she was umpteen light-years away now.

Still, Tia'tan had come all the way to Falanar on the rumor that he and his family were being held prisoner. Kayla wouldn't have even known to look for him in Dolan's lab if not for the Ilmenans. He owed them his freedom. His life. Tia'tan and her promise of a new home on Ilmena were the first things worth believing in in five years.

So he nodded like the answer satisfied him, and her friendly smile returned.

They ate in silence for a few minutes. His lunch really did rank alongside one of Dolan's mildest tortures, but he ate it anyway. Any choice he made of his own free will—to eat or not to eat, what to eat, when to eat—was a luxury.

His gaze drifted to where Corinth sat with Noar. The boy levitated a glass filled to the very top with a translucent pink fluid. Every so often a trickle of liquid would spill over the rim to drip into the bowl below, and Corinth's face would scrunch into a tighter scowl of concentration. It was an early psionic exercise Vayne knew well—learning how to not just lift an object, but to keep it steady, level, completely controlled. From the amount of liquid in the bowl already, Corinth needed much practice.

Noar met his eyes, and his voice sounded in Vayne's head. ::He'll forgive you soon enough.::

Vayne arched a brow at the rudeness of Noar telepathically interrupting his verbal conversation with Tia'tan. On Ordoch that kind of behavior would have been considered quite intrusive, not to mention vaguely insulting to Corinth, who should have had Noar's full attention. Even if you were able to speak directly into the minds of every person in the room, that didn't mean you had a right to.

::Kayla is everything to him:: Noar said. ::You can

understand why he's upset. He'll accept why you insisted we leave, in time.::

Given the chance, Vayne knew he would make the same decision again: leave his *ro'haar* behind rather than suffer being taken prisoner. That didn't mean he didn't hate himself for it, or that he didn't think Corinth should, too.

::Thank you for working with him:: Vayne said, sounding gruff even to himself.

Noar took his ill humor in stride, as he always did. Noar nodded to accept the thanks and turned his attention back to Corinth.

Luliana's voice came over the ship's comm. "We're nearing the drop point."

Already? They'd just done a course correction last night.

"Why are we dropping stream?" he demanded of Tia'tan, who was already rising, heading with her plate toward the sanitizer.

Joffar said something to Ghirhad and his uncle laughed, a jovial sound that grated as badly as ever on Vayne's raw nerves. It drew his attention to where they stood by the viewport in time to see the green-pink wash of the hyperstream dissolve.

Some warning, Luliana. How about, "Hey, we're dropping this second." He grabbed his own plate, intent on following Tia'tan to the bridge to learn what the trouble was, when something out the viewport caught his eye. Several somethings.

They'd dropped back into normal space and he should have seen nothing besides distant stars. Instead, gigantic masses surrounded them, some the dull grey of stone, others with a metallic sheen. Thousands of them. And one in particular, the size of a battleship's front section, hurtled straight for them, or vice versa. Its solid form devoured the other object in the viewport until—

WHAM.

The ship impacted the debris with a deafening boom, the force fracturing the viewport and sending them all flying.

"Corinth!" He lurched to his feet, looking for the boy. "Get out of here, now!" That window might not hold and Kayla would kill him if anything happened to their brother.

Everyone scrambled for the door, squeezing out two at a time while the ship's klaxon blared and Luliana shouted something about raising the shields. Yeah. Nice timing on that.

Tia'tan pressure-sealed the lounge. Noar and Joffar headed straight for the bridge.

"You three," Tia'tan said, pointing at the Ordochians. "Cabins. Strap in."

Vayne grabbed her arm when she turned to follow Noar. "Where the void are we?"

"An asteroid field?" Ghirhad asked.

"Full of man-made debris?" Vayne countered. "Unlikely. And what kind of pilot takes a ship out of hyperstream inside an asteroid field?"

"It's not asteroids," Tia'tan said, freeing her arm easily and hurrying toward the bridge.

Corinth's voice sounded in his head. ::I bet it's the Mine Field.:: The boy's blue eyes were huge. ::We're in trouble.:: Before Vayne could stop him, Corinth shot down the corridor after Tia'tan.

"What the frutt?" Vayne could only follow.

It was a tight fit with everyone on the bridge. Luliana, seated in the pilot's chair, righted the ship and used thrusters to power them around a massive structure that looked like the top ten decks of a luxury starcruiser. Hundreds of other objects of all shapes and sizes filled the viewscreens. Noar and Joffar were already at sensor consoles starting diagnostics.

"Why did you drop us right in the field?" Tia'tan asked, taking position beside Luliana.

"I didn't, something ripped us out." Luliana rolled left to avoid an even larger chunk of rock, flying through a scattering of smaller stones in the process, setting off the ship's proximity warnings. The bridge's two hundred seventy-degree field of view was filled top to bottom, side to side with debris. It looked like the wreck of an entire planet, strung through with enough demolished ships to conquer the empire.

Luliana cursed when the ship glanced off one of the wrecks, sending it spinning into a nearby rock. The shields held but the ship wasn't happy.

::It's the Mine Field:: Corinth said. He must have projected his mind voice to everyone because Tia'tan and Joffar shared a look that Vayne couldn't interpret. Confirmation? Guilt? ::We have to stop moving!:: This time Corinth shouted so loud that Vayne winced.

"I do that and we'll get pulverized," Luliana said. "This field has its own motion."

::You'll bring the rooks down on us!::

Tia'tan's gaze sharpened on Corinth with interest and Vayne *knew*. Coming to this Mine Field was no accident.

"You've been here before? What do you know about the rooks?" Tia'tan asked.

::Almost nothing. We skirted too close to the field on our way from Altair Tri to Falanar and got pulled in. The rooks nearly destroyed us. *Did* destroy at least one of the ships lurking in the field when we arrived. Tore it to shreds.::

Vayne growled and struck out at Tia'tan with his psi powers. He wrapped a tendril of force around her throat, squeezed hard enough to lift her off her feet and shook her slightly. "What have you done? You promised to bring us to safety." The walls of the bridge crowded closer, tighter. She'd tricked him, trapped him...

Tia'tan choked and struggled, her eyes huge in her face. Another psionic sliced through his hold and she dropped to her feet, one hand at her throat. She stared at him as if seeing him for the first time, as if she hadn't imagined him capable of violence.

She had no idea what he was capable of, what he'd done— especially when someone lied to him, manipulated him. His hands curled into fists. "Get us out of here. Now." Psi power and rage thrummed through him, urging him to strike out at someone, anyone.

All of the Ilmenans raised their shields, including Luliana, who was plotting a nimble dance through the looming debris using the GUI in her headset.

"No," Tia'tan said. She regained her composure and squared her shoulders. "This is too important." She called to Joffar without taking her eyes off Vayne, as if by staring at him she could keep him back, hold him in place. "Any sign of the *Radiant*?"

"Nothing. No distress call, no life pods, no central core homing beacon."

"You're here about a ship?" Vayne laughed without humor, sweeping his arm in the direction of the viewport. "Look outside. I think it's safe to say they didn't survive this place."

::*We* won't survive if you don't stop the ship:: Corinth added. ::Movement draws the rooks.:: He stepped beside Vayne, standing shoulder to shoulder, facing off with Tia'tan. Shielding emotions was still a challenge for Corinth, and behind the earnestness the boy projected, a tide of fear lurked.

"Stop the ship," Vayne ordered. He barely resisted marching to Luliana's chair and making his point more forcibly. "Whatever these 'rooks' are, Corinth clearly knows more than you. Do what he says."

Noar flipped through screens at the navigation console. "There's a large asteroid, er, whatever, at seventy-two, negative one hundred thirty, two hundred one that seems to have a fairly stable path."

"I see it," Luliana called. "I can shadow its movements, stick close. Maybe we can blend in as part of the debris' typical motion." She suited actions to words, taking them through some tricky flying before finding a more stable path beside the gigantic hunk of rock. "This is the best I can do, without having somewhere to land."

Tia'tan finally drew her gaze from Vayne long enough to look at Corinth. "Will that do?"

The boy's fear eased somewhat, at least enough that Vayne no longer thought it might bleed into his own mind. ::Slightly better. We need to get out of here.::

"First we need to get our bearings." Tia'tan stepped over to Noar's station without ever turning her back on them. "How big is the Mine Field," she asked Noar, "and what's our relative position within it?"

Noar summoned a 3D display of their immediate surroundings that hovered above his console. He zoomed out. The image got twitchy after a certain point, the coordinate axes warping, the scene bending and folding on itself. Noar zoomed back in then tried again, with the same results. The space around the ship mapped accurately in close scale. The greater the area he tried to map, though, the more indistinct, garbled and eventually nonexistent the image became.

"Navigation sensors damaged in the initial impact?" Tia'tan asked.

Joffar replied from his console. "I'm looking at the diagnostic report now—none of the sensors took damage. The hyperstream drive is a different matter altogether," he added morosely.

"Reboot the sensor array," Tia'tan told Noar. "The *Radiant* is here somewhere, we have to find them."

::They wouldn't have survived the rooks.:: Corinth said, gaze flipping from viewscreen to viewscreen, searching for danger.

"You did," Tia'tan answered. "And the *Radiant* is far more advanced than any imperial vessel." Her voice vibrated with tension. "They'll be here."

The sensor array came back online. When Noar tried to view a larger picture of where they were in the field the results were the same—impenetrable interference.

"We've got movement," Luliana said. The left viewscreen zoomed in, picking out a shape that resembled a massive mechanical squid. Its black metallic body had blue lights dancing along its many flexible limbs and sparkling in greater concentration across its head. As Vayne watched, the ship—creature?—blinked out of existence, dropping out of sight and off sensors, only to appear again hundreds of kilometers closer.

It seemed to curl around the fractured bow of a fuel tanker, limbs undulating, moving slowly, then it blinked again and appeared even closer, skulking in the cover of another asteroid.

"What the void is that?" Vayne asked. "Some kind of ship?" It moved more like a curious animal come to investigate a disturbance in its habitat, dancing between cover as it approached. The proximity alert went off as Luliana nudged them even closer to the rock they shadowed.

"Maybe they don't see us." Noar pulled his fascinated gaze from the viewscreen and checked the sensor display again.

Corinth shook his head, his mind voice pitched higher. ::It—they—know we're here.::

The ship fell to silence as they watched the rook approach.

Vayne jumped when Luliana called, "We've got another one, approaching from the other side." She put the image on the opposite viewscreen. This one was even larger than the first, dozens of times larger than the Ilmenans' ship. "And a third, dead ahead."

Shit.

The rooks circled, their trailing limbs tracing delicate patterns as they swam through space. They blinked in and out, traveling incredible distances in a second. Coming ever closer.

"We have to move," Tia'tan said.

::No!:: Corinth took a step toward her.

"We can't sit here like prey and wait for them to destroy us."

::They're attracted to movement.::

"What about energy signatures?" Tia'tan asked. "IR sensors? Who's to say they can't see us even now, no matter how still we are?"

::Maybe the Mine Field messes with those.::

Tia'tan shook her head. "I won't gamble on that. Luliana, plot a course through the debris."

"Which direction, though?" Luliana asked.

"Away from the rooks, with all possible speed."

"You could be taking us farther into the field," Vayne argued. "You don't even know what the frutt you're doing."

Tia'tan gave him an imperious stare. "This discussion is over. Luliana—do it." Tia'tan strengthened her telekinetic shields as she said it, shifting her feet slightly to give herself a more balanced stance, should he come at her again. Noar and Joffar said nothing as Luliana broke away from their hiding place and darted into the open.

The movement galvanized the rooks. They left off their circling motions and came on, full speed, alternating blink-jumps with sharp zigzags, expertly navigating the debris field.

"They're gaining," Noar said, eyes fixed on the navigation console, and Joffar moved to the tactical station.

Tia'tan finally broke off her stare, apparently convinced Vayne wasn't about to lash out. He wanted to. Everything in him revolted at the idea of leaving the fate of his newly regained freedom in someone else's hands, and he had the irrational urge to strike out, as if that would help.

Luliana dove the ship straight down and the rooks gave chase. They came on faster than Luliana could maneuver.

Tia'tan's voice cracked the silence. "Frag missiles. Hit the smallest one."

"The targeting sensors are scrambled, and the lock drops every time the rooks blink out," Joffar said, his fingers skimming over the tactical controls.

"Do what you can."

The missiles launched, bursts of light that streaked toward the smallest of the rooks. Two missiles veered, clearly off target, and exploded against the wreck of a starcruiser, while another missile's trajectory sent it impacting a jagged hunk of rock. The last missile flew true and hit the rook across the crown in a brilliant flash.

"They don't have shields?" Vayne asked. In that case, the frag missile should have torn a massive hole in their hull. Or skin. Or armor, or whatever it was. Instead the rook seemed undamaged, and nothing in its movements changed. If the rook had any idea it had been blasted with a devastating payload, it didn't show.

"Again," Tia'tan said. "A full spread."

Luliana tracked a crazy, spiraling course through the debris, cat-and-mousing her way across the field as Joffar tried to fix missile targets and the rooks grew ever closer. Joffar hissed in dissatisfaction, then finally launched the full spread of frag missiles.

They lost more than half of the missiles to careening debris. Joffar punched in course corrections as the remaining missiles flew, fighting against the field's sensor disturbance to keep them on target. Three exploded across the rook's crown in rapid succession, and the last two sailed through open space as the rook blinked out of existence.

Gone?

Vayne held his breath a heartbeat. Two. Then the rook reappeared, closer than ever and undamaged. The other two rooks caught up and were zigzagging a path that swept them out to the side of the *Sicerro*.

"I think they're herding us," Noar said from the nav station. From the looks of things, Luliana's trajectory, initially as straight and short-lined as possible, was beginning to show a curve to the right in an effort to keep her distance from the rooks.

Tia'tan snapped out an order. "Prep the plasma cannon."

"In this debris field? We'd be lucky to get a shot anywhere near one of them," Joffar answered.

"Short bursts."

Joffar nodded, already initializing the cannon. The ship cut too close to a rock fragment the size of a tiny moon and Luliana couldn't get them out of the way of a ruined shuttle beyond it as they zipped around its curve, hitting the shield hard over the wing. Luliana looked too focused to curse, but the ship's warning about weakened shield integrity had the same effect.

The plasma cannon let loose a belch of white-hot material in a stream. It shot a hole straight through a decrepit pleasure barge and scorched a streak of molten fire along the smallest rook's side. The thing reared up like an injured animal and halted in place. Its tentacle arms flared out, two sliding over the plasma scar as if probing for damage. An eerie blue light built in the ends of each tentacle pulsed ominously as the rook swished back and forth in place.

"Now we've pissed it off," Vayne said. The tentacle tips of the other two rooks began to glow with a matching blue light. "Correction, we've pissed them all off." Blue lights shimmered down each arm, the pattern increasing in speed. Joffar fired several more bolts of plasma that the smallest rook easily dodged even as it retreated, then blinked out of sight for good.

One down? Vayne could only hope.

"Focus on the closer ones," Tia'tan said, at the same time Luliana said, "They're definitely herding us somewhere."

"Not toward something, away from something," Noar said. He expanded the 3D nav display as far as it would go. Along one side the dots representing debris disappeared in a well-defined curve, leaving blank space beyond. "It's the edge of the field."

"I'm trying to get there, they keep heading me off."

"Designing a firing solution to give us some room," Joffar said. A shot of plasma lanced into the side of the closest rook and it reacted with a flaring of tentacles. It blinked out of existence then reappeared right below them. One of the arms lashed out, striking straight toward the belly of the ship. Everyone not seated in the cabin was thrown as the tentacle speared through the shields with enough force to send the ship into a spin.

How the frutt?

Luliana struggled to right the ship and Tia'tan climbed to her feet. "Get us out of the field, then we'll have enough running room to open a hyperstream window out of here."

"No good," Noar said. "That shot took out the hyperstream drive, and one of our sub-light drives is leaking fuel. If we get out into the open, we'll be sitting ducks without the debris for cover."

Joffar shot a round of plasma into the rook and it blinked out, dropping back. The other rook backed off as well.

"We can't keep running," Luliana said.

Joffar shook his head. "We can't make a stand—the cannon doesn't have enough juice to take out two of these things, never mind if the third one returns."

"We need to hide," Vayne said, hurrying to the nav console. "There, what's that, a freighter?" Noar zoomed in. Looked like a mostly intact long-haul freighter, with row after row of open bay doors. "If we can disguise our movements long enough, we can slip into one of those bays and cut the power. We'll cool right down off the IR scans, disappear from electronic grids, and our mass will blend in with that of the freighter."

"And how are we supposed to shake the rooks long enough to duck into the bay unseen?" Tia'tan asked.

"Fake a crash," Vayne said. "Fly us right by a rock, then unload all of the frag missiles at it in the same spot, simulating us hitting the rock and exploding."

"That's a terrible plan," Tia'tan said.

She wasn't wrong. But what else would work?

Tia'tan had five seconds to consider before a bolt of green energy so bright it left an after-image on the viewscreens streaked across their bow and blew the nearest rook into a million pieces.

Holy shit.

"It came from beyond the field," Noar called, and Tia'tan nodded at Joffar.

"Do it," she said. Luliana skimmed them by the closest piece of debris and Joffar launched the frag missiles in their wake. The remaining rook halted as the decoy payload exploded.

"Luliana—get us to that damn freighter," Tia'tan said.

They slipped into a bay, clamped themselves to the floor and immediately shut down everything, leaving them blind and breathing shallow as the viewscreens blanked and the air circulation cut out. Tia'tan slid the viewscreen aside to reveal the actual glass at the front of the ship and a view out into the field. They didn't need the magnification powers of the viewscreen to see the rook as it glided slowly by, blue lights shimmering beneath its ebony "skin," the bow turning this way and that as if scenting.

Vayne stood frozen in place, unable to even twitch as the gigantic rook slid slowly by. Another bolt of green energy flew past, missing the rook by mere meters. The rook blinked out of existence. Three more shots followed in rapid fire, then... nothing.

::Now what?:: Corinth asked.

Now what indeed.

8

ISONDE'S TOWNHOUSE, FALANAR

Kayla woke that afternoon feeling curiously light. She hadn't realized how much weight had pressed down on her ever since Malkor found her in the swamp. Its sudden absence left her buoyant.

Had Isonde woken only hours ago? Kayla's future had shifted so dramatically because of that fact, it hardly seemed possible.

As she lay in Isonde's bed, the reality of her situation sank in. She wasn't free, at least, not yet. She'd have to continue her masquerade as the princess for the time being, until Isonde regained her strength. And then there was the threat of Bredard hanging over them all. She couldn't leave Malkor and Isonde to face the repercussions of that blackmail alone. Still so much to do. At least now, for the first time in weeks, hope glimmered.

Kayla dressed with the well-learned precision of Isonde. Her hologram was firmly in place as she made her way downstairs for a quick lunch before returning to the rooms that housed the real Isonde.

Isonde remained in her medical pod, lying down as if even sitting was more than her body could handle at the moment. Her eyes, though, were as sharp as ever, and she busily interrogated Ardin on current events.

"I've missed so much," Isonde said, frustration evident in her voice. That was Isonde, all right—all business. Not "Gee, I'm so glad I survived," or "I really need to rest."

"How are you feeling?" Kayla asked.

Isonde lifted a few fingers in a weak gesture. "Toble's keeping me confined to this pod for at least another day, then it's bed rest after that."

"Much to her dissatisfaction," Ardin said with a smile.

"I have too much to do to lie abed." Isonde's gaze sharpened on Kayla. "Ardin's told me your true identity. I wish I had known."

Kayla wasn't sure if she meant "I wouldn't have treated you with such scorn initially," or "I really could have found a way to leverage that knowledge." Kayla replied, "The fewer people who know, the safer I am."

Isonde didn't answer that directly. "Ardin's caught me up on the Game and Trebulan's TNV attack at the attempted wedding. Tell me everything you've done since—and don't leave any details out."

Oh man. This was going to be a long day.

Some hours later, Toble came and insisted Isonde get some rest, saving Kayla from the inquisition. She was all too eager to escape the grilling. Isonde analyzed and catalogued every choice Kayla had made, every word she'd uttered as Isonde in the last few weeks. She hadn't been that thoroughly critiqued since her *ro'haar* training days. As exhausting as it was, it still brought a sense of relief. Isonde was readying herself to take back her life, freeing Kayla to live her own. Not to mention how beneficial it was to have an experienced politician help her navigate her last delicate days as Isonde.

Sadly, her reprieve was short-lived.

She was sitting in Isonde's front solar, sipping tea and enjoying a moment thinking of absolutely nothing at all, when Malkor entered. The grim set of his mouth and his worried brow announced her quiet moment was over.

"Have you seen this?" he asked by way of greeting, stalking

to the vidscreen and flipping it on. Falanar's main news feed appeared, the screen filled with an image of Wei-lu-Wei from space and a chaos of ships around it. Thousands of spaceships, most not even capable of deep-space travel judging by their design, jockeyed for position. Even as she watched, two ships collided, and more ships launched themselves through the atmosphere and into the fray.

What kept them in orbit? Why hadn't they flown away?

"Wei-lu-Wei's citizens hadn't known about the TNV on their planet," Malkor said. "Since the news broke, people have been fleeing the surface by any means necessary."

What a disaster. "Who knows how many of them are infected? They could be spreading it across the entire empire, to all the other uninfected worlds." On screen a giant imperial army battleship cruised into view.

"This is a scene from earlier." Malkor gestured toward the battleship. "The army pulled its battleships from patrol on the Ginesea trade corridor to blockade the planet. They don't have enough ships in place yet to do it effectively."

As she watched, two passenger ships broke from the crowd and tried to dart past the battleship. They were promptly fired on and destroyed.

"Holy shit. The military is killing civilians?" Kayla watched in stunned amazement as the clip repeated. "They could have disabled the ships, instead."

"Those aren't their orders. Apparently the military isn't taking any chances with the spread of the TNV."

"What about all the ships that escaped before the army arrived? Are they going to be hunted down?"

"I have no idea."

How many more people would be desperate enough to get away from Wei-lu-Wei that they'd risk trying to get past the battleships? How many uninfected civilians would die because people feared they might be infected?

"The army is sending reinforcements to make an impenetrable blockade. I don't know what'll happen in the skies above Wei-lu-Wei in the meantime." Malkor flipped to another feed. "And then there's this."

The headline ticker running across the bottom of the screen caught her eye first: *TNV outbreak on Wei-lu-Wei the latest in the Wyrds' terrorist attacks on the empire?*

A politician she didn't recognize gave an impassioned speech about the moral depravity of all Wyrds and the need for the empire to strike back in the face of such villainy. Kayla slammed her tea cup down.

"How *dare* he claim that my people had anything to do with this, that the Ilmenans are responsible for this outbreak?" She was one second from breathing fire. She stabbed her finger at Malkor like a sword. "You brought this on yourselves."

"Hey, don't point that finger at me. I didn't weaponize those nanites."

"And we didn't spread them," she snapped. "Somehow *we* still pay the price." Kayla pushed off the couch to pace. She wanted a fight. A dirty, no-rules brawl. She wanted to strangle someone. "Of all the asinine—" She broke off, unable to speak past the fury.

Long moments passed before she controlled her temper. "What would Ilmena possibly gain by spreading the TNV?"

"Payback seems a pretty obvious motive to me." Malkor was wise enough to keep his distance as he said it.

She gestured toward the vidscreen. "Don't tell me you believe this bullshit?"

He perched on the arm of the sofa out of her way, eyes following her as she walked. "It *is* possible. The evidence found by the imperial army linking the Ilmenans to Prince Trebulan and providing him with a supply of the TNV is pretty airtight."

She made a sound of disgust. "Corinth could manufacture evidence that airtight. It doesn't mean a thing."

It *didn't*.

The Ilmenans had every reason to hate the empire, as many reasons as she did. They wouldn't resort to genocide, though. Wyrds were better than that. Superior.

Malkor crossed his arms over his chest. "I'm not saying they did it, but, how well do you really know these Ilmenans? They came to rescue your family, yes. Beyond that you have no idea what their plans are."

She stopped pacing and faced him head on. "They are Wyrds. That's all I need to know." And she had damn well better be right, since she had entrusted the fate of her last surviving family members to them. "This was *not* a terrorist attack. The TNV has been eating its way through the Protectorate Planets; it was only a matter of time before the infection spread to a Sovereign world.

"Besides," she said, "if your empire's elite had given half a damn about the Protectorate Planets when the TNV first broke out, things might never have gotten this far."

Malkor nodded to concede the point. He looked... tired. And wary. Kayla took a breath and eased out of her defensive stance, standing down from attack-mode. Malkor wasn't saying anything that other people hadn't already said, and he didn't need her jumping down his throat over it.

"Sorry," she said. "You didn't deserve that."

"I knew you'd calm down in a minute or two," he said with a smile. "Your style's mostly 'react first, think about it after.'"

She opened her mouth to argue, but he was right. IDC agents had years of training on how to be patient, calculating, diplomatic, strategic. As a bodyguard, she identified a threat and neutralized it immediately. Questions could wait until after her *il'haar* was safe—if there was anyone left alive to question.

And okay, maybe she was a *little* more overprotective, and a *little* more reactionary than most *ro'haars*.

Maybe.

She continued pacing. "We have to head this 'Wyrds as terrorists' bullshit off," she said. "If the idea of increasing the military presence in the Wyrd Worlds gains traction, it'll undermine our position." One more thing on a long list of worries. *Soon to be Isonde's list*, she reminded herself.

It didn't help. Handing the reins over to Isonde wouldn't

erase Kayla's worry. Too much was at stake for her people to walk away from Falanar without a backward glance when the charade was over.

"We should talk to the Low Divine," Malkor said, surprising her.

"That child?"

"She has a strong influence over the people, and she's always counseled peace as the most desirable course."

The idea of involving any religious figure in politics as important as this seemed ridiculous to her, but Raorin *had* included the Low Divine in his pre-council meeting.

"I'll talk to Isonde about it." Kayla turned to her most immediate concern. "How goes the search for a way to neutralize Bredard's threat?"

"You mean besides killing him?" Malkor managed half a smile, as if it was a joke. The very real option of assassination hung in the air between them. Could she kill someone in cold blood to save herself? Maybe. Could she do it to save Malkor? Yes, unequivocally.

"Assuming it doesn't come to that," she said.

He let out a sigh, scrubbing a hand over his face. "It's complicated. Without knowing what evidence he has against us, I don't know how much counter-leverage we need. Commander Parrel has people going over Dolan's files on who in the IDC and imperial army were complicit with Dolan's experiments, and we have some major hits against high-ranking IDC members. One of those will likely be Bredard's handler, capable of reining him in. I don't know how to flush them out without making the corruption within the IDC public knowledge." His tone echoed her frustration. "Do I want to expose those involved? Absolutely. Am I willing to dismantle the IDC over it, see the entire institution destroyed due to their actions?" He left the question unanswered. "There's still so much good we can do," he said, almost as though he were trying to convince her—or himself—of that fact.

Kayla didn't give a damn about the IDC. With the exception of Malkor and his octet, they could burn to ash while she watched. The organization was bloated, rotting, and about to implode. It wasn't worth saving, not if it meant the men and women who helped Dolan imprison and torture her family went free.

Malkor wasn't ready to hear that.

"Decisions are going to have to be made," she told him, "and you're going to have to choose which side you're coming down on."

Mine or theirs.

His eyebrows rose. "*You're* going to talk to *me* about divided loyalties? About who you stick with, and who you leave behind?" He sounded somewhere between incredulous and furious that she would dare question his loyalty.

Last night, in the midst of near-delirious relief to be alive and see Isonde healed, the tension between them had been forgotten. In the light of day, the choice she'd made wedged itself between them once again.

His mobile comm chimed, cutting off whatever he meant to say. He answered, and the way his gaze flicked to her when he said, "You're certain?" sent a chill of apprehension through her.

Malkor closed his mobile comm with a snap. "Hekkar has a report of the Ilmenans' ship. The army had a run-in with them near the Tucane nebula—just outside of the Mine Field."

"What the frutt are they doing there?" They'd probably pass the Mine Field on their way to Wyrd Space. It was well-marked on imperial star charts; they would know to give it a wide berth. Her worries for Vayne and Corinth kicked into hyperdrive. "Bredard knows. This is what he was talking about when he intimated that they hadn't reached Wyrd Space." Had they somehow been pulled into the Mine Field?

She had to know. Kayla headed for the door.

Malkor moved as if to stop her. "Kayla, don't do anything stupid."

"Stupid? Nah." She was an overprotective *ro'haar* and her

brothers were in danger. Acting stupidly might be out, but recklessly was definitely on the table.

"I'm going to pay Bredard a visit."

Three of Ardin's guards fell into step behind Kayla when she left the townhouse and entered the waiting hover car. The door closed behind her on a cacophony of questions called out by the media from the edge of the property.

Damn. She really had to do a press conference soon, issue a statement about Rawn's death at least. How about "Frutt you, Bredard. I'm coming for you." How would that work as a statement?

If only.

The hover car carried her away from reporters and political concerns for the moment. Her thoughts switched immediately to the impending confrontation with Bredard, which she might be anticipating a tad too much. *Could be a cluster-frutt.* At least she was *doing* something. On the attack instead of waiting for the next punch to land. If Bredard knew anything about her brothers, anything at all, she had to try.

They traveled through the crown district and arrived at the most recently renovated area of the business sector. Old commerce hubs and narrow office buildings—some historical landmarks from before the addition of the Protectorate Planets to the empire—stood shoulder to shoulder with newly built-up lots, ancient stone giving way to modern organoplastic.

The street was blissfully media-free when they arrived. No one shouted questions at her or recorded her every move. Not yet, anyway. The throng on the sidewalk parted quickly for her guards' muscled bulk in full regimentals, and they reached Bredard's office building in no time.

The sight of the future empress sent the entire lobby into a frenzy. Kayla was fast-tracked through security and personally escorted to the office suite of the Gethans. Through it all she maintained Isonde's poise, even while her blood hummed with excitement for the impending confrontation. Her fingers tingled, itched to tap the kris she hadn't been able to bring with her.

Before Kayla could say a thing or their escorts could stop them, her guards flung open the double doors of the suite and took post on either side.

"I like your flair," Kayla murmured, as she passed the closest guard. She struck a pose dead-center in the doorway, chin up, shoulders back, sweeping the interior with Isonde's icy gaze.

There. The office at the back. Had to be Bredard's.

She marched down the aisle between the staffers' desks, guards following behind, ignoring the wide-eyed stares and half-hearted attempts to question her.

When she stopped before the secretary posted in front of the door, the woman stammered, "Are you expected?"

Kayla arched a brow. "I am Princess Isonde," she said, as if that answered everything. She had a heady sense of her own power in that moment. And having two of Ardin's impressive guards flanking her like sentinel towers didn't hurt.

"Of course," the secretary murmured.

Bredard's pet biocybe, Siño, rose from the chair outside the door, smirking all the way. Probably remembering the last time they'd met, when his backhand had cracked across her cheek and she'd done nothing but take it.

Not this time.

Kayla tilted her head toward her guard on the right. "Why don't you two keep Siño here company while I chat with Bredard?" She gave the biocybe an airy wave as the secretary opened the office door, and Kayla sailed past Siño into the room, knowing her guards would block his entrance.

The look of shock on Bredard's face was gratifying. It only lasted a moment, still long enough to savor a feeling of power. She approached his desk like a shadow panthe on the hunt, stopping kitty-corner to him, neither in front of the desk nor totally in his space. Close enough to control the situation, if need be.

He flashed a bland smile and laid his hands flat on his desk. "Quite a ballsy move, coming here."

She shrugged. "Not really. The media will be here any second. Your office is agog with curiosity over my presence, likely alerting everyone they know that they just saw the future empress. Anything happens to me..." She snapped her fingers.

"The same goes in reverse."

She arched a brow. "Does it?"

He leaned back in his chair, letting his right hand trail across the desk's surface toward his top drawer.

Not very subtle.

Kayla swung her right leg over his shoulder and struck downward with her heel in an axe kick that knocked his hand toward the floor. It was a delicate maneuver: too much force and she would have snapped his wrist. Lucky for him, she knew the limits of her strength to the finest degree.

He gasped, gripping his injured wrist.

"No need to get overly excited," she said with a feral smile. "Let's have a friendly chat." She slid the drawer open herself, unsurprised to find a pistol secreted there. She placed it on a table by the door, well away from his reach, and returned to his desk.

Bredard left off rubbing his wrist, once more calm and complacent. "If you don't have my data, *Princess,* then we've nothing to talk about."

The bastard was oh-so-smug.

"I disagree." She made herself keep still, even though she itched with the urge to commit violence. This man killed Rawn, someone innocent in all of this, to make a point. He held the lives of people she cared about in his hand and he was ruthless enough to destroy them all.

"Your bargaining position has changed," she said, trying to keep her tone even.

He arched a brow, settling back in his chair as if perfectly comfortable. "Really? Last I checked, I still held all the cards."

"Then perhaps you need to check again."

He ticked points off on his fingers. "Your real identity, knowledge of you fixing the Empress Game with Agent Rua and the actual Princess Isonde, and let us not forget, the whereabouts of your beloved brothers." He smiled. "I think that covers it, don't you?"

She reached out and curled one of his fingers back into his fist. "About my brothers…"

He stilled, smile frozen on his face.

"I hope you weren't counting on that being your strongest piece of leverage." She let her words sink in.

He lowered his hand and gazed at her, assessing. She waited, feeling for once not at a complete disadvantage. She had knowledge, she had power.

Not enough, though.

She knew where her brothers were, but not why. What the frutt were they doing near the Mine Field? How did Bredard know they had gone there? And how in the void could the Ilmenans endanger her family like that?

She had the urge to lift Bredard by his shirt front and shake the answers out of him. Sadly, he was her only source of information. Better to save some violence for later.

"You couldn't possibly know where they are," he finally said.

"The Mine Field is a pretty big place, so it's hard to know *exactly* where…" She shrugged one shoulder. "They're safe enough with the Ilmenans." A bald-faced lie. They could be dead even now and she wouldn't have known. If they somehow managed to survive the Mine Field, Tia'tan was going to answer to her.

"What do you want, then?" he asked.

"Information. You knew they were headed for the Mine Field. How? What's there that they're after?" It had to have something to do with Dolan, something he'd told the Ilmenans about. And if the Ilmenans knew, then likely Bredard and the shadow elements within the IDC knew as well.

Bredard laughed. "Why would I tell you anything?"

"Because you want your data." Her answer seemed to amuse

him and she itched to punch him square in his laughing face.

"I'm pretty sure the threat of revealing your actions at the Empress Game ensures that I'll get what I want."

"Really? And what proof do you have? It's not like you can quote Dolan as your source, not when so many secrets of the IDC and imperial army are tied to your involvement with him."

"I have other sources."

"Do you?" She took a step closer to him and he leaned back ever so slightly in his chair. Cocky he might be. Invulnerable? Not against her. "Show me your proof. Tell me why I should quake at your threats."

He didn't bother replying. Ah well, it had been worth asking about, anyway. A man like him wouldn't have gone into the blackmail business without solid evidence. Too bad he wouldn't brag about it so they knew how to counter his threat.

"Tell me about the Mine Field," she said instead, switching gears. "Why are the Ilmenans there?"

"Are you going to ask me to death? Real scary, Princess."

She grabbed him by the back of his neck and slammed his face into the desk, holding it there, then wrenched his right arm behind his back, immobilizing him.

His breath rasped harshly in and out, eyes wide with surprise and a flicker of fear.

Kayla leaned in, pulling his arm higher behind his back. "Maybe I'll delete some of your precious data."

"You wouldn't dare."

She squeezed his neck, pressing his face harder into the desk. "Wouldn't I? You'd never even know. Parts of Dolan's wonders could be lost forever."

He stared at her with one eye, judging her resolve.

Test me, you frutter. I dare you.

She wrenched his arm higher. "Tell me what's in the Mine Field."

He grunted in pain as she stopped short of dislocating his shoulder. "Fine. Fine, let me up." She held him down for another second, giving him a taste of the powerlessness she'd felt when he'd held her at pistol-point the other night. When she finally released him, his face was a mottled red-purple. "There's nothing you can do about it anyway."

"What do you know?"

He huffed, straightening his shirt before speaking. "Two Ilmenan ships came to Imperial Space, not one. Tia'tan's ship traveled to Falanar to win the Empress Game. The other ship traveled to the Mine Field."

"It's a death trap."

"There's something *in* the Mine Field, something big, worth risking the trip." He rubbed the side of his face that had been pressed to his desk. "I'm not privy to all of Dolan's research and plans, but he pieced something together to lure the Wyrds with. He counted on the Wyrds' superior tech to get them through the field safely."

That might or might not be all he knew. She sensed she wouldn't get any more out of him today. Time to go.

He tilted his chair, trying not to favor his injured shoulder, his smug smile creeping back. He stared at her like he had all the control in her world. Like she couldn't end him in a second if she wanted to.

She pivoted on her right foot as if to go, then leveled him with a left side-piercing kick to the chest that hit so hard he was flung from his chair, crashing to the floor. She quivered with the urge to do more, but held herself in check.

"That," she said, "was for Rawn."

"Assassination," Hekkar said in a flat voice. "You actually suggested assassinating Bredard to Kayla, a woman who's spent her life training to kill." He gave Malkor the all too familiar "you're insane" look.

"She spent her life training to *protect*," Malkor corrected, vaguely annoyed with his second in command, "not kill."

They stood on the maglev train platform in the city's

crown district, not too many kilometers away from Isonde's townhouse. The humid night air of the city wrapped around them, and at this late hour fog was creeping in.

The other intended passengers stood at the opposite end of the platform, carefully not looking in their direction, which was exactly what Malkor was used to. Normally it was because he was in IDC uniform. The Imperial Diplomatic Corps met with everything from respect to fear to hatred on their missions—everything except pleasure. They had near-limitless jurisdiction and the authority to do, well, whatever they wanted. The IDC got its way but it seldom made friends.

Tonight, though, he and Hekkar were headed across town to the Pleasure District, to a bar members of the imperial army liked to frequent. They were dressed to fit in, and he had to admit that Hekkar, with his red-gold-sunset hair spiked into a fauxhawk and his combination of black on black on black—duster, scarf, outfit—looked unsavory, to say the least.

"It's not like the octet hasn't been involved in its share of assassinations," Malkor said.

"For political reasons, Malk, under orders. To save civilians and depose corrupt regimes." Malkor knew him well enough to sense the unspoken anger behind Hekkar's neutral expression.

"Hey, I never said I was actually going to kill the man."

"Doesn't mean the idea's not there, in the back of your mind." Hekkar knew him too well to deny that. With Kayla's life on the line, not to mention Isonde's… "Damnit, Malk. I knew this whole thing was a bad idea from day one, from that first moment when we saw Shadow Panthe in the Blood Pit. I told you so then."

Malkor had known the plan to fix the Empress Game had been a bad idea way before that, from the moment Isonde and Ardin had first come to him with it. There just was no other way. There never had been.

Hekkar's jaw flexed, a sure sign of him grinding his teeth. "First Dolan held the secret over us, now Bredard—and by extension Senior Commander Vega—has you by the balls." He shook his head. "We're so deep in this shit we'll never get out from under it."

Malkor clapped him on the shoulder. "Well aren't you a bucket of sunshine tonight." The train arrived, saving Malkor's ears from Hekkar's string of expletives. Hekkar believed in the mission, they all did. Some days, though, it was harder to remember that.

They settled into a car by themselves, everyone else choosing to sit much, much farther ahead. Hekkar wasn't wrong. The damn executioner's pistol had been pressed to Malkor's temple since he had chosen Kayla for the ruse, and everything he did only seemed to increase the pressure. They should have been safe by now, Isonde sitting pretty on her shiny throne and Kayla heading back home. Instead every day brought a new complication, a new twist wrapping him tighter and tighter in this unending stratagem.

The city slipped by as the train sped on, and thankfully Hekkar remained silent on the topic.

They arrived at the Pleasure District and it wasn't a long walk to find the bar, Henri's Ghost. Easy to identify it as an army bar based on the clientele coming and going, despite everyone being in street clothes. Some things, like wearing a uniform daily, you couldn't hide.

The bouncer hesitated while letting them in, clearly uncertain if they were brothers-in-arms or outsiders. Malkor pushed past him before the man could decide.

As far as bars went, it was actually kind of homey. Dim lights, loud music and drunken laughter, sure, but without that ominous air most bars had of "we're all strangers here, and the wrong look at the wrong guy might start a fight."

Of course, things would probably change once he and Hekkar were outed as IDC. Imperial army soldiers and IDC agents weren't exactly close.

He scanned the room as he and Hekkar made their way to the bar. Their entrance had been marked by most with no more than a curious glance, and the bartender smiled, friendly enough, when they ordered beers. Good. The last thing he needed was to cause a scene. It helped that he and Hekkar looked more than capable of kicking the ass of anyone in there, and probably several of them in combination. Tended to encourage people to mind their own business.

"In the far corner," Hekkar said, "opposite the door."

Malkor took a swig of beer and glanced in that direction. Sure enough, sitting at a round table with two of his buddies was First Sergeant Carsov, part of the army's Biomech Crimes division. Beyond investigations, his team also handled high-risk biomech containment. Kind of like a bomb squad, except considering the TNV was within their jurisdiction, their job was much, much more dangerous.

Malkor had met the man once before. It had been at the near-catastrophic royal wedding between Ardin and Kayla-as-Isonde weeks back, when Prince Trebulan had tried to release the TNV on all of the empire's rulers, councilors and elite. An attempt Kayla barely thwarted in time. Carsov was the team member sent in to detect if Kayla had been infected with the TNV, and to free her from the containment foam.

Waiting for the diagnosis had been the longest three hours of Malkor's life.

At the time, Carsov had been entirely covered in a copper-colored biomech hazard suit. Now, he looked perfectly at ease in a jumpsuit and boots, beer in one hand and a smile on his lips. He was laughing at something the woman beside him said when Malkor and Hekkar arrived at his table.

"Mind if we join you?" Malkor asked, as he pulled out the chair opposite Carsov and sat, Hekkar doing the same.

"Well, well," Carsov said, still smiling. "If it isn't *Senior* Agent Rua of the IDC." He chuckled and nodded toward the rest of the bar. "Man, are you guys lost."

Carsov's friends were considerably less amused by the arrival of IDC agents, and the air at the table took a tense turn.

"We need to talk," Malkor said, "alone."

Carsov glanced at Hekkar. "Then why'd you bring a date?"

"He knows the score. These two," Malkor gestured to Carsov's friends, "had better not."

Carsov snapped his fingers as if remembering something. "Oh, that's right, your threat to send me—where was it again? The deep nether regions of abandoned space if I ever said anything, to anyone, at any time, ever?" He chuckled.

Carsov's friends looked uncertain, unable to laugh at a joke they didn't understand and unsure if it was even appropriate with two IDC agents at their table.

"I think I'll just ruin your career, instead," Malkor said. That wiped the smile off Carsov's face. Malkor caught a mutter of "frutting IDC" from the woman beside him. Carsov made eye contact with his friends and nodded to the bar. The two cleared off, shooting hard stares that said "one wrong move and your ass is mine." Malkor's gut urged him to reposition his chair to keep an eye on them. Instead, he trusted Hekkar had that covered.

Carsov set his beer down and pushed it away with his finger. "So. Did you come all the way down here simply to threaten me again?"

"You're the one who brought that up, not me." Not that Malkor didn't fully intend to make more threats if necessary.

"What do you want, then?" The man glanced at Hekkar then back to Malkor. Despite the beer on the table Carsov seemed mostly sober, if a little belligerent. Fair enough. Malkor had earned that attitude during their first meeting.

Something behind Malkor caught Hekkar's attention. It clearly wasn't enough to worry him overmuch. Still, he pushed to his feet. "I think I'll mosey on back to the bar for another beer while you two chat." He gave Malkor a fist bump on the shoulder. "I'll be back." In other words, he'd handle it, whatever it was.

"I'm here for information," Malkor said, when he had Carsov's full attention.

"What kind?"

The kind that could start a jurisdiction war at the very

least, and most likely see Carsov dishonorably discharged for providing it. "Information about the TNV." Malkor could have gotten that from a hundred people more qualified than Carsov. What he *really* needed... "Specifically, I need information on Prince Trebulan's supply of TNV."

Carsov's brow lowered.

"It's classified," he snapped. So, Malkor had been right—definitely trouble.

"Of course it is. Would I be here talking to you if I could get my hands on the information another way?" The noise level in the bar increased as someone cranked up a rocking song. Malkor moved closer to be heard without shouting over the din. "I know your squad is the best in the Biomech Crimes division stationed on Falanar. And you were the one chosen to go into the arena with the live threat of TNV at the wedding. That makes you the best of the best. Your squad led the investigation on Trebulan, where he got the TNV and how. Shit, you're the ones that found the other canister he had stashed in Shimville."

Carsov looked uncomfortable with the recounting of his recent activities. He glanced over Malkor's shoulder, searching for something, and shifted in his seat when he didn't find it.

"I need the final report of the investigation into who supplied Trebulan with the TNV."

"Those findings were reported publicly," Carsov said, as if that was the end of it.

Malkor lowered his voice. He had to be careful here, feel Carsov out. He'd researched the man before deciding on this course of action, and that led him to believe this was his best bet to get what he wanted. Still, Carsov was a relative stranger, and making assumptions about a person you only really knew on paper could get you killed.

He studied Carsov's face, alert for any reaction. "Weren't you, after your investigation, surprised to hear that the Wyrds had been denounced as Trebulan's suppliers?"

There. There it was—the flinch, barely noticeable in the

bar's dim light. The acknowledgement of Malkor's implication. He let out a breath in relief. Kayla had been right, her people hadn't done this. He'd been ninety-nine percent sure, but that last one percent had kept him awake at night.

"Why come to me?" Carsov asked.

"I told you, your squad—"

Carsov cut him off. "No, why *me*? I have a squad leader with higher clearance, why not go to him?"

Here it was, test time. Time to see if his profiling skills were as sharp as he thought they were. "Because I know you, guys like you."

"You don't know shit about me, Agent."

"Of course I do. Top marks at school, blowing the roof off test scores in biomechanical engineering. Joined the service straight from there, served three tours in the Altair Sector, turning down a promotion because you were holding out for a spot in the elite Biomech Crimes unit. Youngest biomech containment tech, as dedicated to the job as the army could ever hope for, with a penchant for taking big risks if it meant more civilian lives could be saved.

"Your parents are dead—old age—as is your wife, Carian, and your daughter, Ada. They died in a bioterrorist attack on a maglev train. Her parents are still alive, but you're estranged. They hold you accountable for Carian and Ada's death. Your love for the job had ravaged your marriage, and Carian was leaving you, taking your toddler daughter and going back to her parents' home. That's why they were on the train that day. Her parents still blame you for their deaths, and I sure as shit know you still blame yourself."

Carsov tangled a fist in Malkor's jacket and shoved, damn near knocking him from his chair. "You keep my family out of this."

Malkor held still, hands away from his side, waiting to see if Carsov would throw a punch. The first sergeant looked ready to.

Malkor nodded, indicating he understood, and Carsov

released his grip on Malkor's jacket with a sound of disgust. Aimed at Malkor, or his own loss of control? In the end it didn't matter. Malkor was striking a nerve. So far he'd been dead-on about Carsov. Malkor straightened his clothes, giving Carsov a minute to compose himself. No more than that, though. Time for the push.

"A tragedy like that," Malkor said, holding Carsov's gaze, "it's a crucible. It makes or breaks you. You either go down in a blaze of rum and flames, like my first octet leader, or walk through the fire and come out reforged. That's you. I traced your career from that point on. Commendation after commendation. Innovation, bringing new containment methods for biomech hazards to the team, new safety protocols for civilians. They say you're next in line to lead the squad when your boss retires."

Carsov reached for the beer he had pushed away earlier, took a sip. "So? What does all of that have to do with classified files from the Trebulan investigation?"

"All of that answers your first question of 'Why me?' Your dedication to doing your job at the very highest standards, your dedication to saving lives—squadmates, civilians, strangers— every single day, is why I am here asking *you* for a look at those files, not your boss."

Malkor paused for a sip of his own beer, trying to gauge Carsov's reaction to his speech. Some wheels were turning in the guy's head, that much he could tell. The right wheels? Malkor needed to connect with him, needed Carsov to think beyond the jurisdictional lines of IDC and military.

"The Wyrds aren't responsible for supplying Trebulan with the TNV," Malkor said, driving the important fact home. "I know that, and you know that." Carsov gave no indication either way. "I need to know who is, and I need to be able to prove it."

Carsov leaned back in his chair, shaking his head. "No way. That file's classified ten times over. If I hadn't worked on it myself I wouldn't even know it existed." He shook his head again. "Not gonna happen."

"Carsov, think about it. The Wyrds are a convenient

scapegoat. No one has liked them since they decided they were too superior to have anything to do with us generations ago, and that dislike turned to hate when they wouldn't help us with the TNV."

"Yeah, and?"

Ugh. Soldiers were as bad as civilians when it came to following politics. "And, now the Ilmenans are being pegged as terrorists bent on assassinating every imperial leader who came to the Empress Game." He leaned forward, tapping the tabletop as he made his point. "That's an act of war."

"Wei-lu-Wei," Carsov said quietly. "The TNV outbreak. I saw a story on the news that hinted that the Wyrds might be responsible for that, too."

"And as something of a TNV expert, what do you think?"

"It's bullshit. The TNV has been following that line of space, carried by traders in a trail that leads straight to Wei-lu-Wei. The only 'terrorists' who infected that planet are the frutting scientists who created the TNV years ago."

That's my man, Carsov.

"You know there have been calls in the Sovereign and Protectorate Councils for an increased military presence in Wyrd Space. With all this nonsense going on, there's talk of an all-out war with Ilmena, even."

That last had clearly been more than Carsov had heard. Sometimes Malkor forgot what it was like not to have a toe in the grandest sandbox in the empire.

"Three things," Malkor said, holding up three fingers to mark off the points. "Three reasons the Wyrds need to be exonerated. One, if a war starts, Wyrds who are innocent of any act of aggression against us are going to die wrongful deaths. Two, if you don't give a damn about the Wyrds, then let's talk about your army buddies. Those soldiers are going to die in a war that never should have started in the first place.

"Three. I need to find the bastards willing to infect their own people with the plague. The bastards who *did* supply Trebulan with the TNV. Nothing is more dangerous to the empire right now than those people. Nothing."

Malkor finished his beer and stood, leaving the bottle on the table. He wanted to push the point until Carsov handed over the file. Years of IDC training held him in check. He'd done what he could tonight to make his point; it was time to let Carsov chew on everything.

"You know how to reach me," he said, and turned to search for Hekkar. His second in command looked to be throwing bones with Carsov's two companions, each of whom looked giddier than he'd expected.

Carsov stopped him before he could leave. "Damn," he said. "You're not so bad at your job yourself." He gave Malkor a mock salute and walked off.

Hekkar met Malkor at the door and they exited into the warm, humid night.

"Everything okay back there?" he asked Hekkar.

"Course. The two were getting chatty with their friends about IDC agents crashing their little bar scene, so I challenged them to a game of bones to keep them from starting trouble." He grinned. "I think they liked the idea of bleeding an IDC agent of his monthly salary too well to resist. That, and I might have called them cowards when one of them tried to pass."

Malkor let himself relax for the first time since leaving Isonde's townhouse earlier in the evening.

"How'd it go with Carsov?" Hekkar asked.

How had it gone? Well, he thought. Carsov had at least been listening, and he hadn't misjudged the man. Carsov had a clear morality and was far into the "right" side of "right and wrong." He *was* military, though, and Malkor was asking for the most controversial and confidential file in all of Falanar.

"Eh," Malkor shrugged. "It went well enough for now, I think."

Hekkar stopped walking and stared at him. "You're pegging all our hopes for getting that file—which might be our only chance to dampen this anti-Wyrd hysteria that's rising—on one man's conscience and hero complex, and you're telling me it only went 'well enough?'"

"Hey, I said 'for now,' all right?" Malkor kept walking, grinning as Hekkar's string of expletives followed him down the street.

9

THE *SICERRO*, MINE FIELD

Everyone aboard the *Sicerro* seemed to be holding their breath. A minute passed. Five. Ten. Vayne didn't dare move as they all stood in silence, watching the debris of the Mine Field shift beyond their hiding place in the freighter. A band of tension constricted his chest. It seemed as if any movement, a single movement, would bring back the rook and certain destruction.

And then there had been that blinding green burst of energy that had ripped one of the rooks apart. What the void was that? Friend? Or yet another foe?

Twenty minutes passed before Vayne felt he could take a deep breath, could relax shoulders so stiff with tension they ached.

::Are they gone?:: Corinth asked. No way to know. Not with the ship powered down and no access to sensors. Tia'tan let out a huff of breath and he knew she had reached the same conclusion—waiting would get them exactly nowhere.

"Minimal power," Tia'tan said. "I want sensors, vidscreens, that's it."

Corinth flinched when the faint hum of power rumbled through the ship and the lights flicked back on. Kayla would have known what to do, what to say to steady the kid. Once, Vayne would have laid a hand on Corinth's shoulder and sent a message of calm. Instead his hand hung limp at his side—he had no comfort in him to give.

"The hyperstream drive is definitely down," Joffar said from his station. "Even if we make it to the edge of the field without the rooks reappearing, we won't be able to catch a hyperstream."

"We have a bigger problem than that," Noar called.

What the frutt could be worse than being stranded in Imperial Space, stuck in the deathtrap of the Mine Field?

Vayne moved closer to Noar's station to get a better look. The glowing map showed the curving line of debris that ended suddenly, delineating the edge of the field. They were close. So close.

Then he saw it, the way the curve continued, arcing back. Noar zoomed out and the truth of their situation became clear.

They hadn't reached the edge at all.

They'd reached the frutting center of the field. A wide-open field of nothing that the Mine Field's debris orbited around.

No, not nothing.

A gigantic structure floated in the center, spindle-like. The axis around which the entire Mine Field spun. What in the—

"We found it," Noar said, and the words were almost a question.

"That has to be it," Tia'tan answered. She reached out, touching the dot on the sensor array as if that would confirm its existence. "But where's the *Radiant*?"

Noar's fingers danced across the interface, screens changing rapidly. "No sign," he finally said.

"Damnit, Kazamel," Tia'tan muttered. "Where are you?" The Ilmenans on the bridge pretended not to hear.

Vayne had heard enough. Or rather, not nearly enough at all. "What is 'it?'"

Tia'tan ignored him. "Send the message," she told Noar. "Joffar, bring us to full power, spin up the engines."

"Are you out of your mind?" Vayne reached out to grab her arm but his hand smashed into her shield. She glanced down at the spot as if surprised he hadn't punched through. He could have with his psi powers. He still wanted to. Instead he forced himself to stand down. "Twenty minutes ago we were running for our lives, now you want to go back out there?"

"The rooks have cleared off." She gestured to the map. "You want to wait until they come back?"

"You want to take our chances with something that can liquidate a rook with one shot?"

"They could have killed us and didn't," she pointed out. "And if that's really the *Yari*, then the safest place to be is with that ship."

The word *safe* didn't belong anywhere in this conversation.

"Message incoming," Noar said, before Vayne could press further. Noar played it—garbled bursts of static and jumbles of words. He played it again and all Vayne could make out was something about docking. "They sent the passcode back with it," Noar said. He looked at Tia'tan, and for the first time since they'd been pulled into the Mine Field, someone smiled. "It has to be them."

"Good enough for me," Tia'tan said. "Luliana, take us there."

"Across all that open space?" Vayne said. "We'll be target practice if you're wrong."

Tia'tan gave him a determined look. "We didn't come all this way to be wrong." She turned her attention to the viewscreens as Luliana nosed them out of their hiding space.

Vayne glanced back to where Corinth stood alone. He was white-faced and breathing shallowly, eyes huge as he stared into the Mine Field. Sometime in the last five years, Vayne had lost the ability to feel that kind of terror, not without Dolan's mind-control machine programming it into him. He could remember the genuine feeling, though.

He crossed back to Corinth's side and stood silently with him.

No one spoke as Luliana maneuvered them through the debris. The rooks had been herding them away from the center of the field on purpose, Vayne reasoned. Maybe it was more than fear of what lay at the field's heart, maybe the rooks knew the Wyrds would find help there. It was a slim supposition to hang their hopes on.

Their journey through the last of the debris was anticlimactic compared to their frenzied flight earlier. They reached the edge without incident, and Luliana increased their speed as they launched themselves into open space.

No weapons fire came. No rooks flew after them. The massive spindle-shaped object grew large enough on the viewscreens to make out details.

"Holy shit," Vayne breathed. "Is that—" He recognized the shape of the looming spaceship. Anyone from Ordoch would, in an instant. "When you said '*Yari*,' you meant *the Yari*?" He couldn't even put the impossibility of its existence into words.

Tia'tan nodded, her gaze never leaving the screens, as if to look away would make the miracle vanish. "That's the *Yari*."

"Holy shit," Vayne said again, because nothing else could cover it.

The *Yari* was a piece of history, a relic of time past. It was a gigantic weapons platform built by his people a century ago, at the height of the Second Ilmenan War. It was supposed to be a game-changer for Ordoch, a weapons system so powerful that nothing Ilmena had would match it. It was being towed to its destination, the drives still under construction, when a rogue wormhole ripped open space and sucked it in. The *Yari* had been assumed destroyed when the unstable wormhole collapsed.

A message came through the system as they approached the station, this time the words perfectly clear. "Welcome to the Middle of Nowhere."

10

ORDOCH

Cinni stared at the collection of hyperstream drive parts loaded on the hover cart. A pitiful pile of gently—and not so gently—used components, more like a mad peddler's hoard than Ordoch's one hope for freedom. It represented a month's worth of stealing, dealing and kneeling. It took all the resources the uprising had to scavenge even this small amount of tech, and the meagerness of the collection filled her with fury.

She kicked the hover cart. "Damn those godsforsaken imperials!"

Mishe looked up from where he'd been gathering the last bit of heat shielding to throw on the pile. His sympathetic look only made her angrier, and she kicked the cart again before turning away.

She knew what he thought. What her superiors thought. Everyone walked on eggshells around her now, afraid she'd burst apart if they so much as looked at her wrong. Everyone in the base knew what she had done, what she'd volunteered to do.

Murder her mother.

Execute, she corrected. Execute Hephesta for crimes against her own people. For conspiring with the imperials. For turning traitor. The *blast* of the ion pistol as she'd fired it still echoed in Cinni's head, but it was her mother's eyes, her mother's last look, that haunted her.

"I'll be back," she said over her shoulder, and stalked out of the storeroom. The guards posted outside nodded as she passed, their thoughts written on their faces: was she one of the most dedicated "soldiers" to the rebellion, or the next one in line to lose it over the choices they all had to make?

Get it together, Cinni.

The uprising had recruited Hephesta because of her position and influence, while they'd recruited Cinni for her zeal and dedication to gaining Ordoch's freedom at any cost. That dedication would serve her well, and she'd keep on as she always had this last year—putting emancipation first. A citizen turned into an unlikely soldier.

She strode down the concrete tube that served as the hallway at this sublevel, boots ringing against the stone matrix with satisfying violence. She'd spent so much of her last year learning to walk silently, to be invisible, that it was gratifying to announce her presence with her walk. Here in the base, even if she was one of the foot soldiers, she wielded her own kind of power.

::I'm coming up:: she sent to Aarush, and stomped her way to the magchute. She pulled a flat sheet of foil tabs from her pocket and popped a dreamer into her mouth. The sedative would calm her agitation better than a shot or two of oblivion.

Aarush was in one of the briefing rooms on a mid-level with two senior operatives, going over, for the hundredth time, details of tonight's raid. A raid she ought to be part of. All three turned when she entered. Aarush had a neutral expression on his face. The other two looked relieved.

"Give me a minute," Aarush said to the rebels. They took their chance to escape from Aarush and his obsession with detail.

"We'll miss you tonight, Cinni," one said, and clapped her on the shoulder as he fled out the door.

Cinni waited until the door closed behind them to speak.

"I should be going with them." It was her most oft-repeated phrase since word came down that she'd been pulled from the raid. The official call was that she'd earned some R&R after her solo mission to assassinate Hephesta. The inside word, that Aarush himself had told her, was that the higher-ups were waiting to see if she'd self-destruct.

"I'm fine," she told Aarush. Again.

He said the same thing he'd said every time they'd had this conversation. "It wasn't my call to pull you."

"It's still bullshit." If the uprising had official ranks, his rank would be somewhere in the range of colonel. He designed the strategies for the offensives, trained the Wyrds involved in those missions, and ran the raid side of things.

Aarush sighed. "Honest." It might not have been his decision to pull her, but he could have fought against it if he disagreed.

Blast.

She flinched as she heard that ion pistol shot again, the one she'd unloaded into her mother. She saw that moment of recognition and realization in Hephesta's eyes, when she understood what was about to happen.

Would that one moment mark Cinni forever?

"There'll be other raids," he said, "and your mission's no less important."

"Right. Letting a bunch of space junk hitch a ride on my carbon atoms to make it through the Tear." She tried to sound blasé. He didn't seem to buy it. In truth, stepping through the Tear was more terrifying than attacking an imperial outpost. In an attack her skills came into play. Walking the Tear to the *Yari* was like rolling the dice with your life. No amount of skill was going to change the way those pips came up if the already fluctuating Tear destabilized completely.

She felt the dreamer kicking in, slogging through her bloodstream, calming her.

"The *Yari* is our only hope for ending this occupation any time in the near future," Aarush said. "You know that. Without those parts to complete its stream drive…" His brown eyes, a beautiful anomaly on Ordoch, flicked to the closed door behind her before returning to her face. "Come here," he said softly.

She locked the door and then crossed to his side. She respected the distance he wanted to keep between them as her superior, and never approached him without an invitation, but if an opening presented itself she was damn well going to take it.

He was so beautiful, so confident, so perfect in every way. A star in the rebellion, a leader people would follow into death, and he wanted *her*. Even though no one said anything, she felt her status in the rebellion's ranks elevated because she warmed his bed.

He wrapped her in his arms and she laid her head on his shoulder. The calm of him surrounded her, stilled her frenzied need for action, soothed her so recent loss. Her mother's gaze couldn't find her here, and his dead family's ghosts couldn't haunt him when they were together.

"I wouldn't have sent you through the Tear," he whispered in her ear. "I don't like it."

He didn't say what they were both thinking: one of these days an order to cross the Tear would be a death sentence. A chill raced through her and he held her tighter.

She wanted to reach out to him, mind to mind, to know him on that intimate level. As always, though, he kept himself closed off.

"I'll be fine," she said, hoping that would prove true. The Tear became more unstable each day. It was the most dangerous rollercoaster ride in the universe.

Aarush pulled back sooner than she wanted, leaving her feeling as uncertain as ever.

"So few people know about the *Yari*," he said, in apology. "You wouldn't know if your mother hadn't told you." True enough. The existence of the *Yari* was too important a secret to trust to most of the uprising. The fewer who knew, the safer their hopes.

"And with Gorang dead," she said, "I happen to be the lowest man in the chain who knows. The most expendable."

He didn't deny it. The uprising against imperial occupation was more important than the fate of any one member. More important than all of them. She would sacrifice anything to see Ordoch freed, and though he might care for her, Aarush had the same dedication.

Even if her skills would be better used in the raid tonight, there was no one more appropriate to send through the Tear than her.

"I'll be fine," she said again. Aarush brushed his fingertips against her cheek. He looked like he might do more, but a knock sounded at the door, ending their time together.

"Let me know when you return," he said, instantly morphing back into her intense superior. "Megara will want a full report on the drive's progress." He brushed past her to unlock the door and she felt herself dismissed.

11

ISONDE'S TOWNHOUSE, FALANAR

Three days left on Bredard's ultimatum, Kayla thought, as she made her way to Isonde's room the next morning. Three days left to find a way to undermine him and save their skulls.

She was returning from the quiet memorial service they'd held for Rawn, which Isonde was still too weak to attend. Kayla had never felt like such a fraud as she had at the ceremony, reading the heartfelt words Isonde had written for a man Kayla had barely known. At least Kayla's sorrow was genuine, grief for a life that never should have been taken, a loss she was inadvertently responsible for.

Damn you, Bredard.

Now that she knew where her brothers were, and that they weren't on their way to the safety they'd been promised, it took every gram of self-control not to commandeer a ship and go after them. She couldn't, though, not now. Not with politics crashing down so spectacularly around her.

The TNV, IDC, imperial army, Sovereign Council…

At least when she'd been in hiding things had been simple: keep Corinth hidden, keep Corinth fed, keep Corinth safe.

She missed him, missed his mind voice, his face. His earnest excitement at the whirlwind their lives had become. Missed his hero-worship of the octet and his unwavering faith in her.

Guilt rose when she realized she missed him more than Vayne. Vayne had been nothing more than a memory for so long. Corinth—Corinth was real. He was her family.

I'm coming for you. All of you. Please be safe.

She entered Isonde's room, leaving Prince Ardin's bodyguards behind on the threshold. Isonde was propped up in her medical pod. "Thank you," she said, gratitude and solemn approval in her gaze. She must have watched Rawn's ceremony on vid.

"Of course," Kayla replied. What else was there to say about Rawn's death, when they both felt responsible?

Kayla removed the heavy brocade overcoat she had worn for the occasion and tossed it on the sofa. If only she could shed her role as Isonde as easily, the politics and the struggle. How was she to choose between staying here to help her people, and going after her *il'haars* when they needed her?

"We have to have the wedding," Isonde said, wrenching Kayla from her internal conflict.

"What?"

"The wedding. The sooner the better." Isonde's tone didn't allow for disagreement.

Kayla walked over to her pod and took the seat Ardin usually occupied. "Not sure you're going to fit your wedding gown in that thing."

Isonde batted the joke away with a wave of her hand. "I'll be out of here in a day, maybe two."

Considering she was practically a corpse two days ago, Isonde was healing remarkably well, the medical pod working miracles. Soon Isonde would be up and about and the charade would finally be over.

"The wedding will cement my win at the Empress Game and confirm my right to the throne."

Her win, eh? "I suppose you could have a small ceremony here, once you're strong enough to stand, or at least sit in a chair. We could tell the officiant you'd taken ill."

Isonde shook her head. "It has to be a grand event, the more people the better. Everyone in the empire needs to see me claim my place as Empress-Apparent."

"Gee, how romantic."

"Don't be ridiculous. This whole thing is and always has been a power play, from day one. Everything we did was intended to put me on the Council of Seven with Ardin."

How like Isonde, to see her own wedding in terms of a political event. The kind of determination... Kayla was dedicated to protecting her *il'haar*, ruthless about it even, but never so cold.

"Not cold," Isonde said, making Kayla realize she had spoken aloud. "Practical. I... I care for Ardin." She glanced down, awkward for a moment, almost unsure. "I do." Her face set once more with conviction. "That can't matter more than our goal of ridding the empire of the TNV. It just can't."

Had Kayla become the same? Had her love for her family, her brothers—Malkor—been eclipsed by her need to see her people freed? What kind of person did that make her: self-sacrificing... or foolish?

"We'll have the Low Divine officiate," Isonde said, her mind already moving past the moment and back to business.

"What happened to having that guy from Piran that officiated your parents' wedding?"

Isonde shook her head. "Not big enough. Now more than ever, this wedding needs to make a statement. If we can get the Low Divine to officiate we'll gain popular support. She holds the heart of the people."

Imperials and their "Unity."

"You're not even religious, what if she won't agree?"

Isonde actually chuckled at that. It was perhaps the first time Kayla had ever heard the sound from her. "Who wouldn't agree to officiate the most important wedding in a decade? She'll be at the center of the most-watched event in the empire—her own popularity will go through the roof."

This kind of scheming, the manipulating of popular opinion through social events, was familiar enough to Kayla, being part and parcel of growing up in a royal family, even among Wyrds.

Tech might become more sophisticated as a society advanced, but mob mentality could only evolve so far.

"We'll have it on the front steps of the Basilica of the Dawn, in the center of the city. The grounds are huge; we'll open the ceremony to everyone, citizens and royals alike."

"That sounds like a good way to get yourself assassinated." It was a *ro'haar*'s nightmare. Surely Ardin wouldn't allow her to take such a risk, no matter how powerful the event would be.

One look at Isonde's determined face, though, and Kayla knew he would. The man couldn't deny Isonde a thing. Was anyone powerful enough to withstand a force of nature like Isonde?

"You can make your plans," Kayla said, "but we've only got three days, four, including today, until Bredard's ultimatum. Unless you've got a magic plan to put an end to his threats, the Low Divine will be presiding over our executions."

Talk about a heavily attended event.

Isonde scooted herself a little higher in the medical pod. Kayla didn't help—Isonde wouldn't welcome an acknowledgement of her weakness, no matter what she'd been through.

The medical pod beeped annoyingly, unhappy with something it found in its scans of Isonde. The pitch of its hum deepened, and the low light that glowed within brightened considerably, until some of the tension left Isonde's body.

"Now," Isonde said, when the machine quieted down, "the councils will reconvene tomorrow. Security has cleared everyone remaining on the staff at both locations and everyone's adamant that we won't allow Rawn's death to shut down the government. We need to revise that speech you are about to give."

That afternoon, Malkor nodded to the guards outside of Isonde's room and swept through the doors. "I'm on my way to see Rigger. I wanted to know if you needed—" He stopped short. "What the—" Isonde's medical pod was empty.

Instead, she sat at her vanity, staring at herself in mirror.

"These aren't my teeth," she said, without turning around.

"What?"

"Oh, I know they're technically my teeth, regrown with a laser from stem cells and all that." She ran her tongue over her teeth. "They're not *my* teeth. They feel wrong."

An image popped into Malkor's mind of Isonde lying rigid on the floor where she'd fallen after Janeen had injected her with the toxin, her nose broken and bloody, her teeth smashed in. "I'm sorry for what you've been through."

"Teeth are a small price to pay." She met his gaze in the mirror. "I hope it's the only price?"

Her pod started beeping. Quietly at first, then with more insistence.

"Should you be out of that thing?"

She sighed. "Toble said I could be out for an hour at a time. Guess my hour's up."

"Let me help you back in."

Isonde shot him a look that would have killed a lesser man. New teeth, same old Isonde. She climbed in with visible effort, but not his assistance.

"Any progress on Bredard?"

It was Malkor's turn to sigh. "Not yet. Parrel has people on it, though."

"Then you'll have to give Bredard the data." Isonde said it like it was a foregone conclusion. Problem solved, in her mind.

"Not happening." Dolan's technical files held an insane wealth of knowledge. Beyond his work on psi powers and mind control, he had specs in there for advanced weaponry, spaceship design, galactic communication systems—all courtesy of his Wyrd origins. Commonplace tech for Wyrds was pure gold for the less advanced empire. Dolan had dispensed bits and pieces as he went, gaining himself near-limitless power in the empire, and the priceless resources he'd needed for his experiments.

"If it's our only bargaining chip—"

"Do you think for one second that Kayla would agree to give someone else the chance to do what was done to her family? To her mother, her twin?"

Isonde frowned. "So we don't tell her. Not until afterward, at least. She'll be thankful enough to be spared execution."

"You have no frutting idea what you're talking about. Kayla would die before giving someone the specs to build another of Dolan's mind-control machines." With what had been done to her family…

Dolan had warped the minds and personalities of his Wyrd prisoners at whim, until they were unrecognizable even to themselves. He broke them down to their most base impulses, forcing them to act against their innate natures and do, well, whatever Dolan wanted them to.

Dolan was fascinated by how far he could push a person to go beyond their own morals and decency. Perhaps the worst part about it? Once Dolan turned off the machine the mind control faded and each test subject returned to normal. But the memories of what they'd done, what had been done to them—those never faded.

Thankfully Kayla didn't know the extent of what her family had suffered. Malkor had read some of Dolan's files, enough to be physically ill for days over what Dolan's "experiments" entailed. Kayla hadn't asked to see the files and he hadn't offered.

"Well," Isonde said, "I refuse to die for the sake of data Bredard and his IDC cohorts may or may not be able to make use of. I did not survive paralysis and weeks in a coma, I did not put you at risk by asking you to fix the Game, to give in now. The only way this story ends is with me in a seat on the Council of Seven."

"You can't take the chair if you're dead."

She shot him an annoyed look. "The TNV is eating the empire alive. Our people are dying, suffering horribly in the process, and we've made zero progress in the last five years. We all agreed that Ardin and I sitting on the Council of Seven, working together, is the best way to redirect the course of non-action the empire has fallen into."

She crossed her arms over her chest, as immovable as a

battle cruiser with an empty fuel tank. "I will not let anything stand in the way of saving our people from the TNV. If you don't want to hand over the data, find another way. Find a way, Malkor, or I will."

Malkor slumped in his chair in his office at IDC headquarters, rubbing his stinging eyes with the heels of his palms. A stack of datapads mocked him, loaded with the endless collection of files the traitor in his octet, Janeen, had gathered on seemingly everyone. He could stare at this shit all day and it wouldn't matter—the dirt he needed on Bredard wasn't in Janeen's files.

"Frutt it." He pushed the nearest datapad away in disgust. He was considering dinner when his mobile comm beeped. Isonde.

"Hey," she said. "It's me." All of a sudden he wasn't sure who it was. Isonde's voice and ID signature, which Kayla had been using for weeks.

"Isonde?"

She chuckled. "Only when I have to be."

Kayla, then. Thankfully. He'd had enough of Isonde for one day.

"I know you're crazy busy," she said. "Any way I can convince you to take a sparring break?" She blew out a breath that held a world of frustration. "I've got meetings with Raorin in the morning, then council's in session all day, so no doubt Isonde will wake me at dawn to strategize. If I don't beat the shit out of someone before then I'm probably going to explode mid-council meeting."

That brought a smile to his face. "Sure."

"Thank the stars. Vid offered, but Trinan would be the one kicking my ass if I let Vid spar while he's still healing. Besides," she said, and he heard the smile in her voice, "you're my favorite victim."

He changed and met her out front of IDC headquarters when she arrived with Ardin's bodyguards. "You guys can hang in the lobby," he told them as they all entered the building. "The princess couldn't be safer here." Plus, he didn't want two more pairs of eyes on Kayla while she worked out. She was hotter than a sun when she fought and he wanted her all to himself.

He escorted her to one of the smaller gyms the building held, knowing it would be empty. It always was at this hour. Kayla radiated energy as they walked, and it was infectious. The anticipation he'd felt since she had commed kicked a notch higher. She tapped her thigh as she walked, two fingers beating a rhythm against the pommel of a kris she had hidden beneath an overcoat. Two fingers beating a tempo that his body synced to.

How long since he'd been alone with her?

Too damned long.

She shot him a glance as they entered the gym and it was eerie to see the glint of bloodlust in Isonde's eyes. "We have to get rid of that thing." He made a gesture to his throat, then entered in the code that overrode the locking mechanism on the door, sealing them alone inside.

She arched an auburn brow. Malkor closed the distance and stripped the hologram from her. Kayla's gaze shot to the upper corners of the room, switching from one to the other.

"No surveillance in here," he said, without looking away from her face. "All it would catch is shit-talking, slacking, and the occasional brawl when things got too heated between rival octets."

"Trinan and Vid talking trash?" she said in a mock-surprised tone. "Never." She didn't step back from him, didn't move except to breathe, and he drank her in. Eyes bluer than an arc of electricity, rounded cheeks and a snub nose that seemed to contradict the harshness in her. Beautiful.

"You should hear Rigger," he said.

This time she laughed, a throaty sound, a rusty sound, so unlike Isonde's refined trill. His Kayla.

"So, are we gonna fight or are you just going to stare?" she asked.

He could look at her for hours. Well, maybe not without making love to her first. Then he'd take all the time in the world to enjoy her, to study every line and curve of her before she was smothered beneath the hologram once more.

"We can fight," he said, then gestured to her kris, "if you take those off."

Both of her ebony brows arched, and her smile faded into something much more intent. He reached out, slowly, so slowly, waiting for her to pull back. He pushed aside the edge of her overcoat and touched his fingers to her hip, his eyes on her face the whole while. She said nothing, the breath still in her throat as he slid his hand down her thigh until he reached her kris. He started to withdraw one from the sheath and her hand closed over his, automatically protecting herself from being disarmed, even by him.

He waited, neither moving nor releasing the weapon, watching her. She took a deep breath. Another. Her hand slipped from his, a caress of fingers across skin, and she nodded the barest fraction. He withdrew the kris slowly, then the second one. Holding them, one in each hand, he felt as though he held her power, her soul. She had given him her strength, willingly.

A sigh shuddered from her and her shoulders relaxed. He wanted to drop the blades to the floor and pull her to him, but the moment was too precious for that. Instead he laid the daggers gently on a nearby bench while she watched.

He returned to her, loving the way her gaze followed his every move. He slid his hands inside the collar of her overcoat, fingertips grazing each side of her neck as he moved, thumbs tracing her collarbones through her tank top, then palms on her bare shoulders as he spread the coat wider and coaxed it down her arms. It puddled behind her and her breath picked up, matching his own.

His hands were on her thigh, untying the bindings of her empty sheaths, when she said, "I really did want to spar."

He forced his hands to still. "We still can." Yeah, right. If he didn't make love to her in the next five minutes he was going to lose his mind. "If you want."

"I do want." Her voice was almost a whisper. "So, so much." Then she rose on her toes and kissed him, tentatively, as if he might pull away at any moment, and it was more than he could take. He wrapped his arms around her, spun, and pressed her against the wall beside the door. There was almost a purr on her lips when he claimed her mouth again.

Damn her willingness to leave him behind before, and damn the future when she'd leave him behind again. He had her here, now, and that's all he wanted.

Kayla

12

The next morning, Kayla stared out the hover car window as the city streaked past, her thoughts on Malkor instead of the political labyrinth she planned to enter. He had been tender and rough, dominant and surrendering, and everything that was perfect in her world. The two of them, together in the space of that shared heartbeat, were perfect.

Sadly, life was not.

She'd ached to kiss him goodbye when he returned her to Ardin's guards, to kiss him and never stop. To pretend nothing else existed or mattered. Instead she had walked away, wearing Isonde's face, and slept alone with only dreams of him to comfort her.

It had been worse in the morning as she stared at her own face in the mirror, at the face he called beautiful. *Her* face. She wanted it back. She never wanted to be Isonde around him again. It was as if a stranger stood between them.

That stolen moment in the gym was bliss. That's exactly what it was, though—stolen. They couldn't have what they wanted, not while she was still Isonde.

Maybe, after…

Kayla shook her head, dismissing the thought. There was no after. There was now, as Isonde, and then there was later, as *ro'haar* to her brothers, and no room existed for anything in between. No matter that she loved Malkor, no matter that her heart found refuge and peace with him.

That peace, too, was stolen, for she had another life to live.

The hover car she rode in arrived at the Sovereign Council seat, ending the few moments she had to herself.

Time to play the game.

The summons to an early morning meeting with Raorin wasn't unexpected. The TNV situation on Wei-lu-Wei approached utter chaos, and they planned to use that, use every piece of political leverage they had to secure Sovereign Council votes for withdrawing from Ordoch. It was their only hope for securing the Wyrds' help with the TNV.

Kayla arrived at the same time as Councilor Gi, Wei-lu-Wei's primary voting influencer. Whichever way Gi voted, so would the rest of the Wei-lu-Wei councilors. Thankfully General Yislan hadn't been available. *For the best.* He might support their cause, but his pontificating turned people off. Herself especially.

Kayla stopped short inside the office when she spotted Commander Parrel. He arched a cold brow with a look of "Well? Are you just going to stand there?"

One day soon, they were going to have a reckoning over Malkor and his divided loyalties. She felt it stirring between her and Parrel.

So be it.

Malkor might revere Parrel and Isonde might hope that Parrel could convince the IDC leadership to make a formal statement supporting a withdrawal from Wyrd Space, but if Parrel wanted to have private words with Kayla and a battle for Malkor's ultimate loyalty, he could bring it on.

Kayla swept past him and took a seat as the Low Divine entered, her young face a study in aloof elegance. Kayla had argued against involving the girl. Isonde and Raorin overruled her, saying the Low Divine would sway popular opinion because she held the people's hearts.

Raorin thanked the Low Divine for coming and she inclined her head in acknowledgement of the great favor she had done him. In truth, the girl probably couldn't stay away, despite her dislike for Raorin and his irreverent attitude. She had enough political savvy to know when something big was afoot, and a gathering of disparate elements such as these reeked of intergalactic change.

"Thank you all for making it here so early," Raorin said, immediately commanding attention. "I'm sure you agree that the situation on Wei-lu-Wei has gone from dire to near catastrophic. The army's quarantine of the planet is still incomplete, allowing ships to escape and jump stream to points unknown, possibly spreading the TNV.

"Worse still, no effective isolation protocols have been established on the planet's surface. Citizens are streaming from the cities in considerable numbers in an effort to escape anyone carrying the nanovirus. Who knows how many of them are infected themselves? They're fleeing into the farmland and the wilds, spreading the virus across the planet even quicker than it could have moved on its own. If something isn't done, we're looking at devastation on a global scale of one of the richest planets in the empire."

Councilor Gi's dark skin took on a grayish hue, her lips pinched and white around the edges.

"More than ever," Raorin said, "we need a cure. A way to stop the TNV."

Siminia interjected. "We need to stop people running into the unaffected areas like a mindless, stampeding horde."

"What would you have them do?" Gi snapped. "Stay in the cities and die? Have you never seen the vids of TNV victims?"

"They have to think globally—"

"How?" Gi's furious, shaky voice choked off Siminia's words. "How the stars could they 'think globally' while their children's bodies are broken down protein by protein? Their friends and neighbors destroyed from the inside out by a nanovirus with a 99.9% kill rate?"

Raorin let the moment sit, the words heavy in the air.

The devastation of it, the inexorability.

For the first time, the immensity of the TNV infection hit Kayla. The nanovirus could eat the empire alive, until there was nothing left but rocks and water and the abandoned bones of a once giant civilization.

"We *need* a cure," Gi said, "no matter what we have to do to get it." Even the Low Divine nodded her head at the statement. Everyone looked to Raorin for guidance.

"Now is the time to push," he said, "to demand a full withdrawal from Ordoch. Only the Wyrds are advanced enough to design a counter-nanovirus—fruitless years in our own laboratories have proven that."

Surely they realize that. Kayla's gaze traveled the room, willing those gathered to accept the truth of the situation. *Only my people can help you,* she nearly shouted. *Make the damn withdrawal happen.*

"There are other options," the Low Divine said, her childlike voice out of place.

Raorin shook his head sharply. "We cannot wait another decade for our scientists to advance in their understanding of nanotechnology."

"I meant, other ways of influencing the Wyrds."

Kayla's hands curled into fists at the word "influence."

Raorin stared the Low Divine down. "'Other ways' have not worked to date, and we are out of time."

Without drastic measures, the empire might be too far gone already. Isolationist measures on a planetary scale were required, measures that would sever the interconnectedness of the imperial planets and bring down the intergalactic civilization.

"Low Divine, I implore you," Kayla forced herself to say, and only because Isonde had ordered her to. "Use all of your influence with the people. Sway their hearts toward peace with the Wyrds. Exhort them to prevail upon their councilors to vote for a withdrawal."

The young woman made no response.

"Commander Parrel, you have been much too silent," Raorin said. "I know you favor withdrawal, as do many within the IDC. The IDC can no longer afford to be neutral." Raorin leaned forward in his earnestness, dark braid falling over his shoulder. "The backing of the IDC would almost certainly guarantee a win for us. What say you?"

Parrel held silent so long it seemed he would not answer. He looked at each of them in turn, judging them, and Kayla held her breath. What was he debating saying—or not saying?

"The IDC hasn't changed its official stance." The word "yet" hung in the air after Parrel spoke.

When they did change their stance, who would make the decision—the IDC Malkor proudly represented, or Vega's corrupt faction?

Parrel met Kayla's eyes across the room. This was so much bigger than the rest of them understood.

And much, much worse.

Kayla smoothed down the pencil skirt she wore, its shin-length fabric creased from hours upon hours of sitting during the council session. She'd been on edge the entire time, keeping a tally as the number of their supporters shifted after each councilor's speech.

Her heels clicked down the corridor as she made her way—finally—toward the maglift at the end. She could do without the presence of one of Geth's councilors beside her, still speaking heavily accented Common. Anyone from Bredard's home nation unsettled her.

Though, telling him to shove off was probably out of the question. Damn.

He'd kept her long after the session had ended, he and the councilors from Timpania, arguing against Piran's intended boycott of Timpania's gallenium ore if the workers' conditions didn't improve in their refineries. She'd wanted to say, "Honestly? I have so many other things on my plate right now

I couldn't care less." The councilor from Geth might have some control over Bredard, though, and Timpania could be brought over to the side of Ordochian withdrawal if Piran agreed to delay their boycott. So, as tired as she was from the long string of days, Kayla had lingered and listened.

At least the councilor from Timpania finally let her leave. The Gethan councilor followed her from the chamber, prattling the whole way down the corridor. For once she couldn't wait to reach Ardin's bodyguards; they'd pry the unctuous man loose. Sadly, they were stationed in a room off the front lobby with all the other bodyguards.

They waited side by side for the maglift, Kayla nodding noncommittally to his spiel. Isonde would want to know everything he said. Kayla just wanted to pinch the bridge of her nose over the headache that brewed and tune the tenacious man out. "I'm sure we can continue this tomorrow—" she was saying, when the lift doors opened and a familiar face grinned at her.

Siño, Bredard's pet biocybe.

Before she could react, Geth's councilor launched her into the lift with a shove between her shoulder blades. Siño stepped back, letting her in, his fist clubbing her cheek as she passed. She staggered, catching herself against the wall with one hand as the lift doors sealed her inside with Siño. No doubt the Gethan was fleeing the scene.

The lift didn't move.

Siño grabbed her hair and tried to slam her head against the wall. She locked her elbow, her arm like an iron bar thwarting the attempt. He yanked on her hair instead, jerking her head back, and she elbowed him with her free arm, catching him straight on the nose. Blood spurted and she got a second strike off before he could block it. His hand dropped from her hair and she turned in time to receive a blow to her solar plexus that knocked the breath from her.

Frutting strength augmentations.

She tried to strike with a knee but the frutting skirt Isonde

155

had dressed her in trapped her legs. Instead, still wheezing, she jabbed two fingers into his left eye.

Direct hit.

His answering roar shook the lift.

Siño caught her wrist when she struck again, stopping her fingertips no more than a centimeter from his right eye.

Damn he's quick. And half-blind now, at least.

Her wrist bones ground together in his vise grip, drawing a grunt of pain from her and shooting agony up her arm. She swung with her free hand. He saw it coming and ducked. Blood streamed from his crushed nose. He gave her a gory, crimson grin that promised fun for him and death for her. A very painful death.

As she started her backswing, he straightened from his crouch like a coiled spring let loose. Her blow collided with his ear as he caught her throat with an open hand strike that nearly crushed her trachea. He continued his momentum and lifted her off her feet with a stranglehold that pinned her to the lift wall.

Spots danced in her vision. She scrabbled ineffectually against his grip with her free hand. Nails clawing, fingers twisting for a handhold.

Choking, airless and desperate, training took over. She raised her arm, bringing it down in a hammer fist that struck the inside of his elbow in an attempt to bend the joint and break his stiff-arm hold. It had no effect, not against his biocybe augmentations. Second and third strikes were just as useless.

She gripped his arm at the wrist, trying to hold some of her own weight and take the pressure off her throat. Her vision began contracting, Siño's face becoming her whole world. With the last of her strength she lifted her knees together and kicked out at his stomach.

The sharp points of her heels sank into his flesh but he only grunted. She tried to lift her knees for another strike. Couldn't. She was done.

As the world slid away, he released her, dropping her to the ground in a mess of coughing and choking. She couldn't draw air. She knelt, one hand to her aching throat, the other barely holding her up. Even between gasps, though, she planned her next strike. If she could just... catch... her breath.

Wham!

His foot came down on her back, crushing her flat on the floor. His added weight compressed her lungs and she lay there, sucking in air, waiting for whatever came next. With one cheek ground against the floor and her neck bent at an awkward angle, she could barely look up at him.

Siño studied her a second, his uninjured eye overbright. "Bredard has a message for you," he said finally. That his voice sounded thick due to his smashed nose was her only consolation.

A message? The man had a frutting message? "Worst... messenger... ever," she gasped out.

"He didn't say how I was to deliver it." He pressed down harder with his foot, clearly enjoying the moment.

"Frutter," she huffed, and he laughed.

"You don't know the half of it." Siño wiped blood from his mouth. He had the heel of his other hand pressed against the eye she'd injured. The two puncture wounds in his chest oozed nothing more serious than lubricant.

Must be internal body armor of some sort.

There was a gleam in his good eye that she didn't like when he looked at her again. "Man, what I couldn't do with a woman like you. If you're half this fierce in bed..."

She spat in his direction, the only offensive she had the strength for. Her left wrist might be broken and his foot kept her too neatly pinned to get her legs around for a strike at his standing knee.

"We could find out. This lift's locked down, no one to disturb us."

"Try it... you're... dead," she grated out between labored breaths.

That made him laugh. *Laugh.* The frutter.

"Feisty, especially for a woman who's gone zero and two against me."

"Arrogant... for a half... machine who has to... ambush me." She coughed and spat again. "With help."

His smile faded, his gaze cooling. He pulled his hand off of his gouged eye, blinked it a few times. "Business, then. You're out of time. Bredard wants his data by midnight tonight."

"He said—"

"Things have changed. Midnight tonight."

"I don't... have—" He leaned on her back with his foot, cutting her off.

"Then get it." He watched her for understanding and she glared at him. "Good. Now, I'm leaving. And unless you want a kick to the midsection and some broken ribs, I suggest you stay down until I'm gone." She nodded, though it galled her to do it.

He backed off two paces and took his eyes off her long enough to glance at an open panel in the ceiling she hadn't had a spare second to notice. He jumped and grabbed the edges of it, then pulled himself up with a quickness only advanced biomechanics could achieve.

Then he was gone.

Kayla pushed to her feet, wincing at the pain in her wrist, her knees, her throat. A minute passed before she could stand upright and take a full breath. She shuffled to the lift's controls.

Yup. There it was.

She yanked out the locking pin Siño had inserted, hit the ground level indicator, and leaned against the wall as the maglift descended.

Midnight. She only had until midnight.

Kayla jammed the locking pin back into place, halting the lift. If Ardin's guards saw her like this, roughed up and worse for wear, they'd go into high alert. Or higher alert than they already were. They'd take her directly to the palace and practically imprison her for her own safety. Well, Isonde's, she corrected.

She couldn't afford to be on lockdown, not tonight.

She took stock of her appearance. Her hairdo was destroyed, so she pulled the few remaining clips from it and redid her hair in a simple bun. Not as elegant as Isonde, but it would get the job done. Her heels had survived the collision with Siño's chest. She twisted her skirt back into place and checked the rest of her damage.

When she patted her throat the biostrip was still there, and a look at her unscarred hand proved that the image held. The injury to her wrist wouldn't show until the bruising started. Her neck was likely red and swollen, though, and Siño's blood on the elbow of her suit jacket would give her away in a second.

She stripped off the jacket and turned it inside out. She made short work of ripping the satin inner lining from the sleeve and tying it around her neck like a scarf. It was the right length, and she tucked the torn edges underneath it. She righted the jacket and folded it, bloodied side in, and draped it over her injured wrist. It would do for the short ride from the council chambers to her townhouse.

It would have to.

Kayla reclined on the sofa in Isonde's room—where she'd been since she returned an hour ago—as they went over the Sovereign Council's session. Isonde sat in a green silk wingback chair beside the sofa. She looked fatigued and a little fragile, not that she'd admit to it.

The doors slid open as Malkor entered. His voice cracked across the room even before the doors closed. "What the frutt happened?" He zeroed in on Kayla.

She shifted her position on the couch, thankful to have a break from Isonde's grilling. "Bredard's biocybe sent me a message."

"So you said on the comm. What kind of—" He stopped, his gaze seeming to take in the regen cuff around her wrist, the coolant gel pack adhered to her neck and the blue concoction in her hand that Toble insisted she drink for her throat.

"Eh," Kayla shrugged one shoulder. "I think Siño had a bone to pick with me after my last visit with Bredard." Make that a very large bone. Her voice came out raspy and she took another slug of the drink Toble had prepared. It slid down her throat with a welcome coolness.

"I'm fine. I've had way worse, and Toble's already been to see me." A close-quarters fight with a biocybe half-again her body weight trumped a night in the Blood Pit for pain factor, but it was nothing she couldn't handle after some meds and a coolant pack to reduce the swelling.

Malkor nodded, clearly trusting her assessment, which only made her love him more. He finally looked at Isonde. "Should you be out of your pod?"

"Kayla gets beaten by an augmented human and you're asking if *I* should be in the pod?"

Malkor threw up a hand. "Fine. You're all fine. Tougher than ten agents. Can we get on with it then? What was Bredard's message?"

"I'm here," Ardin said, hurrying into the room and sitting on the sofa closest to Isonde's chair. He took her hand. "Should you be out of bed?" he asked.

Isonde uttered a very un-princess-like expletive. "If one more person tries to stick me back in that pod I'm going to sic Kayla on them. Got it?"

She glared at Malkor, then Ardin, who smiled a little. "You are feeling better," Ardin said.

Kayla cleared her raspy throat, then took another gulp of Toble's blue concoction. "We're out of time," she said.

"How do you mean?" Malkor asked.

"Literally. Bredard moved his deadline to midnight tonight."

"Shit." Malkor checked his mobile comm. "I thought we had more days? That's less than four hours."

"Then we had best figure out what the frutt we're going to do," Kayla said, "or come tomorrow morning we'll be sitting pretty on execution watch.

"Where are we at with leverage on Bredard?" she asked Malkor.

He shook his head. "Not far enough."

"Do we know what evidence Bredard has against us?" Isonde asked. She looked as determined as Kayla had remembered her from before her coma. Maybe more so. "Could we preempt his revealing that with some kind of counter-press conference?"

"I have no idea what 'proof' he has," Malkor said.

Kayla slanted Malkor a glance before speaking. "Killing Bredard would be useless. If we off him, they'll come at us with someone else."

And then who would they face? And what would the body count be?

"Break it down for me," Ardin said. His eyes focused on Malkor, friend to friend, conspirator to co-conspirator. They were in this together, reminding Kayla that these three friends—Malkor, Ardin and Isonde—had charted this course long before she met them. "What options do we have?"

Malkor ran a hand through his hair. Kayla knew the options—they all sucked.

"Well," Malkor said, "we could unleash the info from Dolan's files on all of the corrupt members of the IDC and what they had been involved in, and hope that in the resulting firestorm our blackmailers would A: be taken down before they could do anything to us and B: not be taken seriously if they did file allegations against us. But... that would destroy the integrity of the IDC."

"Fine by me," Kayla said. Malkor frowned. Hey, he'd already heard her opinion on that subject.

Ardin turned to her. "You know nothing of imperial politics and how important the IDC is to keeping the peace in the empire." His tone had too much arrogance for her liking.

"Excuse me?" she said. "What have I been doing here for the past months, playing dress-up?" Though in truth, the intricacies of interplanetary politics in the empire made politics on Ordoch look like a tea party. And she'd never been meant to rule at all, her older siblings Natali and Erebus had been groomed for that role.

"The IDC is too crucial," Ardin stated, clearly his last word on the subject.

Good thing the decision wasn't entirely his to make.

Isonde spoke before Kayla could retort. "We could give them what they want. Trade the scientific data for Bredard's blackmail info."

"No," Kayla and Malkor said at the same time.

"What if—"

"Not happening," Kayla said, her raw throat robbing the words of the necessary force. She reached for Toble's concoction and downed a healthy swallow. If they thought—

"We could trim it," Ardin said, "offer only part. The schematics for advanced bionics, weapons, long-range communication tech."

Kayla shook her head. "The only schematic they'll be satisfied with is the schematic for Dolan's Influencer. And they will never, ever, get that."

She made eye contact with each of them. "Ever."

She held Ardin's gaze until he glanced away. Good. Let him be uncomfortable with her intensity. At least then he'd understand that no one would cross her on this.

"Next option," she said, looking back to Malkor.

"Only two more that I see. One, we disappear. We keep all of the data, possibly to use at a later time, preserve the IDC, and run, staying alive when Bredard reveals the Empress Game cheat."

"Unacceptable," Isonde said. "The last choice?"

Malkor frowned, not at Isonde's words—they were in agreement there—but at the last option they had, clearly his least preferred. "We offer to trade them something else in return for Bredard's blackmail files. Instead of the scientific data, we offer them all of Dolan's personnel files on the corrupt IDC agents and leaders." He sighed. "We'd have to surrender all proof of their collusion with Dolan over the last decade, all of their illegal activities, all of our best leverage to clear the cancer from the IDC."

"Would that really work?" Ardin asked.

"I think so. Dolan's info detailing Senior Commander Vega's activities on Ordoch, her people's interactions with the Wyrd prisoners, even things done on Protectorate Planets under her orders... not to mention collusion with the imperial army. It would be Vega's death sentence."

Malkor continued. "If Vega wants Dolan's tech data, it's safe to say that she's interested in mind-control. The only mind-control worth all this risk is control of the Council of Seven. If they refuse our offer and out Isonde/Kayla as conspirators, the government is in chaos. Isonde is executed. Her position on both the Sovereign Council and the Council of Seven remain unfilled. No rulings can be made with the councils in such an uproar. Vega doesn't want that kind of chaos. It would bring every council action and vote under a microscope, drawing too much attention to her possible machinations."

Kayla agreed with Malkor. Only an idiot would try to override the will of the Council of Seven under such circumstances. Nonetheless, she would have to live knowing that she gave away the evidence that would have brought justice to the people ultimately responsible for her family's imprisonment and torture. The people who funded Dolan, supported him, gained from his experiments.

People who deserved death.

Silence descended on the room as the reality of what they were about to do sank in. Kayla sipped at the now tasteless drink, eyes on the chronometer, ticking, ticking. Could she live with this, if it meant saving Malkor's life?

Her gaze drifted to him and found he had been watching her. Thinking the same thing, she knew.

For Malkor? Absolutely.

More than that, though, it would save Isonde and Ardin and their chance to influence the Council of Seven. Their chance to free Ordoch, their chance to stop the horrific spread of the

TNV across the empire, to save billions of lives.

The decision paired Malkor's life with the fate of her people. Thank the void she didn't have to choose between them.

"That's it, then," she said, "our only real option. Are we agreed?"

Everyone nodded. There was nothing else to say, really, and they had three hours to deadline.

Malkor stood, his expression locked into something neutral. "I'll talk to Commander Parrel."

13

It had taken Malkor a precious half-hour to convince Commander Parrel to make the trade—Dolan's blackmail data for Bredard's. And by "convince" Malkor meant he'd convinced Parrel that he was going through with this, not that Parrel had been convinced it was the right idea.

In the end, it had come down to Malkor asking his commander point-blank: "Are you going to stop me?" He wasn't. He couldn't, really, not unless he had Malkor physically detained for the next three hours or so. Malkor had his own copy of the data he could make a deal with. He needed Parrel to destroy his copy, so that Malkor could prove he turned over every last shred of evidence on the IDC-army cabal from Dolan's files.

Parrel had been furious, but in the end, he had no alternate plan. And while he might not place the value of Malkor, Kayla and Isonde's lives above the worth of that data, he couldn't promise Malkor he'd for certain use Dolan's data to expose the traitors.

"I'll take what I *can* do over what you *might* do," he'd told his commander, and walked out.

Now Malkor sat in the back office of an empty fashion boutique at a quarter to midnight, waiting for Bredard to show—or screw him over.

Malkor had suggested the location, an oft-used "neutral ground" for the IDC to meet with informants, and Bredard had agreed. Kayla and Hekkar were there as Malkor's "muscle," and Rigger had come as well. Complink in hand, Rigger would confirm the validity of the data Bredard would hopefully hand over.

The four waited in tense silence. When Malkor had proposed the alternate trade to Bredard, the damn man had left him hanging with, "I'll contact my people to see if this is agreeable." Now the minutes crept toward the deadline and there was no sign of him.

"They won't go for it," Hekkar said, from where he lounged against the wall. He had his jacket tucked back and away from the ion pistol at his hip.

Rigger looked similarly dour, her blonde hair pulled tight in a ponytail, ion pistol on her belt. Malkor was similarly armed. Kayla might prefer the intimacy of hand-to-hand combat—he planned to shoot the shit out of Bredard and Siño if either of them twitched.

Kayla had come as herself, no hologram this time, and was tapping a finger against one kris, eyes on the door.

"They'll go for it," Malkor said. "We can bury them with this." He indicated the black case on the table in front of him, the indestructible housing that protected the data chip. "And if Bredard doesn't show, I guess we'll be fighting treason with treason."

At one minute to the deadline a chime sounded in the office, indicating someone had entered the building.

Thank the stars.

Malkor stood as Bredard entered the office, followed by the biocybe who had roughed Kayla up. Siño's nose looked recently repaired, and one of his eyes was still swollen and red from Kayla jabbing it. The other eye lit on Kayla with an all-too-pleased gleam.

She assessed the biocybe coolly, then tapped her finger to the outside edge of her eye in silent mockery. Siño grinned. He pursed his lips, sending a kiss her way before taking position behind Bredard.

Bredard placed a bag on the table and sat down, indicating Malkor should do the same.

"So. Are we going to do this?" Malkor asked.

Bredard focused on him. "My superiors are displeased with your offer."

"I bet."

"You know what we want: Dolan's experimental data and schematics."

"I'm going to save us all a lot of time on threats and haggling," Malkor said. Bredard might still be trying to negotiate, but Malkor doubted the man would walk out. "You are never, ever, going to get your hands on that data. You can kill me and my friends here, kill the princess and release what you know about our activities at the Empress Game, and you *still* won't get that data. We will destroy it, and all the technologic advancements contained therein, before we let you have it." Malkor held the man's gaze, projecting deadly honesty as his words sank in. "This," he tapped the case they'd brought with the chip inside, "is all you're going to get from us."

Bredard absorbed the words in silence, his gaze seeming to test Malkor, challenging him to break.

Malkor leaned back in his seat and crossed his arms as if his life didn't hang in the balance. As if Kayla's didn't. Ardin's. Isonde's.

"You think you're so superior," Bredard said. "Breathing the stratosphere, looking down at us." He snorted. "You're nothing but a liar and a cheat who saw a chance to grab power for himself and his friends and took it."

"Isonde and Ardin will use that power for good." The words were out before Malkor realized how they sounded. Didn't everyone who coveted power think the same thing? "We never hurt anyone." *Never helped Dolan torture his own people to mental ruin and death.*

"Not yet," Bredard countered. He tilted his head, appraising Malkor. "How far will you go, I wonder, so that your friends can 'do good?'"

The smug frutter. Malkor wanted to slap the satisfied smile right off the man's face. "Let's get this over with."

"Fine. Just remember—if you were any better than us, you wouldn't be here with me, trying to blackmail us to recover evidence of your own crimes."

Bredard opened his bag and withdrew a complink and an indestructible case similar to the one that held Malkor's chip. He punched a code on the case's lock pad and Malkor did the same on his. A code and a thumbprint scan opened the outer case. A different code and an index fingerprint scan unlocked the inner case.

When both chips were laid bare on the table, Bredard flicked a finger over his shoulder. Siño reached into his vest pocket. Hekkar and Rigger had their weapons trained on him before he could remove it. Kayla looked calmer. Then again, she could probably leap over the table and stab Siño before anyone fired.

"Easy, agents," Bredard said with a chuckle. "Standard procedure at info swaps."

Siño removed his hand, coming away with a white organoplastic box, four centimeters by six centimeters with the Ingalls logo on the outside. He passed it to Bredard who popped it open.

Malkor's turn to chuckle, a bitter sound. If he ever doubted his own agency was behind this blackmail, this was proof enough. Malkor pulled an identical white box from his own pocket. Opening it revealed matching contents to Bredard's: two flat, beige, dissolvable applicator strips, loaded with an advanced formulation of a truth serum available only to the IDC. The cases were identical, down to the serum manufacturer's stamp—ATX-006—embossed on each pad.

"We'll work it this way," Malkor said. "Hekkar will select one pad from your case for me and your biocybe can select one from mine for you. No tricks, no preplanned double-crossings."

"Sounds reasonable."

While Hekkar selected a beige pad and handed it to Malkor

to place under his tongue, Rigger set out her complink and gestured to the chip Bredard brought. "May I?"

Bredard brought out his own complink and the two opposing camps began scanning the data available on each other's blackmail chips.

The applicator pad dissolved sublingually and the calming effect hit Malkor's bloodstream. The truth serum was intricately engineered, way past its origins in the unreliable sodium pentothal used in the pre-space-travel days, but it was still at its very basic level a barbiturate. Hekkar and Kayla weren't only backup in case the trade went south, they were there to get his ass home safely when the drug dulled his reflexes and instincts.

They waited minutes for the drug to be fully absorbed, Rigger scanning through file after file as Bredard did the same. Finally, she nodded, confirming that the file did contain what Bredard claimed: proof of their cheating the Game. Bredard's eyes rounded as he took in the sheer quantity of the files Dolan had kept on all his illicit dealings. "The Wyrd traitor certainly was thorough," he murmured.

"Satisfied?" Malkor asked.

Bredard turned his attention back to him. "Depends." He checked his watch—time enough had passed for the serum to take full effect. He nodded to his biocybe.

"Can you confirm that this is the only copy in existence of these files?" Siño asked.

"Yes," Malkor said.

"Can you confirm that this is the entirety of the information that Dolan had on his dealings with the IDC, the imperial army and members of the Council of Seven?"

Sadly, Malkor's answer to Siño was a firm, "Yes." If only they could have kept some of those damn files back.

Hekkar cleared his throat. "Bredard, can you confirm that this is the entirety of your evidence against any fixing of the Empress Game by any party?" They had agreed to make the question broad enough that he couldn't get away with only providing materials against Malkor, while holding back proof against Isonde or someone else.

Bredard nodded. "Yes."

"And can you confirm that this is the only copy of such files in existence?"

"Yes." Bredard's gaze slid to Malkor. "You got very lucky this time, Agent." He slipped Malkor's chip into the case he'd brought, along with his complink.

Malkor got to his feet, the words provoking enough anger to slip through the relaxing effect of the serum. "If you ever come near us again…" He let the threat hang there.

Bredard chuckled and made his way to the door, Siño covering his back. Before he left, he said over his shoulder, "This isn't done. We *will* get the rest of that data."

The sweet taste of the truth serum in Malkor's mouth mocked him all the way home.

14

THE *SICERRO*, MINE FIELD

"Welcome to the Middle of Nowhere," came over the comms. The *Yari* filled the viewscreen as they approached, stunning in its massiveness. Vayne couldn't take it all in, couldn't believe it. He'd seen the ship in history vids. Everyone had seen the history vids. He'd studied the structure, advanced for its time, and knew the story of its demise. It was a relic so mysterious and ancient as to be arcane.

What had happened to it?

How had it arrived here, in Imperial Space?

Beside him, Corinth's eyes were wide with wonder, his mouth slightly open, looking as dazed as Vayne felt.

This could not be happening.

Even as his mind rejected what he saw, the Ilmenans made their preparations to dock with the impossible.

The Ordochians had never built a ship like it before or since. It resembled an old-fashioned spindle, apparently—that was how all of the history vids described its structure. At one end was a large disc, stories upon stories high, that contained all of the living quarters, science labs and so on. Sticking out from its center was a long shaft. Skinny at first, where it attached to the disc, then bulging in the middle where the massive reactors rested, before slimming down again. It stretched out forever, the spectacular housing of a never-before-seen energy weapon that Ordoch had hoped would decisively end the Second Ilmenan War.

A war neither side won.

Most of the shaft was dark—powered down or powerless, impossible to say—but lights winked from the disc section like eyes of a deep sea creature beneath a ledge. Lights? Holy frutt, the thing was still powered, after all this time...

And who the frutt had commed them?

Tia'tan opened a channel. "The Middle of Nowhere sounds about right. Docking in five."

The *Yari* didn't have docking bays, only pressurized hatches they could sidle up to, and it wasn't long before they were aligned and locked on.

"Well," Tia'tan said, a grin somewhere between anxious and excited on her face as she looked around at her people, "this is it." They looked equally excited, and Vayne wanted to smack the lot of them. They were supposed to be headed toward the safety of Wyrd Space, and there was something very wrong about this.

Instead he followed Corinth off the bridge as the boy nearly stepped on Tia'tan's heels to get to the hatch. Natali met them in the corridor. Her gaze clashed with his for a second before he ducked his head, unable to look at her. She'd glanced away even quicker. In that moment she'd seemed pale and haunted and furious, as if the scream that endlessly raged inside him, clawing its way out, was on the verge of bursting forth from her. She was armed—he hadn't seen her unarmed since escaping from Dolan—and she fell in line with the group the same way she did almost everything these days: wordlessly.

Natali was taller than Tia'tan, almost as tall as Kayla, and better trained thanks to being three years older. At least, she had been better trained, before five years of torture. Her light blue ponytail was pulled so tight it must have been giving her a headache, and her hands clenched and unclenched, clenched and unclenched at her sides as she walked stiffly down the ship's corridor.

Shame and guilt and self-loathing burned in his chest and he had to stop and place a hand on the wall to even catch a breath. It was galling. It was pitiful. Tia'tan glanced over her shoulder as if she sensed something. Her lavender eyes held a moment's compassion, more than he could stand. She half-turned as if she would come back for him and he shook his head hard, once.

It's over, he told himself again. *Over.*

It would never be over, not for him, not for Natali, and not for Uncle Ghirhad, no matter that the man laughed like he wasn't just as broken.

Vayne pushed himself off the wall and followed the others to where Noar was entering the sequence to unlock their side of the hatch.

"Wait, shouldn't some of us stay back? What if it's not safe?"

Too late.

The hatches opened, and standing inside, with a huge grin on her face, was the pilot he would have recognized anywhere. She wore the regulation black jumpsuit, complete with *Yari* mission patches, and her thick sea-green braid fell over her shoulder all the way down to her thigh as she gripped the hatch's edge and leaned sideways toward them. "Hullo!"

"Captain Janus?" Vayne froze in place. He'd clearly gone mad. That last session with Dolan had knocked something loose in his brain and he was very, very not okay.

The captain of the *Yari* laughed, matching sea-green eyes twinkling. "Heard of me!" She gave them a wink and gestured for them to come inside.

He felt a hand slip into his. Corinth.

::Isn't she dead?::

So he wasn't insane. A slice of ancient history really just winked at them.

::It was five hundred years ago, she should be dead.::

Vayne shrugged a shoulder. "Guess not."

A grin broke out on Corinth's face. ::Come on!:: He pulled Vayne through the airlock and into the past.

Only it wasn't the past... was it? Nothing in Vayne's recent memories led him to believe they had somehow achieved the impossible: time travel. What, then? Had the *Yari* leapt forward? That made as little sense.

Dazed, he followed the Ilmenans and their smiling host. She was saying something to Noar, her archaic Ordochian dialect hard to follow considering the light-speed stream of her words. Noar thanked her for destroying the rooks and Captain Janus gave a little "whoop!" and a slap-clap that made everyone jump.

"My shooting not that time, you can thank Benny. His shoot fine." She gestured to her throat as she barreled them along, then mimed speaking with an extravagant wave of her arm. "Used to it soon, indeed. The other Ordochians perfect translate already"

Other Ordochians?

"Wait, Captain Janus—" Vayne started, cut off by her laugh.

She looked over her shoulder at him as she walked. "Calls me that no one. You will call Ida." She winked again and turned her attention back to Noar. Vayne could only follow, his head abuzz with the impossibility of it all, swept along in her bubbling wake like everyone else.

::The ship:: Corinth said, eyes scanning the curving walls of the nearly cylindrical corridor. ::Can you believe it?::

Not at all.

Even in this utilitarian section of the great ship the walls were lined with molychromium, the pink-gold shimmer visible despite the low light. A standard shipbuilding material at the time, today the metal was so rare it would have been cheaper to line the corridor with hundred-creds. Layer upon layer of them.

He reached out and ran his fingers across the slightly rough surface. It felt real. Then again, what was real? Dolan had convinced him a million things were real that had never been. He pulled his hand back.

If he was insane, then they all were.

The Ilmenans, for all they seemed to have been expecting the ship, still glanced around with awe. He wasn't the only one to touch the molychromium, or look at Captain Janus—Ida—as if she weren't quite real.

She spoke in an endless stream as she swept them along. Something about a shipment? And someone named Cinni was coming? Apparently that pleased the captain. And Benny, they were going to meet Benny. By the time they reached the observation deck she had been apparently leading them to, he'd gotten a better handle on her inflection, but following the archaic sentence structure was still tricky.

"Benny!" Ida waved at a stocky Wyrd male who stood on the far side of the observation deck, staring out the windows. "I've found!" She came to a stop, encompassing the entire group with a sweep of her arm, looking like a child presenting a birthday present.

Benny, wearing a ship jumpsuit identical to Ida's, turned to meet them with a raised green-blue brow. "Needed so many? And new ones this time? I've enough of common ones, now more new?" He looked at them uncertainly.

Ida smiled at them. "Is Benny."

By "Benny" she meant Abenifluis Strokar, the *Yari*'s main gunner, the man destined to fire the first ever shot from the massive weapons platform, a shot that had never happened.

Not in the history vids, at least.

He'd come from a very wealthy noble family, and had been known as the biggest stickler for rules, regulations and rank. And now he'd been demoted to simply "Benny" by his commanding officer.

Well, it was to be supposed that five hundred years would breed some familiarity.

Benny stared at them as if deciding whether or not to acknowledge them or treat them as a nuisance to be ignored. He finally offered a bow. "First Weapons Officer Abenifluis Strokar, your service." He glanced at Ida, then gave a sigh. "And, you will call Benny. Ida is not denied frivolity with new ones." The look he shot Ida said, "You owe me."

She grinned and said to the group, "Welcome *Yari* to you."

Vayne had a million questions. He was here, actually here, on a ship that had disappeared five hundred years ago. Everything was just as the schematics had indicated. The observation deck—the top one, based on its layout—was a double-height room, viewports reaching floor to ceiling all along the front wall. There was structural bracing where they met the ceiling, then another set of ports covered the ceiling, allowing for a ninety-degree vertical view of the Mine Field. From here he could see where their ship was locked onto the *Yari*, and the path they must have taken out of the field.

Molychromium shone on the back wall, the bare bones of the ship visible everywhere except beneath their feet, where a thin layer of decking tread had been laid down. The furniture was no more than a few hard benches soldered to the floor. The *Yari* had been constructed in wartime, as quickly as possible, and launched for weapons testing before interior construction had even been finished. It was a military ship with one desperate mission—end the war. There was little thought given to comfort, and huge sections of it weren't habitable when it disappeared.

Still, it was magnificent.

Corinth looked like he wanted to start taking the thing apart and study every component. Tia'tan stood close to the viewports, scanning space in all directions as if searching for something.

"Any word from the *Radiant*?" she asked, and Ida shook her head, enthusiasm dimmed for a moment.

"But," Ida said, her smile returning full force, "soon!"

Benny came forward to join them. "Have to forgive Captain her excitement. Here with us nothing more as company, we bore after a time."

"Never!" Ida protested, but the way her eyes sparkled proved her delight. She impatiently flicked her long braid over her shoulder. "Come now." She linked her arm through Benny's and towed him toward the far end of the observation deck. "To the command room!"

Vayne drew close to Tia'tan as they followed the captain through another set of corridors. ::What the frutt is going on?::

Tia'tan glanced sidelong at him, and spoke in mind voice as well. ::I know it's a lot. Finding the *Yari* was always a gamble. I didn't want to tell you until I was sure.::

::What are we even doing here?:: Not that *here* wasn't mind-blowing. ::Why are we anywhere near this damn Mine Field and not on our way to Ilmena, as you promised?::

::We were never supposed to be here. Our mission was the Empress Game and, well, you. It was the *Radiant*'s mission to rendezvous with the *Yari*. When we never heard back from them, though, we had to come.::

::How did you even know this ship still existed, that it was here?::

::We didn't, actually. Your people found it.::

His people? What the—

Tia'tan continued. ::The rebels on Ordoch came into contact with the *Yari*. That's how we knew it existed. We didn't know where it was in Imperial Space until we got the coordinates for the Mine Field from Dolan.::

::Wait. There are organized rebels on Ordoch?:: Unbelievable. His people hadn't organized for anything in a generation. Not anything to the general good, at least.

::Not all Ordochians are content to hide out the occupation in safety.:: She kept her gaze straight ahead as she issued that challenge.

Despite a lifetime's discipline in modulation, his mind voice turned into a growl. ::I have earned the right to peace.::

She inclined her head. ::Forgive me. You are right, of course. I've been part of the movement to free Ordoch from imperial rule from the beginning and I can't imagine any pure-blooded Wyrd not being enraged by the occupation.:: One hand curled into a fist. ::An inferior race, with the audacity to usurp the rule of one of *our* planets :: She cut herself off. He could practically hear her teeth grinding.

I don't give a damn about that, he wanted to shout at her, shout at them all. The imperials could raze the planet and be welcome to it. All he wanted was escape.

Not all, his mind whispered. True. He wanted his *ro'haar* back. Kayla was untainted by Dolan. Her solid presence would keep him sane, protect him, hold back the demons.

And you left her behind.

The bare metal of the corridor walls streamed past as he walked, trapped in his own thoughts. Minimal lighting on this level gave it the feel of walking through cave tunnels. They reached a lift and split into two groups for the ride to a lower floor. Vayne crowded uncomfortably close to Tia'tan in the small space, recoiled, and bumped first into Luliana, then his uncle. It was all he could do to hold still amid the press of bodies for the ride.

He burst out as soon as the doors opened. It wasn't the close space that bothered him—it was the people. He couldn't stand for people to touch him without his consent. He'd had enough of that in the last five years. *Hands, bodies, skin, close, touching, unable to escape, unable to resist...*

Benny led them down a better-lit section of the ship. Here the bulkheads had been covered with some kind of plastic board, and the entire thing, rounded walls and ceiling, was covered in an intricately painted mural that seemed to spiral on forever down the corridor. Benny indicated a vibrant panel with a smile. "Ariel's."

They made it to the command room, a large circular room filled with display units, monitors and control stations.

"Brought new ones!" Ida said, to the two people in the room. "They are not to eat."

She laughed, but a dour woman sitting at a station with her feet propped on the console frowned. "No joke, that."

Ida waved a hand her way. "You will call Ariel. Grumpy is her lot." She smiled to soften the words, then turned to a cheerier looking man at another monitoring station.

He got to his feet, looking almost as excited to see them as Ida had been, and offered a short bow. "New people have made it! Most welcome. You will call Tanet." He bowed again. "Most welcome."

It was then that Ida wound down enough in her speech to actually ask who they were. "We had expect *Radiant*. Skeleton crew."

An emotion passed across Tia'tan's face that Vayne couldn't read. She didn't comment on Kazamel's disappearance. Instead, Tia'tan introduced their party, explaining where they had each come from. Benny seemed to unbend during the introductions. He moved to clasp Natali's hand when she was introduced as the true ruler of Ordoch. Natali stepped back quickly, eyeing Benny as if trying to decide whether he meant to harm her. Benny seemed not to take offense, thankfully. Instead he laid his hand on his heart and offered her a bow.

::When can we meet the rest of the crew?:: Corinth asked the whole room.

Ariel—Navigations First Officer Navriel Entar—glowered at the question. "We are this. All, with Larsa and Gintoc."

Vayne blinked, certain he'd misunderstood. "Six? A crew of over one hundred and there are six of you left?"

Tanet chuckled. "Now Gintoc is half here. I say we count five point five."

"No joke that either," Ariel reprimanded. She looked somewhat fierce with her frown, her muscular arms crossed over her chest, and her short, spiky aqua hair. "If Gintoc turns *stepa at es* we lose mechanic of the competence most."

Ida waved that away. "Pha. Gintoc won't turn. Solitary is only."

"If that is your say so," Ariel answered.

"*Stepa at es*?" Tia'tan asked. Her understanding of ancient Ordochian sentence structure would be even worse than Vayne's.

"Consumer of self?" Vayne asked.

Ida and Benny exchanged a look. "Is close. Here, now. You have this need." Ida turned away from the subject to rummage through a drawer, one of a set built into the far bulkheads. She returned with a handful of thin necklaces. A chip encased in glass, no bigger than a grain of rice, was attached to each.

"RFID chip so that open doors for you, lock some, and of course, we not to shoot you." She winked and started handing them out. Vayne got the sense she was only half-joking about the not-shooting part.

"How are there six of you?" Vayne asked. "Or five point five? How have any of you survived this long at all?"

The *Yari* crew looked at Tanet. Physicist, if Vayne remembered correctly. The man's full name escaped him.

"Is two parts," Tanet said. "One: time eddy." He made a stirring motion with his finger. "There is 'normal' stream of time we ride. Then—wormhole, and *Yari* pulled through to here. Shunted to edge of time stream, *Yari* whirl around in eddy of the normal flow, time there almost none. Then, *whoooosh*!" He shot his arm forward. "We pulled back into normal again. I decide we eddy years around two hundred."

At Vayne's skeptical look Tanet put his hand out and wobbled it. "Is theory, but, time I have had to think."

"What about the other three hundred years?"

"Two: so simple is boring." Tanet shrugged his shoulders. "Cryosleep."

Vayne made eye contact with Tia'tan, and he could tell she was thinking the same thing as him. Cryosleep science had been very primitive at the time the *Yari* was built. The number of possible malfunctions, the loss of brain function… Unsophisticated cryosleep chambers, used for long periods of time, could wreak havoc on a person.

Which might explain a few things about the crew.

"And now here you are, to help!" Ida said with a smile. She bounded to a display and brought up what looked to be schematics of a hyperstream drive. A *massive* hyperstream drive. "Here and see, it is repairing!" She pointed rapidly to several different points. "New, new, new and here. Plus, parts today arrive." She glanced over her shoulder at Ariel. "Communicate to Gintoc that Cinni brings to us?"

Ariel nodded, for the first time looking a little less bellicose. "He could not be pleased the more."

"Good." Ida returned her gaze to the schematic. "Gintoc has an understanding thus, it makes a sense to him in a way not I."

"Not sense to any of us," Benny agreed.

With every word that came out of the crew's mouths, Vayne felt less certain of what was going on.

Ida turned to Tia'tan with what looked like hope. Or was it resignation? The emotions looked the same to Vayne these days.

"Fuel is carried on your ship as well?"

Tia'tan shook her head. "Not nearly enough. That was… that is the *Radiant*'s mission."

"Ah. Well." Ida offered Tia'tan a big smile and clapped her on the shoulder. "Soon is to be here. Truth. And we are repairing still! Time is enough, time is enough."

"Captain cannot be kept down," Benny said, with something that sounded like exasperation. "Not hundreds years later."

Something beeped at Ariel's station. She sat up abruptly. "It's time." Her fingers flew through a pattern on the console, then she was on her feet and out the control room door. "Benny, preflight," she shouted from down the corridor.

"Make certain has brought food!" Benny shouted back, before taking over her station and calling up a dozen reports on the screen.

"Cinni comes," Ida said. "See in your watching with me." She headed back to the lift and all they could do was follow.

I could stop right here, Vayne thought. *I could stand in this corridor like a stone, refusing to move until I had answers, and still Ida would barrel me along with encouragements and enthusiasm.* The captain's momentum was invincible.

Ida led the group to a different observation desk, with a more limited panorama. Several comfortable chairs had been dragged here and placed in front of the metal benches. The viewports provided the perfect view of black space, the wreck of the Mine Field and—

Holy frutt.

A white, diamond-bright star glinted in empty space a kilometer off the *Yari*'s side. Only it wasn't star—was it? It couldn't possibly be. It looked like someone had slit reality and pulled the edges apart. Beyond, the essence of everything shimmered and glowed and beckoned. It was the twinkle of a star seen from a planet's surface. It was blinding and impossible and he couldn't look away.

Never could he have hoped to find something more amazing than the *Yari*, and yet...

Ariel's shuttle hovered in place, halfway between the ship and the... the... "What the void *is* that?" he asked Ida, without looking away. Beside him, Corinth had a hand pressed flat to the viewport as if trying to touch the miracle.

"We are calling 'the Tear.'"

"Has it always been there?" Was the Tear somehow responsible for the destruction within the Mine Field?

"Not," was Ida's only answer.

A shimmer rippled across the Tear, white light fracturing and coalescing. Something was happening. Vayne imagined a million possibilities—blinding bolts of plasma arcing out like solar flares, a shockwave issuing forth as the Tear was ripped wider, the *Yari* being sucked in... Anything. Everything.

Ariel's shuttle nudged closer as *something* emerged from the Tear. Initially indistinguishable against the brilliant glare, he couldn't identify the object until it was fully through.

A loaded hover cart.

The most miraculous discovery in the history of his race pulsed before them, and it produced a handcart for transporting goods.

He had definitely gone mad.

A gloved hand appeared next, gripping the hover cart's control, followed by the rest of someone—something?—in a spacesuit. The person pulled a second loaded hover cart through the Tear and angled for Ariel's ship.

"Whoop!" Ida clapped. "Cinni this time, our favorite.

Come. We unload and bring dinner sooner. Fresh food!"

Vayne took a last look at who must be Cinni inside the spacesuit maneuvering the carts into the loading bay of Ariel's ship, and, with a sigh, followed blindly in Ida's wake once more.

Tia'tan's voice sounded in his head. ::I can't tell if she's demented or just ridiculously cheerful.::

::Or high, or brain damaged:: Vayne offered. ::Or all of the above. She *has* been alive for five hundred years.::

Tia'tan's lavender eyes looked dazed, as if things moved too quickly and she couldn't absorb it all.

Welcome to his world.

::The Tear:: her voice sounded in his head, soft, lilting. ::Have you ever seen… I mean, it's…:: She shook her head. ::Not even possible. I knew *about* the Tear, the rebels on Ordoch had passed that knowledge along to my superiors. Hearing about it and seeing it are two completely different realities.::

He couldn't wrap his mind around the Tear's existence yet, so he focused on her other words. ::Ordochian rebels are communicating with Ilmena?:: They entered the ship's corridor and Ida's chatter floated back to them.

Tia'tan nodded. ::We're Ordoch's only hope, despite your people's isolationist ways for the last century.::

Isolationist ways meant to mask the unraveling of their society, to hide from the other Wyrd Worlds the devolution into which Ordoch sank.

::Are they from the mainland?:: he asked. The central landmass in Ordoch, and the seat of his family.

::I'm not certain, I haven't had direct contact with any of them. We all have our missions. Mine was to be sacrificed to the Empress Game and live in exile, tearing the empire apart from within their Council of Seven.::

Bitterness? From the intensely controlled and driven Tia'tan? ::You lost.::

She cut him with a glance. ::I abdicated to your sister because she swore she could be more effective. Her loyalties seem to be in question, though. She had better not betray us.::

Vayne twisted a rope of psi force around her upper arm and jerked her to a stop. "Don't you *ever* question my *ro'haar* again." His low voice was harsh.

"I—"

"You know *nothing* of Kayla. Nothing." He let the psi force dissipate and left her staring uncertainly at his back as he walked away.

The rage had been instantaneous, along with the urge to lash out, to defend Kayla from mere words with brute psi force. Uncontrollable rage, and white-hot.

Kayla had come for him.

It had taken five years but she found him. Tia'tan and her people had helped, but it had been Kayla in that chair across from him in Dolan's lab, Kayla fighting with everything she had to connect to her psi powers to save him, Kayla who had offered to give herself to Dolan willingly if only he'd set Vayne free.

His *ro'haar* had fought for him, and in those moments he remembered what it meant to be an *il'haar*, the stronger psionic half of a bonded pair. He was meant to protect her with his mind as much as she was meant to protect him with her body.

She had killed Dolan, and she had brought her *il'haar* back to life.

And he, in his fear of recapture, had betrayed her and left her behind in the empire, even as she begged him not to.

The darkness closed in again, the rage and shame and violent illness that found him after every one of Dolan's "experiments." Only this time, he'd brought it on himself.

Perhaps you are not so unlike me after all, are you, my dear Vayne? Dolan's voice whispered along his spine and teased its way into his head.

"No," Vayne said on a breath, the word without sound. It wasn't the first time he'd heard Dolan's voice since he'd been freed. It was the first time it happened while he was *awake*.

"Vayne?" Tia'tan asked. She'd caught up to him and now looked... was it concerned? Wary?

He shook his head and kept walking.

15

ISONDE'S TOWNHOUSE, FALANAR

Kayla's feet impacted the treadmill's surface in a short, rhythmic pattern. She had the exercise room in Isonde's townhouse all to herself. Considering it was oh-two-hundred, that wasn't exactly surprising. Her breath passed in and out, in and out, steady and even as she started the next kilometer.

Treadmill running was the absolute worst.

Nights like this, when anxiety and doubt and sheer frustration kept sleep at bay, she used to run in Fontana's Park, a woodland on the grounds of her family's palace on Ordoch. The winding trails, with their sculpted beauty, kept the run interesting, even soothing.

The imperial image database lacked any images from Ordoch, so instead she ran kilometer after kilometer with footage from Fengar Swamp on the vidscreen in front of her. The gloomy locale from Altair Tri evoked an odd combination of dislike, familiarity and nostalgia. She and Corinth had spent most of their five years in exile hiding in a shack in Fengar Swamp. It had been as much their prison as their place of safety.

Life had been predictable there. Simple.

And meaningless?

She denied it, but the thought persisted.

"Useless thought." Kayla jabbed the power control to halt

the treadmill. She sprang off it, itching for more activity despite the run, itching for a fight.

Bredard had disappeared from their lives the second Malkor had handed over the data incriminating the corrupt IDC agents. She couldn't trust the silence. She wanted to. The info exchange should have been the end of it. Instead she hung in this tense space, suspended in expectation, waiting for his next move.

It didn't come. Day after day.

And now here she was, rushing from council meeting to secret meeting to diplomatic meeting to who-knows-what-meetings, insanely busy and yet still waiting, waiting.

Bredard and his pet biocybe, Siño, had beaten her twice already, and that was two times too many. She wouldn't be caught off-guard again.

Kayla checked the chronometer—02:35. Plenty of time for drills before trying to sleep.

She focused on footwork, evasive sequences, techniques that would keep her out of Siño's reach until she found the perfect opening.

Faster.

Faster.

The movements needed to be automatic, instinctual—so natural to her body that she reacted before her conscious mind even prompted her to move. Once he was in range, his augmented strength could make short work of her if she didn't have a weapon at hand.

Faster.

She needed to be better. Stronger. Tougher.

She worked the drills over and over. Then over again. Worked them until she had nothing left to give. She leaned back against the wall for support, then sank down to rest, chest heaving, tunic slicked to her body by sweat.

Kayla rested her forehead on her knees as her heartbeat slowed. The exhaustion in her limbs weighed down on her like a heavy blanket. It was comforting, a hallmark of her life as a *ro'haar*, that exquisite expenditure of every last gram of energy.

The chronometer pinged oh-three-thirty and Kayla pushed to her feet. Still a few hours of darkness left, and she could certainly sleep, now.

As she climbed the steps to Isonde's room, her earlier discussion with the princess came back to her. This was Kayla's last night as Isonde. The last night of sleeping in her room, the last night of wearing her face.

Isonde had been recovering at a remarkable pace that could only be achieved by sheer force of will. Despite being still weak and tiring easily, Isonde was ready to resume her life. Kayla would move into what had been Isonde's sick room and re-emerge in society tomorrow as Lady Evelyn, having "recovered from her near-fatal bout with the Virian flu."

Kayla wasn't off the hook yet, though. She would also attend all of Isonde's meetings—in the role of assistant—in order to offer her opinions afterward. Considering she had been the one interacting with everyone during Isonde's coma, it was necessary until Isonde got back up to speed. The only place Kayla wouldn't go was Sovereign Council sessions. Isonde was determined to attend tomorrow's session herself, and the princess would succeed or die trying.

Kayla entered Isonde's room, stripped off her boots, tossed them by the door and headed for the shower. Surprisingly, she felt anxious about missing the council session. Archon Raorin would speak tomorrow, then two delegates from Inja who would harp on the fiction of the Ilmenans being terrorists. Most importantly, the lead councilor from Falanar itself would close out the day, and his words carried enough weight to sway a large section of the council. Even though Kayla had been unwillingly forced into the role of one of Piran's councilors, she was thoroughly engaged by this point. Every moment, every speech, every shift in power was too important to the future of her people and the spread of the TNV to be missed. And now she'd been sidelined.

For which she was thankful.

Truly.

Right?

Isonde will do what's necessary. Kayla had to trust in that.

She peeled off the rest of her clothes, uncomfortable with her unexpected frustration. She flipped the shower setting from sonic to water, and let a cool stream wash over her.

The Sovereign and Protectorate Councils had come to a crucial point where they had to decide on a course of action for dealing with the TNV and present their recommendation to the Council of Seven. The Council of Seven would then make the final ruling, a ruling that would determine how the empire would handle the TNV plague and the Ordochian occupation.

Isonde *had* to be seated on the Council of Seven before that vote happened. And she would be, if the wedding—scheduled for three days hence—went as planned.

Everything Kayla had done, every chance she'd taken since leaving the Blood Pit, came down to that one moment. And finally it was here. Some days she'd thought it would never come. Some days she wore the illusion of Princess Isonde so well she believed she and Isonde had become one and the same.

A chill that had nothing to do with the cool water temperature hit her when she realized that walking away from Falanar and leaving the fate of her people in someone else's hands, even Isonde's hands, would be much, much harder than she'd anticipated.

It shouldn't be. She was a *ro'haar*, not a politician. And yet...

The comm unit buzzed with an incoming message, saving her from her thoughts. Kayla toweled off and then slipped on a robe before answering the comm.

Isonde. Awake and scheming, even at this early hour. "Are you up? I want to go over the details of your last meeting with Councilor Gi."

And back to politicking it was.

16

THE *YARI*, MINE FIELD

Cinni popped the helmet of her spacesuit off and secured it in a gear locker at the back of Ariel's ship's cargo bay, along with the rest of her suit. Her hands trembled, despite her best efforts to control them, adrenaline pumping through her system.

I survived. I survived.

One more successful trip through the Tear. She'd made it; the Tear hadn't closed on her, hadn't crushed her into oblivion.

I made it.

She took a deep breath. Held it. Reached for a sense of relief that eluded her. Tremors. More tremors.

Pull yourself together, Cinni, you have shit to do.

The air escaped her lungs in a whoosh. She pulled a blister pack from her pocket and forced a dreamer through the foil backing. She swallowed it dry, resting her forehead against the locker while the sedative took effect.

Better.

Ariel buzzed the ship's internal comm. "All is well?"

Cinni took a last deep breath, then double-timed it to the ancient shuttle's cockpit. "Thanks for the ride," she said to Ariel, once she'd arrived. She grinned at the usually dour woman.

Ariel snorted. "As if I'd be food wasting when you have

brought fresh." She maneuvered the ship to dock with the *Yari*. "Ida is not to forgive that."

True. The *Yari*'s crew were near-rabid for calorie packs for their food replicators. Bring actual food instead, though? Rapture.

"Gintoc is pleased the most. Liking Phan is not possible." Ariel grimaced at the mention of Phan and Cinni couldn't blame her. Phan might be a genius with engines, but while most of the Ordochian resistance considered the *Yari*'s crew amazing in and of themselves, Phan thought them outdated relics who couldn't possibly understand his brilliance with machines. Without being too impressed by their own importance, the *Yari*'s crew had enough pride to find Phan's superior air obnoxious.

The shuttle docked smoothly and Cinni started back toward the cargo bay. "I better open the bay doors before Ida busts in, looking for snacks."

The captain of the *Yari* greeted Cinni with a huge smile and a "whoop!" of excitement. She hugged Cinni in a flurry, her thigh-length sea-green braid swinging around like a rope. Just as quickly, Ida bustled past to get to the hover cart full of foodstuffs. The real reason Cinni had come, bringing much-needed supplies to fix the *Yari*'s hyperstream drive, was ignored for the moment.

Larsa, Tanet and Benny rushed into the shuttle next, a gaggle of excitement, with "Welcome to you, Cinni!" on their lips and eyes only for the food crates. If it was up to them, she'd be hauling the engine parts out herself.

Not surprisingly, the taciturn Gintoc had stayed with his beloved drive. She didn't take it personally—Gintoc slept in the engine room.

The flood of black flight suits and blue-green hair quickly emptied out into the landing bay with their prizes and merry shouts, leaving Cinni free to exit the ship. A group of about ten strangers waited in the bay, staring at her. Wyrds all, and a mix of modern-day Ordochians and Ilmenans, judging by the instances of blue-shaded and purple-shaded hair. She was three steps down the shuttle's ramp when the full import of the Ordochian faces hit her.

"Highnesses," Cinni breathed in disbelief. Not only was she on the fabled *Yari*, now she stood face to face with four people back from the dead. The discovery of the *Yari* had purged the word "impossible" from her vocabulary, but seeing members of Ordoch's ruling family, alive, after five years…

She'd only had two dreamers. Surely she wasn't hallucinating this. Right?

She recognized Natali, the eldest of the heirs, and Vayne, the second in line, right away. It took another moment to place the child as Corinth, their youngest brother. He had only been eight at the time of their death—disappearance—and not much in the news feeds. Behind them stood their uncle, she didn't remember his name.

Ordoch's rightful rulers. Alive.

"Are there others?" she asked. Did the ruling *ro'haar-il'haar* pair still live?

The uncle said, "We're all that's left of the Reinumons."

Then… Natali was the dethroned ruler of Ordoch. Typically no one ruled without their other half—in Natali's case that would be her *il'haar* Erebus, apparently dead. Then again, these were desperate times.

Natali looked the part. She stood taller than the other three, shoulders back, her chin tilted at an angle that said, "You wouldn't dare challenge me." Her eyes were the first blue hint of a glacier, her demeanor remote. She had an ion pistol on her hip and a sheathed knife stuck through her belt—armed high-tech and low, like any good *ro'haar*.

::Where did you come from?:: The boy—Corinth—must have spoken, and Cinni blinked at the rudeness of not greeting her aloud first.

"Ordoch." The silence between the heirs was at odds with the crew's happy chatter. "Where did you come from?"

"A void beyond your imagining," Vayne said, with no

192

inflection at all. The uncle laughed as if Vayne had made a joke, and Vayne's mouth tightened.

She struggled against staring at Vayne. In her youthful fantasies, when Ordoch had been free and the royal family of no more concern to her beyond their appearances on newsvids, she'd crushed on him—as no doubt half of the population of Ordoch had. She'd dreamed of having his striking cobalt hair. It was the vibrant pigment from which all other blues were diluted. The top half of his hair was pulled back from his face in a stubby ponytail and the rest fell to about jaw-length. His *ro'haar* had a similar, darker color, if Cinni recalled correctly. Vayne's features were almost delicate, all long lines and perfect angles, with red-violet lips she'd spent hours sighing over.

He looked exactly like she remembered, with the exception of his eyes. His aqua gaze was startlingly direct and intense to the point of fierceness. He stared without seeming to blink, those gorgeous lips tight, and the silent agitation about him seemed to translate itself into Corinth, who looked like a mini-replica of Vayne. It was enough to make Cinni glance away, discomfited.

A female Ilmenan with a lavender bob and the look of command stepped forward. "You came through the Tear from Ordoch?" The woman seemed impressed by the fact, though not completely surprised. She must rank high enough among the Ilmenans aiding the Ordochian rebels to be aware of the Tear's existence.

Cinni nodded, gathering the wits scattered by the resurrection of the royal Ordochians. "Cinni Purl, part of the resistance on Ordoch."

The Ilmenan woman smiled. "Well met. I'm Tia'tan, and this is Noar, Luliana and Joffar." The names slid by so fast Cinni knew she wouldn't remember. "I'd heard about the Tear, but to see it…"

"You should try traveling it," Cinni quipped, making her way down the rest of the ramp and into the landing bay, subtly turning away from Vayne and his absently smiling uncle.

Where had they been? How had they survived? What did they plan now?

Gintoc's voice boomed through the ship's comms, thankfully removing her attention from Vayne. "Cinni," Gintoc said into the speaker, "welcome you are. New parts now?"

That was Gintoc, always on task. Cinni walked to the bay's comm and flipped it on. "Right away, Gintoc. Along with a double helping of shallot, truffle and burgundy soup. You'd better have made some progress since Phan's last report or I'm here to fire you, old man!"

She appreciated the chuckle that sounded through the comm, being so rare from him. "I'll be right down to inspect your hard work," she said. He answered with something she couldn't translate, which was probably for the best.

An hour later, Vayne was no closer to understanding what the frutt was going on.

The crew had trundled all the food to the commissary, and Abenifluis—Benny, he reminded himself—cooked a meal that had the crew sighing in pleasure. Vayne was two seconds from standing on a table and demanding answers when Ida finished eating and fixed her attention on him.

"Eyes are boiling from questions, Vayne." She tossed her long braid over her shoulder. "Present them."

Where to start? The Tear? The ship itself? The drive repair parts? Ordochians somehow traveling through space on foot? Or why the frutt the crew was so bonkers over food?

Cinni arrived before he could ask a thing. She was armed with a plasma bullpup and towed a man Vayne didn't recognize by the sleeve. Must be Gintoc, the engine chief. He'd met Larsa earlier, Gintoc's assistant.

Ida's brow rose at Cinni's entrance, and the girl made a so-so gesture with her hand, which Ida seemed to accept with a sigh. Cinni pulled the PDW—personal defense weapon, as they'd called them back in Ida's day—off her shoulder by the strap and stowed it in a rack at the commissary's entrance. The rack held several PDWs, all plasma weapons. Plasma blasts passed through telekinetic psi shields effortlessly.

Cinni and Gintoc made their way to the remains of the buffet Benny had created. Vayne stood, unable to contain his frustration a second longer.

"First off." He turned his attention to Tia'tan. "Why was the *Radiant* bringing fuel to the *Yari*, and what is all this talk about 'fixing?' Are you thinking of flying a five-hundred-year-old ship out of here?"

Cinni answered before Tia'tan. "That's the plan. And not quite 'flying,' more like jumping out of here, catching a hyperstream."

"Is that even possible inside the Mine Field?" He leaned against the cabinet behind him to keep from pacing.

Cinni looked at Tanet, who was scraping the remains of dinner from his plate. The physicist finished a final scoop of the saucy bits, then cleared his throat.

"Seems possible. This space of pocket sufficient."

It was hard to remember that the crew spoke with perfect fluency in their own dialect when they sounded like disjointed children to him.

"To what end, though?" Vayne asked. "What are you going to do with an ancient, half-finished ship?"

"The most important part of the *Yari* is finished," Cinni said. "The weapon systems."

"At this point, I'd say the hyperstream drive is the most important part, or those weapons are useless."

"Correct." Gintoc nodded without looking away from his plate of food. "Utmost importance of the ship being the engine. Always."

"In either case," Cinni said, "the artillery on the *Yari* is still the most devastating combination of weapons to date. Both Ilmena and Ordoch scaled down their weapon programs after the Second Ilmenan War, and the rest fell into disrepair over the centuries as politics in this system stabilized and interplanetary conflict became a thing of the past."

Tia'tan spoke. "Based on the specs we have of imperial weaponry, the *Yari*'s arsenal is still a match for the imperials' current ships."

"Wait—you're not talking about the cannons and missiles. You mean the PD." The idea was so amazingly reckless that he couldn't be right.

For once, Ida wasn't smiling. "If the need is ours."

Vayne looked from one face to the other. "You cannot be serious." They looked damn serious. Cinni most of all. Even Tia'tan didn't seem surprised.

The PD was a "Planetary Decimator." A massive burst from the PD could cause extinction-level events on a planet's surface. The weapon was so powerful—too powerful—that once the fervor of war had passed, each side agreed it was for the best that the *Yari* had been lost before it reached Ilmena.

"Did you all forget?" He looked at each of the crew in turn. "It was the initial testing and power-up of the PD that tore space in the first place and ripped the *Yari* through that freak wormhole. That weapon, not even fired, is responsible for your exile here."

They were insane. Every last one of them. Cinni too, if she went along with it. Frutt, even Tia'tan seemed to buy into this horrific idea.

"It's the best chance we have," Cinni said, sounding a little defensive.

::What about refitting Ilmena's battleships?:: Corinth asked the room. He, at least, looked as repulsed as Vayne about the insane idea of firing the PD.

Noar nodded as if agreeing with Corinth. Okay, so maybe there were three rational people in the room. "We're working on it," Noar said. "It is taking longer than hoped for. We didn't react quickly enough to the coup on Ordoch." Noar's face looked solemn. "I regret to say that we did not take the threat seriously. Even once the empire had made its move on Ordoch, we assumed the Ordochians would take care of them in short order. We waited—longer than we should have—to take any action."

"Then we wasted time with diplomacy," Tia'tan said, cutting a look to Noar, who shrugged.

"It wasn't—"

A husky, rarely heard voice cut Noar off. "Once the imperials had killed our parents and harmed our people, the time for diplomacy was passed. You should have *acted*." Everyone froze, then slowly, all gazes turned to Natali. She hadn't sat when they entered the room, and from her superior height she looked down on them all with condemnation. Everyone except Vayne. Her gaze never wandered in his direction.

"We're acting now," Tia'tan said quietly into the hush. Natali's gaze bore into her, and Tia'tan straightened her spine.

"Right!" Ida said. She rubbed her hands together as if eager to get started. "Action is now. Gintoc! The time is come to showing off your engine. Progress to observe. Yes?"

Gintoc rose without answering, shoveling the last bites of his meal into his mouth even as he walked to the door. Cinni gave Ida an exasperated smile, then followed Gintoc, grabbing her PDW off the rack as she went. Larsa, Benny and Ariel all took one of the plasma bullpups from the rack before following.

Vayne caught Ida before she hustled after them. "What's with the weapons?"

Ariel muttered something about *stepa at es,* and Ida waved it away with a smile, even as she grabbed a bullpup.

"Is protocol, though no one *stephad* in time long. Come. We lead you safe. Ariel!" Ida called ahead. "Finding the parts of Cinni. Larsa, escort."

They both nodded in a way that reminded him they'd been military for centuries, and peeled off into another corridor. Ida looped the strap of the bullpup over her head and held the gun loosely, not quite casually enough to set him at ease.

::Shield:: he told Corinth. Vayne did the same.

What the void were they walking into?

17

FALANAR

Kayla, back in her Lady Evelyn disguise, sat in the interviewee chair on a cozy set at Falanar City's premier news station. Bright lights heated her skin as Madame Lin Fan, seated across from her, scanned her datapad, reviewing the interview questions one last time before the live interview began. A drop of sweat trickled between Kayla's breasts. The fabric of her dress instantly wicked it away and another took its place. Then another.

Her time as Isonde had officially come to an end.

This morning, the morning of the highly anticipated wedding of Isonde and Ardin, Kayla wore a different persona, that of Lady Evelyn. Another false identity it may be, but the face was her own, at least. For the first time in over a month she bared her own face in public. When she spoke, people heard her real voice. It should have been a relief. Instead, she felt exposed, vulnerable, naked.

Madame Lin Fan had wanted to interview Isonde, of course—everyone did. Isonde refused all requests. Lin Fan happily settled for doing the very first interview with "Lady Evelyn" since her reemergence into society. Evelyn was Isonde's chief attendant for the wedding. Essentially the most important person beyond the couple themselves, so all eyes would be watching Madame Lin Fan's broadcast this morning.

The woman positively cackled with glee.

Was it too late to back out?

Then the vidcam activated and Lin Fan's smile glowed to life. "Welcome! Welcome to the show, my friends. Today I have a very special guest with me, Princess Isonde's *dearest* friend, confidante, and of course, her chief attendant at the wedding—Lady Evelyn."

The woman's words slid over Kayla in a happy buzz perfectly suited to today's events. Kayla forced a smile and nodded graciously as Lin Fan enthused about having her as a guest on the show. She segued from there right into the interview.

"It's terrible that you had a bout of the Virian flu. That's a nasty one, and sometimes fatal! I understand you had quite a long recovery."

Kayla nodded. A flu. *Sure.*

"Now that you've battled through it, do you have any suggestions or tips for anyone else out there afraid of catching it?"

Kayla said the first thing that popped into her mind. "Take your vaccinations seriously."

Lin Fan laughed like it was a great joke. She asked a few more questions about "Evelyn," then turned toward the true subject of the interview. She started off easy, asking about Isonde's dress, the arrangements, enthusing about how wonderful it was that the Low Divine agreed to preside over the ceremony when she never performs weddings... then got to the digging:

Was Ardin and Isonde's story truly a love story, or a political ploy? How surprised was Evelyn that Isonde managed to win the Empress Game? Did the world know the *true* Isonde? What was Isonde's association with the IDC? Why wasn't Isonde's father coming to Falanar for the wedding—was there a nasty family split?

The questions came one on top of each other, always with a smile, always with an empathetic "mmhmm" from Lin Fan, but they had needle-sharp accuracy. Kayla found herself wobbling on more than one of them.

"Thank you *so* much for being my guest today, Lady Evelyn," Lin Fan finally said, with a thankful smile and a congenial pat on her wrist.

Isonde owed Kayla one for sticking her with this surprisingly grueling interview.

"Now," Lin Fan said, "I know you need to hurry off and get ready for the ceremony. One last question, if you don't mind?"

Yes, she did mind.

"Of course not."

Lin Fan's teeth gleamed in the intense lighting as she smiled, like a predator with perfect fang alignment. "I understand that Isonde has a close relationship with those... Wyrds." Her nose scrunched on the word, and she made a moue with her mouth as if she'd tasted something sour. Kayla's hackles rose. "Some sort of," Lin Fan lowered her voice here and leaned in, "alliance. Does such an association with suspected terrorists make Isonde unfit to sit on the Council of Seven?"

Kayla's mouth dropped open.

She was so incensed she wasn't even certain what she'd say. A million fiery words leapt to her tongue at the *audacity* of anyone from the empire casting disparagement on her people. When she drew breath to reply, a light, frothy music cut across the audio, blocking any attempt to speak.

"Oh, I'm sorry, that's all the time we have for today," Lin Fan said, with a knowing glint in her eye. "Thank you again for chatting with me this morning, Lady Evelyn, and we'll see you at the wedding!"

Holy shit, the bitch had set her up.

Now the only thing people would remember was that last line hanging in the air, and Kayla's inability to instantly counter the accusation.

Isonde was going to be pissed.

Malkor, in full ceremonial IDC dress, stood alone on the second of the massive steps that led to the Basilica of the Dawn. He, along with billions of others across the empire, awaited the start of the royal wedding.

A breeze had risen with the sun and blown off the clouds. Now the jewel-bright blue sky stretched overhead and the wind settled to a whisper, its breath fluttering the pennants ringing the immense basilica grounds.

Below him, hundreds upon hundreds of spectators covered every available centimeter of lawn. Unease snaked through him as he scanned the immense crowd for potential trouble.

At the moment he stood alone on the basilica's grand steps. The rest of the wedding party would stand with him, above the crowd, when they arrived. At the foot of the steps, gaily decorated barricades blocked access to the wedding party and marked the front of the seated section. Crowded into the gilt chairs were the royally invited guests, people most important to Isonde and Ardin—or their political careers.

Beyond that, the humongous yard of the basilica grounds had been opened for any and all who wanted to attend. A savvy move on Isonde's part. She'd established her position among the leaders of the empire already—today was all about convincing the general populace that she was a leader "for the people."

Of course, most of "the people" of the empire couldn't afford to travel to the Sovereign Planets themselves, never mind Falanar. Nonetheless, the gesture endeared her to the masses. Everyone felt included in her day of joy, in her triumph of becoming Ardin's wife, the empress-apparent and a member of the Council of Seven.

The day should have been blissful, the atmosphere as joyous as the weather. At any other time he'd expect guests in their very finest—gowns, gloves, hats, jewels; enough to bankrupt a Protectorate Planet. Instead the crowd was an uneasy mix of gaiety and trepidation. Fear of the TNV wove tangled threads through the celebration. At least half of the seated elite wore copper-colored gloves of a tissue-thin metallic fabric and masks of one type or another.

Masks.

As if the TNV were only airborne. As if a nanite wasn't small enough to crawl into a skin pore and break the body down from the dermis inward.

Those people shifted constantly in their seats, careful not to touch their neighbors, twitching the fabric of their skirts and robes this way and that to avoid any contact. Beside them the less paranoid elite wore their finery with pride and laughed in the face of their cohorts' fears.

The ranks of commoners beyond the seated guests were an equally volatile mix. Half looked like they were having a day at a fair, and half looked like they'd come to witness a tragedy. The unspoken question, "What will go wrong this time?" hung in the air.

A disaster waiting to happen.

Malkor had said as much to the army colonel in charge of security, who agreed. A large contingent of soldiers patrolled the grounds. More lined the basilica's outer fence and kept guard at the gates, making sure that the crowd outside didn't push inside and turn the event into a mob scene. The soldiers were darkly clad, somber, armed and very, very edgy.

He expected the feeling, considering a fanatical patriot had interrupted the first wedding by trying to unleash the TNV on the empire's leaders. Malkor could still hear Trebulan's shouted words, still see Kayla, in Isonde's wedding gown, leaping from the dais and tackling Trebulan to the ground. Could still feel his heart in his throat as he realized she might have been exposed to the TNV.

Enough. That won't happen this time. It couldn't. Not to Kayla, and not to Ardin and Isonde, two of his closest friends since childhood.

He reviewed the security protocols again.

The imperial army occupied each building adjacent to the basilica square. Soldiers secured every window and stood guard on the rooftops, assuring that all would-be sniper perches were eliminated. No assassination attempt could come from that quarter.

Traffic had been rerouted for kilometers beyond the basilica with the exception of transport for the elite guests, who had biometrically confirmed invitations. Everyone else, rich and poor, walked their way here.

The screening of guests had started at dawn and Malkor and his octet had been here to observe. Technically the imperial army—not the IDC—controlled security inside Falanar. Ardin had granted Malkor and his octet special dispensation to carry arms in this case.

The first screening station, at the outer end of the basilica's long drive, screened for the TNV, biological or chemical weapons. Once a guest passed through successfully, they walked a lengthy "sterile path" cordoned off from the rest of the street. Then they reached the weapons checkpoint. No guests, no matter how highly ranked, were allowed to carry a weapon—bodyguards included. After passing both checkpoints, guests were allowed to enter the basilica grounds.

Many grueling hours later, the last screen had been done, the last person admitted, and all other celebrants were constrained to watch the proceedings from beyond the basilica's fence.

Now, mid-afternoon, Malkor glanced at his chronometer. Kayla, Ardin and Isonde should arrive soon. Would the security measures hold?

He couldn't shake his foreboding. The memory of Kayla, trapped in biocontainment foam, clutching a canister full of the TNV, played over and over in his head.

Finally the horns sounded to announce the arrival of the wedding party. Everyone on watch, including Malkor, tensed. He saw hand after hand after hand check the readiness of a weapon one last time, and fought the urge to do the same. He was here as Ardin's attendant. Ardin and Isonde needed him as a friend now, not an octet leader.

Kayla came down the long aisle first, every head swiveling in her direction. Her gaze found his and even across the distance her smile hit him straight in the chest.

Mine. My love.

The fierceness of the unbidden thought rocked him, as did the primal need to protect. She made the perfect entrance.

And the perfect target.

It took eons for her to travel the distance, and mere seconds. Then she was there, climbing the basilica steps and standing opposite him. She was no more protected here than she had been walking down the aisle, but at least having her close gave him the illusion of safety. Kayla would probably backhand him if she knew he'd spent even a second worrying about her.

"Any trouble?" she asked him in a low voice. Her smile softened to a vaguely pleasant look as she shifted fully into *ro'haar* mode.

"Not yet."

"That doesn't reassure me. The whole place feels… itchy."

A second fanfare sounded, ending their conversation as they both turned to face the aisle.

Two of Ardin's guards led the way, and then the royal couple appeared. Isonde looked magnificent in her pale gold gown. Wide skirts, an endless train, bodice sparkling in the sunlight and her auburn hair streaming down her back—she was a sight to behold.

Ardin was perhaps the only man majestic enough to escort Isonde at such a moment. With his height, wide shoulders, erect posture and bearing, he was royalty to the tips of his boots. He looked proud and pleased and utterly in love.

Everything else was forgotten as the crowd cooed and sighed in delight.

Malkor studied the gathering. All eyes were on the royal couple with the exception of the security battalion. No guest seemed particularly agitated. No one seemed to be secretly planning the doom of the wedding party.

He glanced at Kayla and found her doing the same thing he'd done, sweeping the crowd. Was she remembering those excruciating hours she'd spent trapped in the biocontainment foam at the last wedding, when they'd been certain she'd been infected with the TNV?

Ardin and Isonde reached the wide stone steps of the Basilica of the Dawn and waited at the bottom, as they'd been instructed to do beforehand by the Low Divine.

This was Malkor's last chance to spot any danger. After this he'd have to turn his back on the crowd, take his part in the ceremony and trust his life to the army and his few octet members. Not an easy feeling.

He hesitated one final moment, then shifted to face the basilica. The massive steps topped off in a broad stone terrace, at the other end of which stood the still-shut doors of the basilica.

The crowd quieted, waiting.

An itch began between Malkor's shoulder blades, begging him to take a more strategic position. Kayla, he saw, had already glanced over her shoulder twice.

At last the ancient triple-height doors of the Basilica of the Dawn creaked open with great ponderance. There was a flurry of fabric as everyone in the crowd bowed their head in real or manufactured reverence. One would expect a dragon or something of equal size and import to issue forth from such a portal.

Instead, a slim blonde waif walked unescorted through the giant doors. The Low Divine, a girl of no more than fifteen, strode slowly along the stone toward the most powerful couple in the empire. She brought with her an intense hush. No one dared breathe as she placed one delicate foot in front of the other.

As if she'd known what Isonde planned to wear, the Low Divine was dressed in gold as well. Whereas Isonde's dress was a pale, malleable, mutable gold, the Low Divine's dress was the fieriest golden hue of the sun at its zenith. She blazed with glory and power.

Malkor caught Isonde's narrowed gaze, which revealed she knew she'd been shown up at her own wedding.

Nothing like a power play between two titans to bring out the romance in an event.

The Low Divine wore an ethereal smile as she reached the stairs. Her arms were wrapped from upper arm to wrist in delicate coils of golden filament, and the metal glinted in the sun as she raised her arms to the waiting throng. "Welcome all, to the Basilica of the Dawn." The firmness of her voice through the amplifiers belied her small stature, and she was answered with a thousand greetings in return.

The Low Divine stood there a moment, arms still raised, her gaze taking in "her people" as she offered that soft, welcoming, oh-so-untouchable smile, before she finally acknowledged Isonde and Ardin.

Isonde had met her match in the Low Divine when it came to manipulating people and power.

The Low Divine beckoned the couple to ascend the steps. Isonde and Ardin went, hand in hand, smiles restored. No doubt the rest of the glory would be theirs. They stood together, an overwhelmingly beautiful pair that dwarfed the young girl.

As the balance of power changed to Isonde and Ardin, the Low Divine lifted her arms again and her section of the topmost stair rose, elevating her head and shoulders above Isonde and Ardin on a round platform.

Oh yeah, Isonde had *definitely* met her match.

The stage was set, the players all here. If a terrorist was going to make a move, now was the time. Malkor casually glanced over the left side of the crowd. From where he stood he could only see half of the gathered elite, no farther than that.

Damnit.

The Low Divine spoke and her voice rang throughout the yard. The audience hung on her every word, on Isonde's and Ardin's when they spoke their vows.

The questions were asked, the assent given. The vows pledged, the tattoos borne, the binding ribbon braided and the final blessing called for.

Then it was done.

Ardin and Isonde were one officially, and no one could sunder their bond without their consent.

The Low Divine quieted the voice augmenter to offer her final wedding blessing to the couple in "private," and everyone had their eyes on her, trying to catch a word or two of what would be a famous speech, should the Low Divine or Isonde and Ardin ever choose to release it.

Kayla let out a sigh of relief that Malkor seconded. It was finally over. Their part was done. She smiled at him, one of her rare, special smiles. Before he could return it, Kayla's gaze shot past him in alarm.

"THIS IS FOR ORDOCH!" someone screamed. Malkor whipped around to see a man standing on his chair in the elites' section, pointing a pistol at the wedding party.

"Guards!" Malkor shouted, while the other man screamed, "FREE THE WYRDS! FREE ORDOCH!" in a high-pitched voice that carried over the crowd. The crazed man fired off three shots while Kayla dove forward to try to cover Isonde and Ardin.

Imperial army snipers fired on the man and it was over before Malkor could move. Those three shots and then *SHIZZT*—the man's head was blown away.

Everywhere was shrieking and horror and chaos. Malkor rushed to Kayla, Ardin and Isonde, frantic to see who had been hit. Who had the gunman targeted? Isonde? Ardin? Had he hit them, or had Kayla died to protect them?

It took a second to realize all three were unharmed. Isonde and Ardin lay on the ground, Kayla on top of them as if her slim body could have covered them both. Ardin's guards rushed in from both sides, righting everyone and forming a protective ring around them. Only after Malkor registered their safety did he notice that the Low Divine's platform was empty.

He sprinted around the platform, knocking guards out of his way.

There, on the ground behind it, the Low Divine lay on her back. Her fragile body heaved with coughs while her splayed limbs lay useless, neither flinching nor moving to help her. Red spittle flew from her mouth. Her eyes rolled in her head like the eyes of a spooked horse.

Malkor fell to his knees. This girl, this *child*, had been shot three times without error, center mass, making a crater out of her once delicate breast. Burnt flesh ringed a hole large enough for his fist, and her one working lung spasmed.

The Low Divine died as he watched, a sheen of blood and mucus covering her cheek as the last tortured breath was forced out and death was let in.

18

The newsvids had exploded. The word "uproar" couldn't begin to describe the outrage sweeping the empire.

Authorities confirmed, after a search of the assassin's comm banks, that the Low Divine had indeed been the target. The *so-called* Wyrd supporter had murdered the heart of the people.

Hours after the event, Kayla paced alone in Isonde's townhouse's back parlor, watching the news with impotent fury. She wanted to scream. She wanted to rage. She wanted to flip back the clock and kill the bastard before he ever got a shot off.

This is for Ordoch! he had shouted.

What a crock of shit.

Of course the idiots of the empire were eating it up. News stories swapped between hundreds of thousands of citizens prostrate with grief over the murder of the Low Divine, and various politicians, diplomacy experts and talking heads weighing in on whether or not this was actually a Wyrd plot.

Bullshit. Anyone with a gram of sense would realize that Wyrds would never do anything to endanger what little goodwill they had inside the empire.

Raorin, Wei-lu-Wei's Councilor Gi, General Yislan and Sovereign Councilmember Siminia were doing damage control as best they could, each making statements that they believed the gunman had acted alone, that the Wyrds—Ilmenan and

Ordochian both—had no hand in this, but the opposition grew.

Kayla's gaze focused again and again on the pistol in the assassin's hand when the news feeds showed the fateful moment in a loop.

Same pistol of unknown design as Bredard's.

Figured.

Isonde and Ardin had been moved to the palace immediately following the assassination. Malkor had seen Kayla safely back to the townhouse and left quickly after. He had too much to do to stay and listen to her rage.

Kayla was back in her working clothes—tunic, leggings, knee-high boots and her kris daggers—wanting to do *something* other than sit here. Sitting was her only option at the moment. As Lady Evelyn, she was near-powerless.

So she waited.

Nighttime found her seated in the blissfully quiet dining room, eating dinner. She'd switched off the news feeds long ago, unable to stand the constant loop of wild speculation and intense grief. Now she focused on thinking about nothing at all while eating.

Kayla had set the bank of vidscreens that ran the length of one wall to a view of space. Cold, calm, quiet space. The huge spread of stars drew her in, took her away from the chaos of the moment. Ever since her time on the perpetually hazy Altair Tri, she couldn't get enough of seeing the stars, even the foreign stars of Imperial Space.

A tenderloin steak cooled on the table in front of her. Isonde's chef was divine and the dish one of her best, but the roasted flesh looked so much like the Low Divine's wound that even the promise of a perfect umami experience couldn't persuade Kayla to eat it. Instead she picked at a bowl of greens and shaved truffles, enjoying the pungent, musky aroma that no synthesizer had ever been able to replicate.

The solitary meal and the view of space was surprisingly soothing. Kayla sipped at a deep red wine. Maybe she could stay in the silence and stillness forever.

The comm chimed. "Lady Evelyn, Senior Agent Rua is here to see you," said one of the guards.

"Send him in."

Malkor looked harried when he entered, still in his indigo and jade dress uniform from the wedding. A frown line seemed permanently etched between his brows, so unlike the way he could look, when the world hadn't gone insane. He paused when he entered, and Kayla got the sense he was trying to decide if sitting next to her or across from her would be more appropriate.

She no longer played Isonde, but the mask of Lady Evelyn's identity isolated her still.

The dining room was open on both ends. Anyone from the household staff to the guards could wander by at any moment. Malkor scanned the entrances, then chose the seat opposite her at the table.

Damn. Of course she didn't want to compromise anything. It would have been nice, for once, to sit incautiously close to the man she loved, especially when he'd no doubt come with difficult news. Maybe—stars forbid—even offer a gentle touch of commiseration.

Instead, the silent gaze between them was their only emotional communication. He looked perfect against the backdrop of stars, and she realized he was part of her peace, a place where she could find contentment.

He scrubbed a hand across his face, breaking the moment, and reality crashed in. There would be no contentment for anyone today. Kayla silently lifted the decanter of wine in his direction. He waved it off. "Still too much to do." He eyed her abandoned steak and he swallowed hard, pushing the perfectly roasted meat even farther away. "I have details."

"Excellent. I've been stuck with nothing but the general news feeds all day." She sighed. "Does it make me a bad person that my major concern over the Low Divine's death is for my own people?"

"I feel the same way, and I at least knew her. You didn't." He shook his head.

"So what'd you learn so far?" She tilted the wine decanter and poured, sliding more ruby liquid into her glass.

"The assassin was from the province of Geth, and we still have no idea how he got his invite to the seated section of the wedding."

She stopped with the glass halfway to her lips. Geth. Bredard's province. "I knew we hadn't seen the last of him."

"The gun's make has yet to be identified. I've only had the newsvids to work from—the army has official control of the investigation and they pulled all available surveillance footage, including that belonging to the basilica." Malkor seemed to be simultaneously talking and running through other things in his head, fingers drumming lightly on the table. Kayla caught sight of a bloodstain on his cuff. The Low Divine's probably.

"The IDC's not involved in the investigation?" she asked.

"We have no jurisdiction in this sort of thing." His fingers tapped harder. "Parrel's pushing for involvement, though, based on the interplanetary nature of the crime." The frown lines on his forehead deepened. "We need in ASAP, since the army's likely involved in the assassination. They controlled the security for the wedding, they're the link between the assassin and the weapon."

"I've seen the pistol before," she said.

Malkor arched a brow, looking suddenly cautious. "Tell me it's not actually Wyrd tech."

"Not really." More similar than she was going to admit, though, with her people accused of planning the assassination. "Bredard had something like it that first night he came to 'visit' me."

Malkor still looked uneasy, and his voice had a hint of "official IDC agent" to it. "Is it possible it's tech Ilmena developed, and you're not aware of it?"

Did he really ask her that? "Wyrds are not involved in this. Period."

"Kayla—"

"This is infighting and betrayal among your own frutted

governments and agencies." She set her glass down with a sharp clink.

"I suppose Ordoch had no infighting or betrayal whatsoever before we came along? We imperials corner the market? The Wyrds are too 'advanced' for that?"

That shut her up. The situation on Ordoch had been... less than ideal long before the coup. Troubled and unstable, to say the least.

Malkor signaled a halt. "Wait. Sorry." He sighed, sinking back into the chair. "That was uncalled for."

"No, I was out of line; you're right to look at every angle. I'm just on edge."

"The entire planet is."

Falanar, the Sovereign Planets—the entire empire was on edge.

"I've been listening to imperials malign my people all day," she said. "As if the empire wasn't the aggressor, as if you—they—hadn't started all of this five years ago." The hand not wrapped around the stem of her glass curled into a fist.

Malkor's tired eyes reflected an old pain. Ghosts from the coup on Ordoch haunted both of them.

No time to wallow, Kayla. Focus. Basics, threats. "So. How could the assassin get the gun inside the basilica grounds?" It would have been impossible without inside help.

"One of two ways: either he walked in with it and someone at the gate let him pass through the weapons check, or it had already been stashed on the grounds by someone and he took the handoff once through the gates."

Both plausible.

"Has to be someone in the army," Malkor continued. "Other than my octet, only the soldiers and royal guards were armed. And the royal guards were stationed by the emperor, empress, Ardin and Isonde—they didn't mingle at all."

"I'm certain this was about framing my people," Kayla said. "Raorin and I—well, Raorin and Isonde, I guess—" Stars, what a mess. "We were counting on the Low Divine swaying the general populace toward supporting a peaceful withdrawal from Wyrd Space." Kayla made a swirly motion with her hand. "Something about it being better for their Unity of spirit, or some such. Raorin had been laying into the Low Divine pretty heavily about it, and she seemed to be buying in." With incentives, of course. Kayla never asked what sort of deals Raorin made, though. "Now, if everyone believes the lie that a Wyrd was behind the Low Divine's death, it's pretty much a call to war."

Or further war, since her planet was already occupied.

The word "war" hung between them, separated them. When it all came down in the end, when swords were drawn or treaties were signed, where would Malkor stand?

Where would she?

"Carsov," Malkor finally said. "We need Carsov."

It took a second for her to follow his line of thought. "The soldier from the army's Biomech Crimes division?"

"Yeah, the guy who freed you from the biocontainment foam at the last wedding. He knows who really supplied Trebulan with the TNV. If I can get that proof from him…"

"You think it's the same people?"

Malkor nodded. She could practically see gears turning in his mind, plans being laid. "Has to be. How many intergalactic conspiracies can one empire have at a time?" The joke was so close to the truth of their crazy situation that it fell flat. How many people and factions and agencies were they up against?

The comm chirped. "Lady Evelyn, comm coming in from Princess Isonde."

"Okay, send it through."

It was a short call, Isonde requesting her immediate presence at the royal palace, dressed as smartly and as somberly as she could be.

Great. More politics. This ought to be fun.

Malkor pushed away from the table, back to full business mode as he stood. "I'm going to lean on Carsov, see if I can crack him." He offered her a fleeting smile. "Good luck with Isonde."

"Thanks, I'll probably need it."

* * *

Kayla arrived at the royal palace half an hour later and was ushered into what must be the official press room. A bevy of seats for media faced a podium, and behind the podium a giant screen displayed the seal of the Sakien Empire on one half and the seal of Piran on the other. The imperial seal—an indigo field bordered in brilliant jade, hosting a ship jumping to hyperspace surrounded by a ring of stars—paired perfectly with Piran's deep violet field and the lighter, lavender embroidered pattern of a sheave of wheat topped by an elaborate crown.

Isonde saw her and hurried over, leaving behind the group of Piran's councilors. "Thank you for coming on such short notice." She was brisk and businesslike, dressed in a somber violet gown with her hair pulled back into a neat chignon. Who would have thought that she'd survived both a wedding and the assassination of the Low Divine a few hours ago?

"Ardin and I are making a statement as the imperial heirs. I wanted a strong contingent of Piranians here to show that both me and my people grieve the loss of the Low Divine, and support the Wyrds' innocence."

Isonde was amazing. The first book she ever read as a child was probably a treatise on politics.

"How can I help?" Kayla asked. Isonde seemed to be processing a million things at once. Her gaze darted between the media filling the room, Ardin speaking with his advisors, the Piranian councilors and the datapad in her hand, covered in scrawled notes.

Isonde locked her attention on Kayla. "We're going to get a handle on this, you know that, right?" Her voice had absolute determination. "I won't allow your people to be blamed for this."

The sentiment touched Kayla. Most people who'd had a prominent religious figure assassinated at their wedding would probably call it a day. Not Isonde. Instead she'd ordered a press conference, staying on top of the politics, fighting tooth and nail for their agenda of Ordochian freedom and a cure for the TNV.

"I want you to speak," Isonde said. "I've already written it so you'll just have to read it and you're done. It's a small piece to reinforce our belief in the Wyrds' innocence."

Kayla nodded. That she could do.

Isonde's gaze made another circuit of the room, stopping on Ardin. She watched him in silence a moment, and Kayla spontaneously took her hand, giving it a slight squeeze.

"There will be better days with Ardin," she said. "Happier ones."

Isonde looked at Kayla with eyes full of regret. "Sadly, we all need to play our parts." She gave Kayla's hand a brief squeeze in return. "It's time now. And... thank you."

With that Isonde went to stand beside Ardin as the last of the media entered and the place filled with expectation. Kayla took her place with the Piranian councilors, feeling an odd sense of duality. She'd be speaking as Lady Evelyn, in the name of Piran, but she'd be speaking from the heart for the sake of her own people. Both of those voices had power.

The quiet conversation, coughing and rustling from the media section went silent as the sonic field was engaged, blocking the movement of sound toward the podium. Everyone at the podium would be heard by the entire room, and no one from the media could interrupt until the floor was opened for questions and the field turned off.

Ardin made the opening remarks, expressing their sadness at the events of today. His voice, low and sincere, held the right combination of grief and steadiness. The people could grieve with him and they could depend on him. Isonde spoke next, echoing his sentiments over the loss of the Low Divine. She even managed a quaver at one point and took a quiet second to compose herself while the media looked on, clearly forming their first questions.

"We must admit that there is more than one victim of this crime," Isonde continued. "The death of the Low Divine is a blow we will feel for years to come, but the assassin, by falsely claiming to be working with the Wyrds, has injured them as well."

Beyond the sonic field, the media stirred like a kicked anthill. Hands shot up with questions. Isonde ignored them and rolled on.

"This is the crime of one person, but he is trying to take so many down with him, and we can't let that happen." The princess seemed to be gathering steam. Maybe Kayla wouldn't have to speak after all.

"The Wyrds are innocent of wrongdoing on Falanar—or anywhere else in the empire. The Low Divine was killed not by a foreign power out for blood, but by one of us, her own people." Isonde bowed her head a moment as if personally struck by such a betrayal. Ardin moved to stand beside her, one hand on her lower back to offer support and comfort. Even from Kayla's angle off to the side of the podium she could see that they presented the perfect image—strength, unity, empathy, grief, resoluteness.

"My husband and I," Isonde said, "and all of Piran believe in the Wyrds' innocence. We still believe that a peaceful withdrawal from Wyrd Space is our best chance to gain their cooperation in finding a cure for the TNV. That is why we have allied ourselves with Ordoch's rightful ruler."

Kayla froze. What the— When had she spoken to Natali? How?

Isonde turned to face Kayla. "You've known her as my dear friend Lady Evelyn for many months. We established that ruse to assure her safety."

No.

She wouldn't.

After all Kayla had done for her, surely Isonde wouldn't—

Isonde drew breath to speak and Kayla felt the words coming from a light-year away, powerless to stop them.

We all have to play our parts.

Isonde's eyes held that same regret of minutes ago, even as

the words, half-truth, half-lies, tumbled out.

"I present to you Princess Kayla Reinumon, sole survivor of the Reinumon family and rightful ruler of Ordoch."

19

"I present to you Princess Kayla Reinumon, sole survivor of the Reinumon family and rightful ruler of Ordoch."

The words hit the room like a bomb blast, launching the media to their feet in a frenzy, made all the more frantic for the silence.

Kayla's world lurched, canted to the right, everything off-center and cracked.

This could not be happening.

After all I did.

Isonde waited expectantly for Kayla to approach the podium.

Kayla couldn't move, couldn't think. Five years of hiding. Five years of poverty and pain and dubious safety, all for what? To be trapped on the enemy's homeworld with her cover blown. Ripped away by a friend.

A bubble of self-mockery burst in her chest. Friend? Isonde had never been her *friend*, not for a moment. Ally? Yes. Friend? The word burned in her mind like the lie it was.

The screen behind Isonde changed to two pictures, side by side. One of them was from the wedding this morning, Kayla in the scarlet dress Isonde had picked out for her, hair, still dyed black, braided and wrapped around her head like a coronet. Beside it was a five-year-old picture she didn't recognize. It must have been from the day of the arrival of the imperials on Ordoch. She and her entire family were in attendance, arranged together in a formal grouping as her father and his *ro'haar*, the then leaders of Ordoch, had greeted IDC officials. Malkor had told her there were very few pictures from their time on Ordoch, as her people had been very concerned about that. What pictures there were were classified at the highest level. How had Isonde gotten this?

Had Malkor betrayed her as well?

No. Malkor would never have done this to her. Only Isonde was cold-hearted enough to use anything, anyone, to gain her ends.

In the Ordoch picture Kayla stood beside Vayne, looking solemn and distrusting, her blue hair braided and wrapped around her head, her dress a brilliant scarlet, so alike in color to the one she'd worn this morning.

The likeness was unmistakable.

The images shifted to a close-up shot from that same evening on Ordoch, a slight smile on her lips as she watched something out of view. A picture from this morning in almost the exact same pose appeared beside it. Each of the pictures from Ordoch was stamped with the official seal of the IDC and registered as highly classified.

When Kayla still couldn't make herself move, either to flee the room or strangle Isonde, the princess continued speaking, her gaze back on the incensed media.

"Princess Kayla has been living in hiding since the coup on Ordoch and the murder of her family. The time has come for her to resume her rightful place as leader of the Ordochian people. She came to me and Ardin with the hope that we can, between our two peoples, engender a peaceful withdrawal from Ordoch."

Kayla was neither the true ruler nor in a place to promise Ordoch's cooperation in anything. Isonde had made her a liar before Kayla could even open her mouth.

"Ladies and gentlemen," Isonde said, "Princess Kayla Reinumon, of Ordoch." She and Ardin bowed very formally, and backed away to give her the podium.

The media fell absolutely still, everyone on their feet, everyone breathless, for once more interested in listening than shouting out their opinions disguised as questions.

Isonde waited patiently, knowing, as Kayla did, that Kayla would do nothing to refute her.

Kayla was trapped in a web that had been spinning for five long years.

She approached the podium in a daze, knowing as she did that the move put her smack in the middle of her two images on the screen, bridging the connection perfectly.

Isonde was a frutting mastermind.

Kayla looked down, and there, on a screen embedded on the podium, were the words Isonde had put into her mouth. She took a long breath. Another.

We all have to play our parts.

"It's true," Kayla said, lifting her head and facing the media. "I have come here to forge a peace between our people. I am truly sorry for the loss you have suffered today in the death of your beloved Low Divine." And the words rolled on. Kayla read the speech confirming Isonde's claims succinctly without really hearing the words.

To do anything else, to refute Isonde, would bring all they'd worked for to the ground in flames.

And Isonde knew it.

At the same time, in the center of the city, Malkor sat on a bench in the enormous Nicura Park. *How had Kayla's chat with Isonde gone?* He was curious to learn what Isonde had commed her about, but that would have to wait.

The darkness of the night was lit by hundreds upon hundreds of candles, and filled with prayer and song and tears. The people of Falanar gathered in the park for a memorial of the Low Divine, coming together for comfort and commiscration, in a desperate attempt to make sense of it all.

Good luck with that.

He was on the inside of the scheming and conspiring and he still couldn't make much sense of it.

Malkor stayed far away from the main gathering, in the shelter of the greater darkness pooling beneath trees that lined a less-used path.

The number of mourners was truly astounding. As was the complete lack of fear over the TNV. Not a single soul wore masks or gloves, and no one seemed afraid to be near anyone else.

A raised dais stood at one end of the park, the center of the memorial. Dozens of pictures of the Low Divine's ethereal face glowed on the dais, keeping company with the endless stream of people who took a turn saying a few words, leading those gathered in prayer, or offering a song that everyone joined in on. Thousands of mourners stood at the base of the dais, holding candles, holding each other. More people milled through the grounds, their candles lighting the way. Tonight everyone was brought together in Unity over their grief, everyone was a friend who had lost a loved one, everyone was safe.

Naturally, it was the perfect place to conduct a quiet, clandestine conversation with an imperial army soldier.

Carsov appeared out of the crowd, his civilian clothes blending him into shadow here at the dark end of the park. He held a lit candle in one hand. In his other he held a token of some sort that he quickly tucked away when he caught sight of Malkor. Carsov sniffed once, then cleared his throat as if to shift emotional gears as he took a seat on the bench.

They sat side by side in silence a moment, each holding a candle, watching the mourners. Malkor got the sense that the candle was more than a prop to Carsov.

"This is some crazy shit," Carsov finally said.

That it was. "You check the assassination details out at all?"

"Not my area."

Malkor shot him a sideways glance. "Not what I asked."

Carsov kept his peace, eyes on the dais far away and the Low Divine's images.

"Army's got the investigation, IDC's hands are tied," Malkor said. "I thought, with your previous work on the TNV case falsely attributed to the Wyrds, you might have been curious about this one." Carsov was too upright a soldier, too honest an investigator not to have suspicions.

"I looked."

Of course he had. Malkor let the words sit. Carsov had something to say, something to offer, or some reason to agree to Malkor's request to meet. He hadn't had to ambush the man this time.

"It's..." Carsov shook his head. "Something's not right."

"No shit. You know the only one capable of getting a weapon to the assassin was an army soldier."

"Could be the actions of two 'freedom fighters,'" Carsov countered, "one in the army, one ready to shoot and die for his cause."

"Is it, though?" The question met with silence. "Sure, it could be a totally separate incident that happened to fit perfectly into an empire-wide conspiracy to frame the Wyrds as terrorists and incite a greater military presence in Wyrd Space. I could buy that."

"Little heavy on the sarcasm." The flame on Carsov's candle flickered in a breeze and he shielded it with his hand. Malkor's guttered, died. Carsov leaned over and relit the candle when the breeze had blown itself out.

The flames burned together in the dark while Carsov gathered his confidence and decided which way to leap. After the assassination, Malkor felt fairly certain he could nudge Carsov his way, but didn't want to push too hard in case the man balked.

"Apparently the shooter was from the province of Geth," Carsov said. "Wasn't even supposed to be at the wedding. Somehow he made the list of guests."

"A list the army vetted."

Carsov nodded, but he didn't look happy about it.

"What if I told you another person from Geth, with

connections to Geth's ruler, tried to blackmail friends of mine recently. Friends in very high places."

"Frutt, Rua, what the void are you into here?"

That was the question, wasn't it?

"It's deep," Malkor said. Maybe too deep. They sat in silence, listening to the wails and prayers, the hum of gathered voices and the strains of tuneless songs. More candles lit the night.

"You a religious man?" Malkor asked, seeing the way Carsov stared at the memorial.

"Ask me that three years ago and I'd have laughed in your face. Now?" Carsov kept his sights on the giant image of the Low Divine as she had been at her last, and possibly most powerful—arms raised, giving the benediction over the royal wedding. "Now, Unity is the only thing that makes me feel close to my wife and daughter again. Unity of my spirit with theirs. The Low Divine taught me that.

"I met her once. She personally blessed my team before we headed to one of our first TNV extractions. No more than a girl, but damn if she didn't radiate faith. Never seen the like and I doubt I will again. So yeah. I guess you could say I'm religious."

It was on the tip of Malkor's tongue to say, "Hey, whatever works." Tonight wasn't the night to be flippant, though. "Someone killed her, Carsov, killed that bright, shining girl as part of a power play. It wasn't for love or morals or any shit like that. It was for power, plain and simple. They murdered her to frame the Wyrds, to incite the passion of the people for retribution."

"It seems insane."

"Does it?" Seemed all too logical to him. And it was working. Elements in the councils, the IDC and the army that wanted to annex Ordoch were gaining ground.

Carsov took a deep breath and blew it out on a sigh. "You called me because you think it's the same people who provided the TNV to Prince Trebulan." It wasn't a question.

"Something big is going down and it's starting to look like your people and my people are both involved."

The look Carsov shot him was definitely surprised. "You breaking IDC ranks?"

Malkor nodded.

"First time for everything," Carsov said.

"I can't sit back while corruption eats away at the IDC."

Carsov chuckled, then chuckled again at Malkor's annoyed glance. "That's rich. The IDC's been corrupt from the start."

"Are we really going to get into this old pissing match?" Same brawl, different day. "The army saying we're corrupt because you can't get your heads out of your asses and realize that running an empire needs a combination of strength *and* diplomacy?"

"And people willing to ignore all decency, laws and morality to 'get the job done,'" Carsov added. "You forgot that part."

Malkor gritted his teeth. "If you want to be a dick about this, go ahead. Just not on my time." He rose to leave. "My mistake, thinking you were a man who wanted justice, who wanted honor to mean something, no matter which of us had the power."

Carsov stopped him. "Don't get your frutting panties in a bunch, Agent. You wouldn't be here if you didn't think the same thing I did—the IDC's out of control. Gone too far."

"Actually I'm here because I'm thinking the same thing about the army."

Carsov mulled that over, glanced at the people gathered to mourn, then back to Malkor. "You might not be wrong."

Sensing common ground, Malkor resumed his seat on the bench. He felt Carsov's opinion sliding his way. "Someone in the army's dirty," Malkor said. "You know it, I know it. Someone buried your report on the TNV. I'm admitting the same about the IDC." Though it had taken him too damn long to see it. "I'm here, being honest with you. Some shit is going down, and only good men like you and me can fix it."

"You believe that?"

The words, oddly introspective, caught him off guard.

"What, that we can fix it?" Malkor shrugged. "Trying's better than doing nothing."

Carsov shook his head. "No, that you're still a good man. You believe that?"

It wasn't a question Malkor cared to think about. And in the end, it really didn't matter. "I'm working for something real here, Carsov, something worth caring about—freedom for the Ordochians and the withdrawal of our men before the other Wyrd Worlds get their fleets rebuilt and annihilate us. A possible end to the TNV, with Ordoch's cooperation. Exposing the corruption at home. They're all linked."

Carsov heard him, Malkor could tell by the way the soldier nodded slightly to himself while listening. If he could tip the man over…

"I'd love to give you some kind of bullshit ultimatum like, 'This is your one chance to do right by the Low Divine, by your family, by the empire.' The truth is, I'm going to keep coming back. I need your honesty and I *need* what's in that report about who supplied Trebulan with the TNV and framed the Wyrds."

Malkor's mobile comm buzzed. He ignored it. When Carsov pulled his own comm out Malkor fought the urge to shake the man. *Give me the damn file.*

Carsov's eyes went round. "Wow. You'd better check in with your princess and her 'bodyguard,' Agent. I'd say shit just got heavy."

He had his comm out in a second. One look at Kayla's message had him on his feet. "The file?" he asked.

"You'll have it."

Malkor nodded and took off into the night. *Isonde, what have you done?*

The royal guards had hustled Kayla from the press room so quickly her head spun. She finished reading Isonde's little speech and then *bam*, she was out of there, guarded on all sides like a priceless package. They'd deposited her in a suite of rooms—her rooms now, apparently—in one of the many wings of the palace with an order to stay put, and that was that.

That had been maybe an hour ago. She was still fighting the urge to pack everything she owned and run. The choice was made somewhat easier by having none of her own things with her, not even her kris daggers. Someone was being sent to Isonde's townhouse for them.

And run? Where would she go this time, back to Altair Tri and the Blood Pit?

Kayla paced the square of her sitting room over and over, fight or flight instincts still in high gear even after reprogramming the allowable IDs on her door lock and demanding a weapon from one of the guards outside.

She'd kept her identity a secret for five years with good reason. The empire and Ordoch, while not at all-out war, were still in a military conflict. The army could take her prisoner and use her as leverage any number of ways. As far as anyone on Ordoch knew, she was the last surviving member of the Reinumon family. The army could demand the Ordochians work on a cure for the TNV or they'd kill her. Or they could publicly execute her to show the Ordochians how serious they were about retaining power in Wyrd Space. Or they could torture her for any number of state secrets that could help them consolidate power on Ordoch.

No doubt they'd find other ways to use her as well.

Isonde had made her a symbol. More than that, she had made her a target. And if things went wrong? If anti-Wyrd sentiment continued to grow, went the way of the Low Divine? She had made her a martyr.

Malkor commed the door, breaking her out of her thoughts. When he entered, she couldn't tell from the look on his face who was more furious, him or her. It was a tight race for who could wring Isonde's neck first. Malkor had known her longer, he probably had dibs.

"Did you know?" Deep in her heart, she knew his answer, but she had to ask the question. "Did you know she planned to do that?"

Malkor shook his head. He seemed to have nothing to say and she felt the same. What was there to say about their new reality? *If I had known... If there had been a chance to stop it...* They hadn't and there wasn't. All that was left to be decided now was their next course of action.

"We have to get you out of here," Malkor said. "Somewhere safe, until I can secure you passage to Wyrd Space." Ah, defiance from Malkor. She liked it.

Unfortunately, acceptance was their only option.

"She's gone too far this time," he said, hands clenching into fists. "Kayla, I'm sorry."

"Isonde owes me that apology, not you. This was not your doing." An apology would never happen. Isonde might regret the "necessity" of revealing Kayla's identity, but Kayla doubted the woman regretted her actions, for doing what she thought was essential. "Besides, I can't leave anyway; she's made sure of that."

"How do you figure?"

Kayla sank down onto the nearest couch, drained from the midnight hour and the full weight of Isonde's betrayal. She slouched down, exhausted, and let her head fall back, her eyes close.

"She told the entire empire I was here to sign a possible treaty." Not that Kayla had the authority to do that. "If I disappear now, people will assume a peaceful withdrawal and Ordoch's help is off the table." She cracked an eyelid to look at him. "Not to mention if the only Wyrd in Imperial Space disappears right after the Low Divine is assassinated..."

Malkor cursed.

Kayla closed her eyes again. "My thoughts exactly."

20

THE *YARI*, MINE FIELD

The trip to the engine room from the commissary was surprisingly convoluted and tense. Apparently there was a more direct path from the landing bay to the main engine chamber, which is how they were able to get the parts through the ship. It was far out of the way from the commissary, though. Instead they traveled sparsely lit corridors and took turns climbing down ladders because the lifts weren't active in this section.

"Protocol," Ida had said, without her usual grin.

Vayne was getting a handle on the crew's strange syntax. *Either that or I'm getting closer to Ida's level of wackiness.* At least it made communication easier. They passed through several powered decks, Ida stopping at one point to declare the decks below that level off-limits. Something about safety and *stepa at es*. When they reached the engine room without incident, everyone seemed to breathe a little easier, though why remained a mystery to Vayne.

The bay doors opened to an immense cavern-like room so large it swallowed sound. Here great sheets of a gray material hid the molychromium ribs of the ship—heat and radiation shielding, possibly? The vastness of the room alone was impressive after the close confines of the rest of the *Yari*, but the engine itself demanded all of Vayne's attention.

About eighty percent of the massive hyperstream engine was stunning. Silver in color and ovoid in shape, it seemed to hang from the ceiling like a liquid pendant. All other hyperstream drives looked miniscule in comparison. Graceful struts secured the engine to the far walls and a series of plascrystal tubes extended in a radial fashion from its midsection. When the drive was powered, those tubes would carry the fuel to the drive and siphon off the waste byproduct into giant holding structures deeper in the ship.

The lowest twenty percent of the engine, however, looked like a child's craft project gone horribly wrong. The ovoid shape was unfinished, and bits of the original metal structure hung down like loose teeth. Attached at every odd angle was a conglomeration of parts in various sizes, shapes and colors, some battered, some shining like new, each of them foreign to the original structure and design.

He remembered the vids of how the engine should have looked when fully assembled. If memory served, the remaining necessary parts were supposed to be housed in the *Yari*'s storage bays. What had happened to those?

Ida grinned, looking like a pleased shadow panthe showing off her cub. "Is fantastically coming along, Gintoc." She turned to the party. "Fantastic, no?"

Gintoc grumbled. "Adding this... this..." he gestured to the lower part of the ship, "this *trash* to such a beauty... No right. No right." He wandered off toward the scaffolding built around the engine, muttering to himself.

::What about the original parts?:: Corinth asked, without taking his eyes off the thing.

"The parts lost to us," Ida said. "Some time before this time." She snapped her fingers. "Then we get contact with Ordoch and parts we are having now! Much progress, much progress."

Vayne narrowed his eyes at Ida. Somehow, even with all of her friendliness and apparent openness, he got the feeling that her often cryptic answers were more than "accidentally" evasive.

Ariel and Larsa arrived not long after, coming in from one

of the many other entrances to the engine room. They brought with them the hover cart full of parts that had come through the Tear with Cinni. Gintoc clucked and grumbled over each piece as it was unloaded, inspecting each, tilting it this way and that, alternatively shaking his head and nodding. Corinth wandered closer, clearly fascinated. He selected a piece Gintoc seemed to have discarded and Gintoc froze, eyes narrowed on the boy. Corinth must have said something to him. Vayne could only assume so, because a minute later Gintoc nodded again, completely at ease. They continued their silent communication as the parts were picked over and divided, completely ignoring everyone else.

Vayne interrupted the conversation between Tia'tan, Noar and Ida. "So this is it, this is your grand plan to save Ordoch: patch together a hyperstream drive that's as likely to go nova as it is to actually work, jump the frutt out of here and blast... something... with a weapon destined to do no less than tear the fabric of space apart?"

Ida chuckled like he'd said something funny. And wasn't the entire situation laughable? Unless of course, one happened to be standing in the engine room of such a ship, likely to go out in a ball of flames with the whole damn thing.

"And you don't even have the fuel to run it," he said, looking specifically at Tia'tan. "If the *Radiant* had survived the Mine Field, they would have been here by now." Tia'tan's lips tightened, looking angry at the statement. Vayne held up a hand to forestall Ida when she chimed in. "You know it's true," he said to Tia'tan. She held his gaze, refusing to admit it.

"Even if you could fix it," he went on, "even if you could fuel it and fly the *Yari* right out of here, what then?"

Cinni piped up. "The *Yari* would hold its own in a fight against imperial ships blockading the planet."

"Without using the Planetary Decimator?"

The girl didn't answer.

"Exactly." Idiots. All of them. Reckless idiots. "You can't fire the PD at ships anywhere near Ordoch. The thing has the targeting precision of a catapult—you stand as much chance of hitting the planet as you would hitting their ships." A fact they seemed to be ignoring.

"Then we don't take it to Ordoch." The engine room nearly swallowed Natali's husky voice, but he was attuned to every pained nuance of it. "We take it to *their* homeworld."

Tia'tan was the first to recover from the suggestion. "You're not talking about emancipation—you're talking about all-out war."

More like genocide.

From the corner of his eye, Vayne saw Natali nod once.

Noar frowned, obviously hating the idea. *Well that makes two of us, at least.*

Tia'tan cleared her throat in the awkward silence. "Ilmena hasn't decided what exactly—"

"What is there for Ilmena to decide?" Natali said. "This is an Ordochian ship. Crewed by full-blooded Ordochians, am I right?" All around them the *Yari*'s crew straightened, at attention now, with the exception of Gintoc. Natali pointed at Cinni. "Ordochians have taken the risk of bringing parts through the Tear."

The air between Tia'tan and Natali grew charged, each woman standing at full height, arms held loosely at their sides. "As far as I can tell," Natali said, "the Ilmenans failed at their only task—bringing fuel."

"There's no proof that the *Radiant* has been destroyed," Tia'tan snapped. "And if it has been, my people *died* for this ship." Noar put a hand on her arm. She shook him off. Tia'tan looked pretty pissed, but in a fight, Vayne would bet on Natali any day. Natali had been cut from the stone of prison after five years and was every bit the dangerous animal that he was. Maybe more so, because she at least cared about something: Ordoch.

Natali lifted her chin a fraction. Her low voice held an authority that couldn't be questioned. "As of this moment, the *Yari* is under my orders. Captain Janus will take any and all action that I deem necessary." She glanced around the room at everyone in turn, save him. "Is that clear?"

All eyes fell on Ida. Even Gintoc was paying attention now. The captain clicked her heels together, spine perfectly straight, and snapped off a crisp salute. "Yes, ma'am."

Natali nodded again, then turned her attention back to Tia'tan. "Make no mistake—we're already in an all-out war, and the imperials will pay for what they've done."

After the tense scene in the engine room, Ida declared their guests tired and bundled the Ilmenans and Ordochians off to crew quarters, where they were each given a room. With only six—or five point five, as Tanet had joked—crew members left, Vayne expected the rooms to be empty, possessions packed away.

Instead, everything had been left as it was when the occupant had lived, as if they might return any moment. Or, as if the crew couldn't quite accept that, even after all this time, these people really were gone.

Vayne took one look at his room and balked. Though sparsely outfitted, it had enough personal mementoes to give it an eerie, haunted feel. He lit out as soon as he could and headed for the observation deck, where he enjoyed two blissful hours of privacy.

The observation deck overlooked the diamond-bright impossibility of the Tear. His eyes were drawn again and again to that rending of space. He saw it behind his eyelids when he closed his eyes. As insane as it was, the existence of the Tear made about as much sense as anything else had today.

Someone entered the room and he knew immediately who had come looking for him. He took a subtle taste of her mind to confirm it.

Tia'tan.

She stopped some distance away as if uncertain of his mood, uncertain of her reception.

Fair enough. He had attacked her on her own ship and told

her off on more than one occasion. Which, she had coming. Even now he wanted to shake the shit out of her for getting him into this disaster. Willingly. Knowingly.

His ever-present, churning anger spiked.

Tut tut, Dolan whispered in his mind. *Mustn't be ill-mannered, now.*

"You son of a bitch," he growled in response, and was rewarded with a sharp intake of breath from Tia'tan.

Bah.

"Not you," Vayne said on a sigh, and turned to face her. "Sorry, my thoughts were somewhere else." Some time else.

"Mind if I sit a bit?" She gestured toward the comfortable chairs that had been dragged up to this observation deck from some other part of the ship. He looked at the chairs, back at her. Would "Yes, I mind" be too rude?

She probably heard his answer coming from a light-year away. Naturally, she sat in one of the chairs anyway. She looked at him, at the chair beside her, him again.

So. She hadn't idly wandered here, she'd come for a "talk." Vayne eyed the door. In reality, he had nowhere else to go.

"I'll stand, thanks," he said, and leaned back against the observation window. "I'll save you some breath: you've come to ask if I agree with Natali or not."

She tilted her head to look at him and her long lavender bangs fell over one eye. She tucked them back behind her ear. "Partly. Mostly I came to see how you were doing. With the number of surprises hitting you since we dropped into the Mine Field…"

That moment felt like it had happened a month ago. What had it been, a day? Two? He should probably attempt the impossible: sleep.

Tia'tan looked concerned. Genuine concern, or a calculated concern meant to lull him into some sort of friendship? Would he ever be able to trust in the authenticity of another's emotions ever again?

Unlikely.

And really, not even necessary. All he wanted was peace. A place to live quietly, away from everything. Ilmena would do. It wasn't home, but it also wasn't occupied by imperials or harboring an underground rebellion.

Three months ago he wouldn't have wasted any energy dreaming about such a place. Now, he'd fight with everything he had to get there.

"I'm pretty sure you can guess how I'm doing," he said, "or at least the beginnings of it."

Tia'tan nodded. "Corinth, at least, seems pleased to be here."

"Make no mistake. While the kid is fascinated by all things tech, the only place he wants to be is with my *ro'haar*." And she should be here. With them.

"At least he has you."

That wasn't even worth a response.

Silence fell, Tia'tan looking at him with concerned lavender eyes that made him feel unaccountably guilty.

Her voice softened when she spoke again. "I never meant to bring you here, you know."

He arched a brow. "Then what the void are we doing in the Middle of Nowhere?"

She shifted in her seat, seeking a more comfortable spot. "When we hadn't heard from the *Radiant* in so long, I had to investigate. I only meant for us to stop outside the Mine Field and hail them, I didn't plan on getting ripped out of stream and deposited mid-field."

"Happens to fifty percent of hyperstreams anywhere near the area, Corinth said."

"Yeah, well, our stream drive is more efficient, I thought we'd be fine."

"Clearly, that was not the case." Now he was trapped on an ancient battleship with a crazy crew and other insane Wyrds with a thirst for genocide. "What's so important about the *Radiant* that you risked coming here at all?"

"The rebels on Ordoch can't scavenge the massive amount of fuel the *Yari* will need. And even if they could, it would take forever to transport it through the Tear, considering that's only slightly larger than a person. We need the fuel the *Radiant* is carrying."

"Frutt that," Malkor said. "You had a mission—rescue any POWs and get them to Ilmena. You detoured, putting us all at risk."

Tia'tan let out a quiet breath. "It's Kazamel. He's head of security on the *Radiant*. He's... an old friend, from a while back." Tia'tan shrugged.

For once Vayne felt in sympathy with her. He knew too well the pain that fear for the life of a loved one caused, how the uncertainty ate at you. Some of his resentment bled off as understanding.

"And now we're here," she said, gaze going to the observation deck's windows.

Damn.

It was easier to stay furious when he'd thought her obstinately reckless.

She finally brought her gaze back to him. "You're right about the other reason I sought you, to ask about Natali."

Vayne tensed, every muscle tightening in response to his sister's name. "Yeah?"

"Was she always so... intense?"

Vayne crossed his arms over his chest. "Before she was tortured for five years, you mean?"

Tia'tan flinched, as if she'd forgotten. "I mean— She's..."

He waited while she floundered.

Tia'tan finally decided on, "She came on a little strong."

Everything about Natali was strong. Only he knew what it took to break her.

And of course, me, Dolan whispered. Bile rose to the back of Vayne's throat as his stomach lurched. He coughed, but he couldn't clear the pain away, the taste of it.

"You okay?" Tia'tan asked.

Not remotely. "As for coming on strong, rightful rulers bent on reclaiming their homeworld will do that."

A frown line appeared between Tia'tan's brows. "She's bent on a little more than that."

Vayne shrugged. "That's her prerogative." And he washed his hands of it.

Tia'tan looked less than pleased with his answer. "You're her brother; you could counsel her to temperance."

"Whatever thoughts you're having in that brain right now, stop. I won't 'counsel' Natali. I won't gainsay her and I won't start a conflict. If she wants to blast the entire empire to bits, she's welcome to. In fact, I might cheer her on."

Tia'tan got to her feet, taking a balanced stance—hands loose, shoulders relaxed, eyes up—an excellent ready position that Natali had taught him to identify, back when she used to train him in the early days of their captivity. A stance ready to make a move. "The rebels on Ordoch have been working *with* Ilmena's help," Tia'tan said. "Mutual cooperation."

Vayne shifted off the window to match her stance. "You can't have it both ways. You can't bring in the royal family as a rallying point for the rebellion and not expect them to take control as the rightful rulers."

"'Them?'" Her tone was challenging. "Are you not one of 'them?'"

He shook his head definitively. "Not anymore."

The tension grew between them. Thankfully Noar and Corinth entered the observation deck, ending the conversation.

"The drive's coming along surprisingly well," Noar said, ignoring the undercurrent of conflict in the room. "If the Ordochians are able to get the right parts to us, we might actually be able to complete it."

It was that kind of thinking that scared the shit out of Vayne. "No way I am sticking around for that. We need to get out of here now, before the crew fires this thing up and blows themselves to bits." Seeing Corinth's serious little face made it doubly important they leave. Kayla hadn't spent five years of her life protecting Corinth to have him killed after a few weeks in Vayne's care.

"And how do you propose we leave?" Tia'tan asked, a bite to her voice. "The hyperstream drive on the *Sicerro* is shot to shit and we can't risk flying through the Mine Field again and encountering rooks."

"We could always step through the Tear to Ordoch," Noar offered.

"Absolutely not," Vayne said. He refused to strand himself in the middle of a rebellion. Corinth's eyes glinted, and Vayne stabbed a finger at him. "You aren't to either."

Tia'tan spread her empty hands. "Then...?"

::Kayla.:: Everyone looked at Corinth. ::Kayla will come for us.::

If only. "She doesn't even know where we are. She thinks we're safe on our way to Ilmena."

Corinth shrugged. ::Then we tell her.::

"If there was a way to get a signal through the field, the crew would have done it long ago," Tia'tan said. "The only reason they can contact Ordoch is because the signal goes through the Tear that opens on Ordoch."

::Our sensor emitter tech is five hundred years newer than the *Yari*'s. We've made major improvements.::

Noar's speculative look lifted Vayne's hopes.

"You're talking about using the sensor array from the *Sicerro*," Noar said, and Corinth nodded. "What about the signal interference from the field? Our sensors were scrambled after a short distance."

"And didn't that make fleeing from the rooks a real party," Vayne said.

::We'll dismantle the array, and send the sensors out into the Mine Field. They're tiny enough they shouldn't draw the rooks.:: Vayne could see the idea shaping in Corinth's mind, the boy's focused excitement as his brain jumped steps ahead. ::The first one will only go as far into the field as it can while still having a connection with the ship. Then the next will maintain a link to the first and go out into the field that same distance, then the next and the next, and we'll make a line of sensors heading to the edge of the field. Once beyond that, we'll be able to broadcast a message back to Falanar.:: He grinned, and looked two seconds from doing that slap-clap thing Ida did with her hands when she was excited.

Noar was nodding. "It could work. As far as each sensor determining distance and driving itself—"

::We'll use the guidance array from the weapons system, pair a targeting link with each emitter.::

Vayne took a step toward Corinth, stopped short of touching him. He knelt down so he was on eye level with his brother. "Can you do this?"

Corinth looked at Noar, and they shrugged simultaneously.

"Worth a try," Noar said.

Corinth reached out and laid a gentle hand on Vayne's shoulder, as if he were the elder brother, comforting the younger. ::Kayla will come when she knows we need her. Trust me.::

Tia'tan started, "If she could bring the fuel for the *Yari*…"

Vayne shot her a look, then got to his feet and followed Corinth and Noar from the room.

21

IDC HEADQUARTERS, FALANAR

Sunrise battled the city's haze for dominance as Malkor strode into IDC headquarters on his day off. Not that a man embroiled in Isonde's schemes and investigating an interagency conspiracy really had days off, but, it sounded nice.

The quiet of the building at this early hour gave the impression that all was well, that the empire wasn't rapidly headed toward crisis. The TNV, Wei-lu-Wei, an IDC-army collusion, the assassination of the Low Divine… Yeah, days off were a luxury he couldn't afford.

His two complinks booted and he saw Carsov's report on the Trebulan-TNV situation waiting for him as a secure download on his non-networked drive. He breathed a silent sigh of thanks that Carsov had come through. Malkor collected the file and brooded over it as he ate his oatmeal.

Carsov was as good as his word. Every detail, every finding was in there, nothing redacted, nothing held back.

It wasn't pretty.

After an hour of looking it over, Malkor called together the octet members he could reach. Day off or not, within a half-hour Hekkar, Rigger, Trinan and Vid were on their way to his office. Aronse was away with her family for a long weekend and Gio was handling some "personal business." Malkor didn't begrudge them the time off; they'd been overworked since the start of the Empress Game. Besides, this wasn't exactly an "official" IDC investigation he was inviting them to.

Rigger had the empire's largest mug of coffee in one hand and a stack of datapads in the other as she shouldered her way through the door first. She was oddly bright-eyed for someone who probably hadn't slept in days, with both IDC work and Dolan's scientific data to deal with. Typical Rigger, burning it at both ends.

Hekkar arrived next, his bright red-orange hair still wet from a shower. "Little early, isn't it, Malk?"

"You expect me to believe you've even been to bed yet?"

Hekkar grinned. "True." He commandeered the chair closest to Malkor's desk and sprawled into it, legs straight out in front of him, ankles crossed, arms behind his head. "I'd forgotten what it was like to have a night off—and a morning to sleep in."

Trinan and Vid arrived right after that, the two giants looking as well-rested and relaxed as he'd seen them in a month.

Guilt hit Malkor in the gut. His team should have had a day off.

"How's the physical therapy going?" he asked Vid, instead.

Vid flexed his shoulder, rotating it without a flinch. "Good as new; I'm ready for active duty." Trinan didn't look convinced. Considering the burns and tissue damage Vid had taken a while back, when Janeen kidnapped Corinth, the man was healing with the speed of an adolescent.

"Glad to hear that," Malkor said. "I still demand Toble's okay, first."

"I said the same thing, boss," Trinan said, cuffing Vid on his good shoulder as they both took a seat.

For one minute, Malkor was thrown back to another world—was it only months ago they'd headed to Altair Tri to find Shadow Panthe, aka Kayla? Before they'd all gone quasi-rogue, a dedicated team member had betrayed them, and they'd changed the fate of the empire with the outcome of the Empress Game.

They'd done their jobs back then—shit, they'd *liked* their jobs—and they'd known who they were working for.

Now…

Rigger ribbed Hekkar good-naturedly about his busy night/morning in the Pleasure District while they all got settled in. Within a minute they were down to business. Before they could get their datapads out and styluses in hand, Malkor cleared his throat.

"This is going to be an ears-only briefing."

Eyebrows rose. Hekkar gestured to the door. "Gio and Aronse?"

Malkor shook his head. "Busy."

"So this is an unofficial, 'we were never here' briefing?"

Vid chuckled. "My favorite kind. Lay it out for us, boss."

"So," Malkor started, glancing at his complink display, then back at the group. "Sergeant Carsov came through with his official version of the investigation into who supplied Prince Trebulan with the TNV."

"And?" Hekkar asked. Rigger set her stack of datapads on the floor beside her chair and took a serious gulp of her coffee.

"It's not as straightforward as I'd like." Of course it wasn't. If tracking this info down was easy, Senior Commander Vega, her fellow IDC conspirators and whoever they were allied with in the army would have long ago been busted. "Here's what Carsov's got:

"Trebulan was in possession of two canisters of TNV, the one he brought to the wedding and the one stashed in a hideout in Shimville. Both were regulation biomech isolation canisters used by the army's Biomech Containment teams, as well as various medical and research centers. Carsov's team traced the serial numbers of the canisters—they were issued to the army. Those specific canisters were part of a batch of supplies on one of the army's ships, a ship that carried biomech teams to Thu Tal to help with TNV quarantine there.

"As per mission reports from that trip, no samples of TNV were collected at that time, and no samples were logged in upon return. During a resupply of the ship afterward, the quartermaster discovered the inventory was missing one batch of collection canisters, fifty in all. It was written off as 'ruined supplies, destroyed without proper paperwork.'"

Hekkar whistled low. "Wow. The army collecting and storing TNV samples off the record?"

"Was he able to locate the other forty-eight canisters?" Rigger asked. "Talk about a nightmare, forty-eight unaccounted-for canisters, all possibly full of TNV."

Malkor shook his head. "Not at this time, and the investigation has since been closed."

The impact of what was out there, in who-knew-whose hands, silenced the room.

"That's lunacy," Vid said, pretty much echoing Malkor's thoughts since he first read the report. "How does this info help us with what's going down inside the IDC?"

"Carsov's team pulled every available source of surveillance for the area and was able to put Siño in Shimville, entering the same warehouse two days before Trebulan's attack, carrying the same case the second canister was later discovered in."

"Siño?" Rigger said. "Bredard's pet biocybe?"

"Exactly."

Vid swore. "You should have ended those two at the information drop."

"Bredard's a middle man. Taking him out doesn't solve the problem."

"What's the final consensus on Carsov's report?" Trinan asked.

Malkor scanned Carsov's summary of findings at the end of the file. "Basically, this proves the army is collecting TNV illegally, and trading it to people to use as a weapon. It also proves that Siño and Bredard—imperial citizens, *not* Wyrds—provided Trebulan with the TNV for the attack." Thank the stars. This was a much needed political weapon right now. "He wasn't able to get any farther with Bredard, but..."

"But we have evidence that links Bredard to Senior

Commander Vega, among others in the IDC," Hekkar finished. That was intel Parrel had been able to discover. Hekkar crossed his arms over his chest, face going hard. "So our crazy conspiracy theory is correct—IDC leaders and rogue elements in the army are working together, *against* the best interests of the empire." He shook his head. "Shit."

"Remember when this job was simple?" Trinan asked.

Vid barked out a laugh. "Being an IDC agent has never been simple." That brought nods all around.

Rigger jumped into the silence. "What's our next move?"

Everyone looked at Malkor. What the void *was* their next move? "Honestly, I haven't gotten that far yet. I'll have to speak with Commander Parrel. Thoughts, first?"

"This puts us in an impossible situation," Hekkar replied. "Anti-Wyrd sentiment is rising, even with Isonde announcing that Kayla is here as an emissary of peace. If it tips to the boiling point, the Council of Seven will have no choice but to increase the military presence on Ordoch, which is a waste of resources we need at home."

"Not to mention likely to be ineffective," Trinan added.

Hekkar nodded, running a hand through his tousled hair. "On the other hand, if we let the people know who's really behind Trebulan's TNV attack—and likely the assassination of the Low Divine—the empire will be in major upheaval."

"We can't *begin* to predict the fallout from revealing a conspiracy within the IDC to grab more power," Vid said. The big man tapped his finger unconsciously atop his knee as he thought. "It could bring the entire agency down, and then what would happen to the empire?"

Rigger leaned forward with a shake of her head. "We can't sit on this, it's too big."

"How can we even think of letting the truth out, though?" Trinan countered. "What happens to the army if it gets out that they're storing rogue samples of the TNV and giving it to terrorists? If we dismantle the army, or sideline them while a huge investigation is undertaken, who's going to help quarantine

Wei-lu-Wei and get the situation under control there?"

"There's no controlling the TNV," Malkor said, "not once it gets its teeth into a planet." The best they could do was hope to slow the spread.

The room fell into quiet, each octet member spinning ideas in their heads, looking at the problem from all angles no doubt.

Malkor gestured to Rigger's stack of datapads. "What else did you bring to the party?"

"Hmm? Oh! Yeah, hang on."

"Do you ever sleep, Rigger?" Vid asked.

"Sleep is for the weak, like you guys." She grinned and dug the datapads out from under her chair. "Okay, I've got updates from going through more of Dolan's data."

Yup, she definitely never slept. Thank the stars for Rigger.

She handed Malkor a datapad. "These files are amazing. The amount of advanced tech discussed—weapons, ship design, neurological studies—in the right hands, this data could do a lot of good."

The right hands. Whose hands were those? He wasn't sure he knew anymore.

"I've had your medic friend, Toble, look over Dolan's neurological notes," she said, after another sip of coffee.

"Toble's a generalist, not a neurologist by any means," Malkor said.

"True, but he could make better sense of Dolan's notes than I could, especially when he delved into the latest imperial research on the brain." Rigger glanced at the top datapad in her stack. "Apparently Dolan discovered an area of the brain of imperials analogous to the cartaid arch in Wyrds—the structure responsible for psionic powers. There's a *lot* neither of us could follow. It *seems* Dolan believed he could give imperials psi powers much in the same way he'd been harvesting psi powers from the Ordochian prisoners to reestablish his own."

The words sucked the air from the room.

Malkor was the first to recover. "Imperials with psi powers? That would be a whole new era."

Vid waved that away, still tapping on his knee. "Not possible. Dolan's machine, which I'm assuming is necessary for this process, was destroyed when Kayla and Vayne busted their asses out of his facility."

"Along with most of the building," Trinan added. "Vayne barely left it standing." And none of Dolan's people had made it out alive. No one mentioned that fact.

"The specs to build another one *are* in the data file," Rigger said.

"Yeah," Hekkar said, "but they'd need Wyrds to harvest."

Malkor nodded. "Which would partially explain the IDC cabal's plan to stoke anti-Wyrd sentiment and increase the military presence on Ordoch. On top of needing Wyrds to harvest psi powers from, they'd need Wyrds to train any imperial who received the psi powers. Kayla said mind-control was a high-level skill, it could take a lifetime to learn."

"Moot point," Vid argued. "*We've* got the specs to the machine, not Vega, and *we* certainly aren't building it."

Hekkar made eye contact with Malkor, and Malkor knew exactly what he was thinking before he said it. "We should destroy the files."

Kayla would heartily agree. Rigger argued against it.

"At least the schematics for the Influencer," Hekkar continued. "No good can come of those."

"I'm in," Vid said.

"Same," Trinan agreed.

Malkor scrubbed a hand across his face. They were right, and it would put Kayla's mind at ease. Was that their call to make?

"You know the justifications Vega would use, Malk." Hekkar's voice held quiet certainty. "They'd say the opportunity to give imperials psi powers is essential to our evolution, that there's no harm in harvesting the Wyrds' powers because they could regrow them. You asked for our opinion—that's mine."

Parrel is sure going to love hearing from me about all of this, Malkor thought, not looking forward to the upcoming meeting with his superior at all.

* * *

By mid-afternoon, Kayla had had all the stewing she could handle. She hadn't talked to Isonde since the press conference the night before—which had been for the best. Even now she was trying to decide if it would be better to talk her feelings out, or just strangle Isonde.

Option two was definitely leading the race.

Kayla checked her reflection in the mirror of her room. Knee-high black boots, grey leggings, tight-fitting violet tunic that wouldn't hamper movement, and her kris daggers. Frutt palace security. Now that her identity was out, she'd wear them everywhere she went. The best part of her outfit? Her hair.

Some time in the middle of a sleepless night she'd accepted the reality that she couldn't hide any longer, her secret was out. Despite the new pressures that brought, it freed her from the burden of burying herself beneath a mask. The first thing she did was remove the black appliqué from her brows, lashes, and long blue hair. Now she wore her hair unbound, admiring it. It was the sky's last blue after sunset, as the first evening stars came out.

And it was the most beautiful sight since she'd seen Vayne, alive, after five years.

Am I being vain? You betcha. And damn if it didn't feel great, for one minute, to indulge.

She. Was. Wyrd.

Or, she would be, if she had her psi powers back.

The tiny moment of happiness vanished, escaped like air from a deflating balloon. The emptiness where her powers should be still mocked her. She'd had more than one nightmare where she was back in the chair in Dolan's laboratory, watching the *kin'shaa* torture Vayne while she scrambled with mental fingers against the glass that had sealed off that portion of her mind.

"Frutt you, Dolan. Frutt you."

Kayla squared her shoulders at her reflection. Psi powers

or not, she had protected Corinth for five terrible years. She would find her brothers again and be the best damn *ro'haar* the Wyrd Worlds had ever seen.

Once she got the void off this planet.

With that thought firmly in mind, she exited her rooms and demanded her royal bodyguards lead her to the apartments that Isonde and Ardin now shared. When they balked at traveling to the royal couple's suite without an express invitation, she headed off on her own, making it exactly one step before they agreed to escort her there. Apparently being a Wyrd princess was as intimidating as being Princess Isonde in these parts.

Good.

As much as Kayla hated being confined, it made sense to house her in the palace. She was officially under the protection of Ardin and Isonde, and no one, not the army or the IDC, could remove her without royal permission.

When they reached the apartments, a servant answered the door chime. One of Kayla's guards politely asked if Isonde was available, while two of Ardin's guards assessed them from beside the door. The servant started with a polite, "Not at this time, I'm af—" and so Kayla brushed by her and into the apartment, all four guards rushing behind her. A jumble of arguments and objections trailed in her wake.

"Isonde?" Kayla called.

"In here, Kayla," Isonde answered, from somewhere down the corridor. The suite that housed Ardin and Isonde seemed to be absolutely enormous. She wouldn't have had a chance of finding Isonde if the princess hadn't been in one of the closest sitting rooms and heard her bust in.

Isonde appeared in an arched doorway halfway down the hallway, an amused grin on her face as she took in the scene. "You can all wait outside," she said to the guards, "I'll be perfectly fine with the princess." The men stopped. Trying to decide if they could take orders from Isonde now that she was Ardin's wife? Debating if they needed to hear it from Ardin himself?

Isonde turned away, clearly dismissing them. She bestowed

a smile on the flustered servant. "Leela, thank you for being so diligent. Princess Kayla is welcome to visit anytime I am at home. Understood?" Leela nodded wordlessly. "Perhaps you could bring us some refreshments?" Leela nodded again and headed off down the hall, looking relieved to have something to do.

Isonde chuckled after the girl left. "It's a bit of an adjustment, I'm afraid, my being here in Ardin's suite." She gave Kayla a "you know how it is" smile. Kayla's bland expression must have translated well because Isonde's smile shrank. She gestured to the open door of the sitting room. "Come on in."

The vidscreen on one wall showed a dual display, right side running a feed from Falanar's main news outfit on mute, the left showing a recording from one of the Sovereign Council sessions Kayla attended while Isonde was still incapacitated. Archon Raorin was delivering a blistering speech about the abuses of power.

"One of his best in a while, I'd say." Isonde gestured toward the screen before muting it. That was Isonde, always working, always preparing, always scheming.

Isonde sank gracefully onto a chair situated outside the rays of sunlight that streamed through double-height windows and pooled on the floor at her feet. Tiny skylights high above, cut into stars and filled with birefringence gel, sparkled like diamonds under a gemologist's lamp. Rainbows fractured and hit the walls in a thousand places. It was a cozy room, a room for shared confidences and secrets. The intimate setting only served to darken Kayla's mood.

Kayla perched on the arm of a burgundy settee, one foot on the floor, one swinging as if she were at ease. Isonde's gaze raked over her from boot tip to kris to flowing blue hair, approval in her eyes. No doubt she was pleased to see Kayla reclaim her heritage. She had probably already ordered Kayla a dozen dresses more in line with Ordochian fashion

Presume much?

Of course she did.

Isonde crossed a leg over the other beneath an ivory gown that looked spun from clouds. "So," she said.

Kayla's ire spiked. "So?" she snapped. "So? You reveal my identity to the entire empire—without warning, without my consent—and all you have to say afterward is 'so?'"

A chime at the door halted any reply. Leela entered with a platter full of a variety of finger sandwiches, delicate mugs of some steaming red beverage and two heavily frosted pastries. For one second Kayla imagined upending the entire tray in a spray of red liquid, sugar and violence. Instead she sat still, fingers clenched in her lap, holding her temper.

Five years as a pit whore had tarnished her royal manners. Luckily for her, months of acting as Isonde had polished them to a high gleam again. She inclined her head in thanks until the servant curtsied and left the room.

Isonde reached for a cup of whatever sort of drink it was. As she smiled in appreciation of the beverage, her image split in Kayla's mind. Two women sat before her. One, the woman who had spoken to Kayla as an ally, if not quite a friend, about how they could work together to bring about a peaceful withdrawal from Ordoch. The other Isonde was a woman willing to do anything, use anyone, to her own ends.

Were there really two sides to Isonde, or had Kayla been deceived all this time?

"That was not your secret to tell," Kayla said. "I had kept my identity hidden for five long years with good reason."

Isonde inclined her head in acknowledgement. "I'm sorry, Kayla, it had to be done."

"Had to be done?" Kayla scoffed. "No one held a knife to your throat."

"Anti-Wyrd sentiment is rising, which hurts our cause. I need you to be a tragic figure that proponents for peace can rally around." Isonde said it so matter-of-factly, as if anyone in her position would come to the same conclusion, but there was an apology in her eyes. "I didn't warn you because you wouldn't have agreed."

Of course she wouldn't have. Even now Kayla debated demanding Malkor find her a way to the Mine Field to search for her brothers, despite knowing the damage her disappearance at this crucial point would do.

In a softer voice, Kayla asked, "Haven't you used me enough?"

Isonde closed her eyes, looking pained by the question, looking almost human for a moment. What regrets went through the mind of such a dedicated woman when she lay awake at night?

Isonde took a deep breath and opened her eyes, the moment of weakness gone. "I'm sorry that you have suffered, that your people continue to suffer. What Ordoch is going through is nothing compared to the devastation wrought by the TNV, though. Not even close.

"I need you to understand that I will do *everything* in my power to find a cure for the TNV to save the empire. To save *my* people. Right now that means using you as a rallying point and trying to convince the Council of Seven to withdraw from Ordoch.

"Whatever becomes necessary in the future, I will *also* do. There is no price I won't pay to see this plague halted." Isonde's clear blue eyes were without doubt, without hesitation.

This, Kayla knew, was the heart of who Isonde was. These words were truer than her marriage vows. As real as Kayla's dedication to Vayne.

I can't stay.

Isonde would use her up, bleed her dry in pursuit of her cause. Kayla realized that now. There would never be a day when Isonde was finished with her.

Kayla felt a momentary sympathy for Ardin, who had married a woman who could never love him as much as she loved her people.

"This will work," Isonde said, setting down her cup. "With you as a figurehead, we can get the votes we need."

"With so many moving parts in your government, how can you be certain?"

Isonde shrugged. "I know of no other way to be." She leaned forward, and Kayla sensed she was shifting gears, going from "we need to have a chat" mode to "let's talk battle strategy" mode.

An image on the vidscreen behind Isonde caught Kayla's eye.

Someone in imperial army dress was giving a speech from the steps of *her home*, from the front steps of her family's seat on Ordoch. Kayla scrambled for the controls, hitting the volume on the news feed and reversing it to the beginning of the story. Isonde turned to see what had caught her attention.

"Breaking news from Ordoch: Wyrd terrorists recently broke into the home of engineer Hephesta Purl. Hephesta was murdered while asleep in her own bed, shot point-blank in the chest. Hephesta, a Wyrd engineer specializing in neural robotics, was said to have begun cooperating with army scientists to develop a cure for the TNV. The suspect in the murder case has been identified as Cinni Purl, the woman's own daughter."

The screen flashed back to a news studio, where two "experts" were clearly ready to dissect this new development.

"Mr. Srih," the newscaster asked, "with this latest, shocking evidence of the Wyrds' refusal to aid the humanitarian cause of stopping the TNV, can Wyrd Princess Kayla Reinumon's pleas for peace be considered at all credible?"

"Terrorists?" Kayla's grip on the control piece tightened until the organoplastic casing cracked. "Fighting for freedom on our *own* planet and they dare call us terrorists?"

"It's all spin—"

"Don't." Kayla cut her off with a slash of her hand. "Don't you *dare* say another word to me." She pointed the broken controller at Isonde's heart. "*You* started this, you voted for the occupation." Kayla forced herself to set the controller down very precisely. It was that or wing it at the vidscreen, which felt too much like a temper tantrum.

Kayla took a last disgusted look at Isonde, then headed for the door. "How's your Wyrd-princess-puppet's sympathy rating now?" she asked, and stalked off.

Malkor tucked a datapad in his pocket and exited his office at IDC headquarters. He had one more stop to make before finishing at HQ for the day—the detention cells in the sub-basement.

He tapped his fingers along his thigh as he walked down the hall to the lift at the end. His brain churned over the meetings of earlier, first with his team, then with Parrel. Even with plenty of intel, he still felt like he was trying to assemble a jigsaw puzzle in the dark, with several pieces out of reach. About as productive as banging his head against the wall would have been.

They knew *some* of the guilty parties.

They knew *some* of the reasons why.

They had *some* of the proof.

Malkor jabbed the button to send the lift to IDC's sub-basement level. Parrel's information led them to believe Senior Commander Jersain Vega was the lynch pin, and Malkor trusted Parrel's intel was good. Without a doubt, Vega and her allies needed to be brought down. How to prove their duplicity and illegal activities to the Council of Seven? How to convict them of crimes without destroying the IDC?

"We wait," Parrel had said. "We need more evidence. I don't want to go off half-cocked and bring a shit-storm down on our heads."

Of course Parrel was right to be cautious, of course they wanted irrefutable evidence.

Malkor had had enough of waiting, though. Waiting wouldn't have gotten him Carsov's files, and waiting wasn't going to help him sink Vega and everyone else responsible for terrorist activities blamed on the Wyrds.

The lift hit the bottom and the doors hissed open on stale air. Frutt waiting, it was time for some action.

He checked in at the guard station, got directions to the prisoner, and headed into the I-shaped block of detainment cells. She was in the farthest one on the left, with an empty cell across from her and beside her.

Agent Janeen Nuagyn.

One-time member of his octet, one-time friend. Someone he had trusted, depended on, someone he had liked and respected.

Someone who had betrayed him.

He looked through the one-way field at Janeen, studying her in her four-by-four-meter cell. She sat on her bed, knees to chest, arms around her legs, back against the wall, staring at nothing. She was familiar and foreign and as much as he hated her and what she'd done, he missed who he'd thought she was.

Shit. He hadn't expected the betrayal to hurt all over again.

He palmed the control on the wall beside her cell and the one-way field became translucent, letting her see out, letting her see him.

She bolted upright, feet flat on the floor, back straight. "Sir!" The word was out of her mouth probably before she even realized it. The twist of her lips said she never meant to let that slip. For a minute they stared at each other, old memories crowding close. She'd saved his life once. He'd saved hers. He'd gone to her sister's wedding. She'd gone to his dad's funeral.

He could still remember the day he approached her with an offer to join his octet. The look of surprise on her face then resembled today's wide-eyed stare.

"I didn't think you'd come," she finally said. She relaxed, still sitting on the bed, leaning her back against the wall. He could tell the ease was feigned.

Malkor didn't have it in himself to pretend to be emotionless.

"Isonde's alive," he said.

Janeen closed her eyes for a second, a word of thanks shaping her lips. "No one would tell me."

"She recovered from your attack. Married Ardin yesterday."

"That's good."

Why was he telling her this? His words seemed to bring her some peace, and that was the last thing Janeen deserved.

"I have questions." He pulled the datapad from his

pocket and thumbed through the files he had open. They were all secondary mission reports Janeen had sent to her handler, covert ops she had completed illegally while on legit assignments with Malkor's octet.

Her gaze narrowed on the tablet. "Of course you do. I've told Commander Parrel all I intend to say."

"The only thing you told him was the formula for the toxin you injected into Kayla and Isonde." And if that was the only thing she would ever tell them, he could live with it. That formula had saved Isonde's life. Still, he had to try. He needed more dirt on Vega and her cabal, and Janeen had answers.

"Yup," she said. "So you can take your questions and that oh-so-disappointed look in your eyes back to your office and leave me alone." She turned her head away, lips tight.

"Janeen." She wouldn't look at him. This whole visit reeked of futility, but now that he was here, he found he couldn't walk away. "You were a good agent. A damn good agent."

"So good that both sides of the IDC recruited me," she said, with a touch of self-mockery. "Do you know, when I first enrolled in the academy I was so full of self-righteousness about IDC's mission that if you'd struck a match near me, I would have burned like a sun with it." There was more than a touch of mockery now. "Almost as full of it as you still are." She tilted her head to look at him. "You're a fool, you know that?"

He shrugged. "Maybe." He was fighting his own people for the future of the agency, grabbing at phantoms, chasing rumors.

Suddenly, the words he hadn't known he'd come here to say tumbled out of his mouth. "Why did you do it? Why did you join the other side?"

Janeen blinked at the question. Blinked again. "In all his visits, Parrel never once asked me that. I guess it didn't matter to him, once I'd defected."

"It matters to me." Did it? Honestly, he wasn't even sure. It seemed to matter to her, though, he could see from the

sudden interest in her gaze. If he could use that to reach her...
"So tell me."

She shrugged. "I didn't choose the other side. At least, not intentionally." Malkor waited in silence while she sorted her words in her head. "It started in the academy. One of my teachers presented me with a 'special assignment' for 'enrichment,' because I was such a promising cadet." She laughed. "Frutt. I was so stupid then."

Memories seemed to pull her under. Her eyes shuttered, looking inward. "I was thrilled when Vega took a special interest in me. I thought, 'My career in the IDC will be fast-tracked.' All my special assignments, enrichment reports, field recon, character assessments... I assumed they were training." She bumped her head lightly against the wall behind her as if to shake loose her past. "By the time I started to put it all together, all the cloak and dagger bullshit, it was too late. I was in too deep."

In too deep. Exactly how Malkor felt, how he'd felt ever since Isonde had asked him to help her fix the Empress Game, ever since he'd learned the truth about a conspiracy within the IDC.

Is that how my whole octet feels? Have I dragged them under with me?

Malkor stowed the question for another time—he couldn't deal with that truth now.

"Help me, then," he said. "Give me the names of everyone you reported to. Who wanted what, when. Details." When she didn't answer he pressed forward. "It won't get you out of this cell, but—"

"No way you're about to give me the 'but it could set you free' speech, boss."

"Would it work?"

Janeen made a sound of disgust even as her eyes told a different story.

Malkor slipped the datapad back in his pocket and grabbed his mobile comm. The message he wanted was weeks old, but he knew exactly where to find it. He'd listened to it over and over, kicking himself each time. He should have been there, he should have done... something. That guilt still rode him even though Vid was recovering and Corinth had been rescued without injury.

Malkor held the comm out and hit play:

"*I'm sorry about Vid, I really am. If he'd just given up the kid none of this would have happened. Frutt!*" Janeen took a shaky breath in the recording. "*I never wanted any of this.*"

It was Janeen's message to him right after she'd kidnapped Corinth, nearly killing Vid in the process. There was more, but that was all he needed. Her eyes locked on the mobile comm, face pale, lips bloodless.

"Do you want to hear it again?" He went to hit play and she shook her head.

"Please don't." Her gaze never broke from the mobile comm, as if a voice from the dead had issued forth from it.

Malkor shook the comm at her. "*This* is who you are. A teammate, someone who cares about her friends." He hit play again.

"*I never wanted any of this.*"

She closed her eyes.

"You've made choices in the past that put you here, in this cell. And you deserve to be here." Her head dipped to hang a little lower. "This doesn't have to be the end of your work for the IDC. Make a new choice." Malkor strode forward until he was right against the energy field fronting her cell.

"Janeen." He waited until she opened her eyes, looked at him. "Choose to help."

"Gods, Malkor—" She stared at her hands clenched in her lap. Her fingers curled so tightly that she was likely bloodying her palms with her nails. After an eternity, her shoulders slumped. She blew out a breath. Another. Her hands unfurled.

"If I promise to help," she said, "will you cut it out with the emotional crap?" She half-laughed, half-hiccupped, and looked at him with damp eyes. "I don't think I can take it."

Malkor actually laughed, surprising himself. "Shit. Me neither."

She gestured to his pocket with the datapad. "Let's get this over with, I get chow in an hour and they serve a mean steak-umm here."

She always could make him laugh. *Damn you, Janeen*, he thought sadly to himself.

"Thank you," he said. "And, Janeen? Vid's fine. Healing like a sixteen-year-old."

One tear landed on her cheek, and they both pretended not to notice.

22

ORDOCH

Cinni sighed with relief when she stepped out of the Tear where it ended underground on Ordoch. She struggled to shake off the specter of death that clung to her. The destabilizing Tear threatened to take her life on every trip, and each return was a triumph.

Finding the Tear itself had been a triumph, and an extremely lucky one, at that.

Or perhaps *insanely* lucky was more accurate.

The rebels, by necessity, had gathered around the outskirts of modernized Ordoch, in buildings large enough to provide protection while still run-down enough to avoid extra patrols by the imperial usurpers. It was the rebels' reliance on such structural heaps that allowed them to catch the faint comm signature that had come from the *Yari* through the Tear. The Tear had formed a cavern underground, dissolving reality and carving its own open space beneath an old building. The *Yari*'s distress call issued forth quietly, and the rebellion had heard it.

It had taken three months to tunnel down to the Tear's location without collapsing the cavern. Three months to realize the miracle they'd thought they imagined had in fact happened—the *Yari* had somehow survived and was standing ready to aid them.

Cinni stored the two empty hover carts against the wall of the roughly gouged-out cavern before popping off the helmet of her spacesuit and taking a deep breath of stale air. Ordochian air. She was home.

Mishe leaned against one dark rock wall, her only welcoming party. She'd known he'd be there. If anyone looked out for her, it was Mishe. Cinni smiled to see him. The expression froze when he came out of the shadows and the diamond-bright light of the Tear lit him up. Fury beat in her blood when she saw the bruises on his face and what looked like a rope burn on his neck. One of the imperial dogs Mishe whored for liked to play rough.

She laid her palm along his bruised cheek, her heart aching for what he suffered in the name of their rebellion. Mishe flinched, looking away.

"I'm so sorry," she said, lowering her hand. "Why hasn't this been treated?"

When Mishe returned his gaze to her, the seriousness in his blue eyes hit her dead in the chest. "The others needed it more," he said.

"What 'others?'" *Oh void.* Aarush, the raid. She couldn't bring herself to ask about him. "What happened?" She shucked out of her spacesuit in record time. *I have to see him.* She had to see Aarush with her own eyes, to know that he was okay.

"The raid was a setup. A trap." Mishe shook his head. "I'm glad they pulled you from it and sent you to the *Yari*, instead."

And Mishe? Was he glad he was spared the raid as well, forced instead to whore himself to the imperial bastards for information? Cinni wrapped Mishe—her best friend left on the planet—in a tight hug. "I'm glad you're safe," she whispered, though she knew the word "safe" was very relative at this point in their lives. He clung to her for an instant, then they were both hurrying away from the Tear.

"How many did we lose?" she asked as they jogged to the lift. *Please don't let Aarush be among the dead.*

"Five."

Shit. Five people more than they could afford to lose. Their raids were by necessity small, due to limited resources, headcount, mobility and so on. They had to be strategic. They didn't have the numbers to face the occupation head-on. Most Ordochians seemed to be living in a holding pattern, as if the occupation was some kind of nightmare they'd eventually wake from. The rebellion was in no place to be waging a ground war.

Instead they struck like thieves, each mission tightly planned and executed, each with a specific target and focus.

The lift whirled to life and carried them to the inhabited levels of the base. Cinni caught herself rocking side to side as she agitatedly shifted her weight from one foot to the other.

"Bad intel." Mishe chafed at a rope burn on his wrist, rubbing the skin as if to erase the mark.

Cinni hit stop on the lift. "Tell me. I can take it."

"They had a psychokinetic field destabilizer." A generator that could disrupt all psionic powers in a small area.

"What? How the frutt did they get their hands on one of those?" Even if they had found one, how would they know what it was?

"Your mother isn't the only Wyrd to turn traitor," Mishe said quietly.

Cinni flinched. She saw her mother's face—Hephesta, eyes opening from sleep—heard the *blast* of her ion pistol as she emptied the full charge into her mother's chest.

"Cinni, I'm sorry—"

She shook her head. "No, you're right. She did, it happened." *It happened.* Her mother had agreed to help the imperials with a cure for the TNV. *If we do that, if we give in, they'll never leave.* "She can't have been the only one." Just the one whose betrayal permanently scarred Cinni's heart.

"In any case," Mishe said in his soft voice, "our people couldn't shield, couldn't communicate. Of course the imperials weren't hampered by the field, not having psi powers, so they decimated our team. It's only been a day, we're still not sure of everything that happened."

Cinni nodded, trying to take it in. "And Aarush?" She had to know. Before she faced anyone else in the rebellion, she had to know.

"He survived." Mishe's tone left no doubt that that was not necessarily a good thing.

Survived. Not, "He's okay," or, "He escaped injury." He only survived.

The breath whooshed out of her and she nodded. Nodded again. Over and over.

He survived.

She hit the power button on the lift.

Survived. Like she had, after killing her mother. Like Mishe had after letting those bastards use his body.

We are messed up. So frutting messed up.

The lift doors opened and Cinni hit the hallway with a purposeful stride and her shoulders back. They would survive. They had to, at least until the *Yari* was complete. After that?

She ignored the question and walked on.

The rebel base was situated in an abandoned manufacturing facility, chosen specifically because it sat near where the Tear had opened. It was one on a long list of buildings in this section of the kingdom that were slated for demolition. *Yeah. We'll get right on that, as soon as we kill every last imperial soldier on Ordoch.* It suited their purpose for now.

Cinni made her way to one of the sterile manufacturing rooms, transformed into their makeshift infirmary. Thankfully they saw no one else on the way so she didn't have to adopt a neutral expression. Mishe touched her arm lightly and she stopped outside of the infirmary doors.

"You might not want to see him, Cinni." Mishe's concern sent a shiver of dread through her. "Maybe in a few more days…" It was the "maybe" that sealed it for her. Mishe wasn't even sure Aarush would make any healing progress.

"I have to," she said, and pushed open the door. Mishe stayed behind in the hallway.

The infirmary was eerily quiet and dim. Four figures lay on

beds like corpses on biers. They were covered in a motley of blankets and sheets in different colors and sizes, three of them asleep or sedated. The fourth body drew her eye as a medic worked on his unconscious form, a lamp directing a tight beam on Aarush's face—or what was left of it. Even from the doorway she saw that the right side of his face was a ruined, pulpy mess. A pile of bloody bandages were heaped on the floor beside his bed.

"Not now," the medic said, without bothering to see who interrupted his work. The man directed a regenerating laser into Aarush's filmy right eye. Cinni pressed fingertips to her mouth, trying in vain to stifle a horrified gasp. Aarush's breathing was deep and even beneath the sheet covering him to mid-chest—peaceful almost, in contrast to the carnage. It was a façade. Cinni was no medic, and even she could tell that the damage to his face was beyond the simple application of a medstick to heal.

She turned, about to leave the medic to his work, when an irregularity caught her eye. Each of the other three patients had a perfect trapezoid shape at the end of their bed—the bottom side was the bed itself, the top was their feet, tenting their blankets, and the two non-parallel sides sloped away from the feet, the blankets hanging over the edge of the bed.

Aarush's trapezoid was lopsided.

The left foot held its end of the shape, but the top sloped in an angle right from there to the mattress.

Cinni whirled and barreled from the infirmary, straight into Mishe's knowing arms, who held her while tremors of shock shook her.

It was an hour, two dreamers and a canteen of oblivion later before Cinni could report to Megara on the *Yari*'s progress.

23

FALANAR

The Low Divine's funeral took most of the next day and the entirety of Falanar seemed to come to a standstill. All of the Sovereign and Protectorate councilors were in attendance, not to mention the entire royal family, the Council of Seven members, and anyone with any remote claim to power. People clogged the streets outside the Basilica of the Dawn.

The newsvids were choked with stories of the Low Divine's piety and greatness, and the High Divine even broke his blissful, continuous state of Unity to come down from on high and speak before the gathered masses. He was seen so rarely that at times the novelty of his presence overshadowed the Low Divine's death. The Mid Divine hadn't appeared, but was said by her attendants to be buried in the archives, researching the proper way for the people to regain unity after such a tragedy.

The hoopla finally ended at sundown, but the media would be feasting off this story for another month, at least.

The holy day having passed, the Sovereign and Protectorate Councils were back in session the next morning. The crisis over the TNV situation, Wei-lu-Wei and Ordoch approached a critical point. The Council of Seven was getting ready to convene, demanding plans of action from both councils so that they could use those as their guides for making the final decision on how to proceed. One thing was clear—the empire couldn't afford to wait much longer without acting.

The army or the IDC needed to take control of the situation on Wei-lu-Wei, and if they wanted to stop the TNV from devouring the Sovereign Planets, they needed to push ahead with a plan to secure a cure.

Council sessions ran late into the evening. Still, nothing was decided, and the fate of the empire hung from a rope that quickly unraveled.

Isonde was quietly inducted to the Council of Seven early the next morning.

It had been a private and brief ceremony, she told Malkor afterward, no one willing to engage in pomp so soon after the Low Divine's funeral. For once Isonde hadn't insisted on turning the moment into a high-profile event. Even in that choice she'd played it right, entering into her new responsibilities with humility, solemnity and reverence.

It might have been Isonde's greatest moment of triumph. For Malkor, it was his greatest relief. His part was over. Finally, Isonde was on the Council of Seven and he could breathe deep, no longer tangled in her plans. From here on out it was all up to her and Ardin.

Not that he didn't have his own mess ready to eat him alive.

He arrived at IDC headquarters after hearing from Isonde that all had gone well with the ceremony, to find Hekkar and the rest of his team already at their desks. *Workaholics, every one of them*, he thought with a smile.

His office was as he'd left it yesterday—a mess of reports, performance reviews and paperwork due last week that he couldn't dig out from under if he had a month. Ah, the glamorous lifestyle of an octet leader.

He set his coffee and the datapads he'd brought from home on the pile and powered up his IDC complink. He absently swiped his fingertip across the biometrics reader and entered in his password, surprised out of his mental planning by an angry bleep from his complink.

What the—

[Incorrect password]

Bah.

He retyped it, actually paying attention this time.

[Incorrect password]

Piece of shit.

A third attempt locked him out of his system. Had he missed a prompt to update his password? The IDC had a million passwords for accessing a million different systems and they all needed updating at different times. Total pain in the ass.

He reset his password via the provided link and got to work.

Hours later, a pang in his stomach reminded him it was lunchtime. Thank the stars, his eyes needed a break. But first, he wanted to spend a little more time going through the notes he'd gotten from Janeen.

Malkor unlocked the drawer containing his non-networked complink and plopped the thing on his desk. It wasn't *exactly* IDC standard issue. Then again, every agent had a machine they worked offline with. He swiped the biometric strip, entered in his password and—*bleep.*

[Incorrect password]

The hair prickled at the nape of his neck, his fingers freezing over the keyboard. The two machines weren't synced to rollover passwords on the same day.

Frutt.

He shut the lid of the mobile complink, then glanced at his IDC-linked machine. Suddenly that password reset prompt looked a lot more sinister.

Hacked? How? The system was supposed to be unhackable. Sure, Rigger could crack it. Not many others, though. And his non-networked complink? In order to access that someone had to have been *inside his office.* Senior Commander Vega was behind this, without a doubt.

The lock on the desk drawer looked undamaged. Malkor did a sweep of the room for bugs. Sure enough, the lining on the underside of his chair had been peeled back a centimeter and a tiny surveillance device stuck there.

Mother frutter.

He left it there, for the moment. Mobile complink tucked under one arm, Malkor headed out of his office and over to the cluster of desks his octet occupied. He nodded to Hekkar, and based on the return look Hekkar gave, his second in command knew something was wrong.

"Hey, Rigger," Malkor said, leaning casually into her cube. "You're looking a little ragged around the edges. Wanna grab some coffee?"

His tech specialist didn't miss a beat despite the full cup on her desk. "Absolutely. This report is kicking my ass."

"Let's hit the café across the street. I need a break from that replicated brew."

Her smile was genuine at the mention of real coffee. "You buying, boss?" She locked down her station and he gestured for her to lead the way.

Considering the problem he was about to drop on her, it was the least he could do.

They made inconsequential chat all the way through the building, past the security checkpoint, out the doors, in line at the café, and while choosing a table outdoors. Silence hit as they each sipped the admittedly delicious coffee and Malkor set his complink on the table. He slid it across toward her like a snake about to bite and one of her eyebrows lifted.

"What kind of tech support are we needing this morning?" she asked.

He kept his expression neutral, just two co-workers enjoying a coffee break. "The kind that deals with hacking."

Her other brow rose. No doubt she recognized that as his non-linked machine. "An up-close-and-personal job, hmm?"

She set her coffee aside and flipped open the lid. "Password?"

"Won't work. Locked me out and I haven't done a reset."

"Ah." She started tapping away and Malkor let her work.

He watched the people passing by as she frowned and mumbled to herself, the minutes ticking, ticking.

Fifteen minutes later she sat back in her chair, blowing out a sigh of frustration. She powered the machine down and closed the lid. "Well, you're good and hacked."

"I was hoping for 'they didn't get past the secondary protocols.'" Though, getting jammed at the login screen would have been ideal.

"Whoever did this was good. Not as good as me of course, but damn good." She shook her head, mind clearly still grinding on the problem. "If they hadn't tripped the guard code I put in on their way out, prompting that password change, we might never have known this had happened." Even with her calm tone, he could tell she was as worried as he was. "I don't suppose you last accessed this machine at oh-three-hundred this morning?"

"Nope. It was in the office and I was home sleeping."

"Figured. I hate to state the obvious, but, it had to be an inside job."

"Finding a short-range transmitter bug in my office clinched that." The person on the other end of that little beauty had to be somewhere in the building.

"Sorry, boss." She gestured to his machine. "This is compromised. I hope you have the info backed up somewhere?"

"Of course." Damnit. All of the corroborating info Janeen had given him was on there, the info he'd hoped no one would know he had.

"I assume the same thing happened to your machine in the office?"

"Yup."

She sighed. "Report the hack on your official machine to InfoSec—they'll decommission it, get you a new one and look into the hack. As far as this thing goes," she pushed the complink back across the table, "smash it to bits. Sooner rather than later."

He kept a bland, just-enjoying-my-coffee expression on his face.

"We need to move Dolan's science data," he said, in a low

voice that barely carried to her. "As of right now stop working on it."

Only a slight widening of her eyes gave her surprise away.

"Hide the chip somewhere, and don't tell me—don't tell anyone—where."

"You really think that's necessary? I've never brought it to headquarters at all." There was a mix of caution and disappointment in her tone. No doubt she hated to lose the chance to study all that tech.

"Definitely." Malkor finished off his coffee and grabbed his compromised complink. "And, Rigger? Keep it from the rest of the octet."

"Sure thing, boss."

Midday in the royal palace found Kayla in the gym—grunting, sweating, and generally getting her ass kicked. Infinitely superior to how she had spent the previous week.

Turns out that one of her bodyguards, Jed, was an expert in Nguni stick-fighting, a martial art from his homeworld that she had never studied. It hadn't taken Kayla more than five minutes to convince him to teach her.

The art consisted of fighting with two sticks, one the *isiquili* or attacking stick, and one the *uboko* or defending stick. Jed gave her a tutorial on the basic movements, then proceeded to kick her ass in the sparring ring.

Anna, Kayla's other bodyguard, called encouragement from the sideline. She was clapping for Kayla's particularly nimble dodge when Kayla's guard slipped. Jed cracked her across the face with a killer blow. Kayla's head snapped around and the room fell into silence.

"Princess—" Jed choked off. "Are you—"

Kayla touched fingers to her split lip, then cupped her jaw for a second. *Okay, that might be fractured...* She moved her mandible side to side, testing the damage. Hurt like the void, but probably not broken.

Probably.

She spat out a glop of blood and grinned at Jed's horrified expression. "That'll teach me to let my guard down, eh?" She chuckled. "Damn, you can swing!" She shifted her jaw again. *Hopefully* not fractured.

Jed finally relaxed, realizing she wasn't about to report him or anything. "Well, you did say not to go easy on you."

"Yeah," Kayla agreed. "I had that coming." She spat out more blood and wiped her mouth on her sleeve. Adrenaline coursed through her body, sung to her, urged her to fight on. She spun the *isiquili* in her hand. "Another round?"

Anna chuckled. "I'm not sure Prince Ardin would appreciate his guards brutalizing a foreign ruler."

"Then we don't tell him. Besides, this is the most fun I've had all week." Kayla adopted a ready stance and Jed mirrored her. Before they could close, though, Kayla's mobile comm chirped.

If that's Isonde...

Kayla stomped her way over to the bag where her comm hid. She checked the screen: Rigger's ID.

"Something wrong, Rigger?" she asked.

"Not a bit. I've got a vid message to route to you, top priority." Kayla heard a smile in the woman's voice. "You'll want to watch it in private." And with that she disconnected.

A chill shivered through Kayla. Who could it be? And why the secrecy?

Kayla resisted the urge to run back to her rooms—barely. She set the palace guard on edge just by being Wyrd. It wouldn't go well if she started sprinting through the building with her kris.

Still, the anticipation nearly killed her as she power-walked through the halls.

Back in her rooms she locked the doors with her reprogrammed codes and strode right to the comm. The message indicator on the panel blinked unendingly. It was supposed to only blink the number of messages she had, then pause a few seconds before repeating. Since her true identity had been revealed, she'd received a continuous stream of comms from a billion different people across the entire empire. Thankfully, a secondary light beside the private comm channel blinked only once.

Rigger would have warned her if it was bad news, right? She jabbed the play button, unable to wait a moment longer.

Vayne's face came on the screen and the breath lodged in her throat. The message paused while the system buffered.

Vayne. His image blurred. She blinked. Tears fell.

He's alive still.

When the message came to life again Corinth's head appeared over Vayne's shoulder, staring at the screen as if he could see her through the comm. Her heart flipped over in her chest with a painful thump. *Thank you, thank you.*

Even though he'd hit record to get this message started, Vayne sat still, frozen, clearly unsure what to say. What little she could see behind him looked like some kind of cabin on a ship. Tia'tan's vessel?

"Kayla," Vayne said. His voice was a little choked up, and he cleared his throat before continuing. "I hope this makes it to you. Corinth wasn't sure where to reach you, so we sent this to someone named Rigger. Whom Corinth," who was smiling at this moment, "assured me we could trust. If you get this, please reply with your comm signature so that we can talk. I hope—" He stopped, but he didn't need to say anything, she could see it all in his aqua eyes. *Please let this reach you; please be okay; please forgive me.* "I hope to hear from you soon. Vayne out."

The screen went black. She immediately hit play again, watching the brief message one more time, soaking in the sight of her brothers' faces. *Sweet mother, they're alive.* Then she replied, letting them know how to reach her directly, and that she'd wait all day and night to hear from them.

She thought of comming Malkor, then decided not to. She wanted to hug this truth to her chest alone for a little while. Maybe the rumor of them being in the Mine Field was wrong.

Maybe they were still on their way to Ilmena. Maybe they were perfectly safe and sound.

She didn't believe that lie for a moment.

Kayla pulled her hover chair directly in front of the comm and set it on a rocking cadence. She was prepared to wait for hours to hear from her *il'haars*. Vayne and Corinth must have been doing the same thing on their end because within a half hour they were live on her screen, live and dear and so beautiful it hurt.

"Kayla," Vayne said, breaking into a smile. "I can't believe it worked." Behind him, Corinth did a slap-clap thing with his hands, grinning.

"It is so good to see you. Both of you." Her smile felt like it stretched to her ears. "I was so worried."

"You and me both."

"Okay, I do *not* like the sound of that." She couldn't see much of the background behind him. "Are you still on Tia'tan's ship?" They had better be.

Vayne's smile faded. "Uh... yes and no. Technically at this moment, yes."

Her *ro'haar* instincts kicked in immediately. "Explain." They were supposed to be near Wyrd Space by now, beyond the reach of the imperials.

"Long story, and trust me, you *won't* like most of the details." He shot a look over his shoulder and Tia'tan's lavender hair came into view. She looked no-nonsense as always. "Short version, we're stuck in the middle of the Mine Field."

"What in the name of Zoola were you doing anywhere *near* that voidhole?"

Vayne's brows furrowed. He looked as pleased with the situation as she felt. Maybe less so. "Also a long story."

"I need details, *il'haar*. Report. Now." She left no room for compromise. It was that voice that had snapped him out of his stupor in Dolan's lab, and that tone that, when a *ro'haar* used it, their *il'haar* obeyed without question. Even five years away from his *ro'haar* hadn't destroyed that instinct in Vayne, and he started from the beginning of an almost unbelievable story.

Kayla was following him fine, if furiously, up to the point where the rooks chasing them were destroyed by an unknown energy weapon. After that point, things took a slide into crazy land.

"Wait, what? The feed must have glitched because I thought I heard 'the *Yari*.'" Which, of course, was impossible. Naturally, that's where Vayne's story continued, with Corinth clearly prompting him at times, albeit silently.

Vayne finally ended with, "And that's why we need you to come to the Middle of Nowhere, the center of the Mine Field, to come rescue us."

Maybe she should have called Malkor over. That way he could validate if she had really heard what she thought she'd heard, or if she was so desperate to see her brothers that she had hallucinated the entire thing.

She blinked. Rubbed a hand across her eyes. Nope, still there.

"That is the most insane thing I have ever heard," she said.

That, at least, brought half a smile from Vayne. "You should try it from our side. Seriously, though, we need your help to get out of here, Kayla."

Which of course had her wanting to leave this second. "You want me to fly to the Mine Field, where fifty percent of the hyperstreams in the area get warped toward the field, and ships get ripped out of stream and deposited randomly." Talk about terrible odds.

"Actually, Corinth and Noar have a theory about that. All of the streams trying to go *around* the Mine Field get bent toward it and distorted. But you'll be flying straight into the heart of the field. That should negate any 'bending' effects."

"And this theory would be based on…" She watched Corinth. He squirmed a little, looking away, not meeting her eyes.

Vayne rubbed the back of his neck. "Okay, so, that part of the plan is really more a hunch than a theory."

This got better and better.

"On the upside, we have the exact coordinates in the Middle of Nowhere for you to take a hyperstream to. We rigged a series of sensors in order to get a message from within the field to the outside. The signal bounces from the closest sensor to the *Sicerro*, then the next and next, relaying all the way until it reaches the sensor outside of the field. Without the electromagnetic warping of the Mine Field, the sensor can judge its location in space accurately, and relay that back, sensor by sensor, getting the coordinates of the center of the field based on the distance and direction of each of the sensors in the chain from each other."

"Why does that not make me feel any better about my odds of making it there alive?"

Vayne blew out a breath, hunching down a little in his seat. "Admittedly, this is one seriously shitty plan. Our two alternatives are A: walking through a tear in the fabric of space—a tear which is destabilizing as we speak, by the way—into the middle of a warzone on Ordoch, or B: cobbling together an engine with not-so-gently-used parts and ancient tech, then trying to catch a hyperstream in the galaxy's oldest still-functioning weapons ship."

Incredulity must have shown on her face because he said, "Yup, that's when we decided to call you."

For a moment, all she could do was stare at them. What in the— How in the name of— Impossible. The whole thing was impossible.

Vayne lowered his voice. "I left you behind on Falanar and that eats at me every single day. I'm a failure of an *il'haar*. I've failed you, and I have no right to ask this." The pain in his eyes shot straight through her chest.

"Don't say that, Vayne. You've never once failed me." Even as she'd begged him not to go, not to leave her, she'd understood why he had to do it. Understood his fear of recapture, of being a prisoner again. "I don't have a ship at hand, and things are... tense here right now." So damn tense. "I'll find a way. As soon as I can, I promise. Just sit tight and do not—for any reason—choose option A or B, okay?"

Vayne chuckled. "Got it. I'm sending you the coordinates now."

"Vayne, do something for me," she said, before he could cut the connection.

"Anything."

"Keep you and Corinth safe. No matter what you have to do."

He nodded once, then their image faded from the screen.

Back in his office after coffee with Rigger, Malkor grabbed all necessary datapads, stuffing them into his bag with the compromised mobile complink, before notifying InfoSec of the hack to his IDC complink.

InfoSec booted him from his office and commandeered the complink. Each octet carried dozens of potentially explosive secrets, and an octet leader's complink was top-level classified. Info from various missions, especially delicate and inflammatory political negotiations, wasn't released to other octets except on a need-to-know basis.

Malkor stationed himself at Janeen's old desk. Security swept each of his team members' desks for bugs, but found none.

Good. At least the heat was off his team.

Sunset came and went before Malkor decided he'd had enough work for one day. Everyone had already left—though Trinan and Vid were likely to hit the gym and Rigger was guaranteed to work after she made it home. Malkor stretched his back, popping a vertebra back into alignment with a groan. Too much desk time.

He missed being out on assignment, doing his job as an IDC agent. If things were "normal," he and his octet would likely be shipping out in a week, sent to one of the two Protectorate Planets quickly escalating toward war with everyone's attention focused on Falanar and Wei-lu-Wei.

He couldn't afford to leave Falanar at the moment, not with the IDC situation reaching critical mass. Malkor walked to the maglift, ready to head to the first floor and get the void out of there, when he remembered a question he had for Janeen. He hit the button for the sub-basement with a sigh. *Almost* done with work for the day. He riffled through his bag, grabbing a datapad. *I'll leave it with Janeen overnight.* She could go over the details he still had questions on, shore up the notes and he'd get back to her in the morning.

Check-in through security went smoothly. Malkor anticipated lounging in his chair at home in front of his faux fireplace, feet on the coffee table, as he walked to Janeen's cell.

He froze at the sight that greeted him.

Janeen sprawled on her back on the floor of her cell, both hands in a death grip around her throat.

"Janeen!" He fumbled at the panel, entering his senior agent override codes and cursing as he shut off the electrical field sealing her cell. The field winked out and he dashed into the opening.

"Janeen!"

Too late.

Her face was a mottled blue-violet, her eyes bulging from their sockets, her skin cold to the touch. She looked like a beached fish frozen mid-flop, spine arched upward, heels dug into the floor, struggling, straining, dying for that last breath of air that hadn't come.

Tears stung his eyes. He sank to his knees.

Not like this. Frutting—

Gods. Not like this.

Coroners would do an official cause of death, but he already knew. Only one thing could keep the muscles of her spine bowed like that long after death, could keep her hands clutched, manacle-like, around her throat: dutrotase mixed with the muscle stabilizer known as RDU-7.

Janeen had been killed with her own toxin.

Rage surged inside of him. He boiled with a fierce blast of

hatred that had no outlet. He slammed his fist against the wall. Once. Again.

How could this have happened? *How?* She was under guard day and night. She was in total lockdown, for frutt's sake. Shouldn't alarms have gone off when her vital signs flagged? The guards had a grand total of four criminals to watch at the moment. Frutting four.

I'm going to tear them apart.

He shot to his feet and ran down the hallway. The men at the guard station took one look at his face and launched into panic mode. One cycled through the vidfeed on each of the cells while the other loosened his weapon in its holster and turned to face Malkor.

"What is it? What's happened?"

Malkor grabbed a fistful of the man's indigo tunic. "What's happened? Check your frutting vidscreens." He shook the man, who looked close to choking. "One of your prisoners is dead."

The other guard frowned. "They're all fine."

Malkor thrust the first man aside and knocked his chair out of the way to get to the bank of vidscreens. There she was, in cell twelve. Alive, pacing, walking the length of her room over and over, hands tucked behind her back and head bowed in thought.

Malkor growled at the image. "Not possible." He ran back down to her cell, the two guards jogging to keep up. He thrust his finger at her dead body when they arrived. "There. *That's* the truth." Blood drained from the guards' faces.

"Your security feed has been duped and looped."

"Holy shit," one muttered. They finally had the presence of mind to hit the alarm and recall security procedures. "Check wings one and two," the first one said to his partner, "I'll check three, four and five."

"Don't bother," Malkor snapped, eyes locked on Janeen. "This was personal."

Like the hack in his complinks, the bug in his office.

When the guards finished their sweep, Malkor stalked

back to the security desk to meet them. "Who was her last visitor?" he asked. A guard protested when Malkor sat down and started going through the records, but the look he shot the guard silenced him.

It wasn't hard to find Janeen's last visitor, since it was the last visitor to the cell block in general.

[Check-in time: 04:12 Today]

[Guest ID: Senior Agent Malkor Rua]

[Biometrics: Confirmed]

[Credentials: Confirmed]

[Visual Identification: Confirmed]

[Confirmation completed by: Guard 016, Petres]

The three of them stared at the log, no one moving as the details sank in. It took a full minute for Malkor to process the information, and by then it was too late.

Both guards raised their pistols, covering him in three hundred sixty degrees.

"Agent, I'm going to have to ask you to surrender your sidearm."

24

Kayla woke early the next morning to a blank mobile comm. *No New Messages.*

She hadn't heard from Malkor last night. Her chest ached from holding in the news of Vayne and Corinth, but she didn't want to discuss it over comms. Odd not to have heard from him. Kayla sent him another message, then rolled out of bed.

After a shower and some breakfast, she still hadn't heard back. The need for immediate action drove her from one side of the room to the other, pacing. She needed a ship, needed to get to her family, needed to rescue them.

My people, though...

If she fled Falanar now and abandoned her push for withdrawal from Ordoch, what would happen to her people? How could she abandon her family for the "greater good?" Then again, how could she abandon her people to save two lives?

Another thought brought her up short: *How can I abandon Malkor?*

The idea pierced right to her heart, split her down the center. As much as she wanted to run to her brothers, the thought of leaving without Malkor, of never seeing him again, caused an instant ache in her chest that took her breath away.

She remembered the expression on his face the day she'd tried to leave Falanar on Tia'tan's ship, leaving him behind without warning. The hurt, the loss—stars, the anger. The feelings ripped through her now.

If she left to rescue her brothers, how would Malkor feel when she demanded a ship?

How could she hurt him like that again? How could she hurt herself like that?

Maybe I could convince him to come with me.

An irrational thought. His duty here, to his people, to the IDC, was no less important to him than her *ro'haar* duties were to her.

She needed to talk to Malkor, *now*.

Kayla grabbed her jacket, formulating a plan to storm IDC headquarters. A chime from her vidcomm stopped her at the door. *Finally*. Hekkar hailed her when she opened the channel, not Malkor.

"What's going on?" she asked by way of greeting. Hekkar's tight expression let her know right off the news was bad. He was in Rigger's apartment, and the tech specialist typed furiously at her complink in the background.

"Malkor's in custody for the murder of Janeen."

"*What?*"

Hekkar's frown deepened. "It happened last night. The entire octet is suspended; we'll be brought in later for questioning."

"Who set him up?" Malkor might have wanted some revenge on Janeen, but murder? Not remotely possible.

"As of right now, the evidence points perfectly to Malk committing the crime." Hekkar jerked a thumb over his shoulder. "Rigger tapped into the security files. Someone got into IDC's cell block with a flawless set of Malk's credentials—palm print, retinal scan, credentials—around oh-four-hundred and injected Janeen with her own toxin. She asphyxiated."

Rigger grunted. "It would have been easy to pass as Malkor through security if someone had access to IDC's personnel records. Tough to get, those records are locked down in a virtual fortress. However, *if* they had that info, they could make contacts to match his eyes for the retinal scan and use a polymer biofilm stamped with Malkor's palm print. It wouldn't last long before being dissolved in the skin, but it could have been applied in the lift on the way down. As far as fake credentials? I could have made those even before joining the academy." Rigger continued typing as she spoke. "A cheap hologram with the boss's image would fool a visual inspection. It wouldn't even need a voice replicant program as long as he didn't say much."

An inside job, then.

"Tell her about the hack," Rigger said, without looking away from her screen.

"Malkor's complinks were hacked right before the murder. No doubt evidence was planted that Malkor manipulated security in the cell block before heading down there. Two feeds were clipped and copied, one from Malkor's previous visit to Janeen and one of Janeen pacing her cell looking perfectly healthy. Also, the alarm system on Janeen's cell was disabled using Malk's code, so the guards weren't notified when the cell was opened or when her vitals dropped to nil."

Shit. When the IDC conspired against its own, it didn't frutt around. Kayla banged her fist against the wall. "We have to get him out of there."

"Working on it," Rigger called. Hekkar, however, looked doubtful. Very doubtful.

Kayla's lungs clenched, making it hard to breathe. She lowered her voice. "We have to spring him, Hekkar. If they could get to Janeen, even while she was in custody…"

"I know," he said, his voice running with an undercurrent of frustration and serious worry—worry that sent her pulse spiking higher. "At this point, our only possible lead is to identify the hacker."

Rigger pushed herself away from her desk, sending her hover chair spinning until she faced the comm. She ground the heels of her hands into her closed eyes for a minute. When she opened them, she looked pissed. "Right now identifying the hacker is proving impossible. Malkor's private complink is unnetworked and his IDC-issued one is powered down. Both are in custody at HQ and I can't access them remotely."

"I'm sorry, Kayla," Hekkar said. "At this point—"

"Unacceptable." She looked from one to the other. "I assume you're both banned from headquarters?" They nodded. "Then I'm going to see Commander Parrel. This second." He was the only one with enough clout to get Malkor cleared, and she'd be damned if she was going to let him stay neutral on this one.

She pulled on her jacket as she spoke. "If we can't clear Malkor's name, then we're busting him out. ASAP." It had to be possible. Somehow she had to get in there and get Malkor back. Frutt the damage to his reputation as an IDC agent. "I'll let you know how it goes with Parrel."

She cut the connection and was out the door before the screen had fully dimmed.

The royal guards snapped to attention as she exited. "I need transportation to IDC headquarters."

The more senior of the two cleared his throat. "Has this been cleared, Princess?"

Isonde had stressed that it wasn't safe for Kayla to be loose in the city at this point. Protestors gathered outside the palace with signs of GO HOME WYRD; WYRDS SHOULD BE IN PRISON, NOT A PALACE; TERRORIST IN PRINCESS CLOTHING, and so on. Demonstrations were happening across the planet—the newsvids loved to interview those assholes and broadcast their not-so-clever hate propaganda.

"No," Kayla said, "it hasn't been cleared. And yes, we're leaving now." She headed toward the lift to get to the underground garage. She'd drive her damn self if need be.

The guards hopped to follow, one calling in the excursion while the other pushed the lift button for her as if she were incapable. Kayla stared straight ahead, ignoring them both. The distinct urge to murder someone had her in a stranglehold.

As she slipped into the back of a hover car after her guard, she tried to pull together her thoughts for approaching Parrel. She should probably be cool and logical. What she *wanted* to do was grab the gruff commander by the front of his uniform and demand immediate action. If he tried to dance around his dual loyalties to Malkor and the future of the IDC she'd knock him out.

The drive to headquarters was uneventful. The only scuffle came at the IDC security station when her guards refused to abandon her and she refused to abandon her kris. Her threats of dire consequences if the security officer tried to take her kris didn't have the desired effect, and in the end she and her two guards were forced to go weaponless into the den of inequity.

The only reason they passed the gate at all was because Parrel gave the OK when security paged him. No doubt he'd expected her. IDC security escorted them to Parrel's office, where Kayla left her guards outside and entered alone.

Parrel was finishing a call when she entered, and he held out his hand to silence her while he wrapped it up. Kayla didn't do "cooling her heels" well, especially not today. Then again, she probably wouldn't win him over if she marched to the comm and hit "end" before he was finished, so she forced herself to wait, all the while tormented with thoughts of what could happen to Malkor while he was in custody.

Parrel finally finished his call. Before she could speak, he said, "I really don't have time to deal with you right now." He could have looked less friendly, but only with serious effort. She knew he had issues with Malkor's friendship with Isonde, and apparently that dislike rubbed off onto Kayla. Probably because she *was* Isonde. Or had been, for quite some time. That or he knew her relationship with Malkor divided his loyalties further.

"Tough." Kayla crossed her arms over her chest and braced her feet. "I'll get right to my point—you need to get Malkor exonerated."

Parrel steepled his fingers and leaned back in his chair. "How do you propose I do that? My word against hard evidence?"

"Easy. Counter-attack."

Parrel arched a brow.

"We both know this is a plot by your IDC's secret cabal to discredit him." Parrel didn't reply; agreement enough. "You've been tracing this conspiracy much longer than he has. I know you have evidence of illegal dealings by certain octets and commanders who are under secret orders. Evidence of leaders in the IDC having knowledge of Dolan taking Wyrd prisoners and conspiring with him to keep their existence a secret, allowing for his scientific 'experiments.' Of Janeen being given off-the-book assignments like assassinations and unsanctioned intelligence-gathering. Agents being recruited for shadow ops who, when they refused, were discredited and forced out of the IDC with falsified or manufactured evidence."

"I see Malkor has no secrets from you." Parrel, if he ever liked her, certainly didn't now.

She forced herself to take a breath, calm down a notch. *Get back to facts.* "Add to all of that Carsov's findings on the army harvesting the TNV, and Bredard acting as the IDC's go-between with the army to supply Trebulan with the virus." That in itself should be enough to sink the bastards.

Kayla uncrossed her arms, aiming for a less combative stance. "Go to the press right now with every piece of evidence you've got. I know the IDC answers directly to the Council of Seven but this can't wait to be handled through official channels." Malkor might not survive that long. And Kayla couldn't think straight when faced with the very real chance that he could be dead already.

Parrel was shaking his head, so she continued. "Put every single thing out there for the empire to see, every single instance of conspiracy. Make the biggest stink you can. You're high enough in the IDC, with a flawless record, you can make this real." He *had* to do this. No one else could. "Credit Malkor with finding most of the evidence and everyone will see he's been framed."

Parrel shook his head again. He leaned back in a chair that squeaked in protest. "It's not the right time."

"Commander." Kayla kept her voice level with effort. "This

is the *only* time you have. You have to strike now, before anything else happens." She tapped her finger against the empty holster on her thigh, missing the familiar weight of her kris at times like this.

"If you understood anything of imperial politics," Parrel said, "you would know this plan is a disaster." He did a fair job of making her sound like an idiot. "It would lead to the dismantling of the IDC, right when it's needed most."

And there it was, the one thing holding them all back: the fate of their precious IDC.

"You will *always* think the IDC is 'needed most,'" Kayla said. "*Always.* You believe in what you do and the necessity of your organization. Obviously an empire this large needs something like the IDC. Not something this corrupt, though, and not," she said, making each word crystal clear, "at the cost of Malkor and his octet."

"Believe me, I'd like nothing better than to clear Malkor and launch Vega and all her cronies into deep space." And the way he said it, Kayla really did believe him.

Damnit. Why did he have to fight her so hard when they were on the same frutting side?

Well, *almost.* Only one of them gave a damn about the fate of the IDC.

"If I thought I could do it," Kayla said, "I would release this info myself and take the decision out of your hands. We both know I don't have access to the proof, and I don't have a chance of making the kind of impact that you would with this. So—do it."

Parrel slowly let his chair tip back upright. His eyes narrowed. "Last I checked, you had exactly zero authority to tell me how to do my job." He let that sink in. He might agree with her on some points, but he wasn't going to be pushed around.

We'll see about that.

"I'm one candidate approval away from being promoted to Senior Commander, on par with Vega. Once that happens, then—"

"I can't wait that long." She'd assassinate Vega first. "Look, I know this chafes. Sometimes events take control of your life right out of your hands." Kayla knew all about that. She'd been living that way ever since Malkor found her in the Blood Pit.

She leaned over him, bracing both palms on the desk and staring him down. "Welcome to the new timetable, Commander. Make it happen."

25

THE *YARI*, MINE FIELD

Vayne couldn't stand to sleep in one of the previously inhabited cabins aboard the *Yari*. Each—still filled with the dead crewmember's few possessions—felt like a cross between a shrine and a tomb. Instead he camped out in his old cabin on the *Sicerro*. Everyone else had bunked in the *Yari* over the last week they'd been here, and the silence on the *Sicerro* suited him perfectly.

Tucked away in his cabin on the *Sicerro*, Vayne did push-up after push-up while his demons rode him—hard. His conversation with Kayla played in his mind, and for the first time since being pulled into the Mine Field he felt a spark of hope that they could get out of this alive. Kayla would come through.

Dolan's whispery laugh invaded his thoughts. *You've been here before, haven't you? Waiting for Kayla to save you? Remember how it was when you arrived on Falanar? The hope? That painful, burning certainty dying away, slowly, oh so slowly being ground to nothing as she failed to show, day after day?* Dolan's enjoyment was thick on the words. *I remember. Your faith in your* ro'haar *deteriorated one centimeter at a time. You gripped that fading dream so tightly. Then came the anger. First at her, for not rescuing you, then at yourself for doubting her.* If a ghost could sigh happily, the sound shivered through Vayne. *Those were the wonderful early days of our relationship, weren't they, Vayne?*

The burn of tired arm muscles couldn't drown out the words. Vayne switched his hand position from shoulder-width to making a diamond with his fingers and began his series of push-ups again.

Killing Dolan once hadn't been enough. The man deserved to die a thousand deaths, a million. One death for every gram of physical and mental destruction the *kin'shaa* had inflicted on them.

It still wouldn't be enough. Nothing could ever be enough.

With his triceps ready to give out, Vayne switched to sit-ups. He willed everything away, every thought, every pain, every memory, and worked his body to exhaustion.

Natali had been a master of that, preserving her sanity through physical exertion. Vayne's older brother Erebus, Natali's *il'haar*, had been captured along with them and the two were able to draw strength from each other. When she saw how terribly Vayne suffered without Kayla she had taught him the practice, had given him her own strength so that he could go on. She had, in essence, kept his insanity at bay.

Though that seemed somewhat in question at the moment...

Dolan had allowed them plenty of time to socialize with each other, which all of the prisoners did at first, plotting and planning an escape. An escape that never happened. Dolan probably got the biggest kick out of all their plans, the bastard, knowing as they did not how trapped they really were, how well prepared he was to hold them against their will.

When the mind-frutting started to take its toll, Natali helped all the non-*ro'haars* with the *ro'haar* training. Giving them something to focus on, some way to reclaim themselves, since they were denied their own psi powers most of the time. He might not have made it through without Natali's help and teachings.

Then, of course, everything changed.

Dolan had seen to that.

The prisoners still had the freedom to socialize, but kept more and more to themselves, each trapped in their own private void, with a few exceptions.

His mother had remained bright, untarnished in some small way. She was able to spend time with people without bringing her tortured soul into personal interactions. Maybe that's why she had been Dolan's favorite. At least, as long as she lasted, which, as it turned out, was not all that long.

Then it was Vayne's turn to be the favorite.

Vayne collapsed to the floor, helpless against the memories. The rage closed in. A haze of pain descended, blinding him, and he wanted to strike out like a wounded animal. At anything. Anyone.

Kayla will come, he told himself again. A mantra. *I can escape this, with her help.*

Though what he hoped to escape was left unanswered for the moment.

"Frutt it." Vayne pushed himself off the floor and headed for a shower. As much as he hated the idea, seeking out someone else's company might be the best thing for him at the moment.

Cinni had returned with a hodge-podge of random parts and more fresh food. The crew's excitement over her return—and the subsequent food—had driven him to seek out the silence of the *Sicerro* in the first place. By now some of the furor should have died down.

After a shower, Vayne made his way to the commissary and what would be the remains of an admittedly delicious meal. The door opened on Tia'tan, Cinni and Ida sitting together, heads bent close, empty plates pushed aside. He effectively ended their conversation when he entered.

Ida beamed. "You having emerged, somber one! Excellent!" She gestured to a place beside her. "Sit with us." Cinni looked distinctly uncomfortable at the idea. Dark circles lay heavily beneath her eyes, and her lips looked sealed tight in a permanent frown that was half-sorrow, half-exhaustion. Her hand had the slightest tremor when she reached for her cup.

Tia'tan neither encouraged nor rebuffed him. Instead she watched with her assessing gaze, studying each millimeter of him as if to gauge his mood, his stability. Wouldn't she just love to know that his dead torturer had started speaking to him in his quiet moments. It was fan-frutting-tastic.

Vayne scooped a portion of a fluffy casserole onto his plate, poured himself a centiliter of archan ale—a drink from home that could never be properly synthed on Falanar—and took a seat beside Ida. The captain grinned and hefted her own significantly larger dose of ale, clinking her glass to his. "Meal time is at its best today."

Cinni shifted in her seat. She glanced at him before returning her gaze to the casserole on her plate. Uncomfortable with him, or the conversation he interrupted?

"How are the repairs to the engine coming?" he asked into the quiet after Ida's greeting. He didn't really need an answer. Corinth spent every waking second in the engine room with Gintoc, Gintoc's assistant engineer Larsa, and Noar, working on the thing. His continuous stream of excitement and random updates to Vayne were a bit exhausting. At least his brother seemed to have forgiven him for leaving Kayla behind on Falanar, now that Corinth expected her to arrive any day.

Vayne should *probably* force Corinth to work on his psi skills. It's what Kayla wanted for him. But the boy so much preferred working with electrical and mechanical problems that Vayne didn't have the heart to pull him away. He was almost jealous of Corinth's happiness and excitement over the project, two feelings Vayne doubted he'd ever experience again.

"Is quite well," Ida said. "Gintoc is thinking the end is nearing."

"We're still missing a few crucial components, though," Cinni said, not looking up from her plate. "Our last raid on the manufacturing facility was a complete failure." The last word came out choked. The girl blinked furiously against tears, her frown refusing to admit anything.

Tia'tan patted her shoulder, and even Ida's good cheer seemed to dim for a moment. What had he missed?

Vayne sipped his ale, taking it slow on such a powerful drink. He'd come here for the distraction of conversation, instead he seemed to have stifled it. "How was the ride through the Tear?" he asked Cinni, for lack of anything else to say.

Cinni shrugged in response to his question. "Same as always." She removed a flask from her pocket and took a deep gulp.

Back to silence.

Over the last week, his questions about the Tear's existence had been answered.

Apparently the crew had been trying unsuccessfully to reach Ordoch with a mayday from the day the *Yari* went missing. At first, nothing had happened in response to their signals. Once they were out of the time eddy, however, and back in the normal flow, they noticed that every message sent out caused a tiny disruption in space. These were incredibly brief, gone almost before sensors registered them.

As time went on, however, the microtears grew wider and lasted longer. The crew of the *Yari* was faced with a choice: stop sending messages in an attempt to be rescued and accept that they were going to die here, or send the messages, regardless of the tears, hoping against hope that they might someday reach someone.

In the end it was no real decision at all. Ida refused to let her crew accept defeat. When they realized they needed to enter cryosleep to continue to survive, the ship was set to automatically send the signal out, adjusting the temporal and angular frequency minutely, using frequency-hopping and direct-sequence spread spectrum techniques. If a signal was ever returned, the ship was programmed to kick Ida out of cryosleep.

With the physics of the Mine Field as broken as they were, the only way a signal could escape was to travel through a tear. Tanet hypothesized that the *Yari* had opened as many as sixteen billion tears over the hundreds of years, and one, finally, impossibly, opened into space to end at Ordoch.

On Ordoch's end, the tear had hollowed out a space underground, deep beneath an old manufacturing facility. The signal barely reached the surface. If the rebels hadn't already been using that decrepit sector as a base of operations, it would never have been heard and the *Yari* would never have been found.

By that point the tears were lasting much longer, and it was thought that the answering signal returning from Ordoch helped to maintain the current tear. The thing was by no means stable, though. The fluctuations could result in the collapse of the tear at any time, and the *Yari* would once again be cut off from communication. The odds of another tear opening on an inhabited world approached zero.

No wonder the crew, with Ordoch and Ilmena's help, rushed foolishly ahead with this ridiculous plan of restoring the *Yari's* engine.

The awkward silence in the room was getting to him. Vayne was planning his exit strategy when Ida thankfully came through.

"Ghirhad your uncle, I like him." She smiled, flicking her sea-green braid over her shoulder. "Much fun to be speaking."

He mustered a half-smile. Of course she would like his uncle. Ghirhad was almost maniacally cheery—a creepy state for a torture victim. Something about that ever-ready laugh sent chills right through Vayne.

"And his knowledge of Ordoch history impresses. We are the best of reminiscers. Even we can engage Ariel to join. Sometimes."

"Must be nice to have someone else to talk to for a bit, about the things you all remember from home," Tia'tan said.

"Yes! Just so. Great grasp of history is his."

"Has anyone seen Natali of late?" Vayne asked the group. All three ladies nodded, though Tia'tan looked the least pleased about it.

Ida said, "Following around me everywhere and noting all she sees. Learning of the ship." Approval colored her tone.

"She's been grilling me about the rebellion and its progress," Cinni said, before taking another sip from her flask.

"Same," Tia'tan offered. "Though on Ilmena's side of things. Ilmena has been in contact with the rebellion on Ordoch since they reached out to us and Natali wants to know everything we've done to help." Her voice soured a bit. "Which, apparently, has not been enough."

"What *have* you done?" Vayne asked. Tia'tan's glare had him adding, "I'm curious, not trying to criticize. Honest." The four Wyrd Worlds no longer warred, and they'd all become very insular, having little to do with each other aside from the necessary trade. In Ordoch's case the isolation hid the partial collapse of their society. For the first time he wondered what the other Wyrd Worlds hid.

Compared to the empire's obsession with expansion and pushing frontiers, Wyrd Space had become stagnant.

"Well, we're not able to send supplies or manpower to Ordoch since the empire controls the airspace. After our initial period of..." Tia'tan cleared her throat a little awkwardly. "Of overconfidence in assuming the empire would be crushed after the coup, and our unwillingness to recognize the enormity of the situation, we got our act together." She swept her bangs behind one ear, warming to the topic. "We're focusing on refitting our ancient battleships. They're little more than relics at this point, so it's a massive undertaking. Our other focus has been developing a cure for the TNV."

"Excuse me?" He could not have heard that right. "You're going to give them what they want?"

"*If* they agree to leave Ordoch peacefully. Only then."

"Wouldn't that prove that their aggression was justified?" Vayne shook his head. "What's to stop them from coming back the next time they nearly destroy themselves?"

Tia'tan leaned her elbows on the table. "I don't give a damn what happens to the empire once they're out of Wyrd Space. They can cure each other or kill each other, either is fine by me. I want Ordoch freed *now*. If the empire comes back again in the future," she shrugged, "we'll be more than ready for them. We won't underestimate them again."

"The cure's not ready yet," Cinni added. "It may never be finished." She made that sound like the likely outcome.

Tia'tan waved that away. "We'll figure it out. That's Noar's hope, at least."

"Your plans seem to differ quite a bit from Natali's with regard to the empire," Vayne said.

"We've had our... disagreements."

Vayne tipped his glass in her direction. "Good luck with that." Natali was an immovable object when she made up her mind. Not to mention the legitimate ruler of Ordoch. She outranked Tia'tan by light-years.

Ariel entered the commissary, plasma bullpup in hand. She stowed the weapon by the door and headed for the remains of the casserole. It took no time at all for her to fill a plate.

Ida laughed. "Already seconds?"

Ariel spoke around a biscuit she'd taken a huge bite of. "Have to beat Benny or nothing." She swallowed a bite down, then gave Ida a significant look. "You'll want to be seeing how is Gintoc."

Ida's smile slipped away.

Ariel hadn't mentioned the engine's progress at all, only Gintoc. Was that intentional, or had he mistranslated again?

Ida rose from the table, the solemn look on her face so at odds with her normal character that an inkling of foreboding crept into Vayne. As she reached to arm herself with a bullpup, he asked one of the many questions that still hadn't been answered.

"What's with the armament whenever we leave the three main decks?"

Ida's gaze flicked to Ariel, then back. The navigation officer froze in the act of snagging a second biscuit.

"Is protocol," Ida said.

Vayne stood. "No. I want an actual answer. All we've been hearing since we arrived is 'is protocol.'" He looked at Tia'tan and Cinni, who were also getting to their feet. "Do either of you know?" Duplicate noes answered the question.

"So, why do we have a protocol to carry weapons whenever we visit other decks? Why does the trip to the engine room make everyone so tense? Does it have to do with the *stepa at es* I've heard you mention?"

All eyes went to Ida. She drew herself to her full impressive height, looking like the stern commander she'd been when the *Yari* launched all those centuries ago. "*I* am the captain. *This* is protocol. *You* will follow."

She left with those words hanging in the air.

Ariel abandoned her plate and her half-eaten biscuit on the counter and followed after Ida. But not before claiming a fully charged bullpup from the weapons rack.

26

Malkor had been sitting in his cell for a day and a half now. Stewing for a day and a half. Cursing for a day and a half. Outside the sun would be hitting the horizon, announcing dawn. Down here the lights were still dimmed for the "night cycle."

They had placed him in the cell across from Janeen's and left the electrical field fronting the cell set to transparent when they'd arrested him. Seeing her contorted and purpled body was eerily reminiscent of when he'd charged into Isonde's room after Janeen's attack and saw Isonde lying on the floor, stiffer than quadtanium, her nose and mouth smashed in, her face covered with blood.

Isonde's full-body paralysis had been the result of a severe allergic reaction to the toxin. Janeen's killer must have injected Janeen with a massive dose of the toxin in her chest. That would have solidified the muscles around her lungs, making breathing impossible. It clearly spread to the muscles of her back as well, explaining the fixed upward arc of her spine.

"Damnit." Malkor stood at the front of his cell, hands fisted at his side, unable to look away from Janeen's now empty cell.

Even after they'd carried her body away he could see her, lying there, frozen in a futile gasp. The image was etched into his brain with the permanence of a tattoo.

She hadn't deserved to die like that. And she certainly hadn't deserved to die for no other reason than to frame him for murder. Void. Was there nothing Vega and her allies wouldn't stoop to?

His first concern was for his octet. Had they somehow been implicated as well? He hadn't heard any commotion of new prisoners being brought in, which was a small comfort. Hopefully they were merely suspended pending an investigation. How far their enemies would go with such an "investigation" was another worry entirely.

He needed to get out of here.

And Kayla? Had someone told her what happened? If so, he could imagine her sharpening her kris daggers and painting targets on pictures of Vega. There was little she could do beyond that as a foreign dignitary with no real power in the empire.

He sighed with frustration and forced himself to look away from Janeen's cell, stop visualizing her dead body. Pacing the narrow length of his cell didn't help, it only made him feel more closed in, more trapped.

I should have seen this coming.

How Vega had learned of his visit to Janeen was a mystery. It had given her the perfect setup. Besides putting him away, it allowed InfoSec to confiscate all of his possessions, which included the hacked mobile complink he hadn't destroyed yet, and datapads with all of Janeen's notes. If Vega got her hands on that evidence she'd destroy it in a second. Same with the duplicates he had at his apartment.

Why didn't I see this coming?

The appearance of a guard at his cell caught him by surprise. No one had come to interrogate him about Janeen's death. And why should they? The people who thought he was guilty were probably satisfied with the evidence they already had. And the perpetrators, who *knew* he was innocent? They had accomplished all they'd needed to by having Janeen killed and framing him for it, getting him firmly—and likely permanently—out of their way. They had no reason to speak to him at all.

The guard told Malkor to stick his wrists through the slot in the field to be cuffed with magcuffs like a good little criminal. He almost refused. It was beyond galling.

Instead he complied, too curious about who wanted to see him. He followed the guard to an interrogation room near the front of the sub-basement. The guard opened the door and when Malkor caught a glimpse of an indigo and teal IDC uniform, he had a hope that Parrel might be here to tell him his plan for clearing Malkor's name.

Instead, Senior Commander Vega waited for him.

Any doubt about Vega being dirty fled Malkor's mind. She stood against one white wall in the square room, arms clasped behind her back, her uniform crisp and her expression serious. Vega nodded sharply to the guard and dismissed him before gesturing that Malkor should have a seat at the lone table in the room.

He'd rather his hands weren't cuffed, but he refused to ask her to demagnetize them and give her that display of power. Instead he took his seat with the bearing of a senior agent in good standing, sure of his rank and his worth. He kept his cuffed hands on his lap, out of sight.

Vega sat opposite.

Malkor wanted to shake her composure. Underneath lay a scheming, conniving power-broker with no limits.

"Come to gloat?" he asked.

"Do I really seem the type?"

Not really. She looked comfortably composed, and serious without being severe.

Vega bent to pull a datapad from the case beside her chair and set it on the table. She slid it across to him, not saying anything, just watching his face. The datapad showed the "evidence" compiled against him and it looked damn convincing.

Malkor had been asleep in his apartment at the time of the murder, but the only proof he had was his ID unlocking the place when he got home, and he could have passed that ID on to anyone to enter for him and provide a supposed alibi. It was worthless.

"Quite extensive for a frame-job."

Vega retrieved the datapad. "The 'evidence' is so airtight you're not getting out of this without a confession from the guilty party that they'd done it, as well as an explanation of how they'd done it."

"Since you know I'm innocent, why don't you go get that for me?" *And go hang yourself, while you're at it.*

"I'd be happy to." She sounded perfectly reasonable. It was strange how much she looked the same as always, and how differently he saw her now. "Problem is, I'm terribly busy at the moment. You making noise about an IDC conspiracy, a certain army sergeant making noise about the IDC being involved in that nasty TNV situation with Trebulan…"

Carsov. *Shit.* Of course she'd find out about him.

"Not to mention your friends in the councils making a big push for a peaceful withdrawal from Ordoch—which does not suit my plans at all." Vega leaned back in her chair, totally at ease, crossing one leg over the other. "By the way, Isonde springing your Wyrd princess's identity? I didn't see that coming. Bravo."

Yeah. We were all so pleased with that particular stunt.

"The Wyrd has a chance to be a rallying point for the peace movement." Vega seemed to consider that. "If I didn't think she would make an excellent martyr, even more sympathetic dead than alive, I'd take care of that situation."

"Don't you touch her," he growled.

Vega lifted a brow. "Or what, you'll shake your magcuffs at me? You're worthless to her at the moment.

"Honestly," Vega continued, "it would be easiest for me to let you rot in here."

She could do it, too.

"You wouldn't bother to visit if that was your intention."

"True enough." Vega tugged at one cuff, aligning the jade

piping more perfectly. "I have a meeting shortly so I'll get to it. You have one and only one way to gain your freedom."

"Turning over Dolan's scientific data and tech specs." The moment he saw Vega from the doorway, he knew that's why she was here. "Never going to happen."

"Never's a long time, Agent."

Malkor shrugged. He could hear again Bredard's prediction, made under the influence of the truth serum, that they would get their hands on the data.

Rigger better have hidden it well.

For the first time since the interview began, Vega's mouth turned down in the slightest of frowns. "One way or another—"

"I wouldn't hold your breath."

Her frown disappeared, her mask of professionalism shifting back into place. "You like your sarcastic edge. It's noted in your personnel file." She nodded as if she'd expected it to surface all along. "How about this? You sit there smugly in your little cell and I'll go after your octet. Most of them are loners, true. Agent Aronse, however, has family in Falanar City, doesn't she? And Agent Gio spends quite a bit of his off time in Shimville."

Malkor kept his tone unconcerned with effort, though he lost the smile. "Won't help you any."

"I guess we'll see." Vega got to her feet, smoothed out her uniform, and called for the guard to collect Malkor. "I'll keep you apprised of my progress, Agent, and you let me know when you've changed your mind."

By noon Kayla was speaking with Hekkar again via vidcomm. He had zero info on Malkor's status, and it took all of Kayla's self-control not to rail at the man. The uncertainty of Malkor's safety ate at her until she couldn't think. Now Hekkar counseled her to be patient and she wanted to scream.

She was a *ro'haar*. She did not do patient when it came to protecting the people she loved.

Her mobile comm chirped: Unknown Identification.

"Let me know as soon as you hear something," she said to Hekkar, then ended his call and answered her mobile comm.

Commander Parrel.

If he didn't tell her exactly what she wanted to hear, she *was* going to scream.

Parrel's gruff voice came on. "I'm still patching loose ends and scrambling to close holes. I intend to call a press conference this evening, as soon as I have everything ready."

Thank the stars.

"What can I do?" She was going crazy sitting here, useless.

"You should be there. You're not the most popular person at the moment," he said wryly, "but once I reveal IDC's connection with Dolan's activities, you can speak about your family being held prisoner and what they'd gone through, since you saw it firsthand."

"What time?"

"Be at headquarters at eighteen hundred, though I might not be ready until later. I'm waiting for two agents to commit to coming forward. Parrel out."

He'd barely finished speaking when her door chime sounded. "Kayla? It's Isonde."

"For frutt's sake." She had too much on her mind to deal with the princess right now. Sadly, she couldn't ignore her. The presence of Kayla's two guards outside proved she was here.

Isonde breezed in when Kayla unlocked the door, heading straight for the vidscreen.

"What—"

Isonde shushed her as she flipped on the vidscreen. It was already set to Falanar's main news feed. Kayla had never watched so much damn news in her entire life.

STUNNING DECISION blazed across the top of the screen above a reporter's head, who looked to be standing outside the Protectorate Council building.

"The Protectorate Council released their plan moments ago for handling the escalating TNV crisis. This comes before

the Sovereign Council's decision has been made, an almost unprecedented move for the Protectorate Council. Here's Councilor Abjarni talking about the decision."

The scene flashed to a press room. A stoop-shouldered woman wrapped in voluminous aqua robes stood at the front, against a backdrop of the Sakien Empire flag. Her ebony skin was finely wrinkled and her advanced age showed in her creaking walk to the podium. Her face could barely be seen over the lectern.

"We, the Protectorate Council, have announced our approved agenda and submitted it to the Council of Seven as of eleven hundred."

Her voice was remarkably strong for so aged a figure. It was easy to understand why she was the speaker for the Protectorate Council.

"We advocate, without reservation, the immediate and complete withdrawal from Wyrd Space."

Kayla sucked in a breath and Isonde let out the most unladylike "whoop!" of triumph. She and Isonde had had little involvement with Raorin's plan to sway the Protectorate Council. They'd counted on his contacts and influence to manage that part of it, and as of last night, things had still looked shaky.

"I can't believe it," Kayla said. Isonde shushed her again as Abjarni continued.

"Our responsibilities and interests lie entirely with the great Sakien Empire. Our recommendation to withdraw from Wyrd Space is based on the necessity of such a move if we're to save this shining empire. The Protectorate Planets have been hit hardest by the TNV plague and we are fighting a losing battle to save our homes and the very lives of our people. It is clear that all hope of a cure lies with the Wyrds, and our only way to appease them at this point is to withdraw.

"Added to that, the immense amount of money being funneled to the occupation is desperately needed domestically. With those resources—"

Isonde muted the vid. "Best possible outcome." Her pale eyes gleamed like a glacier hit by sunlight. "Not just withdrawal, *immediate* withdrawal. Not a long, drawn out, three hundred twenty-five step plan to get there after we're all dead."

"This could actually work," Kayla said, stunned. All her efforts for the last few months might not be totally in vain.

"Our first victory!" Isonde grinned. "I have to call Raorin." And she was gone as quickly as she'd come.

Kayla stared at the vidscreen, feeling an unexpected surge of hope as the words *Protectorate Council calls to abandon Wyrd Space* scrolled across the bottom of the screen.

This could really work.

I might actually be able to go home.

She sank blindly onto the nearest sofa, the word "home" echoing in her mind, in her heart.

By the time evening rolled around and Kayla readied herself for the press conference with Parrel, she was wound tighter than a plasma coil.

She'd spoken with Ardin and Isonde about what they could do to get Malkor exonerated—the answer was a frustrating "nothing."

She'd tried to see Malkor while he was in custody and had been denied access. The guards assured her that he was alive and well, and she'd told them where they could shove their assurances.

She'd tried to write notes on what she might say at the press conference. That ended in her flinging the datapad against the wall in frustration.

The only way to get what she wanted, what she *needed,* was to reveal the conspiracy within the IDC.

They should have done it a month ago.

Shit, Parrel should have done it way back when he first caught on to it, before any of this had happened.

The chronometer pinged a fifteen-minute warning before

her intended departure time. She checked her appearance in the mirror one more time.

Sapphire-blue bodysuit that set off her hair, rich purple tunic over that, black boots and her kris and she was ready to go. She didn't want to appear too "Wyrd," but she didn't want it forgotten, either. Her royal torque would have been a nice touch. The imperial bastards had probably looted that from her home.

The sun set as she and her guards exited the garage in an unmarked hover car. The usual protesters stood outside the palace gates, and new signs had been added claiming the Protectorate Council was in bed with the Wyrds, or some nonsense like that.

People and cars clogged the streets on the way to IDC headquarters. The traffic grew worse the closer they got, jammed for blocks and blocks.

"Probably all news crews," one of her guards said. "An IDC announcement, coming so soon after the Protectorate Council's announcement—has to be big business."

And of course Parrel would have called as many people as possible to be there. Good. The more coverage for the fall of the IDC the better.

When they were two blocks away, Kayla noticed that people weren't randomly milling in the streets and on the sidewalks, they were patrolling them. Cars were being stopped and IDC agents, all armed, were questioning the passengers.

Something's not right. "Turn on the news," she demanded, while their car stopped yet again in the endless traffic. Had something else happened in the last few hours? "Do you see Parrel anywhere?" The light quickly faded as the sun sank below the city skyline.

He wasn't visible, if he was even there. She could make out the front steps of the IDC building from her spot in the back seat, and the view set off warning bells. Too many agents. Way too many for a press conference. Their heads turned this way and that, everyone scanning the crowd, the street, the cars.

"*One hour ago,*" the newsperson said, "*IDC Senior Commander Jersain Vega made a startling announcement about a group of rogue agents operating from within the IDC with the help of the Wyrd Princess, Kayla Reinumon. Their leader, identified as Senior Agent Malkor Rua—*"

"Get me out of here," Kayla said. "Now. Right now."

It was a trap. They knew she was coming.

She was the one the armed agents were scanning the area for. No one could snatch her from the palace, but here, in the open, she was vulnerable.

"Now!" she said, when the car didn't move.

"I'm sorry, Princess, the traffic…"

Frutt.

They were still a good dozen cars away from where the agents were stopping people. If she got out now…

She popped open the hatch. "Don't follow me or I'm dead," she told the guards, and slid out of the car. She was way too conspicuous to blend into the crowd—royal guards at her side would make her doubly so. Any second now an agent would recognize her.

Only one option.

Kayla chose a side street at random and sprinted for it.

27

The breath sawed in and out of Kayla's lungs as she sprinted down another unknown street. Shouts had erupted behind her when she'd dashed from the car, but the gathered agents hadn't been prepared to chase her on foot and she'd distanced herself from the scene rapidly.

That advantage wouldn't last long, however. Once they mobilized a coordinated search she was done for. She didn't know the city, she was too conspicuous by half, and combined air and ground searches would locate her shortly. At least the descending night would cover her somewhat.

Gaining distance had been her first priority, and now that transitioned into a need to blend in. Where could she hide?

Her race had taken her through the classier district and into a more downscale section, thronged with a gaggle of people weaving in and out of an enormous number of stores. Street vendors and food markets kept company with massive storefronts and the occasional restaurant. Lights danced around the roofs of the stalls and carts and poured into the street from gigantic display windows. Kayla ducked into a narrow, dark alley between two soaring buildings.

She wiped the sweat from her forehead and struggled to catch her breath. The market district might be the best place to blend in—too bad she wasn't far enough away from IDC headquarters for comfort. She needed more distance, which would require a cab ride, and enough of a disguise that the driver didn't make her.

The tunic was the first to go. Kayla undid the zipup and peeled the garment off. The blue of her bodysuit was too bright for her liking, but it would have to do for now. If she kept to the shadows of the street it wouldn't stand out *too* much. If they released a description of her later as last seen wearing blue and purple, she could foil that somewhat.

Next she stripped off the leg harnesses strapping her kris to her thighs and tossed them farther down the alley. It killed her to leave those behind. Nothing screamed "hey, look at me!" quite so much as wearing daggers in the middle of a shopping center, though, so out they went.

Precious seconds ticked by, each bringing her closer to capture. She wrapped her long blue hair into a bun, grabbed her sheathed kris in one hand and calmly stepped out into the flow of people when a gap appeared. Some shot odd looks her way—probably because she'd come out of an alleyway—but she garnered no more notice than that as she headed deeper into the market.

As the hum of voices and confusion of scents enveloped her, Kayla found herself thankful for her five years spent on Altair Tri's slum side. With the ease of long practice, she filched a black over-the-shoulder bag made of woven ciacha from a store teeming with teenagers. It fit her kris perfectly and kept them out of sight.

Once those were secure she snagged an off-white headwrap that had fallen from the display tree on a corner vendor's shop. It covered her hair without drawing too much attention, even if it was a touch dirty from lying on the ground. All the while she kept moving, moving. Struggling not to hurry when everything in her blood screamed to run.

The urge to push people out of the way and bolt for the other end of the shopping center was too strong to resist, though, and she found herself cutting in front of people and darting faster and faster through the crowd. Ideally she'd get a new outfit, but that would take planning to steal, and the few credits in her pocket wouldn't buy her anything at these prices.

Time to get out of here.

Where to go?

She needed a place to hide for the night. She left the shopping center behind and entered into a large plaza, too exposed for safety. Still, it had the one thing she needed most at this point: transportation. A kiosk stood nearby with a map of the city, and as her eyes searched the layout of the districts, she knew exactly where she could go.

The Pleasure District.

The idea was as revolting as it was perfect. Since the release of her identity by Isonde, a fetish had started, giving rise to a new breed of pleasure workers and sex bots dressed to look like her. Not just her—Ilmenan lookalikes had become popular as well, Tia'tan and Noar especially. Why not make the perversity of the imperials work in her favor? She'd blend in like a TNV victim on Wei-lu-Wei.

Kayla ignored the faster, more expensive bot-driven cabs and hopped on a decrepit transport destined for the Pleasure District. With one credit for a fare, an apathetic driver and a group of passengers disinclined to look too closely at anyone else, it suited her perfectly. The cheap organoplastic windows were nearly opaque and she tried to let that fact calm her.

I'm safe here. This is safe.

Then why did it feel like the IDC was breathing down her neck?

"Come on come on come on," she muttered under her breath at the driver. The sooner she was buried in the heart of the don't-ask-don't-tell district, the better.

The hoverengine wheezed to life as the output pumped like bellows and struggled to lift them off the street and into the flow of traffic.

Low-priced anonymity at its finest.

The lights in the cabin dropped to nothing, cocooning her in the illusion of safety. Kayla pulled her mobile comm out of the bag that held her kris and slouched in her seat. A minute later—Corinth could have done it in thirty seconds—she completed her hack into the low-tech imperial comm system. They'd have her comm signature by now, so she wiped it.

Now no one would be able to trace her. The downside? Friends wouldn't be able to reach her either.

She set the comm to scan the area for sympathetic signals. Of the four passengers and one driver, three others had mobile comms. Kayla mirrored the signal of one of them to her own comm and commandeered the answering and messaging functions. It was a low-grade, very temporary fix. All calls and messages sent to the ID would hit only her comm. Both she and whoever's signal she boosted could make outgoing calls, as long as it wasn't simultaneously. The comm system itself would identify the hack before long so she'd have about a day of use before she needed to switch mirrored IDs.

Content that, for the moment, she'd done all she could to make herself invisible, Kayla took a minute to think.

When, exactly, had things gone to shit?

Last she heard, Parrel was going to break the IDC's secrets wide open. That should have been at eighteen hundred, though, and the newscast reported that Vega had made her announcement an hour before. Vega must have learned of Parrel's plans and preempted him somehow.

Unless that had been Parrel's plan all along.

Had it?

Had Parrel said the one thing needed to entice her to leave Ardin and Isonde's protection at the palace in order to take her into custody and use her as the scapegoat to hide the IDC's corruption? Had she been a fool to trust Malkor's faith in Parrel?

Kayla thrust that thought away. Malkor wouldn't be so blind, not even about a beloved superior. Had to be a mole inside Parrel's camp. One of the very people Parrel had trusted had turned on them, warning Vega what was about to happen.

Shit. Considering Senior Commander Vega had every detail

about her own treason, it would take next to nothing to provide real-life examples of what had happened, and alter the facts to place the blame on Malkor; turn him into an enemy of the state while keeping her name clean.

The octet would have been brought down in a second. Probably incarcerated alongside Malkor. And Parrel? Where was he in all this? The question made her uneasy.

The transport's air intake sputtered and quit, dropping the bus to the ground with more force than the cheap shock-absorbers could handle. Kayla nearly jolted out of the seat. The halt brought her anxiety back to desperate levels. Should she run? Bust out the transport's doors and hit the street?

She tried to see outside through the windows, expecting any second to be caught by an IDC agent rounding the corner. Her breath hitched as the net drew tighter and tighter around her. Vayne's haunted face leaped into her mind. She would never, ever, allow herself to be taken prisoner by imperials.

Ever.

"Happens all the time," the driver called. A minute later the engine kicked back to life and they were on their way again toward blissful oblivion.

Twenty minutes later the transport crashed with the same violence. Apparently that was its natural landing procedure because the doors opened and the driver ordered everyone off.

The second Kayla hit the pavement she was moving, striding away from the half-hearted lighting that lit the transport stop, and rushing into the enveloping warren of the Pleasure District. The other passengers scattered even faster than she had. It immediately became apparent that while the Pleasure District had a polished, upscale, respectable side, she had been dropped at the opposite end of the pool—which suited her needs perfectly.

First stop—wardrobe. "Princess Kayla, Lady of the Night" needed something skimpier than a bodysuit that covered her from shoulders to ankles.

Most of the city's glow globes were burnt out or broken in

this section and she slinked easily in a near-constant cover of shadow. The sidewalks canted at uneven intervals, tripping her up while she looked in all directions for threats.

Door after door after door lined the streets. None had signs, but everyone seemed to know where they were headed. As club doors opened, people came and went, lit by squares of red and blue and strobe lighting, ringed in smoke and followed by music as the doors slammed shut again.

Kayla kept close to the wall, dodging propositions and catcalls. Suddenly the door at her left elbow was flung open, knocking her aside. A man sauntered out with a happy smile and a lightness to his step. He caught her elbow as she reeled. Back on balance, she jerked her arm away, glaring at him.

The man laughed and called back into the establishment. "One of yours, Fantasmo? I might be interested, next time." He winked and went on his way.

Sounds of a string quartet drifted outside on perfumed air, the melody so sophisticated and elegant that she stopped in surprise. Dim purple light fell on the pavers from the open door and a black shadow grew as someone neared from inside. Fantasmo, Kayla supposed. She expected a gaudily dressed, bedazzled dandy oozing charm.

Instead an austere bot stood there, looking at her with unblinking, glowing eyes. It had a silver ovoid face with only two distinguishing features, his eyes and a polite smile etched onto the metal. The rest of his body was made of the same highly-polished silver material, vaguely humanoid in shape—not so much that it threatened a person's perception that it was, in fact, a machine. The words *Butler Extraordinaire 5c* were embossed on his chest where a nametag might be.

"Fantasmo, at your service, my lady." The bot swept her a precise bow. The gently masculine voice held the same elevated accent that Isonde and Ardin employed.

Okay, she had officially ventured into crazyland. An antique household bot had somehow acquired—and ran—an elite establishment in the bowels of the Pleasure District.

How in the...?

The silver head tilted slightly, as if studying the particulars of her attire and possessions. "Are you, perhaps, looking for work?"

What exactly would "work" entail in an establishment like Fantasmo's? She was momentarily transfixed by the oddity.

"Um, I'm looking for clothing."

He continued to study her, golden-lit eyes unblinking.

"More appropriate clothing," she offered.

"Ah. Of course, my lady. I understand completely." Butler bot cum vice-caterer extraordinaire stepped back and invited her inside with an automated arm flourish. "I could see to your needs immediately."

Was she really having this conversation? A glance over her shoulder showed that a well-dressed couple was waiting impatiently for their chance to enter Fantasmo's establishment.

"I provide whatever you desire, my lady. This is Fantasmo's, where nothing is out of reach." He gestured again.

Anyone who could afford to keep an antique bot in such beautiful repair, not to mention cater to such exclusive clientele, would be well beyond the range of her meager credits. "I'll look elsewhere." She started to back away. Fantasmo's multi-articulated arm snaked out with such agility that he caught her off-guard.

"Nonsense. This is on Fantasmo. A gift for a potential friend." That arm movement certainly hadn't been possible with the bot's original build. Someone had cranked this thing to a whole new level of ability, and his fingers were entirely too manacle-like around her arm.

Kayla's fight or flight instinct kicked in and she broke the hold, then beat it out of there. Between one word and the next she had crossed the street and slipped into the alley that led to another section of the Pleasure District.

Within ten minutes she realized she'd hit rock bottom.

Perfect.

Two male whores on a dark corner, one fresh from a blow

job, gave her an excellent tip for an outfitter and she soon found herself in the competent hands of Madame Jessiel.

Kayla ignored the pungent smell of stale bodily fluids in the back room of the shop as she changed out of her bodysuit and into her new clothes. The bodysuit would cover payment for her new outfit, which made sense since it had twice the amount of fabric of Kayla's new costume. She let her hair down and loose.

Kayla exited the backroom in a minidress of shimmery white that barely covered her ass. A sapphire bustier underneath made the most of her modest breasts, and showed through the giant V in the minidress that ended somewhere in the vicinity of her navel. She refused matching sapphire stilettos. Might be de rigueur for showing off her assets, but damn if she was going anywhere in heels where she might need to run at a moment's notice. She kept her boots, bought a cheap hair dye appliqué of ash brown for later, and paid Madame Jessiel the required credits.

Sufficiently hookered-up for appearances, Kayla walked to a bar—Fishy's Bait Shack—a block from Madame's shop. Madame had told her that while it was a popular pickup spot, it was one of the few places nearby that didn't also contain backrooms for frutting around. The owner, "Fishy," apparently couldn't pay the lease for a license.

Once inside Fishy's, Kayla ordered a liquid-nitrogen-cooled cocktail that she didn't intend to drink, and sat in a booth in the corner that allowed her a view of the door, the bar, the bathroom and the single vidscreen above the bar. The screen played the news, the audio obscured by music, swearing and a half-hearted fist-fight in the opposite corner of Fishy's. Kayla had to content herself with reading the scrolling bar at the bottom of the screen.

News of the Protectorate Council's decision to withdraw from Ordoch was playing when the first Tia'tan lookalike approached her. Even though the real Tia'tan had short lavender hair, tight in the back, with long bangs hanging over one eye in the front, this whore had opted for shoulder-length locks. Boys liked long hair, she told Kayla.

The whore tossed a hank of greasy, badly dyed lavender hair over one shoulder and gestured to a particularly eager guy at the bar. "My client says he'll pay us each double if he can watch the two of us go at it."

Kayla waved her away. "Not interested."

"Come on," the woman wheedled. She put her palm on the table and leaned in, blocking Kayla's view of the screen. "I bet you haven't heard a score this juicy in weeks. Caleb is *always* generous, and I've got him well and greased right now."

Kayla shot her a glare that could freeze fire. "Not interested. Now leave." Imitation Tia'tan tottered off in a huff on heels high enough to give her a nosebleed.

Not ten minutes later, as Malkor's image came on the vid, a couple approached her and slipped into the booth opposite before she could stop them. The woman was a startling ringer for Tia'tan. The man was supposed to be Noar, she assumed, based on the purple wig he wore. He was about ten centimeters too tall to play any powerful male psionic on Ilmena, however.

"Princess Tia'tan and I," the man said with a twitter, "were wondering if you'd like to join us for… dinner."

Kayla glanced past them at the news. Without audio, she couldn't make much sense of what was happening. She looked back at the couple, at the excited gleam in their eyes. The male was practically salivating. Over his shoulder she saw a man at the bar glancing her way, clearly biding his time to see if she'd turn down this pair before he made his move.

Kayla swore under her breath. There were at least three other "Kaylas" in the bar, why did people have to keep hassling her? Apparently in this area of the Pleasure District, her "disguise" was a little too perfect. Then again, in this end of the district, blue hair, blue eyes and a tight ass would pretty much kill it.

Frutt. She didn't have time for this shit.

She left the table without a reply. Five minutes later she was back in Madame Jessiel's, trading a few credits for a handful of sedative patches and directions to the more upscale section of the Pleasure District. Here the establishments actually had signs, though the lighting was every bit as low in the streets.

At Caia's Starhouse Kayla was given a thorough once-over by the host before being allowed entrance. Score some points for having her own teeth and actually showering this week. Kayla slipped into a cozy lounge, halting by the entrance, and began scanning the patrons. It was getting late—or early—and considering that she'd barely slept in days, she needed at least a few hours of sleep to keep going. Who knew how long it would be before she'd have another chance.

Several people gave her the eye as she stood in the entryway, so she quickly selected her mark: the best-dressed guy in the place. He had the confident look that came with having plenty of credits to burn.

A drink, some flirtatious talk, a proposition whispered in his ear and they were out of there, on their way to a hotel. The second they locked the room's door he got handsy.

Kayla calmly gave him a hammer fist to the temple that knocked him out cold.

"Sorry, guy. Just not your night."

She made short work of hogtying him with cords pulled from the blinds, and once he was bound hand and foot, she slapped a sedative patch on his arm and rolled his unconscious body into the closet. Even cheap sedative patches should keep him out for about eight hours. Plenty of time.

Kayla turned on the vidscreen. Finding any news was a challenge. Four hundred streams of porn and one lousy news stream. She pulled a kris from the bag, unsheathed it, and then slung the pack back over her shoulder before lying down on the bed, boots still on. Kris in hand, curled on her side, she stayed awake long enough to learn that some of Malkor's octet had evaded capture, including his second in command, before she fell asleep.

* * *

She woke five hours later to the sound of her would-be lover's snores coming from the closet.

Thank you, Madame Jessiel.

The guy had a healthy supply of credits in his pocket and Kayla helped herself, then sent a text-only message to Hekkar. Long shot, because he might have dumped his mobile comm, but she had no other option.

A minute later her mobile comm chirped. Thank the stars for tech specialists with the skill for sophisticated comm hacks.

"Kayla. Good to hear from you," came Hekkar's voice.

"You too," she said into the comm. "I wasn't sure if any of you made it out." The sound of Hekkar's voice released some of the tension in her shoulders. She might be neck-deep in a conspiracy that could end in her death, but at least she wasn't alone anymore.

Hekkar hesitated a moment. "We had warning."

Now that begged some questions...

"I've got Rigger, Trinan and Vid with me. We're holed up in Shimville, the safehouse we used when your family was rescued. Do you remember it?"

"Vaguely." Everything had been such an emotional blur at the time.

Hekkar gave her the coordinates. "Meet us here and we'll talk more."

"I'm heading out." She could definitely afford a cab ride to the outskirts of Shimville now.

"Be careful. The entire city's looking for you."

Of course they were. Because who didn't enjoy a manhunt?

Kayla said goodbye and fussed with her miniskirt, trying to cover a little more ass. While the outfit worked wonders last night, she needed something a little less... well, actually, she was going to need something a whole lot more. Like fabric. She applied the mousy-brown hair dye appliqué in the bathroom and then studied the results. It was a hideous and oh-so-common color—no one would look twice at her hair. She twisted it into a tight bun at her nape and made her way down to the lobby.

The early morning sun hit her eyes when she exited, sending her into a squint. The Pleasure District was decidedly less alluring by day. She hurried to a clothier down the street and exited twenty minutes later wearing a pair of shaded glasses and a beige pantsuit that said, "Hi, I'm a generic worker bee, don't mind me." She was light-headed from lack of food but didn't want to waste any time tracking some down.

After a cab ride and a lot of walking, she arrived at the safehouse. The building showed every sign of collapsing in a strong wind. Lines of mildew and algae crawled across the beige organoplastic façade where water overflowed plugged gutters and ran down the exterior wall. The front was windowless, sign-less and depressing enough to turn even the most desperate of thieves away.

When she knocked, Hekkar opened the door and blinked at her a second. "Kayla? Wow, talk about blending in." He stepped back to let her enter, gaze shooting past her to see if anyone was taking notice. He closed the door behind her.

"Thanks, I think." The inside of the building was as she remembered it, a complete one-eighty from the outside. Clean and bright, if utilitarian. High-tech complink and communications equipment could be seen through an open office door. The floor was scrubbed, watertight and thankfully mildew-free. A long table dominated one wing of the building— the "war room"—where any number of ops were planned, and an opposite wing had a cozy collection of chairs and couches for down time. As she remembered it, a storage room below held enough weapons and tactical gear to host a private war.

Something they might need soon enough.

Rigger, Trinan and Vid, huddled over the table in the war room, gaped at her entrance for a moment. Then Vid grabbed her in a bear hug and Trinan slapped her on the back.

Rigger grinned. "Knew they couldn't catch you. Where'd you spend the night?"

"Don't ask." She looked at the four of them. "Man, am I glad to see you." She glanced past them to the table. Looked like they had been studying schematics of some kind. Hopefully a layout of IDC HQ in order to break Malkor out. Her stomach growled, demanding attention. "Glad you made it out. Now—where's the food synthesizer? I'm starving."

The five of them packed into the kitchen, queuing the synthesizer and grabbing seats at the round table. When they were settled, Kayla, Vid and Trinan with food, Hekkar and Rigger with coffee, Kayla asked the obvious question. "Where are Aronse and Gio?"

That brought the happiness of the reunion crashing to the ground. Smiles faded, jokes quieted, and everyone waited for someone else to speak first.

Finally, Hekkar cleared his throat. "They made deals with Vega."

"You're shitting me." How could anyone make a deal with Vega? "What the frutt happened yesterday? I went in, planning to support Parrel in revealing the IDC conspiracy, next thing I know Malkor's public enemy number one, you're all rogue operatives that need to be arrested, and I'm the foreign power that initiated it all."

"Vega flipped everything on us," Vid said. "Got the jump."

Trinan nodded. "Us, you, Malkor, Carsov, Bredard, Janeen—all co-conspirators. Not to mention dozens of good agents, agents I'd stake my reputation on."

"Some dirty ones, too, though," Rigger added. "She even named a few senior commanders, all of whom have been in on her illegal dealings."

"Mixing truth with lies to make it more believable," Hekkar said. "I bet the dirty ones were challenging her authority, or at least they were liabilities. Looked like she was cleaning house."

"And positioning herself as the hero at the same time," Rigger said with disgust.

"Where the frutt was Parrel during all of this?" Kayla asked. That was the key question, as far as she was concerned. Malkor had been counting on him to be the spine of the movement to reform the IDC.

"Haven't heard anything." Hekkar clearly had some suspicions. "Aronse and Gio plan to testify against Malkor, and confirm Vega's 'evidence.'"

Vid threw his napkin down with a violent swear.

Hekkar shot him a look. "It's understandable. Aronse has family here. Two girls and a husband she adores. Not to mention she's still looking after her dad. You know she's supporting them all. No way she could afford to go rogue and leave her family behind."

Vid continued to grumble. Trinan, sitting beside him, shouldered him good-naturedly. "Knock it off."

"And Gio?" Kayla asked. She'd never really cared for the man. Too cold and slippery for her, even if he was a brilliant linguist and an essential part of the octet, according to Malkor.

"Vega has him by the balls," Rigger said. "Gambling debts. The kind that get you killed when you can't pay. Or worse."

"I didn't know," Hekkar said, and she could tell from his tone that he blamed himself for not knowing. "An IDC agent salary can't support that kind of addiction, not at the level he was at."

"Hey, none of us knew," Rigger said.

When Hekkar answered, "We should have," no one argued.

Guilty silence enveloped the room. The weight of friends failed and bonds broken dragged them down. Kayla's heart ached for Malkor. Even if he understood, rationally, why Aronse and Gio made the choices they did, the defection was still going to cut through him.

"So Malkor's supposedly in charge of the Trebulan-TNV situation?" Kayla asked. Hekkar nodded. "And Bredard and Carsov are his 'co-conspirators' on that?" Another nod.

"And Vega asserts he killed Janeen to keep her quiet about the conspiracy when she threatened to expose him," Vid said. "Really, the list of crimes Vega is pinning on him—*her* crimes—is a kilometer long."

Shit.

"Bottom line," Hekkar said, "Malkor's the fall guy, and us along with him."

Trinan smiled. "Wouldn't have it any other way. If the boss is going down, I'm right there beside him."

Quiet agreement circled the table.

The situation sucked. Nothing new, really. Kayla's life had been one big pile of suck since the coup. Rescuing her family from Dolan, meeting Malkor and getting to know the octet were the three shining moments in five long years of struggle.

"At this precise moment," Kayla said, "I have only two objectives: rescue Malkor and get the frutt off this planet." Rescuing her brothers was a very close third, but that required completing the first two. She wasn't leaving without Malkor, not now.

"I'm on board," Trinan said.

Vid nodded. "Same."

"Hekkar? Rigger?"

"You know I'm in," Hekkar said.

"This is what we do, right?" Rigger said. "Thwart the bad guys, save the day, and then haul ass outta there. Let's do this."

"Okay," Kayla said, eager to get to details. "Busting Malkor out of the IDC cell block. How challenging is that going to be?"

"Damn near impossible," Hekkar said, "and that's the easier of the two pieces of our plan. Getting an appropriate ship?" He shook his head. "None of us could have afforded one before, and now that all of our 'legal' accounts have been frozen, it's a no-go."

"Malkor might have had the clout to get one requisitioned through IDC," Vid said. "You know, if he wasn't an intergalactic traitor."

And as far as Kayla was concerned, Parrel was out of the equation. Too many unanswered questions there.

Kayla looked into her coffee cup. Empty, much like their store of allies was. "We're left only one option—Ardin and Isonde. They can get a ship for us, easily." They'd better. They owed her, and Malkor, at least that much.

"Um, you need to see this," Vid said. "It was released this morning." He turned on the vidscreen and scrolled to a story headlined: *Empress-Apparent Breaks Silence Over Accused Enemies of the State, Senior Agent Rua and the Wyrd Princess Kayla Reinumon.*

Vid raised the volume and hit play.

"*Moments ago, Empress-Apparent Isonde Veriley gave a speech denouncing her long-time friend, IDC Senior Agent Malkor Rua, and the Wyrd princess, calling them both traitors to the empire. She expressed her shock and disbelief over their actions, claiming that she had no notion that Senior Agent Rua had been working covertly within the IDC for years. She also noted that she had believed the Wyrd princess's motives to be genuine, and expressed sorrow over her duplicity.*

"*The Empress-Apparent went on to call their attempted TNV attack at her first wedding 'criminal' and 'unforgivable.' Her final quote of the interview was: 'This is a betrayal from which I may never recover, and I stand with Senior Commander Vega's intent to prosecute them as traitors to our empire.'*"

The vidscreen showed a grimly determined Isonde, the perfect picture of an innocent woman who had been misled by criminals. The image was replaced with the male reporter.

"*It should be noted that Emperor-Apparent Ardin did not accompany his new wife to the interview or make any statement to echo his support of her claims. The Empress-Apparent made no mention of him during the interview.*"

The coffee cup fell from Kayla's numb hand and Vid turned the news feed off. She blinked, uncertain that she'd seen and heard what she thought she'd seen and heard. "It can't be true," she whispered. "She wouldn't have done that to him."

Kayla pushed to her feet with enough force to send her chair skidding across the kitchen. "It's not possible. They've been friends since childhood. Malkor's done everything she's asked of him. *Everything*." Her gaze darted from one face to the other. "Right?"

"I'm sorry, Kayla," Trinan said, "it actually makes perfect

sense." He looked pained even saying that much.

"How?" she demanded. "How does throwing her best friend under the bus, instead of standing by him when he needed her most, make any sense at all?"

Trinan exchanged looks with Vid, and she realized that for all her posturing as Isonde for the last two months, every member of Malkor's octet had a lifetime's worth of understanding imperial politics that she lacked.

"Isonde has a long history of friendship with Malkor," Trinan said, sounding apologetic. "It's well-documented. Of course there's going to be concern that he has an influence over her. Initially it was idle talk through the rumor mills."

"Now, though," Vid added, "Malkor's been implicated— very believably—in an empire-wide conspiracy. He's been arrested by the IDC. Speculation is rampant that Isonde had a part in the conspiracy. General consensus, before her statement, was that she should be investigated as well, possibly even brought into custody."

"Malkor is a sinking ship," Trinan said, "dragging Isonde down into the muck, undermining all of her political power."

Kayla nodded, the pieces coming together. "Not to mention me," she said. Isonde had vouched for her presence in the empire, claimed that Kayla was here on a mission of peace, and had brought Kayla under her official protection. "Now that I'm accused of aiding Malkor in his so-called TNV terrorist activities and instigating a conspiracy, I'm an even greater political liability than Malkor is."

Isonde had to distance herself.

Hekkar had his hands clenched on the table, fury clearly riding him hard. "Isonde is one cold-hearted bitch. Always has been. In order to keep her political power, to remain above question, she had to strike first." Hekkar pounded the table with a fist. "By denouncing you she's separating herself from any actions you take, putting herself above question *and* making herself look even better in the process by being the victim of a vicious betrayal."

Something in Kayla's chest fractured with a cracking *snap* that echoed in her ears.

Her last thread of obligation to Isonde, having grown more and more brittle over the last few weeks, finally snapped, freeing her.

I'm trying to save your people, Isonde had said.

Bullshit. Every word out of her mouth—bullshit.

The shock that had numbed Kayla melted away, sublimed in the heat of her gathering fury. Rage, so cold it burned, so hot it melted, roared through her, replacing, for the moment, the ache of betrayal.

She had trusted Isonde.

Trusted.

Surrounded by an empire's worth of enemies, Kayla had believed Isonde was one of the few she could rely on. Malkor should have been able to depend upon Isonde and Ardin to protest his innocence, demand the Council of Seven carry out a full investigation.

Hekkar had it right, Isonde was a cold-hearted bitch.

And I'm going to bring her down.

Kayla's searing thoughts turned to Ardin. Ardin, probably Isonde's greatest victim of all. Ardin, who hadn't been at her interview or publicly made any similar statements about Malkor being guilty of Vega's crimes.

Ardin probably had no idea what Isonde was about to do.

Just like Isonde had sprung the surprise of Kayla's identity-reveal on everyone, before Kayla could object, Isonde had probably held this interview without giving Ardin any notice of her intentions.

It was the only hope they had at this point.

"I'm going to see Ardin," Kayla said, surprising the octet.

Vid frowned. "I don't think that's wise, not after Isonde's stunt."

"He's been Malkor's friend as long as Isonde has," Kayla argued. "Just because Isonde betrayed him to save her own political career doesn't mean Ardin would do the same."

"That's a big if," Trinan said.

"I have to risk it. He's the only one left I can go to about getting us a ship."

Trinan rubbed the back of his neck, looking doubtful. "That's if we can even free Malkor."

Kayla leaned over the table, palms flat on the organoplastic. "You will. I refuse to accept any other outcome." Simple as that. She was not leaving here without Malkor, no matter the consequences.

Rigger quirked a grin. "I've always liked your style, Kayla. You can be in my octet any day."

Vid chuckled. "Then there'd be six of us: you, Kayla, the boss, Hekkar, me and Trinan."

"No way I'm joining a group called the sextet." Kayla managed a smile, looking around the table. *These* were people she could trust. Malkor's people. Her people, now. "Keep it a six-person 'octet' and I'm in."

"Deal," Rigger said. "Now, about getting in to see Ardin…"

"Can you get me a comm line to him directly, without it routing through the palace comm system?"

Rigger made a sound of disgust. "I can't believe you asked me that." She was already headed to the office. "Let's do this. The sooner the boss is out of custody, the better."

28

Setting a meeting with Ardin went almost too smoothly—or maybe that's just how it felt when you worked with the best IDC agents in the galaxy.

Ardin instantly agreed to see her. The octet fabricated a false identity for Kayla as an interior decorator Ardin was considering hiring, now that he was married and Isonde wanted to make changes to their suite. She was slotted in as his fifteen hundred appointment.

Rigger got busy inserting her fake credentials into the imperial citizens identification database; meanwhile Hekkar calibrated contact lenses to match the ocular scan specs Rigger provided, and Trinan sculpted the palm print negative for the polymer printer. Vid had a little too much fun altering her features in the complink's facial recognition program, and sent the details to a low-end hologram biostrip.

Kayla slapped the hologram on and looked in the mirror. "Thanks for the underbite, Vid."

He laughed. "All in the name of disguise."

The contacts would take care of her eye color, and Vid had given her heavy lids, a unibrow and a protruding jaw.

"I owe you one," she threatened with a smile. A slightly yellowed smile. Kayla popped the contacts in—a lovely muddy brown that suited her newly dyed hair—and turned for a second opinion.

"Perfect," Trinan said. He opened the printer case and pulled out the sheet of transluca with the biofilm of the palm print on it. "Remember, you've got about twenty minutes from when you apply this biofilm to your skin until it dissolves, so don't put it on until you arrive." He put a second layer of transluca over the print and slid it into an envelope.

"And the hologram's low-tech," Hekkar said. "It only disguises your face, nothing else."

"Kris?" Vid held out a hand.

Kayla groaned. Worst part of the whole thing—having to leave her weapons behind. She pulled them from her bag and handed them over, then slid the envelope with the palm print into her bag. "If I come back and those are damaged in any way…"

"I'll guard them with my life."

Kayla punched Vid on the shoulder. "You better."

"Ready?" Hekkar asked. He ordered a cab to meet her in a nearby section of Shimville, far enough away to keep their location secret.

Kayla looked herself over once more and Rigger pushed her to the door. "We do this shit all the time. Don't worry, the fake ID will pass."

Kayla's short smile faded quickly. She looked at the octet members, their faces full of their typical confidence and "ready for a fight" attitudes, and realized how much she'd come to depend on them.

"If I don't come back tonight…" She couldn't get more than that out.

Hekkar nodded. "Same here," he said quietly.

They all gave her a pat on the back and sent her out the door.

The long ride across town went by in a blur of traffic and noise. Their progress evident as the roads gradually became cleaner, the pedestrians grew more fashionable, and the buildings began to soar. The architecture in the Royal Sector wasn't as inspired as in Ordoch's grand cities, but it was still the best Falanar had to offer, with clean building façades, statuary and the occasional tower.

When the palace came into view and the driver was occupied trying to find a parking spot, Kayla applied the preprinted biofilm to her left hand. The cab set down gently and Kayla hit the sidewalk at a brisk pace. She needed to make it through security and fast.

For the first time in—shit, weeks?—luck favored her, and she breezed through security. An aide led her through the halls and wings and floors until they reached Ardin's apartments and a pair of stoic guards. The aide checked her datapad. "Ms. Leedenma is here for the prince's fifteen hundred appointment. She's all checked in."

A nod from a guard, a brisk entrance, a departure by the aide, and there she was, standing face to face with two people—one her only hope, one her newest enemy.

Neither Ardin nor Isonde smiled. Each wore a different air of silence. Ardin looked grim. Isonde, in contrast, was caught by surprise by Kayla's entrance. She had a moment of bewilderment she tried to hide.

Good. Ardin hadn't told Isonde beforehand, hadn't given her a chance to scheme.

Isonde assumed a superior, polite air. "I don't believe we've met, Ms. Leedenma, is it?"

Kayla ignored her and spoke to Ardin. "Is there somewhere we can speak in absolute privacy?"

"Let's go to my office." He gestured for her to follow, and Kayla realized that his frown wasn't directed at her. She let out a tight breath. Even better.

"Ardin?" Isonde asked, trailing behind. "What's going on?"

It was hard—damn near impossible—for Kayla to stop herself from spinning on her heel and punching Isonde flat out. It would at least take the edge off of the wave of anger she rode.

Sadly, that might make too much of a spectacle for the servants, so she followed Ardin in silence. Isonde also shut her mouth when Ardin didn't reply.

They arrived at the office and Isonde slid into the room before Kayla could shut the door in her face.

Could I get away with throwing her out on her ass?

Kayla looked to Ardin for a hint that he wouldn't mind, but he ignored Isonde and crossed the room to the sideboard. The office had a warm vibe to it. It was richly paneled in wood to waist height, then painted in a deep red tone that lightened and transitioned to orange, then yellow, then to white at the very top, leading to a brightly lit ceiling.

It seemed entirely too tranquil to host the storm that brewed between the three of them.

"Drink, Kayla?" he asked, without turning around.

"Please." Kayla pulled off the hologram and dropped it into her pocket. No need for secrecy now.

Isonde arched both brows.

Catching Isonde unprepared, probably for the first time in their acquaintance, was delightfully satisfying.

Glass chinked as Ardin poured, took a good shot from his glass, and poured again. Isonde glanced sidelong at his back, not speaking. Angry words hung in the air, either screamingly unsaid or echoing from an earlier confrontation between these two. The quiet violence reverberated in the room. It was all Kayla could do to take a deep breath in the smothering atmosphere.

Ardin handed her a glass of amber fluid. The liquor matched his eyes, and the volatile fumes wafting from the glass matched the pain and anger she saw in his gaze.

He propped himself on the corner of his desk, still not looking at Isonde, which clearly upset her.

What finally pushed him too far, Isonde?

Isonde hid her annoyance behind a smile. "I'm glad you came, Kayla, I had no way to reach you. I was worried."

For a moment Kayla was speechless, glass halfway to her

mouth. She took a drink while she processed Isonde's unending audacity.

"You're actually going to try to bullshit me?" Kayla asked. "Now, after all you've done?" The thought was incredible.

"All I've done is—"

Isonde's placating tone sent Kayla through the roof. "'All you've done' is *ruin* Malkor," she said in a growl. "And me, though that's less surprising." She set her glass down on a nearby bookshelf before she threw it. "You've been using me from the beginning, so why not burn me to the ground if necessary. But Malkor?"

Shit. Kayla's chest ached at the thought of such a betrayal, of how Malkor would feel when he learned of it.

Ardin stared at the liquid in his glass, swirling it, as if it had a truth to reveal.

"After all Malkor's done for you," Kayla said, her voice a furious tremble. "Everything he's sacrificed. Everything *I've* sacrificed." She curled her hands into fists, curbing the urge to do violence. "You wouldn't be where you are without me, and you damn sure wouldn't be within ten thousand light-years of where you are if Malkor hadn't helped you at every step."

Kayla shook with rage. She wanted to cut Isonde open with words, wanted her to bleed. When she spoke, her voice was low with unrealized hatred. "You were never worth a second of his time."

"You don't know what I've sacrificed," Isonde said, as if she were misunderstood in all of this. "Everything I did, everything I do, is for—"

"Shut up." The quiet words came from Ardin, shocking them both.

Isonde blinked. "Excuse me?"

Ardin tossed back the rest of his drink, set his glass down very precisely, and got to his feet. "I said— Shut. Up." The command actually forced Isonde back a step.

In any other moment Kayla would have laughed to see that expression on Isonde's face—the astonishment of a lifetime.

Not now. Not when the words came from so deep inside Ardin's private hurt that they throbbed with feeling.

Isonde opened her mouth and Ardin took one step toward her.

Holy shit, was he going to strike her?

Ardin had much better self-control than Kayla had, and stopped after only that step.

He pointed his finger at Isonde's face. "Not another word."

She shut her mouth with a snap, her face blanched, pale eyes huge. No doubt Ardin had never used that tone on her before, never looked at her with such anger.

"I have listened to your 'for the good of the empire' reasoning all my life. I've watched you justify every action you've ever taken with that same damn speech, serving it flawlessly time and again. And I am *tired*, Isonde." His volume rose, filling the room with word after long-denied word. "I am so damn tired of it. Of you, hiding behind your 'I do this for the people' rhetoric, and crossing every line of morality, of legality… of decency."

Ardin's body vibrated with anger, with a fever pitch that Kayla feared would shatter him. His fury held the room spellbound, trapped them all in a tableau thirty-two years in the making. Kayla couldn't have moved if she wanted to.

"Malkor is like a brother to me, the only brother I've ever had." His lips twisted into a mockery of a smile. "I can't say you feel the same about him, since I know about your relationship."

Isonde swayed and reached out to steady herself on the back of a chair. "What relationship?" Her voice was whisper thin.

Kayla jumped when Ardin laughed, an ugly, wrenching sound.

"In the face of all this, you would lie to me?" he asked. "I may have been a hopeless, lovesick idiot where you are concerned, but I'm not blind. I knew when you and Malkor hooked up years ago, just as I knew that it would pass, that you'd choose me in the end." He turned his head toward Kayla. "Ask me how I knew."

Ardin was dangerous like this. Dangerous and glorious. He

was capable of anything in this state and for the first time since meeting him, he'd earned Kayla's full respect.

"How?" Kayla asked, unable to do other than follow where he led.

"Ambition, of course. Isonde's ambition wouldn't allow for anything less than the throne at my side."

He turned a smile on Isonde that mocked her as much as it mocked him. "I told myself you'd come to love me as much as Malkor, in time. More even." When he spoke again his voice was brutal, any trace of a smile gone from his face. "And I believed myself. The greatest of my follies.

"I believed when you spoke of our future together, told me, 'Together, we can be a force for good.' I wanted that." He closed his eyes a moment. "Gods, how I wanted that."

Isonde's shock melted in the heat of Ardin's words. She seemed to be gathering herself for a speech.

Ardin opened his eyes and fixed Isonde with a stare. "It was all bullshit, wasn't it? In your heart it was you and only you from the start. From the moment we met as children."

He rolled on when Isonde tried to interrupt.

"You care about me, sure," he said. "We're 'friends.' But you used me, like you use everyone." Ardin paused, as if letting those words sink in to his own consciousness. Kayla held her breath, uncertain what might come next.

He nodded to himself as if a truth was finally clear. When he refocused his gaze on Isonde, his voice rang with conviction. "Malkor never asked for anything of us. Not *once*. You—we— abused his position as a senior IDC agent again and again, and he never once insisted on concessions for himself.

"What you did today," he said, drawing himself straight and looking every inch the ruler he was born to be, "denouncing Malkor—the very best friend we, either of us, have ever had— when he needed our support most, is unforgivable." The words were a decision, binding and irrevocable. A sentence levied on a criminal.

"Ardin, please," Isonde said, in a placating tone, "be

331

reasonable. If I am to retain my position of influence I have to distance myself from him. Surely you see that."

Ardin turned away as if he couldn't bear to look at her a moment longer. Instead he met Kayla's gaze and spoke only to her. "I know what Malkor means to you. I am sorry for everything he has suffered at our hands."

She respected him for owning his part in this tragedy, but regret, no matter how sincere, wouldn't help them now. "I need more than your apology."

Ardin nodded. "Anything, you name it. If it is within my power to give, you will have it."

She cut a glance to Isonde.

"Leave us," Ardin commanded without looking at Isonde, his tone unquestionable. Even Isonde couldn't argue. She marched from the room with her head high.

The tension left with her, leaving Kayla alone with the ally she hadn't expected, the ally she couldn't do without.

"I need a ship," Kayla said without preamble. "With Malkor and the octet on the official 'enemy of the state' list, none of them have the wherewithal to obtain a vessel capable of getting us to Wyrd Space."

"I can do that." The wounded soul disappeared behind the aloof mask she was used to from Ardin. "When do you need it by?"

She blinked. Somehow she hadn't expected it would be that simple. "ASAP." *Otherwise known as, "No frutting idea, just have the damn thing ready."*

He seemed to get the silent message. "Understood. You have a plan to 'liberate' Malkor, I assume?"

If only. "Still working on that. Let me know as soon as you have a ship ready. Don't bother with a captain, I know someone who could fly it." Probably every one of the octet members were trained to pilot any number of craft. If not, she'd figure out the particulars as she went. It was imperial tech, how complex could it be?

She meant to head for the door. Instead she found herself

pulling Ardin in for an awkward hug. It was stiff and uncomfortable and so what she needed that tears stung her eyes when he finally hugged her back. *You were so brave today,* she wanted to whisper. He wouldn't appreciate the reminder of all the days he'd let himself be Isonde's puppet.

She pulled back and looked at him head-on. "Thank you." She couldn't put enough emphasis on the words to do them justice. "From one person who loves Malkor to another." She squeezed his arm, trying to impart all of her feelings at once. "Thank you."

He cleared his throat and stepped away. "Better head off, now. Mind the hologram."

Kayla pulled out the biostrip and slapped it on. She walked to the door, then looked over her shoulder at Ardin. This might be the last time she ever saw him.

He raised a hand in farewell.

When Kayla exited the office, she saw Isonde standing halfway down the hallway. No doubt she was waiting for another chance at Ardin.

She gave Kayla a cool look. "I bet you're pretty proud of yourself," Isonde said with faint hauteur, "turning Ardin against me."

Kayla struggled to get a grip on her temper. The hallway was not private. Here, she was an interior decorator facing the Empress-Apparent, and a linen maid down the hall looked on with round eyes.

"Everything coming to you, Isonde, you brought on yourself," she said in a low voice, anxious to get out of there before she blew her cover.

Isonde scoffed. She straightened her shoulders, squaring herself to Kayla. "If you knew anything about—"

"You know what I know?" Kayla interrupted, on the balls of her feet now. She looked down the hall—empty, the maid had fled.

Isonde arched one imperious brow and it was all Kayla needed. She took a double step to gain momentum and kicked the bitch square in the solar plexus with a heel kick that could have broken concrete. The sole of her boot sent Isonde staggering into the wall. Isonde rebounded and dropped to her knees, retching.

Kayla knelt beside her while Isonde gasped and choked, braced on all fours. "That's how Malkor's going to feel when he hears how you've betrayed him."

Isonde's coughing, the helpless spittle dripping down her chin, and the green tinge of her skin gave Kayla a rush of satisfaction.

A male servant appeared in the hallway in response to Isonde's pitiful hacking noises. Kayla offered him an innocent smile while Isonde gripped her stomach.

"The princess is coming down with something. Could you help her into the bed she made? I think it's best she lie in it, now."

Kayla sauntered down the hall, humming a *ro'haar* training song.

29

THE *YARI*, MINE FIELD

Vayne stood at the windows on the smaller observation deck of the *Yari*, studying the tear in space. It fluctuated and twinkled, blinding in its radiance and impossibility, offering escape from the Middle of Nowhere.

Except escape to his besieged homeworld was no escape at all. The Tear's promise mocked him.

Benny and Tanet sat down a ways in the comfortable chairs that had been dragged to this deck. Farther back in the room, Noar sat on the hard benches with Luliana and Joffar, taking a rare break from working on the hyperstream engine. The three Ilmenans quietly discussed when Ilmena might be able to send another fuel ship to them. Tia'tan had contacted Ilmena with the request, giving them the same coordinates Vayne had given Kayla. Coordinates they'd figured out when the last sensor reached the edge of the Mine Field and could translate its location back to the others, measuring the distance between them until the Middle of Nowhere's actual position was fixed.

Foolish to request a ship from Ilmena now, considering they hadn't even proved Corinth, Tanet and Noar's theory yet, that taking a hyperstream straight into the heart of the Mine Field would avoid disruption.

Tia'tan stood beside Vayne at the glass, ignoring her fellows.

Instead of looking at the Tear, her gaze traveled farther, to the curve of the Mine Field debris that ringed them. She concentrated as if summoning something from the wreckage.

The *Radiant,* no doubt.

No one had mentioned the ship in the last week, the unspoken consensus being that it had been destroyed. Hard to argue any other outcome considering how long it had been missing.

Vayne glanced at Tia'tan's solemn profile.

The unexpected urge to offer her comfort caught him off guard. How long had it been since he'd worried about anyone's pain besides his own? He looked at her again. She was worlds away. The right words wouldn't come to him, and he'd just be interrupting her. He could only offer her privacy, and the silence of one who knew that sometimes, nothing could make it right.

::I've finally pulled Gintoc away from the engine room.:: Corinth's mind voice halted the downward spiral of Vayne's mood. ::We're coming to the observation deck. Gintoc says, 'View most impossible is restful,' or something like that, so I think he wants to watch the Tear for a while.::

Sleep would be better, but it sometimes seemed as if the crew never slept. As if they feared that if they closed their eyes for one moment, they would never wake again.

Besides, building a makeshift hyperstream drive from castoff parts was pure insanity. Why not have a slightly off-center, sleep-deprived engineer working on it at all hours?

Corinth entered first, his face alight with excitement. ::You'll never guess what we figured out.:: Everyone in the gallery straightened with interest when he spoke. Corinth latched onto the engineer's wrist and pulled him forward when the man froze in the doorway.

::Gintoc will tell you. Noar! We were looking at that coolant siphoning system all wrong.::

Vayne's eyes remained on Gintoc, unmoving in the doorway. Gintoc's gaze swept over everyone. The engineer was an odd one, to be sure. Taciturn didn't begin to cover it, though he seemed to get along well enough with the few people who could speak the language of his beloved engines.

Now, Gintoc's mouth twisted into a frown. "Not to rest with the enemy." His gaze turned cold, suspicious.

Benny called to him from the other end of the room. "You never like the new Ida bring." He smiled and waved him over. "They are not so new now. Come. Have a sit."

Gintoc shook his head. "Princess Natali is where? She knows the enemy."

True enough. Natali's world seemed blocked out into two categories: "on her side," or "needs to be defeated."

::Come on.:: Corinth tugged at his sleeve. Gintoc held firm, glaring first at Tia'tan where she stood with Vayne, then at the gathered Ilmenans.

"Pah." Gintoc made a sound of disgust and spat on the floor. He wrenched his arm from Corinth's grasp and left.

Tanet finally broke the awkward silence. "Is solitary, is all. Gintoc likes very few, isn't to worry."

"Overtired," Benny said, and both crewmembers seemed to agree with that assessment.

Corinth shrugged. ::I'll check on him, Vayne. See you.:: Then he was gone as well.

The confrontation was typical of any interaction Vayne had with the engineer, but the fact that he asked for Natali, saw her as an ally even though she didn't know a thing about engines, stuck in Vayne's mind.

The sooner Kayla got here, the better—for all involved.

ORDOCH

Midnight, Cinni thought, or close to it. Down here in the bowels of the rebel base it was impossible to tell.

She stood in the corridor outside the makeshift infirmary. Weak lighting set the hallway in perpetual twilight, and the smell of dust and damp concrete permeated the air. Through the square window set in the infirmary door she saw Aarush's prone body. He lay still as death, the blue sheet covering him looking more like a shroud than bedding, and she shivered with premonition.

Stupid, really. An amputated foot, massive burns and an eye that may or may not recover from shrapnel wounds didn't kill someone. To her, though, it felt as though he'd already died. The image she always had of him, utterly competent, quietly commanding, a rebel star on the rise, was forever shattered. The man she loved was gone.

More than a week had passed since the failed raid and still she couldn't bring herself to visit him.

Inside the infirmary darkness enveloped the beds, the gloom broken only by a single lamp at Aarush's bedside. Mishe sat there, reading something to their commander. Mishe was the only reason she knew anything about Aarush's progress—or lack thereof.

Mishe visited him regularly. Aarush's biggest fear, Mishe said, was that he had suddenly become useless to the rebellion because he couldn't lead any more raids. It horrified him. So Mishe kept him in the loop. Brought him reports, updated him on everything from raiding plans to the *Yari*'s progress to the dwindling medical supplies. Made him feel included, if not exactly useful again. It gave him a future to hope for, Mishe told her.

Mishe had also told her that the damage to Aarush's right eye was extensive, and that it was uncertain yet whether the tissue regeneration would take effect. Currently, he could only see vague shadows in that eye and the other one was gone completely.

Then there was Aarush's foot. Cinni sighed, placing her palm against the door and leaning closer. The effect of the dreamers she'd taken whooshed through her bloodstream, blurring lines, washing away tension. Mishe was a familiar and much-loved haze of brown in the chair, the lamplight a puddle of butter on the pillow, but that gaping cavity at the end of the bed, that depression in the sheet where a foot should have been, was as crisp as the first time she'd seen it.

"Nothing to do," she whispered, remembering Mishe's report. "Nothing to do."

The leg had been severed halfway up his shin. Before the occupation, it would have been a dramatic, if not necessarily life-altering injury. They'd had access to the medical equipment necessary to regrow the limb and reattach it.

Here? In this rat hole? Even if they had possessed the equipment they certainly didn't have a surgeon capable of completing a reattachment. It's not like you could stick the two ends together, slap a regen cuff on it and call it done. Not something that complicated.

Cinni sighed, feeling the mellow overtake her. One dreamer too many? Possibly.

She pushed away from the infirmary door, steadied herself, and started down the corridor slowly. She needed bed. And sleep.

And there was nothing to be done.

30

SHIMVILLE, FALANAR

Kayla made it back to the octet's safehouse at sunset. Her blood still sang from her final words to Isonde. The promise of a ship from Ardin buoyed her.

They could do this.

The octet was gathered around the long table in the war room, the surface covered with a dozen schematics. Trinan and Vid seemed to be in the middle of a vehement argument about sewers, of all things, and Rigger slouched in her chair, head hanging over the back as if she couldn't look at the schematics for another minute.

Hekkar, bent over the table, palms spread wide to brace himself, looked up at her entrance. "How'd it go?"

Trinan and Vid left off arguing, the topic tabled only briefly, based on their belligerence, and Rigger clearly thought Kayla's appearance was a divine interruption.

"Went well." Kayla dumped the hologram biostrip on the table, popped out the contacts and looked around for her kris as she spoke.

Hekkar straightened, and then passed Kayla her kris. "Ardin came through, then?"

"In a big way." She gave them the short version of the conversation. "Bottom line, we have a ship. I assume one of you can fly it, whatever it is?"

"Yes," they said in unison.

Kayla chuckled. "Figured. Now. Your turn to wow me. How are we springing Malkor?"

"Well," Hekkar said, "I've got some shitty news, followed by more shitty news. What do you want first?"

"Bring it on." He hadn't said Malkor had been killed, and that's the only thing she couldn't work with. Everything else she could bend, break or twist her way through, if it meant saving him.

"The Sovereign Council retired their session while you were gone," Hekkar said, "and presented their recommendation for the Council of Seven, which will convene in the morning."

Kayla waited for the verdict.

"They've outlined a plan for full-scale militarization of the occupation. This includes sending troops and more ships immediately, along with increasing personnel recruitment, weapons manufacturing and battleship production."

"So far we've only barely held Ordoch," Rigger said. "Now we're talking planetary annex-level militarization."

Annexation. Making Ordoch part of the empire, their foothold into Wyrd Space.

"Not in my lifetime," she spat.

Rigger shrugged. "If the Council of Seven votes that way, it's going to be a frutt of a lot harder to free your planet."

All that work. Weeks of it. Months, even. Studying the empire's political power players, laying the groundwork for Isonde's master plan, swaying council members. The speeches, the concessions, the debates—all of it, every last second of being Isonde—for nothing if the final vote didn't go their way.

"What's the rest of the news?"

"We've been over every millimeter of the schematics for IDC headquarters. Twice," Hekkar said. "We'll keep at it for a few more hours, but, I'm telling you now—it's impossible to bust Malkor out of there."

* * *

Sometime around twenty-three hundred Kayla and the octet finally surrendered to the reality of Hekkar's earlier statement. There was no possible way to gain access to the cell block, not without an army that outnumbered the mass of IDC agents in headquarters, and multiple hacks into the many security systems that governed the place. Every scenario they ran through the complink ended in failure.

And that was unacceptable. Unacceptable and inevitable.

The octet broke for the night, everyone grabbing a few hours of sleep before they were back at it the next morning.

By then everyone had come to the same decision: it was time to call Vega to deal.

Kayla ate a quick breakfast alone, leaving the octet arguing over locations for the Vega meet/Malkor hostage exchange and different exit strategies. She could fight her way out of a mob armed with only a fork and a really bad attitude, but she happily left matters of strategy to the IDC agents. She was a bodyguard, pure and simple. She knew how to assess threats, rank risk levels, and protect a single person with her life. She wasn't a soldier and her training in tactics didn't scratch the surface of what the octet knew.

Besides, she needed time to wrestle with her demons.

She'd sworn, time and time again, that she'd destroy Dolan's data—with or without the octet's blessing—before handing it over to Vega. After what her family had suffered with the Influencer, what Vayne had suffered at Dolan's hands...

The idea that anyone, *anyone*, could be subjected to that kind of soul-destroying torture made her physically ill. And here she was, agreeing to hand it over to Vega.

The breakfast she'd eaten threatened a return.

Who had she become, that she would allow this? Who was she that she would let someone else suffer the pain that had nearly broken her twin?

A woman in love.

That's who she had become.

The *ro'haar*, the weapon, the ultimate bodyguard she was

born to be had fallen in love. And not just in love, in love with an imperial. And so in love that she would sacrifice nearly everything to save him. Her ideals. Her morals.

She'd sacrifice the happiness of someone else's tomorrow for her chance to save Malkor today. The faces of Vayne and Corinth swam before her suddenly watery eyes. Pray that the choice never came down between Malkor and her brothers—she wouldn't survive.

Instead of joining the others, Kayla went downstairs to the weapons room, looking for a way to sharpen her kris and ease her soul. Her kris-sharpening kit and round diamond file had been left in her apartments at the palace after her mad flight for freedom.

Now here she sat, with fine-grit sandpaper wrapped around the cylindrical handle of a medstick, trying to sharpen the wavy edges of her kris without marring the metal too badly. Thankfully her kris were fairly demure in design, with only a few mild curves on each side. Anything tighter would be a bitch to sharpen.

Hekkar came down the stairs quietly and found a stool in the corner to perch on. An oddly companionable silence bloomed between them, when for so long she'd felt that Hekkar was, if not her enemy, her biggest hurdle to winning the octet over. Now he watched her with respect and she felt joined to him in a purpose. No one loved Malkor more than these agents, with the exception of Ardin, and perhaps no one more so than Hekkar. In this, she and Hekkar were equals, and that awareness settled on them both.

"Why kris daggers?" he finally asked, as if the question had been bugging him since they met. He gestured to the pointed tip. "I mean, they're sufficient for stabbing, and the curves give it a wider blade track without the weight of a wider weapon, but…"

Kayla chuckled. "Believe me, I know. Kris are rarely sharpened and hardly hold an edge. When it comes to cutting and slicing, a straight-edged dagger beats them for sheer utility."

"Why would you use a blade that is less than perfectly efficient?"

"Credits. It's all about the credits." At least it had been when she was on Altair Tri and desperate for a way home. "This isn't a *ro'haar* ceremonial weapon or anything. It's an affectation, pure and simple. Showmanship." Kayla looked at the wavy edges of the weapons that had surprisingly become her dearest possessions. "On Ordoch I trained with every type of weapon conceivable—and even things that you'd never think of as a weapon." She smiled at the memories of fighting with a rolling-pin, a shoe, a musty piece of fabric. "You never know what you'll have at hand when your *il'haar* needs protecting." She shrugged her shoulders. "Sure, I went around armed with a plasma blaster, but my people had long ago figured out how to disable advanced weapons electronically. I couldn't count on that. So I also wore two knives. Armed with low-tech and high, like a true *ro'haar*.

"When I landed on Altair Tri and realized the only way to get Corinth home was to earn an obscene amount of credits and purchase a ride back to Wyrd Space, I adopted the Shadow Panthe persona."

"And fought in the pits," Hekkar said.

"Exactly. Fighting in the pits isn't about skill. I could have beaten most of my opponents armed with a pickle." Kayla set her kris aside, its edge perfectly sharp. "Fighting in the pits—and drawing the biggest purse per fight—is all about showmanship. I learned that early on."

"And so the kris?"

She nodded. "No one fought with kris daggers. They were unique. Exotic. They played into my mysterious Shadow Panthe persona. I made them work. And in the end, I could demand more credits per fight based on my 'alluring mystique.'"

Hekkar seemed to take that in. It was refreshing to discuss weapons with a person who understood the balance between form and function, who valued lethality above all. Just as she'd been taught. A *ro'haar* did not plan to detain their *il'haar*'s attacker. A *ro'haar* killed first, and investigated the attack after their *il'haar*'s safety was assured.

"Will you give the kris up once you return home?" Hekkar asked.

The kris had served her well, kept her safe for five years in exile. Would they serve her as well when she and her family retook Ordoch?

"Depends on what my *il'haar* needs," she said. The answer came without hesitation.

Rigger summoned them from upstairs and Hekkar got to his feet.

"What about Malkor?" Hekkar asked, without looking away. "What if Malkor needs something different from you?"

"That can't matter," Kayla said in a tiny voice, the sound almost swallowed by the darkness.

Could it? Could what Malkor wanted make a difference once they escaped from here?

"You might want to think on that one," Hekkar said.

After a debate, it was decided that Hekkar would host the call to Vega and keep Kayla's presence with them a secret. All Vega knew was that Kayla was in hiding, not that she'd teamed with the octet. Kayla watched the vidscreen from an angle, keeping out of sight when Vega appeared.

The senior commander looked perfectly composed, as if she received calls about illicit prisoner exchanges daily. She took the call in the back of a hover car, based on the plush seating, dim lighting and occasional glimpse of scenery behind her.

"Good to hear from you, Agent."

"Wish I could say the same," Hekkar said.

Vega nodded to acknowledge that. "I assume you're contacting me about a trade?" The woman brought a new level of professionalism to the term "all business."

"Malkor in exchange for Dolan's scientific data." Hekkar's voice was grim, and Kayla could practically hear him adding, "and your head on a platter, while we're at it."

Too bad that outcome seemed unlikely.

Vega muted the comm to say something to her driver, then resumed. "I want all of it, Agent. Not just specs on advanced weapon design."

"You'll get what's there."

She shook her head. "Not good enough. I *know* the information about his Influencer is on that chip."

"Influencer? That's what we're going with?" Hekkar made a sound of disgust. "Pretty benign term for a machine that strips a person of their free will."

"Do you want your octet leader or not?"

"We'll deal," Hekkar said. What choice did they have?

"I assumed so. I took the liberty of selecting the exchange location. I'll send coordinates a half-hour before. You'll have enough time to get there for nineteen hundred."

Vega stared him down. Neither was willing to give the other the advantage. Then again, neither was willing to risk ruining the deal.

"Fine," Hekkar finally said.

"Nineteen hundred it is. Bring all of the data or don't bother coming at all, in which case I'll simply kill Agent Rua."

"You wouldn't dare."

Vega arched a brow. "Why wouldn't I? He's already played the role I needed him for, quite admirably. His only worth at this point is as collateral."

She'd do it, too. They all knew that. Her reasoning was perfectly logical, if frighteningly cold.

"We'll be there," Hekkar said, and ended the call. He swiveled in his chair, looking at the group. "Well?"

"I'd like to kill her," Kayla said.

Hekkar smiled. "Noted. Anyone else?"

Vid raised his hand. "I second Kayla's idea."

The joking broke the tension. The situation was bleak, but at least they had a plan.

31

THE *YARI*, MINE FIELD

Vayne's boot heels echoed on the plate decking that ran the length of the corridor's floor. It was the only sound on this abandoned level, five below the last "safe" level, according to Ida. The lighting was non-existent. When curiosity overcame caution and his need to know what the crew of the *Yari* feared became greater than Ida's stern warnings to keep to the three main decks, Vayne had popped a maintenance hatch and climbed down ladders until he'd dropped out here.

Of course he'd had to repeat the journey in reverse to grab a light to clip to his shirt. He swung by the commissary, thankfully empty, and armed himself with a plasma bullpup before heading back down.

For the first time in too many days he had something to *do*, even if it was walking empty corridors in the dark. Better than the endless brooding, the mistrustful looks from Gintoc, the infuriating conversations with Dolan's ghost and listening to everyone else's whacked-out plans to fire up the PD weapon.

The flashlight's thin beam glanced wildly off the gorgeous rose-gold molychromium walls. The priceless metal, seen now only in works of art and classic buildings on Ordoch, provided the bare bones of the entire ship. In the darkness, with the surrounding air of abandonment, Vayne felt a little like he was robbing a tomb.

What was down here that required weapons as protocol?

In all likelihood the answer was simply nothing. The crew had all spent time in cryochambers—too much time. History vids commented on the rudimentary design of the *Yari*'s cryosystems, the inadequacy of them for long-term use. Without saying as much, the vids intimated that the crew of the *Yari* had basically intended to travel to Ilmena, shoot the shit out of it, and come home. There was no long-term end game in Ordoch's plan to win the Second Ilmenan War.

Who knew what had happened to the crew's consciousness in all the intervening time?

"I'll probably find spiders the size of hover cars." Despite his flippant words, something about the abandoned corridor made him stalk lightly, gripping the bullpup close.

The first sound came as he took a step, half-hidden beneath his boot-fall. Imagination? The natural shifting and settling of an ancient ship?

He halted, turning this way and that, looking for anything out of the ordinary. Doors lined the corridor, each sealed shut, refusing to open when he waved the RFID Ida had given him across the access panel. Each door had a small window set into it, and a quick peek inside with his light showed abandoned crew quarters.

He waited, muscles tensed, for another sound.

What he got instead was an awareness of his own foolishness. *There's nothing down here.*

"Time to head back," he muttered. Instead, something urged: *Farther. The answer to the mystery is around this bend.* He'd been listening to that feeling fruitlessly for an hour, and yet, he kept going. What was the harm? He had nothing better to do.

He'd only taken one step when a banging sound made him jump a meter. A pipe rapping against the molychromium? Bang bang bang—pause—bang bang bang—pause. It was impossible to tell if it came from behind or ahead. No bulkheads had been set into the walls here; it was only the metal frame, waiting in vain to be completed. The sound echoed all around him.

Vayne set his ear to the nearest wall once the sound stopped and held his breath.

Would it come again?

Maybe it was a motor firing, groaning to life to maintain the correct nitrogen-oxygen levels on this floor.

Bang bang bang—pause—bang—pause—bang bang— pause—bang bang bang—pause.

The sound shot through him, raising his hackles. That was no automated generator.

He shielded with his psi powers. Wouldn't do shit against a plasma weapon, but hey, he was the one holding that, at least.

He crept down the hall as the eerie banging continued. The way it reverberated defied all attempts to pinpoint it. Above? Below?

Without closing his eyes he sent his senses outward. His mind flowed like silk over everything, filling the hall like water, breaching metal barriers. He reached outward and upward and downward in a cloud of mental taste and touch, seeking, seeking...

There. A touch. Ice cold. An icicle stabbed into his brain and the sense was lost.

He was alone again in the corridor.

But he was not alone on these abandoned levels. Not by a long shot.

Vayne checked the charge on his bullpup. Full. He crept forward again, shining his light in every conceivable crevice. The banging had become syncopated, its nonsensical rhythm messing with his head. What the frutt had he wandered into?

He rounded the corridor and stopped dead. A door had been breached. The oval slab of metal hung on perfectly balanced hinges, the entire piece of molychromium leaning away from its ruined lock to gape open into the corridor. Thirty degrees of darkness grinned at him from the opening while the pipe pounded away, ringing in his head.

I should call someone. Who? Ida wouldn't answer his

questions. Anyone could have busted this door open. It could have been one of her own crewmembers, after decades of curiosity, if she refused to tell even them anything more than "is protocol."

Vayne approached the door, feeling that he was about to slip in over his head. The beam of his flashlight fell on the gouged and twisted metal of the door's lock. Impossible to tell if it had been jammed, filed away, melted or all of the above. One thing was certain—

The door's lock had been compromised from the inside.

He toed the door open and peered in.

His light fell on a scene of chaos, of passion and insanity and genius and filth. It was indeed crew quarters, judging by the bed—standard size for an imperial female, which would accommodate males fine—the storage unit built into the wall and the ravaged desk.

The overpowering stench of the place made him drop back for a second, gasping in clean air from the corridor before entering the room. The sheets, standard military issue, were torn and twisted, knotted into something that resembled a quipu—a primitive record-keeping system, with many of the strands appearing to be dyed.

The floor, walls, and in some corners, the ceiling, were covered in scribbling. No, not scribbling, diagrams. Battle plans. Star charts. Escape plans. It was like a mad scientist had been locked in this box for a dozen years and made use of every available material. While the floor, walls and ceiling looked to be covered in etchings, the surface of the desk had been pulled from the wall and covered in impermanent markings, used like a primitive tablet or notebook. Based on the stench rising from the thing, the writing medium used was feces.

Vayne covered his nose and mouth with his sleeve and studied the rest of the room.

A portable food synthesizer had been installed in one wall. Below it, a stack of trays waist-high, some still crusted with what appeared to be food, waited for no one. The legs of the desk had been snapped from their frame and were shaped into everything from a spoon to a stylus to a shiv. He looked to the inside of the door.

They apparently made an adequate crowbar, as well.

The sanitary unit was the main source of the stench, though Vayne had his own suspicions about some of the materials used to dye the strands of the sheet quipu. The door to the sonic shower was broken, the fixture ripped off the wall, and the sink had suffered a similar fate. Water, such a precious commodity in a closed system like a spaceship, dripped wastefully from a busted spigot. The privy was filled to overflowing with shit, and the waste dribbled and oozed onto the floor. Five seconds in the putrid space was all Vayne could stand before he ran out into the hallway, kicked the door closed and vomited.

Being outside the room wasn't far enough.

He strode meters away from the cesspool before retching again.

Halfway down the corridor, far enough away he couldn't even see the room, the queasiness finally settled. Vayne collapsed against the rose-gold wall. The banging had stopped, replaced by the sound of his blood roaring in his ears.

Whatever they'd held in there, for however long they'd held it, had escaped.

He had to call someone. He shakily reached for his comm and pinged Tia'tan. "You have to come see this," he said, when she answered. "And bring a weapon."

As he wiped his mouth and leaned weakly against the molychromium wall, it occurred to him how odd it was that Tia'tan was his first choice.

Kayla would be his primary ally, of course, but she wasn't here. He felt closest to Corinth second, but he and Kayla shared a goal of shielding and protecting the boy. Five years ago he might have considered Natali or his uncle, but not now. Never again. Of the other Ilmenans, Joffar, the eldest of the bunch, was quiet. Though that was preferable to Luliana, who watched Vayne like he was about to go feral any moment.

Then again, she was probably closest to the truth. No matter how in control he felt—and the word "control" was an overstatement—a fierce animal rage lurked beneath the surface on even his best days.

Cinni wasn't here, and despite being a fellow Ordochian, he wouldn't have called her anyway. She struck him as somewhat immature. He liked some of the crew—Benny, Tanet, and even Ida—but none of them felt like allies.

So why did Tia'tan?

She was the one who had gotten them into this mess, who had lied about taking him to safety on Ilmena.

She was also the one he understood best. Tia'tan had taken a chance for a friend, refusing to leave Kazamel behind for dead even though she risked her own mission. He could respect that. She was driven and capable, just like Kayla. With her, he felt almost like part of a team.

The wild, crazy-assed, unpredictable super-psi-power part of a team, but part of a team, at least.

Right now, Tia'tan was the closest thing he had to a *ro'haar*, though she had never been trained as such. Ilmenans didn't follow the *ro'haar-il'haar* tradition the way Ordochians did.

When she arrived, Vayne pointed down the corridor. "Take a look for yourself, fourth door on the left. Can't miss it."

He didn't follow her, he didn't need to. The horror of the room had imprinted itself on his brain.

When he heard her retching and trying to catch her breath a few minutes later, he called her back. "It's easier to breathe over here."

Tia'tan returned and steadied herself with a hand against the wall. "I don't know what the frutt is going on," she said, wiping a hand across her mouth, "but we need to confront Ida about it. Now."

The syncopated banging began again. Was something else down here?

A call to Ida brought her, Benny and Ariel into the corridor like a storm. Ida, furious, ordered Tia'tan and Vayne out of there—and not politely, either. Ariel "escorted" them, vaguely at gunpoint, off the level and back to the command room. Once she'd ordered them to stay put with "wrath of Ida isn't to risk," she disappeared again.

Vayne and Tia'tan debated theories about who, or what, exactly, had been locked in that room, only to fall silent when the ship lurched slightly, as if nudged by a giant hand.

The ship's klaxon blared to life. The *Yari*'s "high alert" audible could split someone's head in two. Vayne figured out how to silence the alarm in the command room while Tia'tan found the reason for the alert.

"Shit. The docking hatch." Tia'tan pointed to a screen which showed docking hatch IIJ blown wide open. The *Sicerro* had been thrust away from the *Yari* in the blast and resulting depressurization. Tia'tan's ship rotated slowly, damage visible on its port side where the ships had been linked.

Tia'tan activated a second screen, one keeping track of the *Sicerro* while the other showed the damage to hatch IIJ. Definitely the result of explosives rather than simple mechanical failure. Vayne didn't even know what to think at this point.

"We have a serious problem," Tia'tan said over ship-wide comms. "The *Sicerro*—"

Exploded.

The ship glowed red-hot, then burst apart with amazing violence. The resulting shockwave rocked the *Yari* and set off a new round of alarms.

Tia'tan froze, half-bent over the console, gaze locked on the screen that showed her ship flying apart in a million pieces. "That did *not* happen." She replayed the feed, watching the destruction a second time.

Vayne checked the weapons log. "No one on the *Yari* fired at it."

"Self-destruct," she said, her voice strangled. She hit the comms again. "For the love of the void, *get back here!*"

Tanet made it there first, then Ida, Benny and Ariel rushed in. Ariel knocked Tia'tan out of the way and took command of the vid feeds. Tanet replayed the explosion while Ariel reversed the security feed in the docking hatch. "There," she said, jabbing a finger at the screen.

On screen, a figure crouched at the base of the hatch, laying down what looked to be blocks of explosives. He or she had matted teal-green hair and wore the official black jumpsuit of the *Yari*'s crew, torn in a dozen places.

"Who the frutt is that?" Vayne asked. The figure—female, it seemed—kept glancing over her shoulder every few seconds as if expecting discovery. Her furtive motions and twitchy behavior mimicked a wild animal. Ariel reversed the feed farther and the woman could be seen creeping out of the airlock from the direction of the *Sicerro*.

The crew of the *Yari* was silent, as if unwilling to admit what happened.

Vayne turned to Ida. Damn if she wasn't going to answer his questions now. "Who is that? Is she the one who escaped from crew quarters on level C-18?"

Ida, gaze still glued to the vidscreen, nodded. She looked weary. Heartsick.

Tia'tan, in contrast, looked ready to tear someone apart. She paced near the doorway, no doubt in silent communication with the other Ilmenans.

"That's Itsy," Ida finally said.

"Oritzi Engar," Ariel clarified dully, "weapon systems specialist. Became *stepa at es* time ago." She tapped her temple with a finger and translated. "Consumed by cryo."

"So in other words, crazy."

Ariel nodded.

Perfect. Because what this ship really needed right now was more crazy. "How many other *stepa at es* are out there?"

"Uncertain to say." Ida finally looked away from the vidscreen to meet his gaze. "Not all captured, not all alive."

At least the bullpup protocol made sense now.

::Someone's here! She hurt Noar and Larsa, I don't know if they're dead, and Gintoc's—::

Corinth's shout must have hit everyone at once because Tia'tan grabbed the bullpup she'd set down when they first got there and took off down the corridor. Vayne was half a second behind.

Ida left Tanet and Ariel to hold the control room, then she and Benny were right on their heels. It was a frantic race down dark corridors, tight access ladders and one slow lift ride.

"I can't reach Noar," Tia'tan said, as they sprinted down the long corridor leading to the engine room. "If that crazy Itsy hurt him—"

"Same for Corinth," Vayne said. Cold gripped his insides. The last words Kayla said in their recent conversation rang in his head: *Keep you and Corinth safe. No matter what you have to do.* He was not going to fail her.

Tia'tan waved her RFID at the engine room doors, and rushed through when they opened. She tripped over something and sprawled headlong into the room, her bullpup spinning wildly away from her. As she was kicking free of the dark shapes tangling her feet, Vayne caught sight of faces—Luliana and Joffar, burnt by plasma blasts and still as death. A plasma bolt hit the floor centimeters from Tia'tan's hand.

Shit. *She's as good as dead, defenseless like that.* He threw a psi shield around her instinctively, even knowing it wouldn't save her from a plasma weapon.

The hover cart full of random engine parts sat just beyond her. It would provide adequate cover, if he could get her there.

With no more thought than that, Vayne leapt over the bodies and vaulted into the room. He ducked low, grabbed Tia'tan under her armpit and dragged her to the cart, every second expecting the fiery burn of plasma to hit him.

"Get her out of here," Natali hissed, from farther inside the engine room. He could barely see Natali beyond the edge of the cart. She stood in the open, unarmed and disconcertingly calm considering the chaos of their situation. She had her hands out to her sides as if trying to reassure someone she wasn't about to make any sudden moves.

"Corinth!" Vayne called out.

::I'm here, I'm here, I'm not hurt. But Gintoc—he's not okay.::

The way Corinth said "not okay" put Vayne on edge. What the frutt had they walked into? He didn't dare look over the cart. Beside him, Tia'tan was flat on her belly, spreading her fingers out beyond their cover and trying to grab the strap of her bullpup.

Ida, still in the corridor braced against the doors as cover, peeked her head out for a split second to gauge the situation. Whatever she'd seen had been enough to convince her she wasn't in mortal danger. She gave Benny the command to stay put and stepped into the room. She had her weapon ready, and step by step made her way past them and over to Natali.

"Captain!" Gintoc called. "Three of the enemy down, see?" His strident voice echoed in the huge chamber.

Vayne couldn't take not knowing where Corinth was. He rose slowly, leading with his weapon. Tia'tan used his distraction to grab her weapon.

The scene that greeted Vayne chilled his soul.

Gintoc stood on the scaffolding surrounding the engine, his arm around Corinth's chest, holding the boy in front of him. Corinth's eyes were huge. Gintoc waved a bullpup around while he spoke, gesturing wildly, pointing the gun at Corinth as often as not, though he didn't seem aware of that.

"Knew Itsy was against us. Over to Ilmena's side," he said, waving the weapon like a wild man. "Infiltrated us. Had to kill her."

"Itsy was sick," Ida said.

"Not sick!" Gintoc demanded. "Traitor. She harmed my crew!" He swung the weapon around to indicate Noar and Larsa lying on the ground beside the body of Itsy. Itsy's face had been blown away. Blood pooled beneath Noar's head, and Vayne couldn't judge Larsa's injuries.

"Not my boy," Gintoc said, tucking the muzzle of the bullpup under Corinth's chin. "Him I be safekeeping. I save life. I save Corinth." He gripped Corinth tightly to him, half choking the boy, inadvertently using him as a body shield.

The man was crazy. Full on *stepa at es*.

Vayne reached out with his psi powers only to encounter a massive shield around Gintoc and Corinth—as strong a field as he'd ever felt. In his panic, Gintoc was pouring all his power into shielding. There was no way Vayne could punch through and pull Corinth away or knock Gintoc unconscious.

Gintoc pointed the bullpup at Itsy's dead body. "She let them in! Let the Ilmenans board us!" He gripped Corinth tighter. "At least two of the enemy taken out." He pointed toward the bodies in the doorway.

"Gintoc," Ida said quietly, "Joffar, Luliana and Tia'tan are not enemies."

"We to win the Ilmenan War!"

Beside Vayne, Tia'tan choked on her rage, cursing Gintoc. Vayne couldn't bear to look away from Corinth.

"The war has been over, now, Gintoc," Ida said. "Remember?"

"Lies. All of you lies." He looked at Natali. "Our princess understands. Ask her. Ask!"

"You're right," Natali said calmly. "And you did well. We're here now, and everything's safe."

Gintoc's eyes flashed across the group. "No! None safe. Keeping my Corinth safe."

Luliana groaned from the doorway. From the corner of his eye Vayne saw her try to rise.

::Stay down:: he ordered her. She seemed oblivious, likely from the pain. Everyone held their breath as she rose on one elbow. ::You have to stay down!::

"See!" Gintoc screeched. He fired two blasts into her back. "See?"

Tia'tan roared with fury and surged to her feet. Vayne grabbed for her tunic but missed as she took aim at Gintoc.

"No!" Natali shouted, flinging out her arm. Tia'tan's bullpup flew straight into Natali's hand. The one shot Tia'tan had managed to get off flew wide and Vayne yanked Tia'tan down behind cover as Gintoc returned fire.

"He's the only one who can fix the engine!" Natali hissed.

::Vayne—help.:: Corinth's voice was a whimper.

Vayne looked over the top of the cart again. Gintoc inadvertently burned Corinth on the chin when waving the still-scalding muzzle of the bullpup around. His shouting became muddled, his mental state unraveling before their eyes. Ida and Natali answered his shouts about "enemies coming for us!" with words of assurance. Vayne saw only Corinth's huge eyes pleading with him, and Gintoc's finger getting tighter and tighter on the trigger.

Keep you and Corinth safe. No matter what you have to do.

::As soon as his hold on you weakens:: Vayne told Corinth, ::run to me. Run as fast as you can to cover, you understand?::

Gintoc, incoherent and enraged, fired another blast into Itsy's dead body and Vayne took his chance. He surged to his feet without a sound and shot Gintoc straight in the head. No psi shield in the universe could stop the plasma bolt. As soon as Gintoc was struck, the shield dropped. Corinth must have pushed the man away with all his might because the body went flying. Corinth leapt the three meters to the ground from the scaffolding and sprinted to Vayne.

Everywhere was shouting and movement and cursing. Corinth shuddered in his arms as Vayne wrapped him tight. Relief dropped them both to their knees.

He's safe. He's safe.

It was over. Corinth was safe. He hadn't failed Kayla.

Natali stood perfectly still, gaze locked on Vayne. Her eyes glowed with loathing and pain and betrayal. "I should have known it would be you, brother."

32

SHIMVILLE, FALANAR

Hekkar didn't like the feel of this exchange. Not at all.

It went against the grain to let Vega pick the location, but she hadn't given them another option. Now he, Rigger, Trinan and Vid were in a different section of Shimville, gathered across the street from what looked to be a drug manufacturing facility—and not the legal kind.

Every warning bell rang in his head when they arrived and he realized Vega wasn't there yet.

"A trap," Trinan muttered. They couldn't be certain—the meet time hadn't passed yet. Still, he would have expected Vega to be in position well ahead of the appointed time.

"Damnit, Vega," Hekkar said.

The words seemed to summon her. A sleek, unmarked hover car skimmed down the street and parked directly in front of the drug lab. Vega got out, followed by two other agents Hekkar didn't recognize.

"Where the frutt is Malkor?" Kayla asked over comms. She was out of sight, stationed in the building next door as their secret weapon. To the best of their knowledge Vega still had no idea she was in hiding with the octet. They needed any advantage they could get.

Hekkar marched to the hover car. The interior of the passenger compartment was empty, and two other agents sat in front.

"No sign of him."

Kayla swore in response.

"Of course not," Senior Commander Vega said calmly from the other side of the car. "Do you really think I'd bring my most valuable bargaining chip to this drop in person?"

Now what? Hekkar's first instinct was to call the whole thing off—no way he was trading Dolan's data for anything less than Malk's life.

"Don't worry," Vega said, "he's close by." She arched a brow at the tactical suits they wore, and then headed into the drug lab with her two agents following.

Hekkar ordered his team in after her. The whole op had already gone sideways, but what else could he do?

He found Vega and her men standing on one side of a battered and scarred workbench, looking at their mobile complink as it booted. A datapad already lay on the bench. Hekkar took position directly opposite Vega, Rigger beside him and Trinan and Vid bracketing them.

Vega looked them over. "I have to admire Senior Agent Rua," she said. "He certainly knows how to form a loyal octet."

"Best of the best," Hekkar said. "Now, proof of life or this ends right now."

"You've got the chip?"

He nodded, and Vega seemed to take him at his word. She knew he wouldn't risk not bringing it.

Not when I'm planning on screwing you over anyway, bitch.

Vega powered on the datapad and handed it to him. On the screen, Malkor sat in a chair, wrists and ankles manacled to it. The lighting was bright in that one area, deeply shadowing everything else. He could barely make out rotting pallets in the background. A warehouse?

Great, only a million warehouses in Shimville.

Hekkar's mobile comm triple buzzed—high-priority alert—but he didn't dare check it. Who knew what would set Vega off?

Rigger surprised him by setting the chip case on the lab

bench before he okayed the move. He shot a "what the frutt are you doing?" look that she ignored while reaching for her mobile comm.

Everyone in the room tensed. Rigger raised her other hand non-threateningly. "I need my comm to unlock this."

Vega nodded to her agents to relax and Rigger took out the comm.

Thank the stars for Rigger. The case didn't need a signal from her comm to open it. No doubt she'd adopted the ruse to read the alert they'd received. She glanced at the screen and keyed in an entry.

"I got your message, Rigger," Kayla said in his ear a second later. "Parrel says Malkor's being held two blocks over, warehouse for Alvano's?" Parrel must have sent that to all of them. He wouldn't have known Kayla's mirrored comm signal, which is why Rigger took the risk to send it to Kayla.

Vega hit a button on the datapad, opening a comm link to the warehouse.

"Talk to your octet leader," Vega said. "You've got ten seconds."

"Are you real-time, boss?"

"Hekkar?" Malkor said. "Yes. And don't you dare trade that data for me, that's an order."

Vega reached over and hit mute on the datapad. "Satisfied?"

"I don't trust Parrel," Kayla said in Hekkar's ear. "But I trust Vega even less. I'm going after Malkor. No way she's keeping her end of the bargain."

There was no way for Hekkar to stop her without giving away that he had a man outside.

"Stall her," Kayla said, "and jam comms so she can't get any warning from the warehouse."

Vega powered the datapad down. Now more than ever Hekkar worried what was going to happen to Malk. *Hurry, Kayla.* He gave Rigger the prearranged sign to jam all signals. Hopefully Vega wouldn't notice for a while.

Vega smiled slightly. "Let's get a look at that data."

Kayla sprinted down the stairs and out the backdoor of the building she'd hid in. She could almost see a timer counting down, and felt the squeeze as her window of opportunity to rescue Malkor—before Vega figured out something was wrong—started to close.

Damn tactical suit, she cursed as she ran.

She'd been baking alive since putting the tac suit on. The last time she'd worn one was during the rescue of her family, and she'd forgotten how hot the damn things were. If it didn't promise at least two shots' worth of protection against an ion pistol blast she would have ditched it long ago.

Kayla crossed the street at a dead run and rounded the next block in thirty seconds. Alvano's warehouse looked especially decrepit, even for Shimville. Rotting pallets and abandoned crates filled the alleyway. Sheets of metal hung over the windows. Only half of the windows were secured—she had her choice of ingress.

No time to be choosy. If Malkor's captors didn't hear from Vega in short order they would know something was wrong, and then Malkor's life would be over.

Thankfully he should be sparsely guarded. Vega had loyal people, but she didn't have endless resources to trust with something as controversial as freeing an enemy of the state in exchange for the plans to the Influencer. Something this high-level would have as few people involved as possible.

Kayla jogged the perimeter of the building, looking for the easiest point of access that wasn't the front doors. High-pitched chittering drifted out to her from every window. She didn't have time to analyze the sound as she decided on a side window that already had crates stacked under it.

The metal sheeting was razor sharp on the edge. As she slipped underneath it and shimmied onto the window ledge, the sheeting caught her across her back, tearing into her tac suit and slicing her skin. Hopefully the injury was a good sign, meaning no one expected this window to be used. She pulled herself up and over, then dropped to the floor inside the warehouse. The chittering she'd heard outside increased in volume and frequency, and a stench powerful enough to make her gag hit her nose.

Shit. Bats—and she'd sent them into a tizzy of chirping communication.

At least they weren't mobbing her... yet.

She crouched low and crept forward. The rickety floor she'd landed on seemed to run the entire length of the building as a second level of sorts, with an office at one end and assorted junk strewn about the rest of it. The smell of years of bat shit piled on top of more bat shit was enough to keep most people from claiming even a temporary residence here. Motley floodlights lit the warehouse floor, but she was in shadow for the moment.

"You might as well come out," someone called from below.

Frutting bats.

"You tripped the perimeter alarm."

Ah. That would do it, too.

"I've got orders to kill the agent if anyone gives me trouble, so if you were planning on making trouble, quit it." She recognized that smug voice.

Siño, the biocybe.

Hekkar watched as Rigger took her time opening the case carrying the chip with all of Dolan's scientific data.

Two biometric scans and two sequences of numbers shouldn't take that long. Rigger managed to make it look like an intricate art as she went through the process.

She finally finished opening the case and proffered it to Vega. Rigger looked as cool as the other side of the pillow handing over a chip that contained enough info for Vega to create a new Influencer. Hekkar was on edge. Their entire plan to foil Vega rested on a virus Rigger had written this afternoon. His basic understanding was that it was a two-stage virus. Stage one: the first time the chip is accessed the virus is activated and primed to deploy. Stage two: the second time the chip is accessed the virus launches and writes over the data, rewriting and rewriting ad infinitum so that the data can never be recovered.

Rigger's virus would work as planned. He just hoped no one on Vega's side knew how to look for it.

Vega handed the case with the chip still in it to one of the agents. "Let's see what surprises you have planned for us."

The agent took his time examining the chip with microglasses, no doubt looking for a burn strip that would fry the chip the second it was powered up in a complink. The octet had debated installing one but decided against it in the end. Vega had to walk away believing she had access to everything she wanted in order to get Malkor back. The two-stage virus was the only way to assure that.

Vega's agent finally decided the chip hadn't been tampered with and inserted it into the complink, then started tapping away. Vega let him do his thing without looking at the screen—the agent must be searching for viruses, not accessing the actual data yet.

Hekkar itched to be out of there. He wanted to be on the rescue mission, kicking down doors, cracking skulls and pounding the shit out of IDC conspirators. Instead he was on "stalling" duty, for frutt's sake. He had to rely on Kayla for the skull cracking and give her as much time as possible.

At least Vega's agent was helping him out by being thorough.

By the time the agent finally passed the complink to Vega to delve into the files, Hekkar felt ready to snap. Instead, he forced himself to relax and distract her.

"Don't know why you're so hot for those files," he said. "Without Dolan to hold your hand, you'll never be able to build another of those machines."

Vega raised her gaze from the complink with a slow smile. "Whatever gave you the idea we need to build one?" She chuckled at the stunned look he couldn't hide. "We have version three, Dolan's newest. The one your little Wyrds destroyed was version two."

Holy shit. This went way beyond "worst possible outcome."

"We don't need the schematics to build one; we need Dolan's files on how to *use* it."

Not possible. "Without a Wyrd to control it…" He drifted off. That one fact should be the death knell to all her plans.

Vega smiled at him. Her lips never moved, but her voice sounded in his mind as she said, ::I have that part handled, don't you worry.:: Then she turned her attention back to the complink.

Holy frutt.

Hekkar glanced left at Vid, silently asking, "Did you hear that?" He saw the same fear running through Vid's mind as his own: even with Malkor's life in the balance, even with Rigger's virus in place, could they really let Vega walk out of here with all that data, knowing she had gained psi powers?

"You might as well settle in," Vega said, eyes still on the screen. "Our deal's not complete until I'm certain I have everything we need."

Kayla froze when Siño's voice came from below, calling her out of hiding.

She pulled her ion pistol and checked its charge.

Damnit!

Frutting damn, it had been disabled.

Wyrds had the tech to disable advanced weapons that relied on digital firing sequences. It didn't work on weapons that relied on mechanical systems. Not that it mattered, since she didn't have old-style weapons on her.

Dolan really didn't scrimp on the tech he handed over to the imperials, apparently.

Frutt.

Shooting Siño in the head from here was her best, and probably her only chance to beat him. For once, having her kris didn't fill her with total confidence.

She peered over the edge of the catwalk. Malkor sat in a chair in the center of the room, cuffed to it hand and foot. He'd been roughed up, swollen face, bloody nose—Siño had probably gotten bored. Her gaze skimmed over him, checking for any other signs of injury. Malkor seemed alert and calm. She eased out a breath in relief. Part of her had feared she wouldn't be in time.

The biocybe stood at ease beside Malkor, an old-style firearm on his hip that he hadn't bothered to draw. He knew whoever came would be disarmed by the disrupter tech.

Smug bastard.

Siño drew a knife from a boot sheath and held it to Malkor's neck. "I'm getting a little fidgety down here, so if this is a rescue mission, might as well get on with it."

No way to surprise him from here. Two well-lit sets of stairs led to the floor, and Siño had situated himself with a view of both. The drop from her height to the ground did not look like a good time, and a broken ankle was no way to start a fight with an augmented human.

"You've got three seconds to show yourselves. One."

Kayla stood and waved. "I'm here. Didn't want to tax your brain with more counting."

Siño grinned, knife still at Malkor's throat. "I knew it would be you. Got anyone else up there?"

"Got anyone else down there?"

He shook his head. "You've got me all to yourself, Princess. And I know you like to work alone, so why don't you come on down and we'll settle this."

"Take that knife from his neck and you've got yourself a date."

Malkor's eyes blazed, and if he could have opened his mouth without slitting his own throat he would be shouting at her to get the void out of there and leave him. As if she could ever do that when he needed her.

Siño chuckled and lowered his knife hand. Malkor drew

breath to shout something and Siño punched him in the solar plexus, driving the air from his lungs. Malkor doubled over and Siño grabbed his hair, yanking his head back up. "No interruptions, Agent. I'll deal with you soon enough."

Kayla jogged to the closest set of stairs, scanning the rest of the warehouse as she went. It seemed Siño hadn't lied. The place was emptied out, and unless someone hid in the office, there was no one else here. And why would there need to be? With modern weapons deactivated and Siño's enhanced— well, everything—he was more than a match for anyone. Or any two. Or three. And Vega knew there were only four octet members left on the loose.

As Kayla picked her way down the stairs, Siño's smile of anticipation found an answering fire in her heart. He'd gotten the best of her twice before. He'd had a hand in murdering Rawn. He'd beaten Malkor.

He was going to die. Right here, right now.

Or she was.

First, though, she had to get him away from Malkor. That close Siño could lunge at any time and sever an artery before her eyes.

She hit the ground floor and crossed to her right, widening the distance between her and Siño, hands at her side, ready to draw her kris. Her tac suit was useless now; it wasn't designed to stop ballistic projectiles, and she wished she could toss it.

She glanced past Siño to Malkor, barely visible beyond Siño's huge shoulders.

I'm getting you out of here, if it's the last thing I do.

Kayla forced her concern for Malkor into a mental box. She fixed his location in the room so she'd always be aware of keeping the fight from him, and let go of the rest. This was all about her and Siño now. She'd need all of her concentration if she was going to beat the biocybe.

That and a miracle.

"Don't be shy, Princess," Siño called. He beckoned her with

two fingers. At least he showed no indication of drawing his gun.

"Hey, I came down a whole floor for you. Gotta meet me halfway." And get the void away from Malkor.

Siño chuckled, enjoying himself way too much for her taste. *Let's see what we can do about that.*

He took a few steps toward her, holding the knife out in front, ready but not yet engaged. She held her ground even as her survival instincts warned her to run.

She rested her hands casually on the pommels of her kris. "I see you brought the right party favor this time."

He turned his hand so the knife glinted in the light. "Only fair to let the weaker opponent choose the weapon, don't you think?"

Score a point for Siño. "In that case, how about tossing that cannon in your belt over yonder." She made a sideways motion with her chin, indicating the far end of the warehouse.

"I don't believe in playing quite *that* fair." His grin was evil and eerily compelling at the same time. In another universe, she could almost imagine enjoying sparring this man.

Today, she'd enjoy killing him.

Kayla shrugged one shoulder. "Suit yourself. You'll be that much more embarrassed when I beat you."

He laughed, genuinely amused. "Frutt, woman, if I didn't have orders to kill you I'd be taking you against the wall right now." He thought it over. Then, his eyes never leaving hers, he slowly drew out the gun. He cocked the hammer and pointed the barrel straight at her. Kayla forced herself not to react. *Breathe. Breathe. He doesn't want to kill you like this, he wants full gratification.* Her heart slowed as she controlled her breath.

"All that talk and now you're cheating me out of a good time?" She faked a disappointed sigh. "Men these days."

He uncocked the gun and flicked his wrist, sending it spinning across the floor and underneath an abandoned pallet. "Just for you, Princess."

Thank the stars. One shot would have blown her wide open, kris or no kris.

He drew a second knife from his other boot sheath. "Let's do this."

She pulled her kris. The adrenaline that had been on a slow burn since getting Parrel's message spiked. When he started to circle her, dropping into predatory mode, her sweat turned icy. Their previous fights flashed into her mind as she matched his steps. Him, choking her to near unconsciousness. Him, beating the shit out of her in the lift... It wasn't pretty, and it certainly wasn't inspiring.

His augmentations were his strength, but also his weakness, as he relied so heavily on them. Time to see what flawless *ro'haar* skill could do against brute force.

He closed in on her like an over-ardent lover, unable to wait another second.

Typical male.

Siño's left hand flashed forward, driving the blade toward her face. Kayla dipped and came up with a high-rising block under his wrist, guiding the hand over her head. She side-stepped right at the same time and let his momentum carry him forward past her. She scored a hit on his hip—a weak attack—and then he went for her again.

This time he led with an upward attack aimed at her armpit. She deflected the blow and barely stopped his other knife from punching through her gut. She stepped into him before he could swing again and sliced his arm above his elbow, hoping to sever a ligament. Her blade skipped over metal, his augmentations shielding his ligaments.

Damnit. That strike would have left a normal person with one useless arm. She backed out in time to turn his strike for her neck into a cut across her ear. As they traded blows, it quickly became evident that he wasn't as proficient with knives as he thought he was. His strength more than made up for it, and every block she made square on instead of deflecting hit like a hammer blow. He was going to beat her down.

She needed to end this. While she could deflect and dodge for a while, he could maintain this force and pace all night thanks to his augs.

I need to get in close.

Considering his extra strength and superior grappling ability, close was the last place she wanted to be. But if she couldn't get a vital strike in soon, she and Malkor were dead.

Kayla ducked Siño's lead arm and guided his second attack off-center, opening his defense for a split-second. She struck, aiming for his carotid artery. A drop step saved him. Her kris penetrated his chest below the collar bone. Her cross guard slammed into the bone and cracked it as her blade finished its upward track and punched through the muscle to appear out the other side.

Siño roared with fury, dropping his off-knife and clutching at the wound, trapping her kris there. She let it go and danced out of range, but not before his lead knife came down, carving a deep furrow in her right arm. Only a lifetime of intense training kept her grip on her one remaining kris as part of her muscle flayed and blood poured down her arm.

Yup. That'd kill her soon enough.

Kayla took a double-step back to gain distance and quickly switch her kris to her good hand. She didn't take her eyes off Siño as he lunged for her, free hand grasping like a claw. If he got a hold of her it was all over. That augmented grip would never release her no matter what she did.

Footwork, Kayla, footwork.

She couldn't stand in an open front stance and take blows head-on like a target dummy. The predictable shifting of L-stances forward and back wouldn't get her where she needed to be. If she wanted to get in close enough to get a mortal strike she had one shot at this. One shot, and if she missed he'd pummel the life out of her in about five seconds. Maybe less.

She switched to the ginga style, a constantly moving flow that used a triangle pattern to keep an opponent off-balance.

Start low, deep step back with one leg, keeping the opposite arm raised for protection, then a step forward and out to the side, and repeating the pattern with the opposite leg dropping back. She could move in a circle, covering plenty of ground.

Siño hesitated, tried to track her movements as he lost focus on her centerline.

Keep it low and fluid, she heard her mentor say in her head. *Be ready for your moment, use the step's inherent torque to your advantage.*

Siño double-stepped in, coming on like a maglev train. Kayla fell backward in a queda de quarto, feet planted, catching her weight on her hands like an inverted crab. Siño's strike soared over her prone body. She dropped to her back and brought her feet up, catching him low in the stomach and launching him over her head with his own momentum. She flipped to her feet in time to see him tumbling away. His augs made him quick, though, and he was standing in no time, coming for her with murder in his eyes and blood running down his chest.

Kayla's right arm was numb and her blood made the floor slick in spots. She'd already slid on a smear once. With his augs it was nearly impossible to incapacitate any of Siño's limbs or reach his vital organs, plus he protected his head well, like a bare-knuckle brawler.

The injury to his collarbone only seemed to make him fiercer, faster, while Kayla's own was threatening to black her out. He had enough meat to sustain the blood loss so far, whereas her injury was worse and she weighed less.

Down to my last shot.

A man might let a doctor augment a lot of things, run wires and metal bracing and tubes throughout most of his systems in the name of better defense and offense. But there was one area most guys would refuse to let a doctor use like a wiring panel: his groin. Biocybes who allowed it have suffered from impotence. Siño seemed to have a raging libido tied permanently to his bloodlust, so that was the sweet spot—his weakest area and her last hope.

Great, now she was staking her life on a man's love of his own dick.

Kayla swung back and forth in ginga, waiting, waiting, waiting. She needed the perfect attack on his part. Weakened by the constant movement, Kayla realized she was going to have to lure him into it. She waited until he faced her in an opposing L-stance, then faked a slip and went down into a split. Siño shifted forward in his L-stance, the quickest way to close the distance, allowing her the opening she needed. Just as he grabbed her ponytail to yank her to her feet she slammed her kris into his groin—cutting through his testicles she'd guess, based on the sound he made.

She completed the movement, slashing her dagger to the side and severing his femoral artery. Siño screamed like a dying horse. Blood spurted everywhere. He fell to his knees, his rapidly draining brain unable to decide if his hands should be gripping his ruined privates or his mortal injury. He fell on top of her, his weight threatening to crush her, his blood hot on her, soaking her.

One of his hands struggled for her throat but she beat him off with her good arm.

"Shoulda. Got that. Augmented," she coughed out, light-headed. He fought feebly for a minute. She wrestled her leg around and kneed him in the groin, putting an end to that.

Kayla lay on the floor, staring at the warehouse ceiling, so cold against Siño's lifeblood. Shock, she knew. Blood loss. She was going to need help.

Siño shuddered out his last breath and she tried to heave him off.

No luck.

It was nice here, she thought. Quiet. *I'll only rest a minute. Get my strength back.*

She closed her eyes.

"Kayla!"

"Kayla, get up!"

Kayla. Kayla. Kayla.

Shhhh.

"Kayla! For the frutting love of the frutting void, get the frutt up!"

The sound followed her, echoed back at her in the warehouse. It was a roar. Then epithets. Fantastic epithets. Even she was impressed.

"Get *up*, Kayla. Now. You need help. Get me loose!"

She groaned. Ugh. That voice was pissing her off.

"I swear by all the gods, if you don't get up…"

Angry, angry voice. Fear. It held so much fear. Odd; she felt fine. Cold, really, but Siño's blood was helping that.

"I'm fine," she croaked. "Leave me alone." She closed her eyes tighter. So nice here, with her Siño blanket.

"You're *not* fine. Get your ass up right now. *Now*, Kayla."

She grumbled, opened an eye. Now that she thought about it, she was pretty uncomfortable. One leg was fully extended in the split still, and one awkwardly crushed beneath Siño. Her hand, still gripping the kris, was trapped between them. Something—the cross-guard?—dug into her index finger and thumb.

Ugh. She groaned again.

"Get *up*, Kayla! Get me the void out of these cuffs so I can help you. Do it!"

Why did that voice sound so sweet while it was pissing her off?

"Kayla—"

"Fine!" She tried to move her right arm and grunted at the pain. "Fine. Just. Quit." She took several deep breaths. "Nagging. Me." She couldn't push the biocybe off. Instead she rolled under him, left her kris embedded in his crotch, and dragged herself free of his weight with her good arm. She finally made it loose and sat up.

"Sweet holy frutt. My arm is bleeding," she said, looking down at the ruined thing.

Someone laughed at her. Half-relieved, half-maniacal. "Yes, yes it is. Now get the magcuff key and get me out of here so I can help you."

That someone was handsome. And crying, his cheeks wet with tears. And laughing. And still shouting while she stared.

"Malkor."

"Yes. Yes, Kayla love. Now get the key. Hurry."

She flopped like a dead fish over Siño's body, searching pockets, dragging her useless arm. When she got to her knees and pulled off his belt, the cuff controller fell to the floor. Kayla stared at it a moment. Malkor was shouting something again. That *was* Malkor, wasn't it? She'd been here to save him?

"Yes! Push the button, push it." More swearing. She leaned forward, pushed the de-mag button on the controller, and fell on her face.

The last thing she was aware of was Malkor running toward her, ripping his shirt off and pressing it to her arm.

Vega finally nodded her head. "Looks like we're good here."

Shit, Hekkar thought. They were out of time. *Kayla, you better be as good as I think you are.*

Vega shut down the complink and put the chip into the carrying case she'd brought. As she and her agents headed for the door, Hekkar couldn't think of a single way to stall her that wouldn't be suspicious. Vega turned back halfway there. "Agent Rua's at Alvano's warehouse. Judging by your expression and the silence of our comms, you already knew that."

She gave him a serious look. "I don't expect you to believe me, but I really would have met my end of the deal if you hadn't interfered." Then she shrugged. "His death is on you."

The second she left, Trinan and Vid lunged for the rear exit, and Rigger and Hekkar followed them out as they sprinted to Alvano's, only to find that Kayla really was every bit as good as he'd hoped she was.

33

THE *YARI*, MINE FIELD

It had taken some time after the carnage in the engine room to get all of the wounded and dead transported to the medical triage center one deck below the command room. The triage area was one of dozens strategically placed throughout the ship. Vayne asked about going to the main medical floor but Ida told him it wasn't secure.

Ida had ordered Vayne's uncle to stay in crew quarters where it was safe, and Tanet and Ariel still guarded the command center. Everyone else packed into triage. At the far end of the room the bodies of Gintoc, Itsy, Luliana and Joffar lay under sheets. Vayne hadn't expected their deaths to hit him so hard. He'd lost so many family members and friends over the last five years—he'd thought he was finally away from all that.

Now these brutal deaths, one at his own hands, rocked him.

Corinth sat on a chair, knees to chest, arms wrapped around his legs, weeping in that silent way of his. Tia'tan sat beside Noar on a gurney. Noar's head was wrapped for the moment to staunch the bleeding. Itsy had surprised them all in the engine room and bludgeoned Noar with enough force to knock him out and give him a concussion. He was alert now, if a little unsteady. Tia'tan had her head close to his, speaking softly. It didn't look like a gentle conversation. Her lips moved rapidly, her fingers twitching now and then as if to drive home a point, and she had the look of someone struggling to control her rage.

Larsa, Gintoc's engineering assistant, lay on her stomach while Benny tended to her two plasma burns. She'd been able to dive out of the way when Itsy had commandeered a bullpup from the rack, so Larsa's burns were luckily shallow.

Ida sat at the back of the room beside Gintoc's body. A sheet covered his ruined head, but his arm hung off the edge of the bed. Ida held his hand, patting it. She hadn't spoken to anyone since they'd arrived in triage with his body.

Vayne couldn't bear to sit, not with all that had happened. He paced, going over and over the scene in the engine room, trying to see if there was anything else he could have done. Nothing came to him, though. He played it in slow motion again and again and knew he had taken the shot he'd needed to take.

And if the rest of them didn't agree, so be it.

"Larsa," Natali said, from where she stood in the doorway. "Are you capable of completing the hyperstream drive?"

Vayne whirled on her. "How can that be your first question? Four people are *dead*. And who knows how many others might have died. How can you even think of the engine right now?"

Natali acted as if he didn't exist. "Larsa, can you?"

"Is doubtful."

Larsa should be sedated, doped up on pain meds, not answering questions.

"With Corinth and Noar's help?" Natali's cold voice held no hint of sympathy, only purpose.

Larsa gasped as Benny dabbed at her wound. When she had her breathing under control again she said, "Unlikely. Needed Gintoc. He sings the language of engines."

Natali looked like she would change the answer through sheer force of will. "Try. The others will help. After you're feeling better, of course." She added that last grudgingly, then left triage.

Everyone in the room seemed to exhale when she left. Natali had taken the most volatile currents of tension with her.

"To the void with the drive," Vayne said. "We need to talk about our safety. How many other *stepa at es* are loose on the ship?" No one answered him. He hated to interrupt Ida, who looked devastated by Gintoc's loss, but he needed answers. "Ida? How many?"

She spoke without turning around. "Numbers to be uncertain. Thirteen of my crew unaccounting."

Shit. Thirteen crazy people running around on the ship?

"Some we had contained," Benny added.

Obviously, that had failed. "What happened to the rest of the crew?"

Ida sighed, her shoulders falling as with great weight. "Twenty-two locked in cryosleep. Not to survive awakening. Forty-two the malfunctions in cryo have killed. Twenty-one of our crew we have killed, they being *stepa at es*. And we awake are six." She swallowed convulsively. "We are five, now."

He could tell by her broken posture that she felt every one of those deaths as if they were her fault. She squeezed Gintoc's dead hand tightly and kissed the back of it.

"Gintoc's turning has been coming, Captain," Benny said. His eyes were full of sorrow. "We have all ignored. And hoped."

Ida nodded, still not looking their way.

"The cryo damages create paranoia," Benny explained. "They forget. They fight our old war in their minds."

Which explained why Itsy destroyed a ship of Ilmenan design and Gintoc killed Luliana and Joffar. Thank the stars Gintoc saw Noar as part of his "engineering crew" or he would have been another casualty.

"So," Vayne said, trying to wrap his mind around how much danger they were really in. "Thirteen *stepa at es*."

"Hide mostly," Ida said. "Burrow, carve out dens in the walls. Stockpile. Wait."

Like soldiers trapped behind enemy lines, living in fear of capture. It was that "mostly" part, though, that set him on edge.

"When Kayla gets here, we can get you off the ship."

Ida shook her head before he finished speaking. "I not to abandon mine."

"Nor me," Benny seconded.

It was a fight for another time, when things weren't so raw.

"Have you heard from Kayla?" Tia'tan asked. She had an arm around Noar, supporting him while he slumped, glassy-eyed, against her.

"I haven't." And he was trying not to worry about that. He had no idea if she'd managed to procure a ship, if she was on her way right now, or if she was still tied to the planet.

::We've sent two messages with no response:: Corinth said to the room. The worry in his mind voice hit everyone. Vayne had been hoping to keep Kayla's comm silence between the two of them.

"So for now," Tia'tan said, "we're stuck on a ship that's unlikely to ever fly out of here, counting on a rescue from someone we've lost contact with, and the *Yari*'s crew is trying to kill us."

::We could go through the Tear:: Corinth said.

Vayne slashed the air with a hand. "Absolutely not. I am not getting stuck in the middle of the war on Ordoch with no way off the planet. And you," he said to Corinth, "are not going either."

"We just wait, then?" Tia'tan asked. He could tell waiting wasn't in her blood.

Waiting. Again. He'd spent the last five years waiting for a rescue that he thought would never come.

In the end, Kayla had come.

How long would the wait be this time? And would anyone still be alive when she finally got here?

* * *

Cinni waited in the dark of Mishe's room for him to return from visiting Aarush. She sat on his bed, back against the wall, legs crossed in front of her, a canteen of oblivion in her lap. Mishe was a better person than her, making daily trips to the infirmary. She still hadn't gone to see Aarush.

She put the canteen to her lips and drank deeply. The fire of it going down couldn't burn away the pain in her heart. Why did it have to be Aarush? Why did it have to happen to him? His beautiful face—ruined. That amputation would put him in a chair for a very long time; getting around the base would be a nightmare.

And Mishe.

She stroked the blanket beside her as if she could wipe away Mishe's trauma. He'd always been pretty. Ethereal. Striking in a way that stole your breath the first time you saw him. He wasn't a fighter and he'd been born without psi powers. He believed in the rebellion with all his heart, and served the best way he could—infiltrating the imperials as a whore, gathering crucial secrets from pillow talk and unguarded datapads.

What it did to him, though...

Cinni hung her head. He kept it all inside, never complaining, but his eyes... It was always there, silent, in his eyes.

She took another drink, and as she did she heard the sound that haunted her day and night, waking and sleeping. The *blast* of her ion pistol firing, unloading its full charge into her mother's chest. She heard it over and over.

Blast.

Blast.

So loud in her ears, it sometimes drowned out everything else. The stench of charred flesh accompanied the sound, as did the last look of surprise on Hephesta's face when Cinni killed her.

Hello, Mother.

Blast.

Damnit. She should have taken a dreamer before she came here. Mishe wouldn't have any in his room, he never touched the stuff. She took another sip of the oblivion. Nasty, brewed in the base, and powerful as all get out.

She laid her head back against the wall and closed her eyes.

"Where are you, Mishe?"

She needed him tonight, needed her best friend.

He finally arrived at his room and flicked on the lights. It was blinding and she squinted against the spike of pain in her skull. Mishe instantly dimmed them to almost nothing.

He didn't look surprised to see her. They had open invitations to each other's rooms, each seeking the other out for comfort at every odd hour. Each time Mishe came back from a night out, he sat in the chair in her room in the dark, not speaking. Sometimes she talked for both of them. Sometimes she even slept. He just needed to be near someone who understood.

Mishe joined her on the bed, sitting beside her, shoulders touching, leaning his back against the wall. She offered the canteen to him wordlessly and he shook his head. For the best. Tonight she might need the whole thing.

They sat side by side in near darkness for an unknown amount of time, not speaking, just being there. The world blurred around her, thanks to the oblivion.

"How is Aarush?" she finally asked.

Mishe's shoulders lifted in a shrug. "The same. Mostly sedated to avoid the worst of the pain. Desperately angry and terrified—but stoic." He said the words with tenderness. Cinni could imagine Aarush holding it in, not wanting to burden anyone. Typical Aarush.

"You're good to see him."

Mishe said nothing.

"I can't make myself go in there. I try—"

"You should go."

"Can't." She took another sip from the canteen.

"You know, Cinni, sometimes it's not all about you."

That brought a bitter laugh. "You sound like my mother." *Blast.*

Mishe sighed and reached for the canteen. "Might as well share." He took a sip, then coughed. "That shit is wretched."

That was her Mishe. She smiled.

Time slipped by in the dark as they passed the canteen back and forth between them, not saying a thing. She didn't need words with Mishe.

Her head fell to his shoulder. He tilted his head onto hers. They'd emptied the canteen some time ago.

Sleepy. So sleepy. And snuggly. She curled into him, wanting his warmth. Needing it. Needing him. Everything else in her world was ruined. Gintoc was dead, her mother was dead, Aarush might as well be dead.

But not her Mishe.

He was so perfect, so beautiful. His face hadn't been burnt, his gorgeous eyes still worked. "So perfect," she whispered.

She turned into him, put her hand on his chest, felt his heart beating. The pulse of it drowned out her mother's death.

He was so beautiful and so close and so alive.

And hers. He would always be her Mishe.

She shifted enough to nuzzle his neck. He lifted his head and she moved closer, lips touching that pale, perfect skin, tasting him. Her Mishe. Her hand slid down his chest to the flat of his abdomen and he drew in a sharp breath, fully awake now.

Oh yes. This is what she needed.

She turned and pressed into him, breasts against his arm and chest, her lips moving up to trace his jawline as her fingers slid to the latch of his pants.

"Cinni," he said, catching her hand.

She ignored the quiet warning. He wanted her, she knew it. He was her Mishe.

"Cinni, stop it," he said in his soft voice. She loved that voice. "You're drunk." He tried to push her away and she suddenly felt frantic to have him. She crossed her leg over his lap to straddle him, reached for his face. If she could just kiss that luscious mouth.

He tried to move back. The wall held him there and she slammed her lips to his.

He thrust her away by the shoulders, sending her sprawling backward off the bed and onto the floor.

"What the frutt, Mishe?" She pushed herself off the floor.

He jumped to his feet, his hands in fists at his side. "I said *no*, Cinni." The breath rasped in and out of him, hot and hard.

Fury erupted in her chest. "What, you'll whore for the rebellion, but not for me?"

The second the words were out she knew she'd gone too far. The harshness of them struck her flat in the face, knocking her dead-sober.

Blast. The sound ricocheted through her mind.

Mishe froze, the blood rising in his face. "Get the frutt out of here, Cinni. You're drunk and looking for an Aarush surrogate."

"What would you even know about it?" she flung back, horrified at herself, unable to stop. "You've never been in love. You don't even know what I'm going through."

Mishe took an angry step forward. "You think you're the only one who cares about him? You don't even visit him! You're too selfish, thinking only of how his injuries affect you. How about how it affects him?" He stabbed his finger at her. "Have you ever, for one second, thought about *his* needs?"

Mishe's rage rolled out like a tidal wave, crashing into her, battering her with the truth.

Mishe is in love with Aarush.

"Get out," Mishe growled, and Cinni fled.

Somehow Cinni made it back to her room. She couldn't quite remember the journey. She only knew she was lying on the floor, half-covered in a blanket, her face wet with tears and snot and an empty pack of dreamers beside her. She floated in and out of consciousness. Faces appeared before her, hovering above her.

Her mother—eyes wide and surprised in death.

Mishe—devastated, furious.

Aarush—burnt and unseeing.

Every time she thought she might finally escape the night in sleep, a *blast* in her mind shot her wide awake.

Stars. How many dreamers did I take? And the oblivion?

She struggled to a seated position, leaning miserably against the edge of her bed. What the frutt was she doing? What were any of them doing? Rebels? What, a single busload of people against an army that controlled all the utilities, the power grids, the travel on the mainland? Covered the planet with warships?

She spat, wiping her mouth, and then her nose, with her sleeve.

The rebellion was suicide. Everyone she loved was hurting or dead. The crew of the *Yari* was crazy. For all she knew, Gintoc could have been building the galaxy's largest teapot over there. The royal family was back from the dead, but one of them didn't speak, one of them wanted nothing to do with Ordoch, and one of them was so bloodthirsty Cinni knew she'd get them all killed.

Cinni pulled her ion pistol out of its holster on her hip, stared at it. She hadn't used it since she killed her mother.

Maybe she'd never use it again. Maybe she'd quit this whole thing, run away with Mishe—

Oh gods, Mishe. She buried her face in her hand, tears coming again.

She finally subsided into hiccups, swiping angrily at her wet cheeks, smearing everything. The pistol wavered before her gaze.

Hello, Mother.

Blast.

Cinni flipped the safety off and the gun hummed to life, drawing a full charge.

Maybe she'd use it just one more time.

She tucked the muzzle under her chin, seeing her mother's dead face.

"Well hello, Mother."

Cinni squeezed the trigger.

Blast.

34

ARDIN'S STARCRUISER, FALANAR

Kayla woke when someone tried to rip off her arm.

"For frutt's sake, I need that," she grumbled.

"She's awake," a familiar voice called. Toble, Malkor's medic friend. "How are you feeling?" he asked her.

"Touch that arm again and I'll let you know exactly how I'm feeling." She opened her eyes and took in her surroundings. Low lighting, medical bed, a pump sending a synthed blood transfusion into her... A ship's infirmary? "We made it?"

"Was there ever any doubt?" Hekkar said. She turned her head to see him sitting on the next bed over.

"'Best Damn Octet There Ever Was,'" Rigger said, sitting beside Hekkar.

Kayla tried to smile but her face hurt. Actually, everything hurt. "How 'bout a syringe full of pain blockers, Doc?"

Toble shook his head. "I need to know if there's any nerve damage first. Can you feel this?"

Kayla's four-letter answer set Hekkar and Rigger laughing.

From the looks of things, they had actually pulled the rescue off. "We made it to Ardin's flight strip?"

Hekkar nodded. "Carried your sorry ass right outta there without a problem. Soon as Toble's done patching you, he's out of here and we're taking off."

"Vega?"

Hekkar's grin faded. "She's got everything. And it's way worse than we suspected."

"Which," Malkor said, as he walked into the infirmary, "we can discuss later." He gave his two octet members a "button it" look. "Besides, with Rigger's virus, we've got nothing to worry about."

Kayla sighed. "I really would have liked to have killed her."

"It'll give you something to do next time you visit," Toble said.

Hekkar and Rigger exchanged a glance. There would be no next time. Everyone understood that once they took off, they'd never be coming back to Falanar.

The room fell to silence while Toble worked. His intense expression unnerved her. She glanced at her flayed arm but couldn't look for more than a second. The sight of her own lacerated muscle fibers made her stomach lurch and she broke into a sweat, breaths coming quicker.

"You can fix it, right, Doc? Just as good as new?" Her voice wavered.

Malkor came to stand beside her bed and took her good hand. "Course he can." His confident smile looked forced, especially when Toble made no response. Kayla squeezed Malkor's hand, needing his strength.

Rigger and Hekkar slipped out of the room. Toble applied an anesthetic to her arm and left her and Malkor alone for a few minutes while it set in. The creeping numbness was almost more disturbing than the pain had been, as if her arm had been severed from her body, the way her role as *ro'haar* would be severed from her soul if the wound didn't heal perfectly.

Malkor's expression turned tender. Somehow his battered face only made him look more dear to her. "You had me worried for a bit," he said softly.

"Pfft. As if one little biocybe could take me down." Her heart filled as the reality of their safety hit her. Malkor was alive, alive and safe from Siño, Vega, and anyone else who wanted to do him harm. He squeezed her hand and she squeezed back, unable to look away from him. Such a wonderful sight. Everything askew in her world righted itself, now that he was here with her.

"I love you," she said. She hadn't meant to blurt it out, they had a dozen difficulties to discuss, but when she opened her mouth those were her only words.

He leaned down and kissed her forehead. "I love you, too."

Someone cleared their throat awkwardly from the door.

"Go away," Kayla growled.

Toble re-entered the infirmary. "Malk, your team's starting the launch sequence. We have to go."

"'We' are not going anywhere. Finish patching Kayla's arm, then you get home."

Toble looked at Kayla, then back at Malkor. "A word?"

They moved to the doorway and spoke with voices lowered. The conversation reached her nonetheless.

"I am *not* dragging anyone else down with us," Malkor said. "The octet made their decisions, but you—"

"That is not the kind of wound I can slap a regen cuff on and call it done. Did you see the damage? Multiple layers of muscle and fascia need to be sutured and she needs to be closely monitored." Toble brushed the hair back from his forehead, sighing. "If she's going to regain full use of her arm we need to reduce the creation of scar tissue, and, more importantly, avoid any denervation of the myofibers."

Kayla's heart tripped, then thudded in her chest. *"If she's going to regain full use of her arm."*

If.

Toble tapped Malkor's chest with a finger. "Do *you* want to be the one to tell her she might never fight again if I leave?"

Malkor looked back at her, clearly torn. It was all she could do not to beg Toble to stay. She bit her lip to keep quiet, knowing desperation showed on her face.

"Exactly," Toble said. He returned to Kayla's bedside and started laying out tools. "Besides, it'll take a while to get wherever you're going. Once I'm sure the injury is healing well, you can drop me off at the nearest spacestation and I'll make a big fuss out of being kidnapped by the infamous rogue octet and pressed into service." He winked at Kayla. "Let's get this lunch meat slapped back together, shall we?"

The engines kicked to life, vibrating the hull. Her head throbbed in concert. Still fifteen minutes until launch—Kayla felt likely to pass out before then. Her drooping eyelids lifted, though, when Ardin strode into the infirmary.

"For frutt's sake, people, the sterile field around this bed is only so strong," Toble griped.

"I'll just be a minute." Ardin joined Malkor at Kayla's bedside.

"Thank you for this," Malkor said, gesturing with his hand in a way that encompassed so much more than the ship.

"This is the very least of what I owe you." Ardin clapped him on the shoulder and they stood, looking at each other a moment, a lifetime of friendship passing between them wordlessly.

"I wish things had gone differently." Malkor pulled him into a hug, their final goodbye.

Ardin then turned his attention to Kayla. "I cannot repay—"

She shook her head, stopping him. "You gave me the means to rescue Malkor. I couldn't ask for anything more." And she meant it. Ardin couldn't have done anything greater for her.

She reached out her hand to him and he squeezed it.

"Be well," he said. "Both of you."

Malkor nodded. "Give us a head start, then report your ship stolen."

Ardin left with a final wave and a look of deep regret. Malkor gazed at the empty doorway until the ship's comm sounded.

"Ardin is clear," Vid said. "Are we go for launch, boss?"

"Let's do this."

Malkor pulled a chair beside her bed and sank into it wearily. He took her hand again, his gaze going over every centimeter of her as if proving to himself that she was here, that she was real. The sadness in his eyes broke her heart.

"Do you want to watch the city as we launch?" she asked him. "It might be the last time you ever see it."

He shook his head.

She couldn't help but feel the depth of his loss. Everything he'd worked for—gone. His reputation—ruined. Any good he'd ever done—erased by Vega and her minions. All his efforts, his status, his influence—his whole world—gone.

"I'm sorry, Malkor."

"Don't be," he said, "I have the most important thing of all—you."

"Not only me. You have the best damn octet that ever was. Four of the most loyal people you could ask for."

A tired smile lit his face. "You're right. And I wouldn't be a free man without the five of you."

He kissed her, then rested his forehead against hers, both of them ignoring Toble. Their breathing settled into the same pattern, their hearts found the same rhythm.

"More than that," she whispered, "you have Vayne and Corinth. We are your family now."

He chuckled. "I don't think Vayne likes me very much."

"He'll come around, and Corinth adores you." She lifted her good hand to his cheek. "We'll make this work, my love." Her eyes fluttered closed. "Now, excuse me while I pass out."

Kayla was alone when she woke, but blissfully, deeply rested. Better rested than she'd been in months.

She pinged the ship's comm. "Who's making me breakfast?"

The entire gang entered her room a few minutes later. Trinan helped her sit up in bed and Vid handed her a tray with enough food for three. Malkor took the chair beside her again.

"How long was I out?"

"At least twenty hours," Trinan answered. "And *damn* can you snore!"

She chuckled, trying to ignore the fact that she still couldn't feel her right arm. At least whatever Toble had done was hidden beneath bandages. The food smelled delicious, and she was halfway through breakfast when the gravity behind the octet's usual teasing became obvious to her.

"Are we being pursued?"

"Of course we are," Rigger scoffed. "Not that they'll catch us."

"What else?"

All eyes went to Malkor.

"Gee, thanks, guys." He sighed, sending Kayla into bracing mode. "The Council of Seven made their decision."

"Already?"

"Record time," Rigger said.

Malkor continued. "They've adopted the Sovereign Council's plan to send more forces into Wyrd Space and expanded it, increasing the amount of manpower and ships beyond what the Sovereign Council proposed. They're calling it Operation Redouble.

"With that kind of manpower, they're either going to annex your planet or destroy it—assuming your people still refuse to develop a cure for the TNV."

The words washed over her, taking a minute to become real. Everyone held their breath, waiting for her reaction. There were a dozen variables in play—Ilmena could finish refitting their battleships, Ida and her crew could make the *Yari* fly again, a cure for the TNV could be found—all in a race against time with the empire. The Wyrds could and would eventually beat back the empire, but, before her homeworld was ripped apart in the process?

Even in the face of all that, a question lingered. She had to know. She *had* to. "How did Isonde vote?"

"Isonde voted for a peaceful withdrawal in the hopes of a full reconciliation with Ordoch," Malkor said, "as did Ardin and the Protectorate Council representative. They were outvoted by the emperor, empress and the two Sovereign Council representatives."

Despite all Isonde had done, the ways in which she betrayed

them, she still kept her end of their bargain. Maybe she really did care for her people as much as she claimed...

It didn't matter now, only one thing was certain:

The game was over.

The war had begun.

ACKNOWLEDGMENTS

Every book of mine starts with a huge "thank you!" to my critique partners, Jen Brooks and Diana Botsford. These two wonderful writers and friends improve my writing with their insightful critiques. In addition, they keep me accountable for meeting my goals. I couldn't do this without them! I'm also lucky to have a supportive network of writers in my SHU family – the alumni and faculty of Seton Hill University's graduate program in Writing Popular Fiction.

Thanks must go to the wonderful people at Titan Books who have been so supportive of the Empress Game trilogy – you make me feel like a rock star. A special thanks to my editor, Natalie Laverick, who took the reins on book two and helped me sharpen everything. Thanks to my agent, Richard Curtis, for all he does behind the scenes to keep things moving, and for all he does to keep me sane.

Most importantly, thank you to my family and my husband. I wouldn't be who I am today if not for all of you. From the bottom of my heart, thank you.

ABOUT THE AUTHOR

Rhonda Mason divides her time between writing, editing, bulldogs and beaching. Her writing spans the gamut of speculative fiction, from space opera to epic fantasy to urban paranormal and back again. The only thing limiting her energy for fantastical worlds is the space-time continuum. When not creating worlds she edits for a living, and follows her marine biologist husband to the nearest beach. In between preserving sea grass and deterring invasive species, she snorkels every chance she gets. Her rescue bulldog, Grace, is her baby and faithful companion. Grace follows her everywhere, as long as she's within distance of a couch Grace can sleep on. Rhonda is a graduate of the Writing Popular Fiction masters program at Seton Hill University, and recommends it to all genre writers interested in furthering their craft at the graduate level.

You can find Rhonda at www.RhondaMason.com.

THE HIGH GROUND
MELINDA SNODGRASS

Emperor's daughter Mercedes is the first woman ever admitted to the High Ground, the elite training academy of the Solar League's Star Command, and she must graduate if she is to have any hope of taking the throne. Her classmate Tracy has more modest goals—to rise to the rank of captain, and win fame and honor. But a civil war is coming and the political machinations of those who yearn for power threaten the young cadets. In a time of intrigue and alien invasion, they will be tested as they never thought possible.

"Melinda Snodgrass just keeps getting better and better."
George R.R. Martin

"Space opera with a social conscience as well as lots of sprawling action." David Drake, bestselling author of *With the Lightnings*

"Written with an easy elegance. The opening salvo of what promises to be a grand space opera." Bennett R. Coles, author of *Virtues of War*

For more fantastic fiction, author events, exclusive excerpts,
competitions, limited editions and more

VISIT OUR WEBSITE
titanbooks.com

LIKE US ON FACEBOOK
facebook.com/titanbooks

FOLLOW US ON TWITTER
@TitanBooks

EMAIL US
readerfeedback@titanemail.com